WARRIORS
SUPER EDITION

ONESTAR'S
CONFESSION

WARRIORS

SUPER EDITIONS

WARRIORS

SUPER EDITION

ONESTAR'S
CONFESSION

ERIN
HUNTER

HARPER

An Imprint of HarperCollinsPublishers

ISBN 978-0-06-305045-7

22 23 24 25 26   PC/LSCH   10 9 8 7 6 5 4 3 2 1
❖
First Edition

Special thanks to Cherith Baldry

ALLEGIANCES

WINDCLAN

LEADER

TALLSTAR—large black-and-white tom with amber eyes

APPRENTICE, **MORNINGPAW** (tortoiseshell-and-white she-cat with amber eyes)

DEPUTY

DEADFOOT—lean black tom with a twisted left paw

APPRENTICE, **ONEPAW** (pale brown tabby tom)

MEDICINE CATS

HAWKHEART—stone-gray tom with flecks of darker brown fur

BARKFACE—short-tailed dark brown tom

WARRIORS

STAGLEAP—dark brown tom with amber eyes

WRENFLIGHT—brown she-cat

MEADOWSLIP—gray she-cat

MISTMOUSE—light brown tabby she-cat

DOESPRING—light brown she-cat

PIGEONFLIGHT—dark gray tom with white patches

LARKSPLASH—tortoiseshell-and-white she-cat

APPRENTICE, **ASHPAW** (gray she-cat)

ASPENFALL—gray-and-white tom

MUDCLAW—dark brown tabby tom

TORNEAR—gray tabby tom

CROWFUR—black tom

RUSHTAIL—light brown tom

OATWHISKER—creamy-brown tabby tom

DARKFOOT—blue-gray tom

CLOUDRUNNER—pale gray tom

RABBITEAR—pale brown she-cat with a fluffy white belly and yellow eyes

FLYTAIL—snowy white tom

BRISTLEBARK—black tom

RYESTALK—gray tabby she-cat

QUEENS   **SORRELSHINE**—gray-and-brown she-cat

ELDERS   **HAREFLIGHT**—light brown tom

REDCLAW—dark ginger tom

HICKORYNOSE—brown tom

APPLEDAWN—pale cream she-cat

PLUMCLAW—dark gray she-cat

THUNDERCLAN

LEADER   **SUNSTAR**—bright ginger tom with yellow eyes

DEPUTY   **BLUEFUR**—thick-furred blue-gray she-cat with blue eyes

APPRENTICE, RUNNINGPAW (light brown tabby tom)

MEDICINE CATS   **FEATHERWHISKER**—pale silvery tom with bright amber eyes, long whiskers, sweeping, plumy tail

SPOTTEDLEAF—dark tortoiseshell she-cat with a distinctive dappled coat

WARRIORS   **BRINDLEFACE**—pale gray tabby she-cat

SPARROWPELT—big, dark brown tabby tom with yellow eyes

REDTAIL—tortoiseshell tom with a ginger tail
APPRENTICE, MOUSEPAW (brown she-cat)

THRUSHPELT—sandy-gray tom with white flash on his chest and green eyes

ROBINWING—small brown she-cat with ginger patch on her chest and amber eyes

PATCHPELT—small black-and-white tom with amber eyes

DAPPLETAIL—tortoiseshell she-cat with beautiful dappled coat

SPECKLETAIL—pale tabby she-cat with amber eyes

LEOPARDFOOT—black she-cat with green eyes

FROSTFUR—white she-cat with blue eyes

THISTLECLAW—gray-and-white tom with amber eyes

LIONHEART—golden tabby tom with green eyes

GOLDENFLOWER—pale ginger tabby she-cat with yellow eyes

TIGERCLAW—big dark brown tabby tom with unusually long front claws

WHITESTORM—big white tom

ROSETAIL—gray tabby she-cat with a bushy reddish tail

QUEENS

WILLOWPELT—pale gray she-cat with blue eyes (mother to Darkkit, dark gray tabby tom)

ELDERS

SWIFTBREEZE—tabby-and-white she-cat

with yellow eyes

POPPYDAWN—long-haired, dark red she-cat with a bushy tail and amber eyes

GOOSEFEATHER—speckled gray tom

FUZZYPELT—black tom

ADDERFANG—mottled brown tabby tom with yellow eyes

SMALLEAR—gray tom with very small ears and amber eyes

WINDFLIGHT—gray tabby tom with pale green eyes

ONE-EYE—pale gray she-cat, blind in one eye

RIVERCLAN

LEADER   **CROOKEDSTAR**—light brown tabby tom with green eyes and a twisted jaw

DEPUTY   **TIMBERFUR**—brown tom

MEDICINE CATS   **BRAMBLEBERRY**—white she-cat with black spotted fur and blue eyes
APPRENTICE, MUDFUR (mottled light brown tom)

WARRIORS   **RIPPLECLAW**—black-and-silver tabby tom
APPRENTICE, MALLOWPAW (tortoiseshell tabby and white she-cat)

VOLECLAW—gray tom

ECHOMIST—pale gray she-cat
APPRENTICE, MISTYPAW (pale gray she-cat)

CEDARPELT—mottled brown tabby tom

FROGLEAP—gray tom

OWLFUR—brown-and-white tom

BLACKCLAW—black tom

OTTERSPLASH—white-and-pale-ginger she-cat

SEDGECREEK—brown tabby she-cat
APPRENTICE, DAWNPAW (ginger-and-white she-cat)

BEETLENOSE—tom with crow-black fur

REEDTAIL—pale gray tabby tom

SOFTWING—white she-cat with tabby patches
APPRENTICE, STONEPAW (pale blue-gray tom)

SKYHEART—pale brown tabby she-cat

WHITEFANG—white tom with brown paws

LEOPARDFUR—unusually spotted golden tabby she-cat

LILYSTEM—pale gray she-cat

SHIMMERPELT—black she-cat

PIKETOOTH—dark brown tabby tom

PETALDUST—tortoiseshell she-cat

LAKESHINE—mottled gray-and-white she-cat

OAKHEART—reddish-brown tom with amber eyes

LOUDBELLY—dark brown tom

WILLOWBREEZE—pale gray tabby she-cat with amber eyes

GRAYPOOL—dark gray she-cat with yellow eyes

SUNFISH—pale gray she-cat

ELDERS

FALLOWTAIL—brown she-cat

BIRDSONG—tabby-and-white she-cat

SHADOWCLAN

LEADER

RAGGEDSTAR—large, dark brown tabby tom

DEPUTY

CLOUDPELT—white tom with blue eyes

MEDICINE CATS

YELLOWFANG—dark gray she-cat with a broad, flattened face

RUNNINGNOSE—small gray-and-white tom

WARRIORS

BLIZZARDWING—mottled white tom

WOLFSTEP—gray tom with a torn ear

DEERFOOT—light brown tom

TANGLEBURR—gray-and-brown she-cat

BLACKFOOT—white tom with black paws

FLINTFANG—gray tom

FERNSHADE—tortoiseshell she-cat

RUSSETFUR—dark ginger she-cat

BOULDER—gray tom

CLAWFACE—brown tom

BROKENTAIL—dark brown tabby tom
APPRENTICE, STUMPYPAW (brown tom)

BRACKENFOOT—pale ginger tom with dark ginger legs

HOLLYFLOWER—dark gray-and-white she-cat

MUDCLAW—gray tom with brown legs

LIZARDSTRIPE—pale brown tabby she-cat with yellow eyes

TOADSKIP—dark brown tabby tom with white splashes and white legs

FEATHERSTORM—brown tabby she-cat

SCORCHWIND—ginger tabby tom

NEWTSPECK—black-and-ginger tabby she-cat

ASHHEART—pale gray she-cat with blue eyes

AMBERLEAF—dark ginger she-cat with brown legs and ears

FROGTAIL—dark gray tom

NETTLESPOT—white she-cat with ginger flecks

FINCHFLIGHT—black-and-white tom

NUTWHISKER—brown tom with amber eyes
APPRENTICE, CINDERPAW (gray tom)

ROWANBERRY—cream-and-brown she-cat with amber eyes

MOUSEWING—black tom with long, thick fur

ELDERS

DEERLEAP—gray tabby she-cat with white legs

ARCHEYE—gray tabby tom with black stripes and thick stripe over one eye

CROWTAIL—black tabby she-cat

POOLCLOUD—gray-and-white she-cat

NIGHTPELT—black tom

LIZARDFANG—light brown tabby tom with one hooked tooth

ASHFUR—gray tom

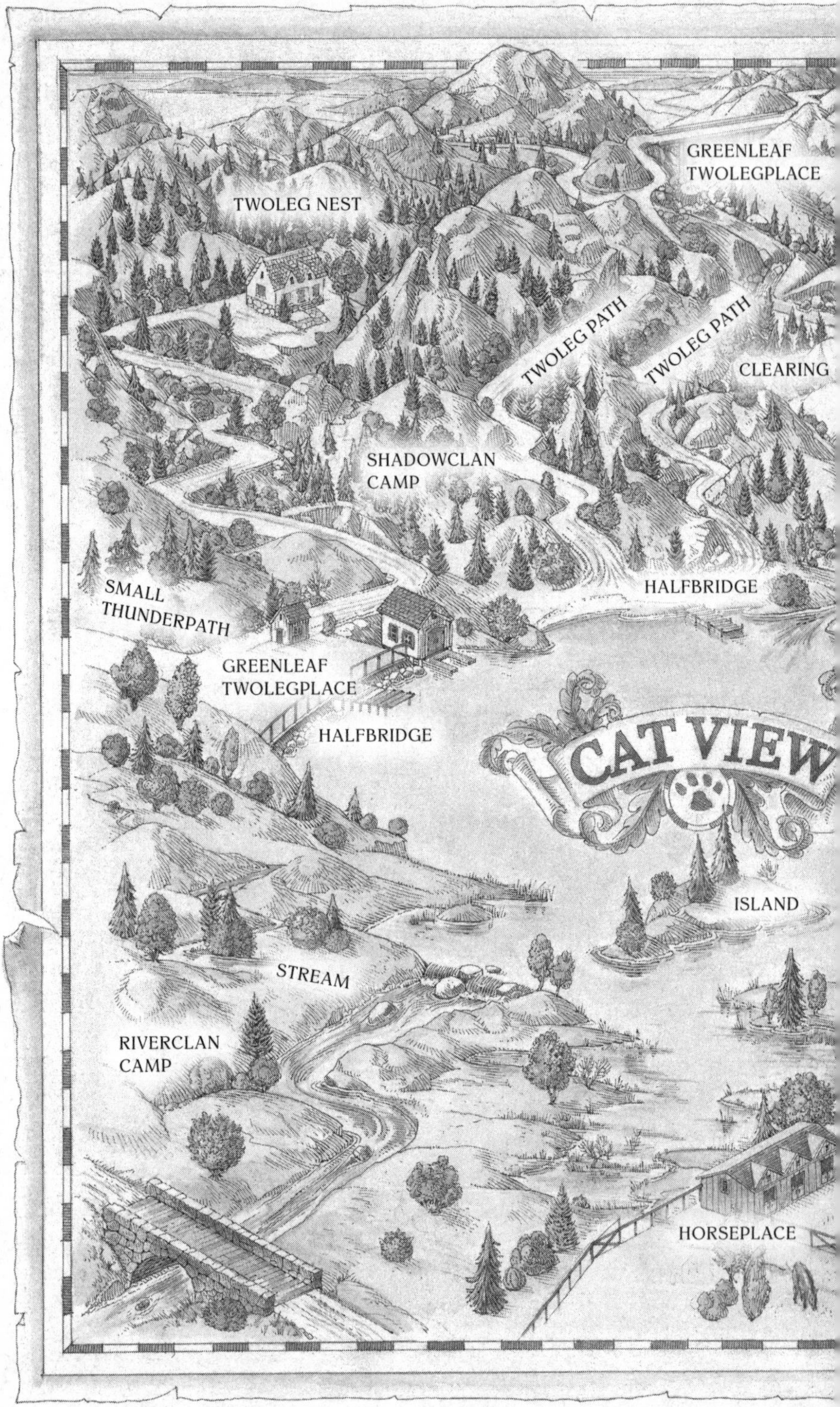

GREENLEAF
TWOLEGPLACE

TWOLEG NEST

TWOLEG PATH

TWOLEG PATH

CLEARING

SHADOWCLAN
CAMP

SMALL
THUNDERPATH

HALFBRIDGE

GREENLEAF
TWOLEGPLACE

HALFBRIDGE

CAT VIEW

ISLAND

STREAM

RIVERCLAN
CAMP

HORSEPLACE

HAREVIEW
CAMPSITE

SANCTUARY
COTTAGE

SADLER WOODS

LITTLEPINE
SAILING
CENTER

LITTLEPINE ROAD

TWOLEG V

LITTLEPINE
ISLAND

RIVER ALBA

WHITECHURCH ROAD

KNIGHT
COPSE

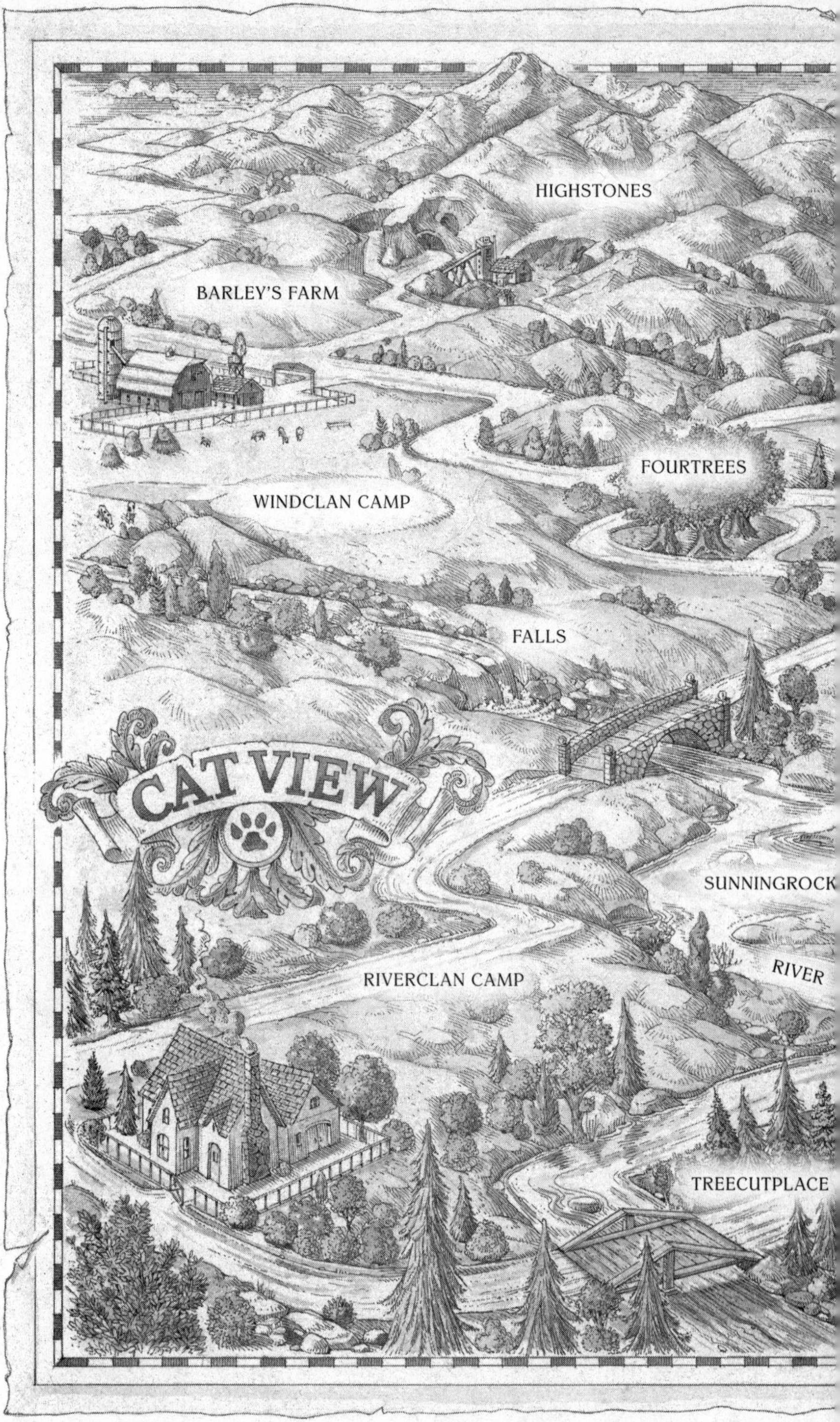

HIGHSTONES

BARLEY'S FARM

FOURTREES

WINDCLAN CAMP

FALLS

CAT VIEW

SUNNINGROCK

RIVERCLAN CAMP

RIVER

TREECUTPLACE

THE OLD
FOREST
TERRITORIES

CARRIONPLACE

SHADOWCLAN
CAMP

THUNDERPATH

OWLTREE

GREAT
SYCAMORE

THUNDERCLAN
CAMP

SNAKEROCKS

SANDY
HOLLOW

TALLPINES

TWOLEGPLACE

KEY
To The
CLANS

THUNDERCLAN

RIVERCLAN

SHADOWCLAN

WINDCLAN

STARCLAN

NORTH

DEVIL'S FINGERS
[disused mine]

WINDOVER FARM

NORTH ALLERTON ROAD

DRUID'S
HOLLOW

WINDOVER MOOR

DRUID'S
LEAP

TWOLEG VIEW

RIVER CHELL

MORGAN'S FARM
CAMPSITE

MORGAN'S
FARM

MORGAN'S LANE

THE OLD
FOREST
TERRITORIES

NORTH ALLERTON
AMENITY TIP

WINDOVER ROAD

WHITE HART WOODS

CHELFORD FOREST

CHELFORD MILL

CHELFORD

KEY To The TERRAIN

DECIDUOUS WOODLAND

CONIFERS

MARSH

CLIFFS AND ROCKS

HIKING TRAILS

NORTH

PROLOGUE

Don't let go! Onestar screeched silently.

He felt the pebbly lake bed fall away beneath him, leaving him to flounder in deeper water. Above his head, gray light filtered down from the surface. His instincts were telling him to kick out, to force himself upward, back into the life-saving air. But he forced them down and kept his forelegs clamped around Darktail's shoulders, his claws digging deep into the white tom's pelt. His hind legs battered against Darktail's belly, and he glimpsed a spurt of dark blood, soon lost in the roiling water.

Darktail lashed at him with one forepaw, tearing at his pelt; the other forepaw gripped him by the throat. The rogue's teeth were bared in a soundless snarl, and the blue eyes that glared at Onestar were glittering with hatred.

How did things go so wrong? Onestar asked himself in the midst of his struggle. *My son truly hates me, and his hate has cost me and all the Clans so much. . . .*

As his chest grew tighter with the need for air, Onestar realized that he and Darktail were both going to die. They were clamped too tightly together for either cat to escape and reach the surface.

This is where it ends.

The realization brought Onestar a curious relief. It was over now: the seasons of regret, and all the lies he had told, especially these last few moons, when he had betrayed every cat in the lake territories by refusing to fight against Darktail and his Kin.

Darktail, his son and his enemy. The enemy of all the Clans.

As they grappled, the two cats sank deeper, the daylight dying; blackness had begun to creep into the edges of Onestar's vision. But he could still see Darktail's face pressed close to his, and Darktail's eyes, blue and furious, just as they had looked on the day of the terrible battle. Onestar heard again what Darktail had said to him then, the words echoing in his mind.

What do you think will happen to a cat who rejected, and then killed, his own son? Surely that cat would end up in the Dark Forest.

Darktail could not have known that Onestar had only one life remaining. But terror of the fate he had foretold had sent Onestar fleeing from the battle, calling his Clan to retreat with him, tilting the balance of the fight against the Clan cats.

Digging his claws deeper into Darktail's shoulders, Onestar saw terror flare in his enemy's eyes. But he found that his own fear had left him. All he felt now was a desperate hope: that perhaps he had redeemed himself by ridding the Clans of the cat who would have destroyed them all.

Then darkness enfolded him utterly, and his senses swirled away.

* * *

Onestar opened his eyes into a dazzle of light. He could breathe easily, and his fur felt warm and dry, as if the sun were gently caressing him. When his vision cleared, he found that he was lying at the bottom of a shallow dip in moorland; a soft breeze stirred the grass, bringing with it rich scents of growing things and prey. Above him the sky was blue, dotted with small puffs of white cloud.

It's like WindClan's territory back in the old forest, before Twolegs destroyed it.

Raising his head, Onestar began to look around. Shock coursed through him like a shower of icy rain as he spotted Darktail standing a couple of fox-lengths away from him, fixing him with a cold, malignant gaze.

Onestar braced himself for an attack, but the white tom didn't move. Instead he opened his jaws to speak, but no sound came out. The look in Darktail's eyes changed to horror as his form began to fade, dissolving into air until nothing was left except a curl of white mist in the grass. Then even that was gone.

His heart thumping uncomfortably, Onestar stared at his own paws, expecting that he too would fade away. He slid out his claws, as if that might anchor him in the tough moorland turf. But nothing happened—nothing except the sound of a cat clearing their throat somewhere behind him.

Onestar glanced over his shoulder and saw a cat standing at the top of the hollow, outlined against the sky. He couldn't make out any features or the color of the cat's pelt, but after a moment he recognized the rangy silhouette and the tall tail pointing straight upward.

"Tallstar!" he gasped.

He sprang to his paws and spun to face his former leader, dipping his head in the deepest respect. When he had last seen Tallstar alive, the older cat had been exhausted, dying under a bush at the end of the Great Journey to the lake. Now, as he padded slowly down the slope to join Onestar at the bottom of the hollow, his muscles rippled beneath a sleek black-and-white pelt. His eyes shone with health, and starshine shimmered around his paws and his ears.

"Greetings, Onestar," he meowed.

"Greetings, Tallstar," Onestar responded, his heart pounding with excitement. "It's so good to see you again." When Tallstar said nothing more, he added hesitantly. "I know I'm dead. Right? But I don't know what this place is. It doesn't look like the Dark Forest, but . . . but surely I don't belong in StarClan. Or do I?"

"That's a question that will take some answering," Tallstar replied. "And because of that, you've been sent here to wait while StarClan discusses what to do with you."

"Oh." Onestar was bewildered. He had always believed that once a cat died, their destination had already been decided. "Er . . . do I need to do anything?"

"No. Just wait." Tallstar stepped forward and touched noses with Onestar. His eyes were brimming with affection. "Even if you weren't perfect," he continued, "I know you always tried to put WindClan first, and protect your Clan."

With a dip of his head he turned and padded away, over the lip of the hollow.

Onestar watched him until he disappeared out of sight. *I know I've made mistakes,* he thought miserably, his tail drooping. *But I've made good choices, too. I've done my best all my life . . . haven't I?*

Sinking down into the grass, Onestar began to think about the path his paw steps had followed to bring him here. *How can I account for it all now?* he asked himself. *An entire lifetime?*

Like a stream running back toward its spring, Onestar's memories carried him through Darktail's invasion, beyond the Great Battle against the cats of the Dark Forest, to the Great Journey, which had ended so unexpectedly in his becoming leader. And at last his thoughts flew all the way back to when he was first made apprentice and went hunting with his mentor in the hills of the old territory. . . .

CHAPTER 1

A stiff breeze blew across the moor, streaming through Onepaw's fur and making his eyes water. He breathed it in eagerly, alert for scents of prey as he padded after his mentor, Deadfoot. The air of early newleaf was still cold, but Onepaw scarcely noticed the chill. Every hair on his pelt was tingling with excitement.

There's nothing better than this! he told himself, feeling that his heart would burst out of his chest with pride. *Being an apprentice, and hunting to feed my Clan.*

He scanned the stretch of moorland carefully, hoping that he might be the first cat in the patrol to spot prey. But it was Onepaw's mother, Wrenflight, who drew Deadfoot's attention with the touch of her tail on his shoulder, angling her ears toward a rabbit that had just emerged from a burrow in a rocky bank.

Instantly Onepaw dropped into the hunter's crouch, making sure that his paws were tucked in correctly. He extended a paw, beginning to creep toward the rabbit—only to halt as Deadfoot flicked out his tail in front of him.

"Keep still," his mentor murmured, his mouth close to

Onepaw's ear. "You won't catch the rabbit like that. There's no cover, and as soon as it spots you, it'll vanish back into its burrow."

Onepaw looked up at the black tom, his excitement fading. "Sorry," he muttered.

"It's okay," Deadfoot responded. "At least you reacted quickly. And that was a good crouch."

While they spoke, Wrenflight had begun to move off in a wide curve, her belly fur brushing the grass. Onepaw realized she was trying to work her way around to get between the rabbit and its hole. Mudclaw, the fourth member of the patrol, was doing exactly the same in the other direction.

Deadfoot crouched down behind a tussock of longer grass and motioned to Onepaw to join him. "What can you tell me about the wind?" he asked.

"It's blowing toward us," Onepaw replied. "So that means the rabbit can't scent us."

His mentor nodded approvingly. "Until . . . ?"

Onepaw had to think about that for a moment. "Until Wrenflight and Mudclaw get behind it?" he asked hesitantly.

"Quite right. What do you think the rabbit will do then?"

Again Onepaw needed to think, trying not to squirm under his mentor's questioning gaze. "It'll run away from them . . . and toward us!"

Deadfoot let out a soft *mrrow* of laughter. "You see, there are more ways of catching a rabbit than tearing after it across the moor."

Onepaw glanced at Deadfoot's twisted paw. He had been

born with it, and it meant he didn't have the speed of other WindClan warriors. Yet he was still known as one of the best hunters in the Clan. Every cat had respected Tallstar's choice when he was made deputy.

"Yes, I can't run fast," Deadfoot mewed, clearly noticing the glance. "That means I have to be sneaky instead. Now you move over a bit in that direction." He gestured with his tail. "If the rabbit heads for you, you know what to do."

Onepaw slid off to where Deadfoot had indicated, flattening himself to the ground and hoping that his tabby fur would blend into the green-and-brown moorland grass.

By this time Wrenflight and Mudclaw had reached the bank where the rabbit had its burrow. The rabbit had ventured farther out and was nibbling at the grass. Suddenly it sat up, startled, and let out a terrified squeal: it had spotted the hunting cats. It darted toward the bank, but Wrenflight and Mudclaw were barring its way to safety. The rabbit skidded to a halt, then whipped around to race away with the two warriors hard on its paws. Onepaw's eyes went wide with a mixture of nerves and excitement as he realized it was making straight for him.

Oh, StarClan, please don't let me mess this up!

As the rabbit drew closer, Onepaw rose up out of the grass, letting out a furious snarl. He sprang at the rabbit, forelegs extended, and felt his claws swipe through its fur. The rabbit veered away, unhurt, and for a heartbeat Onepaw felt utter shame and despair at having missed the catch. Then he spotted Deadfoot leaping forward in a strong pounce. His mentor's claws fastened around the rabbit's neck, and he killed it with a swift bite to its throat.

"Thank you, StarClan, for this prey," he meowed.

Mudclaw and Wrenflight dashed up, panting, and looked down with satisfaction at the limp body of the rabbit.

"That was a neat bit of teamwork," Mudclaw remarked.

Onepaw padded over to join them, his head drooping. "I'm sorry I missed it."

"Sorry?" Deadfoot gave him an encouraging purr. "You have nothing to be sorry for, youngster. You headed it off exactly right, so I could catch it. Good job."

Onepaw's chest swelled with renewed pride. He wasn't sure that he had done as well as Deadfoot said, but he had been part of the team, and they had caught their prey. Water flooded his jaws at the succulent scent of the fresh-kill. They would eat well in camp that evening.

"Do you want to take this back?" Mudclaw asked Deadfoot. "Or should we bury it and try for more?"

"Bury it," Deadfoot instructed him. "I want to go have a look at the RiverClan border."

Wrenflight gave him a doubtful look, the fur on her shoulders beginning to rise. "At the last Gathering, Crookedstar reported that a RiverClan patrol had seen badgers there, on our side."

Deadfoot nodded. "I know. That's exactly why I want to have a look. If badgers are on our territory, we need to know about it. And if they're not, we might pick up a few voles by the river."

Mudclaw slid out his claws; a growl came from deep within his throat. "Badgers or voles, they'd better look out."

Onepaw swallowed nervously as the patrol set out again. He had been apprenticed for barely two moons, and so far he hadn't seen any badgers. But he had heard plenty of stories about them, told by the elders in their den while he was clearing out their bedding or removing their ticks. They sounded like fearsome creatures; Onepaw wasn't sure whether he wanted to meet one or not.

Mudclaw took the lead as the patrol headed for the River-Clan border. The moorland sloped gently downward, and in the distance Onepaw could hear a dull roar; when he had toured WindClan's territory for the first time with Deadfoot, his mentor had told him it was the sound of a waterfall across the RiverClan border.

"If there are badgers, stay back and let us warriors deal with them," Wrenflight instructed Onepaw as they padded along at the rear of the patrol. "They're far too dangerous for a new apprentice to tackle."

Onepaw muttered something that he hoped sounded like agreement. Privately, he had no intention of staying back. *Like I'm going to hide, as if I were still a kit! Anyway, Wrenflight isn't my mentor.*

Wrenflight was giving him a doubtful look, but before she could say any more, Mudclaw suddenly let out a yowl and dashed off, his pelt bristling with anger.

"Mudclaw!" Deadfoot called after him, but the dark brown tom took no notice. He quickly vanished behind a fold of the moorland. "Stupid furball," Deadfoot growled. "Wrenflight, go after him. We'll be right behind you."

As his mother took off, Onepaw turned to his mentor. "Is it badgers?" he asked, not feeling quite as brave as he had a few moments before.

Deadfoot began limping along in his Clanmate's paw steps, tasting the air as he went. "What do you think?" he asked.

I've never smelled a badger, Onepaw thought, but he opened his jaws and let the air flow over his scent glands. He could pick up the ordinary moorland scents, traces of water from the nearby river, cat-scent . . .

"Cats!" he exclaimed. "But they're not WindClan cats, or RiverClan. Strange cats on our territory!"

Deadfoot nodded. "Well scented. Trespassers. No wonder Mudclaw was angry, though he should have more sense than to charge off like that."

Even at Deadfoot's slower pace, he and Onepaw soon caught up to their Clanmates, at the point where the Wind-Clan border turned to run alongside the river. Mudclaw and Wrenflight were confronting a brown tabby-and-white she-cat. From her plump body and sleek fur, Onepaw guessed she was a kittypet. Two younger cats—about Onepaw's own age—were crouching just behind the she-cat and gazing at the Clan cats with wide, scared eyes.

"What do you think you're doing here?" Mudclaw's lips were drawn back in a snarl. "This is *our* territory. WindClan territory."

"Take it easy, Mudclaw." Wrenflight touched her

Clanmate's shoulder with the tip of her tail. "You don't have to frighten them out of their fur."

The kittypet held her head high, though there was a quiver in her voice as she responded. "We're sorry—we didn't realize this place belonged to any cat. We were just exploring."

Onepaw blinked in surprise. He hadn't thought that any kittypet would dare to set paw outside their own Twoleg garden. *Exploring—just for fun? That's really brave!*

Deadfoot seemed to share his surprise. "Why would you want to do that?" he asked.

The she-cat dipped her head toward him. "I want my kits to learn how to be strong," she explained, "and how to survive without the help of housefolk. So we were practicing hunting."

"Housefolk" must be what kittypets call their Twolegs, Onepaw thought.

"Hunting?" Mudclaw snarled. "Did you catch anything?"

The mother cat shook her head.

"I nearly caught a mouse!" one of her kits, a sturdy ginger tom, boasted.

"*Nearly* fills no bellies," Mudclaw growled. "And you're lucky it was only *nearly*. This is our territory, and our prey. Deadfoot," he continued, "we ought to teach these trespassers a lesson. I could do with some kittypet fur to line my nest."

The mother cat let out a gasp; her shoulder fur fluffed up and she slid out her claws. Onepaw couldn't help admiring her courage, that she was ready to stand up to three experienced warriors. His belly lurched at the thought of what his Clanmates could do to her and her kits.

To his relief, Wrenflight stepped forward. "Keep your claws to yourself, Mudclaw. They're not doing any harm."

Deadfoot nodded. "Wrenflight is right. These kittypets just made a mistake. We'll escort them off our territory, and that will be the end of it. Where did you come from?"

"That way." The mother she-cat gestured upriver with her tail.

With a brusque nod Deadfoot took the lead again; the she-cat followed, closely escorted by Mudclaw and Wrenflight, one on each side. Onepaw brought up the rear with the two young kittypets.

At first they padded along in silence. The mother cat was the first to speak, her voice bright and friendly now that the danger was over. "My name's Bailey," she mewed. "What's yours?"

Mudclaw kept a hostile silence, and it was Wrenflight who replied. "I'm Wrenflight, and this is Mudclaw. The cat up ahead is Deadfoot. We're WindClan cats."

"Wind . . . Clan?" Bailey sounded confused. "What's that?"

Onepaw heard Mudclaw mutter, "Great StarClan!"

Once again it was Wrenflight who explained. "A Clan is a group of cats. We live together and we help one another."

"And we fight off intruders," Mudclaw added, with a glare at Bailey. "Now stop asking so many questions. It's really none of your business."

Bailey fell silent, though Onepaw could see from the flick of her tail-tip that Mudclaw's hostility was irritating her.

Onepaw was aware of tension rising again, but the young

ginger tom looked quite cheerful as he turned toward him. "Are you a—a WindClan cat, too?" he asked.

"Of course I am," Onepaw replied, and added proudly, "I'm an apprentice. My name is Onepaw."

The young she-cat, brown tabby and white like her mother, gave Onepaw a puzzled stare. "But you have four paws," she mewed.

"Well spotted." Onepaw stifled a snort of laughter. "*Paw* at the end of my name just means I'm an apprentice. When I finish my training, our leader, Tallstar, will give me my warrior name."

"Cool!" the ginger tom exclaimed. "Hey, Melody, we could be apprentices. You'd be Melodypaw and I'd be Leopaw!"

Onepaw thought those names sounded weird, but he didn't say so. "To be apprentices, you have to have a mentor," he explained. "Deadfoot is mine. He's tough on me sometimes, but he knows loads."

By this time the cats had traveled some way upriver and were approaching a wooden Twoleg bridge, like the one farther downriver that RiverClan used when they went to Gatherings. A Twoleg den and a cluster of smaller buildings lay just beyond it, and farther away Onepaw could make out the rooftops of a small Twolegplace.

"That's where we live," Bailey meowed, waving her tail toward the Twolegplace. "We'll be fine from here."

Wrenflight dipped her head politely. "Good-bye, and may StarClan light your path."

"What's StarClan?" Leo asked, but no cat answered him.

Bailey turned away to lead her kits across the bridge, but she had scarcely set paw on it when a terrible stink wafted over Onepaw, so strong that he almost choked on it.

"What's that?" Melody asked.

At the same moment, Deadfoot yowled, "Badger!"

Onepaw whirled around to see a huge animal lumbering toward them. It was black, except for a white stripe down its head and muzzle. Its eyes were tiny, cold, and berry-bright; its paws were tipped with strong, blunt claws. Its jaws gaped, showing rows of sharp teeth.

A thought flashed through Onepaw's mind. *The elders didn't tell me the half of it! This creature is terrifying!*

At the same moment Mudclaw let out a fearsome screech and hurled himself at the badger. Wrenflight was a heartbeat behind.

Both warriors darted in, raked their claws across the badger's flanks, then sprang back out of range of its claws. The badger tossed its head from side to side, as if it didn't know which cat to attack first. While it was confused, Deadfoot slid underneath its chest, slashed at its belly, and rolled out between its fore- and hind legs. The badger let out a bellow of rage and pain, swiping at Deadfoot with one massive paw, but the black tom limped rapidly away, unhurt.

Onepaw braced himself, trying to remember his battle moves, then leaped up to scratch the badger's nose. Falling back to the ground, he stumbled; a heartbeat later he was staring down the badger's throat as it loomed over him, jaws parted to engulf him.

A paw batted him from one side, forcing him to slither backward away from the threatening teeth. He realized that Mudclaw had thrust him out of danger; now the brown tom had leaped up to fasten his teeth in the badger's shoulder and was battering at it with his strong hind legs.

Panting, Onepaw tottered to his paws. To his surprise, he saw that Bailey had joined in the fight, copying the Clan cats as they darted forward to attack the badger, then leaped away before the slow-moving creature could land a blow.

"Your mother is amazing," he told Leo and Melody.

The two young kittypets were huddled together at the end of the bridge, watching the fight with wide, wondering eyes. Onepaw guessed they didn't realize that this could end in death. They both turned to him with pleased purrs when he praised their mother.

"We can help," Leo meowed.

"Yes, show us what to do," Melody added.

"You can help by staying back," Onepaw declared. "You saw how I nearly got myself killed, and I've had some warrior training. If you try to fight, you'll just get in the way."

"Will not," Leo muttered, but Melody seemed to agree, just dipping her head to Onepaw.

I'd better stay with them, Onepaw thought. *If the badger heads this way, I can try to protect them.*

The words had scarcely gone through his mind when the badger swiped at Deadfoot, catching him in the side and hurling him tail-lengths away. Deadfoot hit the ground with a thud and lay still. Mudclaw and Wrenflight were briefly distracted, and in that moment the badger broke away and began to tramp on heavy, determined paws straight for the three young cats at the end of the bridge.

Onepaw gathered all his strength, sliding out his claws. His heart was pounding, and every hair on his pelt rose in terror. "Run!" he snapped at the two kittypets, but neither of them obeyed him. They stayed at his side, trying to imitate his crouch.

All of his muscles were telling him to flee across the bridge, but he didn't move. *I'm a warrior apprentice. We don't run away!*

Then a tabby-and-white shape flashed in front of his eyes. To his astonishment, Bailey leaped straight for the badger's muzzle and raked one set of foreclaws down it while with her other paw she slashed at its eyes. "Not my kits, flea-pelt!" she screeched.

After dropping to the ground, she crouched with bristling fur, ready to attack again. Wrenflight and Mudclaw dashed up to support her, and all three cats snarled defiance at the badger.

But the badger had had enough. Turning away, it lumbered up the moorland slope away from the river and disappeared over the crest.

Every cat flopped to the ground, panting and limp with relief. A few tail-lengths away, Deadfoot had heaved himself to his paws, and he walked unsteadily across to join them.

"Are you okay?" Wrenflight asked, scanning him anxiously as he approached.

"Fine." Deadfoot's voice was hoarse in his throat. "Just

winded. Great StarClan, I thought we were finished," he went on. "But you all fought well." His gaze rested on Bailey. "I saw what you did. That was truly brave."

"For a kittypet," Mudclaw muttered.

"For any cat." Wrenflight's voice was sharp. "Bailey, you saved your kits, and our apprentice. WindClan honors you."

Bailey dipped her head and gave her chest fur a few embarrassed licks. "It wasn't anything," she murmured. "I didn't have time to think about it."

"You were amazing!" Leo meowed enthusiastically, while Melody nuzzled her mother's shoulder, letting out a loud purr. Bailey turned her head and licked her daughter's ears.

"We're all very grateful to you," Deadfoot declared. "Have a safe journey back to your Twolegs."

Instead of leading her kits across the bridge, Bailey hesitated. "Actually . . . ," she began hesitantly, "could we come to your camp? I'd like to speak to your leader."

"Why do you want to do that?" Mudclaw asked, suspicion instantly flaring in his eyes.

Onepaw admired Bailey even more when he saw that she wasn't intimidated by the brown tom's harsh tone. "I'm interested in what I've heard of warrior life," she replied, meeting Mudclaw's gaze steadily. "I'd like to know more. Maybe my kits could be apprenticed to become warriors."

"Yay!" Leo squealed, bouncing up and down with excitement. Melody seemed more doubtful, rolling her eyes at her brother.

"Really?" Wrenflight sounded disbelieving.

"I'm worried that they won't be able to take care of themselves if they rely on our housefolk all the time," Bailey continued. "I've seen housefolk abandon their kittypets, and the kittypets were quite helpless on their own. I don't want that for Leo and Melody. Being part of a Clan might be a better life for them. Surely we have something to offer WindClan that would make you want to help my kits become warriors?"

Wrenflight looked thoughtful, but Deadfoot was disapproving and Mudclaw outright hostile, glaring at Bailey as if for a couple of mousetails he would spring at her with his claws extended.

"I don't think that would work," Onepaw explained, glancing doubtfully at the two younger cats. "Kittypets aren't welcome in the Clans. They're just not cut out for Clan life!"

Bailey dipped her head, acknowledging what he had said. "I appreciate your concern," she mewed, "but all the same, I'd like to talk to your leader and plead our case."

"Fox dung!" Mudclaw snarled. "WindClan already has apprentices, and we don't need kittypets making trouble and eating our prey. You all need to head back to your Twolegplace and stay there!"

"Hey, Mudclaw, that's not fair," Wrenflight protested. "Bailey was incredibly brave, fighting off that badger. Besides, Onepaw and his two littermates are the only apprentices we have right now. WindClan *could* use more young cats."

"Yes, true Clan cats, not soft, useless kittypets!" Mudclaw snarled at her.

At his words Leo sprang forward and faced him, his ginger

fur fluffing up. "Who are you calling soft and useless?"

Bailey stepped forward and nudged her son away from the WindClan warrior. "Leo, that's enough."

Leo bared his teeth and let out a furious snarl, his glare almost the exact copy of Mudclaw's, but he said nothing more.

Deadfoot thrust himself between them, raising his tail for silence. "That one has spirit, at least," he meowed with a nod to Leo. "And Mudclaw, hurling insults benefits no cat. In any case, it's not up to us to accept or refuse these kittypets. We'll take them to Tallstar and let him decide."

"And Tallstar will say no!" Mudclaw spat.

Mudclaw doesn't have to be so rude about it, Onepaw thought. *But he's probably right.*

CHAPTER 2

There was already a stir of anticipation in the WindClan camp when Deadfoot led his patrol over the edge of the hollow. Onepaw guessed that some cat keeping watch on Outlook Rock had spotted them escorting strange cats across the territory.

As soon as the patrol reached the center of the camp, Onepaw's littermates came rushing across to him, their eyes alight with curiosity.

"Who are they?" Ashpaw demanded, flicking her tail toward the newcomers. "They look like kittypets!"

"Are they prisoners?" Morningpaw asked.

"No—but yes, they are kittypets," Onepaw replied. "You'll never guess what happened this morning!"

He settled into a huddle with his littermates to tell the story of how Deadfoot's hunting patrol had met Bailey and her kits beside the river, and how Bailey had helped them fight off a badger.

"You fought a badger?" Morningpaw's eyes stretched wide. "You lucky furball! I've never even seen one."

"I didn't feel so lucky when it was about to eat me," Onepaw responded, shuddering at the memory.

"And Bailey really attacked it?" Ashpaw sounded disbeliev-ing. "But she's a kittypet! Anyway, that doesn't explain what they're doing *here*."

"Bailey wants Leo and Melody to join WindClan," Onepaw explained. "She thinks they'll have a better life as warriors than if they stay kittypets."

"Well, she's not wrong there," Morningpaw mewed. "But will Tallstar let them stay?"

While the apprentices were talking, Deadfoot had called Tallstar out of his den. The WindClan leader paced into the center of the hollow and stood facing the three kittypets. The rest of the WindClan warriors gathered around in a ragged circle; Deadfoot, Wrenflight, and Mudclaw found places at the front.

"Come on!" Onepaw urged his littermates. "Let's find out."

Together the three young cats scampered forward and wriggled through the crowd until they found a vacant spot beside Barkface, the WindClan medicine cat.

Tallstar gave the kittypets a long, thoughtful look; Onepaw realized that Deadfoot must already have told him the story of how they came to be there.

"So . . . ," the Clan leader began at last. "You want to join WindClan."

Before he could continue, he was cut off by yowls of protest from the crowd of cats around him.

"That's mouse-brained! They're kittypets!"

"Kittypets can't be warriors!"

"*I'm* not hunting for them!"

Mudclaw stepped forward until he was standing at the Clan leader's shoulder. "Listen to them, Tallstar. The Clan is no place for kittypets. You should send them back to the Twolegplace right now."

Tallstar narrowed his eyes, glaring at Mudclaw as if he didn't like a warrior telling him what to do. Then he raised his tail for silence. When he could make himself heard again, he went on. "Kittypets can be brave, at times. And Deadfoot tells me that these are not ordinary kittypets. Their mother fought off a badger. She saved her kits—and a WindClan apprentice."

This news was greeted with gasps of astonishment; cats exchanged bewildered glances as if they couldn't believe what they had just heard. Onepaw could see that some of them were having second thoughts.

"*I* think Tallstar should let them join," Morningpaw murmured in Onepaw's ear. "Having more apprentices means less work for us, and more time for hunting and battle training."

"You've got a point there," Onepaw purred.

"If we take your kits into the Clan as apprentices," Tallstar asked Bailey, "what do you plan to do?"

Bailey was obviously ready for the question; her voice as firm as she replied, and she let the Clan leader's gaze steadily. "I could help in the nursery, or maybe assist your medicine cat. I do know a bit about herbs—our housefolk grow them in their garden."

"She seems to know a lot about how Clans work," Ashpaw commented. "Has she been spying?"

Onepaw shook his head. "Wrenflight told her some stuff when we were heading back to camp," he explained. "I think she really would like to see her kits join."

"I'll make myself useful if you let me stay," Bailey continued, "and once my kits are trained, competent warriors, I'll leave."

Tallstar turned to the Clan's medicine cat. "Barkface, what do you think?"

The medicine cat rose to his paws, gave his short tail a twitch, and dipped his head to his leader. "I could use an assistant," he replied. "And Sorrelshine is near to her kitting; she's old to have her first litter, and I'm sure she wouldn't say no to having a more experienced cat helping her in the nursery."

Once again Tallstar lapsed into a thoughtful silence. "I have considered this carefully," he meowed at last. "If I allow the kittypets to stay, there will be conditions. These young cats must prove their worth to the Clan. If they do not, they will be driven out."

"I understand that," Bailey agreed.

"And your presence here must remain secret from the other Clans," Tallstar went on, his voice becoming stern. "You will not come to Gatherings, and no cat outside WindClan will know anything about you unless and until the young cats become warriors."

"That's a good idea," Onepaw whispered to his littermates. "It would be so embarrassing if the other Clans thought we were desperate enough to take in kittypets."

"You have to realize, too, how unusual this is," Tallstar

continued. "As a leader, I wouldn't normally consider allow-ing a kittypet to become a Clanmate. But my warriors admired your courage, Bailey, when you attacked the badger, and you seem to understand how hard the training will be."

"I *want* it to be hard," Bailey responded. "I want my kits to learn to survive."

Her words seemed to impress Tallstar, and after a long pause, he nodded. "Then these kits will become WindClan apprentices," he announced.

"Tallstar, are you sure?" The speaker was Onepaw's father, Stagleap, stepping out of the crowd. "I can't see this ending well—and if it all goes wrong, it will be on your conscience."

Tallstar gave the dark brown tom a measured stare. "I have no problem with that, Stagleap," he meowed.

Stagleap nodded curtly in acknowledgment.

"Then we will hold their apprentice ceremony now," Tall-star declared. "Leo, Melody—"

"Just a moment, Tallstar," Mudclaw broke in. "Has any cat asked these two young kittypets if *they* want to be warriors?"

"Good question," Ashpaw muttered.

Tallstar looked annoyed at the question, but his tone was mild as he responded. "Well, kits?" he asked. "*Do* you want to join WindClan and train to be warriors?"

"Yes!" Instantly Leo let out a squeal and started jumping up and down.

Melody looked less certain; she exchanged a glance with her brother, who nudged her so hard he almost knocked her off her paws. "Yes, okay," she mewed at last.

"Then come and join me here, in the center of the circle," Tallstar instructed, beckoning them with his tail. "This is a completely new life for you," he told the kittypets when they were standing in front of him. "So you must have completely new names." Touching Melody on her shoulder with his tail-tip, he announced, "From this day forward, this apprentice will be known as Tansypaw. Wrenflight, you will be her mentor. You are a wise and loyal cat, and I know you will pass these qualities on to your apprentice." Bending his head, he spoke more quietly to the newly named Tansypaw. "Now go and touch noses with your mentor."

Blinking nervously, Tansypaw headed across the circle to where Wrenflight had taken a pace forward to meet her, then reached up to touch noses. Wrenflight gestured with her tail for Tansypaw to sit beside her.

Now Tallstar turned to Leo, resting his tail-tip on the ginger tom's shoulder. "From this day forward, this apprentice will be known as Brushpaw. Mudclaw, you are a brave and skillful warrior, and I trust that you will be an excellent mentor for Brushpaw."

Mudclaw gave Tallstar a resentful look; clearly the last thing he wanted was to be given a kittypet apprentice.

Without waiting to be told, Brushpaw scampered up to his new mentor, touched noses with him, and sat next to him, his eyes gleaming with excitement.

"*Mudclaw?*" Ashpaw mewed worriedly. "Won't he be mean to Brushpaw, since he didn't want the kittypets here?"

"No, I think Tallstar's being really clever," Onepaw

responded. "Mudclaw doesn't want the kittypets to join us, but he won't let Brushpaw fail, because that would make him look like a bad mentor."

"Yeah," Morningpaw agreed. "And Mudclaw is too loyal a WindClan cat not to try to be the best mentor he can."

"I suppose . . ." Ashpaw still didn't sound convinced. "Anyway, we can help them too," she added, brightening up. "There's lots we can tell them about Clan life."

"Lots!" Onepaw let out a *mrrow* of amusement. "I can't wait to show them how to pick ticks off the elders!"

"You remember the fight against the badger?" Mudclaw began. "How we darted in to slash at it, then darted out again, out of reach of its claws? That's the first thing you're going to learn. Dart—slash—dart. It's easy."

The morning after their apprentice ceremony, Mudclaw and Wrenflight had taken their apprentices out for the tour of the territory. Now it was past sunhigh; Mudclaw and Brushpaw had joined Deadfoot and Onepaw for battle training just outside the camp, while Wrenflight and Tansypaw had joined a hunting patrol.

Brushpaw nodded eagerly at his mentor's instructions. "I get it!" he meowed.

"Okay, then," Mudclaw continued. "We're going to pretend this rock is a badger. Onepaw, you've learned this move already. Show him what to do."

Onepaw dashed toward the rock, remembering to time his paw steps so that when he reached the imaginary badger, he could gather his hind paws under him for a leap, while his forepaws were free to deal a double blow. He kept his claws sheathed as he raked his paws across the rock, then spun around as he landed, and sped back to Brushpaw and their mentors.

"Not bad," Deadfoot grunted with an approving nod. From him that was high praise.

"Now you," Mudclaw ordered Brushpaw.

The new apprentice hurled himself enthusiastically at the rock, but his timing was all wrong. His hind paws skidded, and he hit the rock with his forepaws splayed out; he staggered back and struggled to regain his balance before limping back to the others, his tail drooping.

"Great," Mudclaw muttered. "You've just given the badger a tasty meal of cat."

Onepaw winced at the harsh comment, but Brushpaw was too far away to hear it. When he reached them, looking crestfallen, Mudclaw's tone was far more understanding.

"Tell me what you did wrong," he meowed.

"Well, I . . . when Onepaw did it, he was in the right place to leap up and strike. My hind paws were too far away."

Mudclaw nodded. "Quite right. Onepaw, show him again, but slowly this time."

Onepaw repeated the move, faintly surprised at how patient Mudclaw was being with the apprentice he hadn't even wanted.

When Brushpaw tried again, Mudclaw made him do the move slowly, too, and as he repeated it, speeding up each time, he gradually improved his timing until his paws were striking accurately on the rock.

"Of course, the badger doesn't sit there waiting for you," Mudclaw pointed out when he was satisfied with his apprentice's progress. "It will try to lash out at you. So this time, Onepaw will be the badger. Claws sheathed, both of you."

Brushpaw's eyes sparkled. "This is fun!" he exclaimed, and added to Onepaw, "Watch out, stinky badger—I'm coming to get you!"

Mudclaw rolled his eyes at Deadfoot. "Apprentices!"

Onepaw and Brushpaw practiced the move together several times. At first Onepaw dodged Brushpaw's blows easily, or managed to land a return blow before his opponent could spring away. But the ginger tom didn't give up; soon he was aiming better and dodging more quickly. *He's going to be a great fighter,* Onepaw realized.

Finally, as the sun was beginning to go down, casting red light over the moor, Mudclaw called a halt. "Not bad, for a first try," he told Brushpaw. "We'll go back to camp, and you can choose something from the fresh-kill pile."

Onepaw and Brushpaw headed back to camp side by side, their mentors following more slowly. When they reached the hollow, Onepaw spotted his two littermates sharing fresh-kill. Tansypaw was with them, but as her brother approached, she sprang to her paws and bounded up to him.

"I went hunting!" she exclaimed. "I chased a rabbit!"

"Did you catch it?" Brushpaw asked.

For a moment, Tansypaw looked crestfallen, but then she

brightened up. "No, but Wrenflight said I *would* have caught it, if it hadn't vanished down its burrow. Wrenflight is great!"

Onepaw was pleased to see that Tansypaw seemed to have gotten over her hesitation about becoming a member of the Clan. They joined his littermates beside the fresh-kill pile and chose pieces of prey for themselves. In between mouthfuls of rabbit, Brushpaw described how he had fought a rock, and then Onepaw, and how Mudclaw had praised him.

"He's okay, when you get to know him," he mumbled with his mouth full.

"I want to learn that," Tansypaw mewed. "Just think, Leo—I mean Brushpaw—when we know how to fight, we could attack that horrible dog in the garden next door."

"No, we couldn't," Brushpaw responded. "We won't be going back there. We're WindClan apprentices now."

Tansypaw looked briefly disconcerted; Onepaw wondered whether she had realized that she wouldn't ever be returning to her Twoleg den. Then she shrugged.

"So the dog escapes our wrath." She gave a little *mrrow* of amusement. "Pity."

"Are there many dogs in the Twolegplace?" Morningpaw asked, ruffling up her tortoiseshell pelt. "I wouldn't like that."

"There are, but they don't bother us much," Brushpaw replied. "The one next door can't get through the fence. It just yaps all day. A cat can't sleep in peace."

"Yeah, and it makes stinky messes in the flower beds," Tansypaw added. "It never even learned to bury its dirt!"

Onepaw exchanged a glance with Ashpaw. "So what do you

do all day, in the Twolegplace?" he asked. "You're not fighting or hunting. . . ."

"We sleep, we eat . . ." Tansypaw seemed a bit confused by the question. "Sometimes we go to visit other cats, and sometimes our housefolk pick us up and stroke us."

Ashpaw's eyes stretched wide with shock. "And you *let* them? Why do you think you've got claws?"

"We wouldn't claw our housefolk!" Tansypaw sounded equally shocked.

"Yeah, they might stop feeding us," Brushpaw put in. "Anyway, being stroked is . . . kind of nice."

Onepaw stopped himself from rolling his eyes at his littermates. *These kittypets have a lot to learn,* he thought. *But I think they'll be good Clanmates once they get to know what it's like to be a warrior.*

"Onepaw! Tansypaw! Wake up!"

Onepaw opened his eyes in gray dawn light. Above his head, clouds surged across the sky, driven by a blustering wind; the weather was still cold for newleaf, and threatening rain. He was curled up in the apprentices' den, a sheltered spot between two large boulders. His denmates were sleeping around him in a furry huddle.

"Come on!" Wrenflight was perched on one of the boulders, gazing down into the den. "You're going to do the dawn patrol with me and Deadfoot. Onepaw, give Tansypaw a prod, will you?"

Onepaw obeyed, poking Tansypaw in the belly with one forepaw. The tabby apprentice let out a long, soft growl and wrapped her tail over her ears. Onepaw had to give her another, harder prod before she looked up.

"Why did you have to go and wake me up?" she asked crossly. "I was having a lovely dream about eating a big bowl full of fish and cream."

Onepaw didn't like the sound of that. It had been nearly a moon now since the two kittypets had become apprentices, and he didn't think that Tansypaw was settling in well. *Is she really committed to WindClan if she's dreaming about eating Twoleg food?*

Wrenflight twitched her whiskers in annoyance, but her voice was calm as she said, "Well, I'm sorry there's no cream here, and if you want fish you'll have to go to RiverClan. Right now we're going to do the dawn patrol, and by the time we get back there'll be plenty of prey on the fresh-kill pile."

"But I'm hungry *now*," Tansypaw muttered, struggling to her paws. "And I'm fed up with rabbit, rabbit, rabbit every day."

Wrenflight leaped down from the boulder and disappeared as if she hadn't heard that. Onepaw hoped she hadn't.

Side by side, he and Tansypaw headed out into the camp, where Deadfoot and Wrenflight were waiting, then followed their two mentors toward the border.

Wrenflight looked back over her shoulder. "Tansypaw, we're unlikely to see cats from any other Clans, but if we do, stay out of sight."

"Yes, Wrenflight," Tansypaw meowed. She plodded along beside Onepaw, her head and tail drooping, the wind buffeting her fur. "Being an apprentice is just stupid," she grumbled.

"It takes so much work to get even a few mouthfuls of miserable rabbit, and we have to be outside in the cold all the time. There isn't even anywhere comfortable to sleep. In my housefolk's den I had a cushion!"

Whatever that is, Onepaw thought. "But don't you like being out in the open?" he asked. "The air is so fresh and sparkly, and up here on the moor we can run forever!"

"I don't *want* to run forever," Tansypaw retorted. "And I don't want Wrenflight ordering me around."

"Keep your voice down," Onepaw warned her. "You don't want our mentors to hear you. Anyway, I thought you liked Wrenflight."

Tansypaw looked uncomfortable. "I sort of do," she admitted. "I can see she's a great cat. I just wish she weren't on my tail the whole time."

"She's your mentor. She's supposed to be—"

Onepaw broke off as Wrenflight turned back toward them. "RiverClan cats!" she exclaimed. "Tansypaw, get down here."

The brown she-cat was pointing to a split in the hillside where a narrow stream tracked between thick clumps of moorland grass. Looking beyond her, down the slope that led to the border with RiverClan, Onepaw saw four cats—clearly the RiverClan dawn patrol. They had paused to glance up at the WindClan cats; one of them raised her tail in greeting.

"Hide! Now!" Wrenflight snapped.

"But there's water!" Tansypaw protested.

"So there's water." Onepaw could tell that Wrenflight was making a huge effort to hold on to her patience. "Do you want the RiverClan cats to see you? Have you forgotten what Tall-star said about keeping you and Brushpaw secret from the other Clans? Now get down there."

"All right, I'm going," Tansypaw mewed sulkily. She slid down into the stream, and an indignant wail rose up from where she had disappeared. "It's *cold!*"

"StarClan give me strength," Wrenflight muttered as she followed Deadfoot down the slope.

Onepaw bounded after them to greet the RiverClan patrol at the border. To his relief, no cat mentioned spotting Tansypaw. Even better, the RiverClan cats were heading in the opposite direction, toward Fourtrees, so pretty soon they moved on, and Wrenflight called Tansypaw out from her hiding place.

She came slowly and reluctantly, shaking each paw in turn to dry it, and stood in front of her mentor with a sullen look in her eyes.

"Don't you *ever* do that again!" There was the hint of a snarl in Wrenflight's voice. "When your mentor tells you to do something, you do it. You do not argue. Do you understand? Well, do you?" she added when Tansypaw did not respond.

"Yes, Wrenflight," Tansypaw muttered at last.

"Then let's get on with this patrol," Deadfoot meowed. "If we're not careful, the sunset patrol will catch up with us."

Back in camp, Deadfoot told Onepaw to help himself to prey, and then rest until sunhigh. Tansypaw was about to follow him to the fresh-kill pile when Wrenflight barred her way with her tail.

"Not you," she meowed. "I've got a job for you."

"But that's not fair!" Tansypaw protested. "I patrolled, just like Onepaw."

"No, not just like Onepaw." Wrenflight's tone was icy. "You disobeyed a direct order, and you spent the rest of the patrol moaning and complaining with every paw step. I'm sick of it, Tansypaw, so now I'm going to give you something to complain about. Go and find Barkface, and get him to give you some mouse bile to deal with the elders' ticks."

"What?" Tansypaw gaped in outrage. "I'm not doing that! It's gross!"

Onepaw cringed. Part of him could sympathize with Tansypaw, who was trying to fit into a completely different kind of life from the one she'd always known, but another part of him couldn't believe what a mouse-brain she was being.

"I'll go with you and show you," he offered.

Tansypaw whipped her head around and glared at him. "I said I'm not doing it!" Turning, she bounded off across the camp, but instead of heading for the medicine cat's den, she vanished into the nursery.

"Go after her," Wrenflight told Onepaw. "You might be better at showing her how stupidly she's behaving—before Tallstar gets to hear about it."

"I'll try," Onepaw promised.

He raced across the camp and slipped inside the nursery. Sorrelshine had kitted the day before, and her tiny kits were snuggled into her belly, sucking eagerly. One of them had a pure white pelt that glimmered in the dim light of the nursery.

Bailey was there, giving Sorrelshine a gentle grooming,

while Barkface was feeding some herbs to the exhausted queen; their tangy scent filled the nursery.

"Bailey!" Tansypaw was wailing as Onepaw entered the den. "Wrenflight says I have to pick off the elders' ticks, and I don't want to!"

Bailey looked up from where she was licking Sorrelshine's shoulder. "Wrenflight is your mentor, isn't she?" she inquired mildly.

"Yes."

"And you're her apprentice?"

"Yes."

"Then you'd better do as she tells you, hadn't you?" Bailey went back to her licking.

"It's so not fair!"

"We all have to do it," Onepaw mewed, padding up to Tansypaw and giving her shoulder a friendly nuzzle. "Come on, I'll help you."

"No you won't." Barkface's tone was stern, though his eyes were filled with amusement. "What would Wrenflight say if she saw you doing the task she gave Tansypaw? But we'll show you what to do. It's not so bad, once you get used to it."

"I don't *want* to get used to it," Tansypaw muttered. But clearly she had given in, because she followed Barkface out of the nursery with her shoulders hunched.

Once Onepaw had seen Tansypaw supplied with a twig with a ball of moss soaked in mouse bile, and pointed her toward where the elders were enjoying a gossip near the fresh-kill pile, he went to find himself a piece of prey.

Onepaw's littermates and Brushpaw were crouching

around a plump rabbit. "Come and share," Morningpaw invited him with a wave of her tail. "There's plenty."

"What was all that about?" Ashpaw asked him as he settled down beside her and tore off a mouthful of the prey. "What did Tansypaw do? I've never seen Wrenflight so angry."

Onepaw shrugged. "Nothing much." He didn't want to go into detail when Tansypaw's brother was sitting right there. "She's just finding it hard to settle in."

Over by the group of elders, Tansypaw was probing through Plumclaw's dark gray fur, carefully checking her for ticks. *At least,* Onepaw thought, *after all that fussing, she seems to be doing the job right.*

"We heard you getting into trouble," Appledawn meowed to Tansypaw, licking one cream-colored paw and beginning to wash her ears. "But don't worry. It will all be forgiven and forgotten tomorrow."

Onepaw couldn't hear what Tansypaw responded, but it made Redclaw prick his ears up.

"You're lucky to have the chance to become a warrior," the dark ginger tom meowed. "Remember, your mentor is there to help you."

"Apprenticeships are always hard at first," Plumclaw declared, wriggling her shoulders under Tansypaw's touch. "But you've got gentle paws. I feel so much better with that huge tick gone."

"Do mine next, Tansypaw," Appledawn coaxed her. "And I'll tell you a story about the time when LionClan and Tiger-Clan walked the forest. . . ."

When Tansypaw had finished dealing with the ticks,

Wrenflight padded up to the group of elders. "Did she do a good job?" she asked.

"She did a marvelous job," Plumclaw responded.

Wrenflight looked slightly skeptical. "I'm glad to hear it," she mewed. "Okay, Tansypaw, find somewhere to wash that mouse bile off your paws, and then you can get yourself some prey. And I hope that from now on you'll have a better attitude about your training."

Onepaw and the others had finished eating by the time Tansypaw came stalking over to the fresh-kill pile, her tail flicking irritably to and fro.

"Are you okay?" Brushpaw asked.

"What do you think?" Tansypaw snarled. She clawed through the fresh-kill pile until she found a vole. "I know I should be grateful to be trained by the warriors," she added, seeming calmer after a bite or two of prey. "But to be honest, I miss the Twolegplace. Life there was so easy and comfortable. I miss our friends, too—don't you, Brushpaw?"

"I do, a little bit," Brushpaw confessed. "But I wouldn't give up being a warrior—not for anything."

Onepaw exchanged a glance with his sisters. He was surprised that the former kittypets could find anything good to say about their previous life, not now that they had experienced life in a Clan.

"I have to admit, I'm curious," he meowed. "I wish I could see what the Twolegplace is like."

"Well, why don't you?" Brushpaw asked, his eyes gleaming with mischief. "We could sneak off tomorrow, after we've done our apprentice duties. Tansypaw and I will show you around."

"Oh, yes, let's!" Tansypaw gave an excited little bounce, throwing off the last of her bad temper. "You can meet all our old friends—and you can try kittypet food!"

Ashpaw let out a shocked gasp; Onepaw felt just as shocked, but at the same time there was a flutter of excitement in his belly. *Kittypet food must taste really good, if Tansypaw misses it so much.*

Morningpaw's eyes were wide and her jaws parted as if she had just spotted a succulent bit of prey. "Should we?" she asked. "If we get caught, we'll get into *huge* trouble."

"We might not get caught," Onepaw responded. With every passing heartbeat he became more and more intrigued, even though part of him knew that it was a really bad idea. "I'm up for it," he declared at last.

"Me too," Morningpaw agreed. "What about you, Ashpaw?"

Ashpaw hesitated, then shook her head. "I think you're mouse-brained," she replied, though there was a tinge of regret in her voice. "You'll end up on tick duty for moons."

Brushpaw let out a snort of amusement. "We can't *all* end up on tick duty," he pointed out. "There aren't that many ticks in the whole of WindClan!"

"Well, we've decided," Onepaw mewed determinedly. "Sure we can't persuade you, Ashpaw?"

"No," his sister responded. "But I'll do my best to cover for you while you're away. Only, for StarClan's sake," she added, "be careful."

CHAPTER 3

By *the time he and his* Clanmates reached the outskirts of the Twolegplace, Onepaw felt like his paws were ready to drop off. He hadn't realized that it was quite so far. His respect for Bailey and his denmates grew; it must have taken courage for kittypets to explore so far away from their home that they had ended up on WindClan territory.

Brushpaw had taken the lead, and now he came to a halt at the edge of a small Thunderpath. Onepaw remembered the stretch of hard black stuff on the far side of the territory, curling along their border like a wide, flat snake. He remembered too the monsters growling up and down, their harsh colors glittering in the sunlight. Deadfoot had warned him how dangerous it was even to set paw on the surface.

"Do we have to cross this?" he asked Brushpaw, trying to keep his nervousness out of his voice.

"Of course we do," Brushpaw replied. "You don't need to worry," he added, sounding pleased with himself that he knew something the Clanborn cats didn't. "Crossing is easy."

He and Tansypaw strolled across without even checking for monsters. Onepaw exchanged a glance with Morningpaw before looking both ways and sniffing the air for the acrid tang that would tell him a monster was approaching.

"Okay, I think it's safe," he mewed, then bounded across with his sister by his side.

On the far side of the Thunderpath was a row of Twoleg dens. "Is this where you lived?" Onepaw asked the former kittypets.

Tansypaw shook her head. "Oh, no, our housefolk's den is *much* nicer than these. You'll see. Come on, it's this way."

To Onepaw, all the dens looked alike, built of the same red stone, and he wondered what it was that made Tansypaw's so much better. But she was already trotting off alongside the Thunderpath, stopping every few paces to look back and urge them on with gestures of her tail.

"I hope it's not much farther," Morningpaw muttered after they had rounded a few corners and crossed another Thunderpath. "My paws are sore, and I think it's going to rain."

Onepaw looked up at the bulging gray clouds overhead. When it rained on the moor, there was always shelter to be found in the lee of rocks or inside a disused rabbit burrow, but he didn't know how to find shelter here, unless they went inside a Twoleg den.

And I'm not doing that!

"Where is this den of yours?" he asked Brushpaw.

"It's down here . . . I think," Brushpaw replied as they came up with Tansypaw, who was waiting for them at the next corner.

"What do you mean, you *think*?" Morningpaw asked, beginning to sound annoyed. "Don't you know?"

"Well . . ." Brushpaw hesitated, giving his chest fur a couple of embarrassed licks. "We didn't used to go far from our den, unless Bailey was with us."

"Great StarClan!" Onepaw exclaimed. "You never told us that." *And what's going to happen if we never find it?*

"I think we should go home," Morningpaw added.

"No, don't do that," Brushpaw protested. "You have to see our den; you'll really like it. And you have to meet all our friends. It'll be great. Come on, I'm pretty sure it's this way."

Brushpaw took the lead again, stopping every now and then to look around or taste the air. Onepaw did the same, trying to memorize the way they were going in case the kitty-pets couldn't find their way back. *At least we can follow our scent trail,* he thought.

Peering through a gap in a Twoleg fence, he spotted a pretty gray she-cat playing on the grass, batting at some strange, brightly colored object. *Maybe we could ask her,* he thought, pausing, but just then Morningpaw called out to him and he had to run to catch up to the others.

When they rounded the next corner, both Brushpaw and Tansypaw drew to a sudden halt. "This can't be right," Tansypaw meowed, sounding confused. "These aren't like our den at all."

The rows of Twoleg dens that stretched ahead of them were bigger than the ones they had passed up to now. Their gardens were bigger, too, and some of the dens were hardly visible behind trees.

"We'll have to try a different way," Brushpaw declared.

He had hardly finished speaking when a loud howling

broke out behind the fence at the corner where the apprentices were standing. It was followed by a spate of furious barking. The fence around the Twoleg garden was made from thin, flat strips of wood; it began to shake as if something huge and heavy was hurling itself at the other side.

"Run!" Morningpaw gasped.

All four cats whirled around and fled. *Maybe now we can give up and go home,* Onepaw thought when the sound of barking had faded away behind them and they felt safe enough to halt, panting.

"This is taking too long," he meowed. "We need to get back to camp before we're missed."

Brushpaw heaved a sigh. "Okay, this time," he agreed. "Maybe we can try again in a day or two."

The apprentices set off again. But after they had turned one or two more corners and crossed a Thunderpath, Onepaw was pretty sure that this wasn't the way they had come. He was certain of it when Brushpaw led them down a narrow alley between two dens.

I've never seen this place before—we must be lost. Oh, StarClan, is there anything else that can go wrong?

He was about to suggest following their scent trail back when fat raindrops began pattering on the ground, and within heartbeats the rain had become a deluge, beating down so hard that Onepaw could hardly see anything beyond the next den.

"Stop!" he yowled. "We've got to find shelter."

His denmates crowded around him. For a few moments no cat seemed to know what to do. Their fur was plastered to their sides, and raindrops were dripping off their whiskers.

Then Tansypaw turned and began splashing her way through a wide gap in the nearest Twoleg fence. "Let's try in here," she meowed.

"You don't know what's in there!" Onepaw called after her.

But Tansypaw didn't respond, quickly disappearing through the driving rain.

"Fox dung!" Onepaw muttered. He knew he couldn't let her go off on her own and maybe get separated from her Clanmates for good. "Come on," he growled. "We'd better follow her."

As he padded after Tansypaw into the Twoleg garden, Onepaw made out a small den standing beside the bigger one. It was gaping open, and Tansypaw was standing in the entrance.

"Hurry up!" she called. "It's dry in here!"

All three of her Clanmates bounded forward to join her in the small den. Onepaw drew several deep breaths of relief, and shook the worst of the water off his pelt before he took a closer look at their refuge.

The floor was made of flat gray stone, and the walls were the same red stone as the big dens. Various Twoleg things were stored around the edges, but the center was clear. The air was full of an acrid scent that Onepaw recognized at once.

"Monsters have been here!"

Morningpaw nodded. "You know, I think this must be a monster den," she mewed, her voice quavering. "What if it comes back?"

"It won't," Brushpaw told her, though he didn't sound confident. "Anyway, if it does, we'll hear it coming, and we can get out."

"And *I'm* not going anywhere until the rain stops," Tansy-paw meowed. She had found some ragged pelts on the floor and was sitting there to lick herself dry. "It would be nice if you *thanked* me for finding this place," she added peevishly.

"I think we've got to stay," Onepaw murmured to Morning-paw. "We can't leave these two on their own, and maybe if we rest here, we'll be able to find our way home after the rain."

Morningpaw still looked doubtful. "I suppose so," she agreed reluctantly.

Onepaw realized how exhausted he was. He found more of the pelts and curled up there after giving his fur a few per-functory swipes with his tongue.

Kittypet life is terrible, he told himself as he sank into sleep. *I'm never coming back to this awful Twolegplace again!*

Onepaw woke with a start and realized that it was dark. He could just make out the sleeping forms of his Clanmates in a weird orange light that was coming from the Thunderpath beyond the garden. He was shivering with cold, and his fur had clumped into damp tufts. He felt as hungry as if he hadn't eaten for a moon.

At least the monster that lived here had not returned. Struggling to his paws, Onepaw padded to the entrance of the little den. The rain had stopped, though he could hear it dripping from the trees. Looking up, he saw that the sky had cleared, and though it was hard to tell against the harsh Two-leg light, he thought that dawn couldn't be far off.

Oh, StarClan, no!

Onepaw dashed back into the den and began shaking and

prodding his Clanmates. "Wake up!" he meowed urgently. "It's so late! We have to get back!"

The other cats began to stir, yawning and letting out groans of protest. "What's the matter?" Morningpaw mumbled. "Is it a monster?"

"No, but we have to head back *right now!*" Onepaw repeated. "It's almost dawn!"

"*What?*" Morningpaw jerked upright. "Oh, we're going to be in so much trouble!"

Brushpaw and Tansypaw were waking too, blinking and arching their backs in a good long stretch. Onepaw didn't think they seemed nearly worried enough about being caught away from Clan territory.

"We're probably in trouble already," Brushpaw pointed out. "We might as well stick around and see if we can persuade a Twoleg to give us some food."

"No, that's a really bad idea." Onepaw felt irritation rising inside him. "If we go now, there's still a chance we can sneak back without being spotted."

"Fine, but we don't know the *way!*" Tansypaw wailed.

"Let me try." Onepaw padded out into the garden, away from the reek of the monster den. The acrid smell still clung to his fur, and drifted in the air of the Twolegplace, and the heavy rain had washed their own scent trail away. But when Onepaw took a good long sniff, he thought that he could recognize, very faint and distant, the scents of the moor.

"Follow me," he meowed.

"Are you sure?" Morningpaw asked nervously as she padded along at his shoulder.

"No, but what choice have we got?" Onepaw asked. "Brush-paw and Tansypaw have no idea where we are."

Gradually, as they hurried along, the moorland scents grew stronger, so that first Morningpaw, then Brushpaw and Tansypaw, could pick them up too. By the time they reached the edge of the Twolegplace, they were racing along, across the small Thunderpath and finally past the cluster of farm build-ings near the river. The sky had grown pale, the warriors of StarClan winking out, and ahead of them a rosy glow on the horizon showed where the sun would soon rise.

"Maybe it'll be okay," Onepaw panted. "If we can catch some prey on the way back, we can say we went out for an early hunt."

But as their paws pounded across the Twoleg bridge and onto WindClan territory, Onepaw felt his heart jolt in his chest as if a badger had kicked him. Appearing over the crest of the slope that led up from the riverbank was a WindClan patrol: his father Stagleap in the lead, with Mudclaw, Dead-foot, and Tornear behind him.

"Oh, no!" Onepaw exclaimed, skidding to a halt.

The patrol bounded down the hillside to meet the appren-tices beside the river. "Thank StarClan you're safe!" Stagleap exclaimed.

For a heartbeat Onepaw hoped that the senior warriors would be so relieved to see them home and unhurt that they wouldn't be too angry. But his hope died with one look at the fury in Deadfoot's eyes.

"Onepaw, I trusted you," his mentor growled. "I thought you had more sense than to go sneaking off into the Twolegplace.

Do you have any idea what might have happened to you?"

Tornear let out a contemptuous snort. "They all have bees in their brain," he snarled. "Do you know that the whole Clan was searching the territory for you, until Ashpaw finally gave in and admitted where you were?"

"Sorry," Onepaw muttered, staring at his paws. Waves of heat and cold were sweeping over him as he struggled with his growing shame. "I'm really sorry."

His denmates echoed his words, but the senior warriors weren't at all impressed.

"It's what I might have expected from kittypets." There was a biting edge to Mudclaw's voice as he glared at his apprentice, Brushpaw. "But Clan cats should have known better."

"Back to camp, right now," Stagleap ordered.

The four apprentices trailed back across the moor with the patrol of warriors escorting them. When the gorse bushes around the hollow came into sight, a second patrol appeared, heading from the far side of the territory. Onepaw recognized Wrenflight and Bailey, along with Ryestalk and Tallstar himself.

The patrol plodded along with heads down and tails trailing over the ground, but when they spotted the apprentices, they seemed to find new energy, racing to meet them at the edge of the camp.

Bailey was the first to arrive. "Where have you *been*?" she demanded, her eyes wide with distress.

"The Twolegplace," Stagleap replied as Tallstar and Wrenflight caught up. "Ashpaw confessed after you left," he explained. "We set out to find them, and we met them by the Twoleg bridge."

Bailey, Onepaw could see, was torn between relief that her kits were safe, and anger at what they had done. She began by covering their faces with frantic licks, then stood back to give each of them a sharp cuff over the ear. Onepaw looked at his own mother, Wrenflight, and could see nothing in her eyes but deep disapproval.

I should never have set paw off Clan territory, he told himself, feeling hot all over with guilt. *And it was all for nothing—we didn't get to see the kittypets' den or try Twoleg food.*

"Into the camp," Tallstar ordered the apprentices with a wave of his tail. "This must be dealt with."

"What will he do?" Brushpaw muttered into Onepaw's ear as they wriggled through the gorse bushes and padded down into the center of the camp.

Onepaw shook his head. "I don't know. We've never done anything like this before."

Tallstar bounded across the camp and leaped up onto the Tallrock. "Let all cats old enough to catch their own prey join here beneath the Tallrock for a Clan meeting!" he yowled.

Onepaw felt as if a heavy stone were lodged in his belly. *This is going to be really bad, if Tallstar is calling the whole Clan to see us punished.* He and his denmates stood huddled together at the foot of the rock, and Bailey came to stand beside them. Onepaw was grateful for her support, even though he doubted that it would do any good.

While the Clan was assembling, Ashpaw slipped up to

Onepaw's side. "I'm really sorry," she whispered. "I tried to cover for you, but when you were still missing at dawn, I had to tell them the truth."

Onepaw had to admit to himself that his sister had been right when she'd warned them that going to the Twolegplace was a bad idea. He rested his tail on her shoulder. "It's okay," he reassured her. "It's not your fault."

"Cats of WindClan," Tallstar began when the rest of the Clan was sitting below him around the Tallrock; Onepaw saw with another pang of guilt how tired and annoyed they all looked. "Most of you spent last night searching the moor for our missing apprentices. In fact"—he let his glance travel around the hollow—"some of our Clanmates are still searching. So I think it's only fair that you should all hear how I intend to punish them. Tell me," he continued, fixing the apprentices with a gaze as hard as stone, "what made you think that sneaking off into the Twolegplace was a good idea?"

Onepaw saw Brushpaw gulp, then raise his head boldly. "It was my idea, Tallstar," he admitted. "I wanted to show the others our old den in the Twolegplace. I thought it would be fun." His voice quivered on that last word.

"Fun!" some cat in the crowd exclaimed; Onepaw thought it was Tornear.

"You thought it would be fun to take your denmates into danger and have the whole Clan turn out to look for you? We have all been frantic with worry, thinking that you might have fallen victim to a fox or that badger." Tallstar shook his head, heaving a deep sigh. "Clearly, I made a mistake when I decided to allow kittypets into the Clan. Maybe you *can't* learn to be warriors like Clanborn cats. We should stop this experiment now."

Stop this experiment? Does he mean to send them away? Another hot tide of guilt swept over Onepaw. He had never expected that going on an adventure to the Twolegplace would lead to the kittypets being driven out of the Clan. Glancing at Brushpaw and Tansypaw, he could see the fear and regret on their faces, and beside them Bailey, gazing at Tallstar in shock and disappointment.

When Onepaw turned to Morningpaw, he could see that she felt just as guilty. *We can't let Brushpaw and Tansypaw take all the blame.* As if she had picked up his thought, Morningpaw gave him a slight nod, and together they stepped forward, gazing up at their Clan leader.

"Tallstar, it was as much our fault as it was Brushpaw's and Tansypaw's," he declared. "We were just curious about the Twolegplace."

"And it wasn't Bailey's fault at all," Morningpaw added. "She never even knew about it."

The worst of Tallstar's anger was fading from his face, his bristling shoulder fur beginning to lie flat again, but his voice was still harsh. "Thank you for saying that. At least you aren't trying to hide behind your friends. But your adventure could have put you all in serious danger—and if you kittypets truly wish to join us, you must learn that your place is on WindClan territory."

"Does that mean we can stay?" Brushpaw asked hopefully.

"It does." Tallstar ignored a few yowls of protest from the crowd of cats around the Tallrock. "But all four of you will be punished. Until further notice you will be responsible for hunting for the elders, our medicine cat, and the nursery— and that is on top of all your other duties and training. Are you prepared for that?"

All four apprentices nodded. *Thank StarClan!* Onepaw thought with a sigh of relief. *It will be a lot of hard work, but it could have been so much worse.*

"Then the meeting is at an end." Tallstar leaped down from the Tallrock.

"I want a word with you two." Bailey stepped forward and gathered her kits closer to her with a wave of her tail. "Are you completely mouse-brained?" she asked, frustration clear in her bristling fur and twitching tail. "We could all have been kicked out, back to the Twolegplace. What were you *thinking*?"

Brushpaw and Tansypaw crouched down, listening to their mother with wide, apprehensive eyes. Seeing that no cat was paying him or his sister any attention, Onepaw gave Morning-paw a nudge. "Come on," he murmured. "I feel like a nap after all that."

Morningpaw stared at him; she opened her jaws to protest, but the movement turned into a yawn. "Okay," she mewed at last. "We'll work better when we've had a rest."

Onepaw began to lead the way toward a convenient rock near the edge of the hollow. But he hadn't taken more than a couple of paw steps when he heard a voice behind him.

"And just where do you think you're going?"

Onepaw and Morningpaw whirled around to see Deadfoot glaring at them.

"Do you have bees in your brain?" he demanded. "Or did what Tallstar said go in one of your little furry ears and out the other? You're in *trouble*, and don't you forget it. Get your tails into the nursery and clear out the old bedding."

Onepaw stared at his paws while his mentor was scolding them. "Yes, Deadfoot. Sorry," he meowed at last, and scurried off to the nursery with Morningpaw hurrying after him.

Sorrelshine was sleeping in her nest, with her kits cuddled up in the curve of her belly. Onepaw and Morningpaw began working around them, gathering up the soiled moss as quietly as they could so as not to wake them. Some of Onepaw's guilt and regret began to melt away as he gazed at the newborns.

Not many moments passed before Brushpaw and Tansypaw came to join them, stomping into the nursery in the foulest of foul moods. Sorrelshine half roused, yawned, then settled back to sleep.

"Shh!" Morningpaw murmured. "You're as noisy as a couple of badgers."

Tansypaw let out an annoyed hiss, but she quieted down as she began pulling at the moss. "No cat seems to care about what *I* want," she grumbled. "That's why I miss the Two-legplace so much! Maybe I should go back to my housefolk and stay there," she added with an irritated shake of her pelt. "Every cat here treats me like a mouse-brain, and all warriors do is work."

Brushpaw shrugged uneasily. "You do have a point. . . . But

I'd miss the hunting, and the stories the elders tell. . . ."

Onepaw cast a glance at his sister and saw his own concern reflected in her eyes. It sounded as if the kittypets were thinking of leaving, and he didn't want to lose them. *How can we convince Brushpaw and Tansypaw to stay?*

"But being a Clan cat is the best life!" he asserted. "Once you get used to it, you'll understand that. Surely you don't want to go back to the soft, weak lives of kittypets?"

"And don't you care about your mother?" Morningpaw added. "She's going through a lot so you can learn how to defend yourselves."

"But we never *had* to defend ourselves in the Twolegplace," Tansypaw retorted. "Our housefolk took care of everything."

Onepaw let out a low growl. "Why would you *want* that boring life?" he demanded. "You're a cat, not a Twoleg kit!"

"You have to stay. We just got in trouble for you," Morningpaw pointed out. "Please, give it some time. You'll grow to love it, you'll see."

Onepaw could see that Tansypaw, at least, wasn't convinced. As they all set to work again, he regretted the whole adventure. *And yet I can sort of understand that Tansypaw misses her home.* Everything there was so different, and he would have liked to learn more about it. *And it's a pity we never got to meet any of the kittypets there. That gray she-cat I saw in the Twoleg garden—she was so pretty. . . .*

CHAPTER 4

Onepaw gave the pellets of kittypet food a good long sniff, then took a big bite. "Yuck!" he exclaimed, spraying pellets everywhere. "They're *hard*! Do you really eat this stuff?" *I thought it would be delicious the way Tansypaw is always whining about how much she misses it!*

Stifled *mrrows* of laughter came from behind him; he turned to face the group of kittypets, spitting out the last of the disgusting mouthful. Brushpaw was with them, his eyes brimming with amusement.

"No wonder warriors don't eat this stuff," Onepaw grumbled. "It's horrible!"

Almost two moons had passed since their first disastrous expedition into the Twolegplace. At first, Onepaw had vowed never to set paw there again. But finally Brushpaw had persuaded the apprentices—even Ashpaw—to give it another try.

Coming here is fun, Onepaw thought. *And as long as we're back in camp when we're needed, it's not doing any harm.*

"Come on, Onepaw," Brushpaw urged him. "Tell them about the fight we had with the ShadowClan warriors."

"Yes, please do." The speaker was Smoke, the pretty gray

she-cat Onepaw had spotted on his first visit. "I love hearing your stories!"

"Well, Brushpaw and I were on a border patrol with our mentors," Onepaw began. "And when we got to the border with ShadowClan, some of their warriors were trespassing on our territory!"

"What did you do?" Nutmeg, a brown tabby kittypet, asked.

"Well, we couldn't let them get away with it," Onepaw went on. "Deadfoot, our Clan deputy—he's my mentor—challenged them right away. And the ShadowClan cats just leaped into battle!"

Gasps came from several of the kittypets who were listening. "What happened then?" Smoke breathed out.

"Well, Brushpaw and I know so many fighting moves," Onepaw replied. "We stood up to those ShadowClan mange-pelts!" Dipping his head modestly, he added, "I think Deadfoot might have been killed if I hadn't leaped in between him and the ShadowClan cat who was attacking him."

"That's right," Brushpaw agreed. "And I fought together with Wrenflight to chase them back into their own territory. I think they might still be running!"

Even while he was telling the story, Onepaw felt uncomfortable. *It didn't happen* exactly *like that.* In fact, the ShadowClan cats had trespassed unintentionally because a heavy shower of rain had washed out the border scent markers. Claws had slid out, but no cat had struck a blow, and in the end the two patrols had settled on where the border should run, and had marked it on both sides. Onepaw and Brushpaw had been there, but they hadn't actually needed to do anything.

It doesn't matter that we've made up a few details, Onepaw told himself with an inward shrug. *We're just telling a story to entertain the kittypets.*

"You're so brave!" Smoke gazed up at Onepaw with admiring blue eyes. "It must be so exciting, living in the Clans."

Nutmeg gave an exaggerated shudder. "No thanks, I'm happy here," he declared. "Being a warrior sounds dangerous."

Onepaw and Brushpaw exchanged a glance, their whiskers twitching.

"Of course, it takes a lot of courage to live in the wild like we do," Brushpaw meowed smoothly. "We have to fight dogs and foxes and other Clans of ferocious warriors every day. But we're tough enough to handle it." He turned his head to give his shoulder fur a complacent lick. "After all, we've been through so much training—which only the best warriors survive."

"I think that's *wonderful!*" Smoke exclaimed.

Onepaw puffed out his chest and tried to look both brave and modest; it was a tricky mix to get right, but he'd perfected it over his last few trips to the Twolegplace. "Oh, it's nothing really," he mewed. "Not when you're a Clan cat."

"*Please* tell us more," Smoke begged. "Your stories are *so* exciting!"

Onepaw was tempted, but he realized how long he and Brushpaw had been away from camp; there would be trouble again if they didn't get back soon.

"I'm sorry," he responded, "but we have to be going home

now. Our Clan can't do without us for long, you know."

"Right!" Brushpaw agreed, puffing out his chest.

After saying good-bye to the kittypets, Onepaw and Brushpaw hurried back toward WindClan territory. Glancing at the sky, Onepaw saw that the sun was sinking, casting long shadows over their path.

"Deadfoot said he wanted us on an early evening patrol," he reminded Brushpaw. "So we'd better get a move on."

As he bounded along beside his friend, Onepaw reflected how much easier it was to slip off to the Twolegplace in pairs. *That was our mistake the first time, going in a big group.*

Even though they'd gotten away with their visits so far, Onepaw still felt a trickle of guilt. He knew that the senior WindClan warriors wouldn't approve, and he, Tansypaw, and Brushpaw would be in even worse trouble if they were caught a second time. *But I really like going there.* In WindClan he was just another apprentice, but in the Twolegplace the kittypets admired him and looked up to him. *It feels so good. Especially when Smoke looks at me with her big blue eyes!*

When Onepaw and Brushpaw returned to the WindClan camp, they found Deadfoot organizing a hunting patrol.

"There you are!" he meowed as the two apprentices slipped unobtrusively down into the hollow. "We're just about to leave. Let's see if we can find some really good prey."

Onepaw and Brushpaw followed Deadfoot out onto the moor again. Mudclaw and Pigeonflight made up the rest of the patrol.

It wasn't long before Onepaw realized that neither he nor

Brushpaw was doing their best. Maybe it was because they were both tired after their long trek into the Twolegplace, but for some reason the hunting wasn't going well. Onepaw managed to catch a mouse, but a rabbit that started up almost underneath his paws managed to outrun him and dive into the safety of its burrow.

As for Brushpaw, he couldn't seem to do anything right. He tackled a rabbit that came straight at him, fleeing from Pigeonflight's claws, but when the creature battered at him with its enormous hind paws, Brushpaw let go with a yowl of pain. The rabbit vanished into the dusk. Pigeonflight pursued it, only to return a few moments later, empty-pawed.

"Stupid apprentice," he growled. "We should have had that."

Brushpaw hung his head. "Sorry," he muttered.

His mentor, Mudclaw, let out a hiss of annoyance. "*Sorry* fills no bellies," he snapped.

Onepaw couldn't help thinking that the senior warriors were right. They were both tired, true, but Brushpaw really did need to spend more time practicing his hunting skills. *Instead of going to the Twolegplace.* The uncomfortable reminder crept into his mind, but he shrugged it away.

"We might as well finish for the night," Deadfoot meowed. "All five of you apprentices will be having your warrior assessments tomorrow, so you need a good long sleep."

Assessments tomorrow! Excitement raised every hair on Onepaw's pelt, but when he looked at Brushpaw, he thought that his denmate seemed worried, his ears flattening and his tail trailing on the ground. "Are you okay?" he asked.

Brushpaw shook his head, dropping behind the rest of the patrol as they padded back to camp. "I'm not sure we're ready—me and Tansypaw," he admitted.

Onepaw had to agree, though he said nothing; he didn't want to worry his friend and sap his confidence even further.

"It's too much pressure," Brushpaw continued. "If we fail, we'll be kicked out, back to the Twolegplace with Bailey."

"You'll be fine," Onepaw reassured him. *Surely Tallstar would give them another chance.* Bounding down into the hollow, he nudged his friend toward the fresh-kill pile. "You just need to remember what Mudclaw taught you."

At sunrise the next morning the sky was clear. The sun was shining as Onepaw emerged from the apprentices' den, and he breathed in the lush scents of greenleaf.

"A good day for hunting," Deadfoot announced as he strode across the camp to Onepaw's side. "Let's go."

Onepaw followed him out of the camp, while the other mentors arrived to join their apprentices. A few fox-lengths from the hollow, Deadfoot halted.

"Okay, from now on I'll be watching you, but you're on your own," he meowed. "I suggest you head for the river. That way you won't get in the way of the other apprentices."

Onepaw gave his mentor a brisk nod, then prowled away from him across the moor, pausing every few paw steps to taste the air. His ears were pricked and all his senses alert for signs of prey. Aware of Deadfoot watching him from a distance, he focused firmly on remembering everything his mentor had taught him.

Please, StarClan, don't let me mess up like I did last night! he begged silently.

Before long, Onepaw caught the scent of a rabbit and spotted it nibbling at something underneath a thornbush. It was too far away for an easy catch, so Onepaw flattened himself to the ground and began to creep up on it, making sure that he stayed downwind and that his tail was tucked along his side.

Gradually Onepaw drew closer to the rabbit. But the thorn branches formed a barrier, keeping it safe; Onepaw knew he'd have to scare it out of its shelter before he'd have a chance of catching it.

But if I go for it too soon, it might outrun me.

Onepaw crept up until he could see every hair on the rabbit's pelt and on its white puff of a tail. Then he rose to his paws, letting out a ferocious growl. The rabbit started up, squealing in terror, and fled.

Pushing off with powerful hind paws, Onepaw hurtled in pursuit. He exulted in the feeling of cool morning air rippling through his pelt, and the movement of his muscles as they bunched and stretched.

This is being a real WindClan cat!

The rabbit vanished over the crest of the hill, but Onepaw was only heartbeats behind it. Racing down the slope on the other side, he caught it a couple of fox-lengths away from its burrow and bit down on its neck until it went limp.

"Thank you, StarClan, for this prey," he meowed, feeling

even more grateful than usual.

Carrying the rabbit, he headed back to find Deadfoot. Triumph flowed through him like a sparkling moorland stream. It had been such a tricky bit of stalking; surely his mentor would be pleased and decide he'd passed his assessment.

"I see I've managed to teach you something" was Deadfoot's only comment, but the glow of approval in his eyes was enough for Onepaw.

When he and his mentor returned to camp, several of the Clan were out in the hollow, waiting for the results of the assessments. Onepaw saw that Ashpaw and Morningpaw had the same glow of triumph about them, but Brushpaw and Tansypaw were standing close together, their tails drooping.

Oh, no! Onepaw thought, padding over to them. "What happened?" he asked quietly, even though he knew what the answer must be.

Tansypaw didn't reply, turning her head away as if she couldn't bear to look at him.

Brushpaw hunched his shoulders. "We failed," he muttered. "We're going to be kicked out, and Bailey will be so upset."

Tallstar appeared from his den and padded over to the apprentices, beckoning with his tail for their mentors to gather around.

"Congratulations," he meowed to Onepaw and his littermates, then turned to the two former kittypets. His whiskers twitched as he took in their dejected appearance. "Mudclaw? Wrenflight?" he asked. "What happened?"

"Not a lot," Mudclaw growled. "Brushpaw strolled past a

rabbit hiding in a tuft of grass as if there were nothing there. I don't know what he thinks his scent glands are for."

"Tansypaw tried hard." Wrenflight was obviously trying to soften her apprentice's failure. "She managed to find a mouse, at least, but she forgot about setting her paws down lightly. The mouse felt her coming and disappeared among the roots of a gorse bush."

"So you can't advise me to make them warriors?" Tallstar asked.

Both mentors shook their head.

Onepaw noticed that Bailey had approached from the nursery as the mentors were reporting to Tallstar. She halted beside her kits, looking utterly devastated at the news of their failure.

"I'm very disappointed in you," Tallstar told Brushpaw and Tansypaw. "I took a chance, letting you be trained in the Clan, but you've only proven to me that I was right in believing that kittypets can't be warriors. Even before your assessment I heard from Wrenflight and Mudclaw that you were falling behind."

At Tallstar's words, sudden outrage seized Onepaw like the grip of a massive claw. *Why did their mentors let them be assessed if they knew they weren't ready?* Shocked at his own boldness, he took a step forward and faced his Clan leader.

"That isn't fair!" he announced. "Setting them up to fail and be embarrassed in front of the whole Clan is just cruel. If you knew they needed more time, you should have given it to them. You would have done that for a Clanborn cat!"

Several shocked gasps came from their nearby Clanmates.

"Onepaw, be quiet!" Wrenflight exclaimed.

"Yes, remember you're still an apprentice," Deadfoot told him, heavily disapproving. "You're not supposed to argue with your leader."

Oh, great StarClan! Onepaw thought. *What if they don't let me become a warrior after all? But I don't care,* he added stoutly to himself. *What I said is true.*

Tallstar gave Onepaw a long, calm look before he responded. "You make a good point," he admitted, "and for some time, I've been wondering whether it was a mistake to let Brushpaw and Tansypaw join us at all. I wanted these kittypets to do well and prove me wrong. But now it's clear that my fears were correct. You're right, Onepaw—letting the kittypets stay and keep failing would indeed be cruel."

What? Onestar's pelt prickled with irritation. *He completely misunderstood! I meant we should give them more time—not kick them out of the Clan!*

But Tallstar was still speaking. "WindClan has no room for kittypets playing at battle," he continued. "I'm sorry, because I understand that Bailey has been a big help to Barkface, but it's time for the kittypets to leave. The Clans are no place for them!"

For a couple of heartbeats there was a pause, until Tansypaw drew herself up. "Okay, then; I'll be glad to go." Her voice was clear and steady. "This isn't where I belong. I want to be Melody, not Tansypaw; that's who I've always been." For a moment she glanced at Brushpaw, who was staring at her in disbelief. Then she turned to Wrenflight and dipped her head respectfully. "I'm grateful for all you taught me," she mewed. Wrenflight responded by touching noses with her, deep disappointment in her eyes.

As Melody finished speaking, she looked at Bailey, who just shook her head slowly, as if she was saddened by her daughter's choice.

Behind him, Onepaw could hear a couple of the warriors muttering together.

"It's only to be expected."

"Yeah, whoever heard of a kittypet becoming a warrior?"

Tallstar turned to Brushpaw. "It's time to go."

For a moment Brushpaw hesitated.

Onepaw gazed at him, his throat choked up at the thought of losing his friend. He leaned into Brushpaw and whispered into his ear. "Please, you have to stay. We're going to be great warriors together. I know you can do it!"

Brushpaw gave him a doubtful look, then straightened up and spoke to Tallstar. "I want to stay," he meowed. "I'm sorry I failed my assessment today, but I won't fail again. In my heart I know that I'm a WindClan cat."

Tallstar was silent for a moment, looking reluctantly impressed. Eventually he nodded. "We'll see about that," he meowed. "I will give you one more chance to pass your assessment—and only one." With a glance at Bailey, he added, "I think that's fair, don't you?"

Bailey dipped her head gratefully. "I do, Tallstar," she replied. "And may I stay as well? I know that Tansypaw—I mean *Melody*—will be safe in the Twolegplace without me. I'm sure our housefolk will take her back."

Melody's whiskers drooped at the realization that her mother wouldn't be going with her, but she kept her head high. "I'll be fine," she assured Bailey, then added to her brother, "Good luck, Brushpaw. I know you'll make a great warrior."

She touched noses with him, then with her mother, and gave them one last look before turning away. She bounded up the side of the hollow and disappeared.

Onepaw watched her go. *She's a great cat. But WindClan isn't the right place for her. She never wanted to be a Clan cat; she hated it right from the start. It was so hard for her, knowing that her mother and her brother wanted to be here.*

His thoughts were interrupted by Tallstar's voice, raised in a yowl. "Let all cats old enough to catch their own prey join here beneath the Tallrock for a Clan meeting." To Onepaw and his littermates he added, "It's time for your warrior ceremony."

A thrill of excitement passed through Onepaw, every hair on his pelt tingling. He could see from his sisters' bright eyes that they shared his feeling. While the Clan assembled, he gave himself a quick grooming until his tabby pelt shone, aware that he had to look good on the most important day of his life.

Tallstar was standing at the base of the Tallrock. When the Clan had gathered in a circle around him, he beckoned Onepaw to join him. Onepaw kept his head and tail high as he padded up to his Clan leader. His belly was churning as if a whole nest of bees was buzzing around in there.

When Onepaw halted in front of him, Tallstar turned to Deadfoot. "Has your apprentice studied the warrior code, and has he learned the skills of a warrior?" he asked the Clan deputy.

Deadfoot nodded. "He has, Tallstar."

A trickle of guilt passed through Onepaw's fur, as if a drop of rain had fallen on him. *Would Deadfoot say that if he knew about my visits to the Twolegplace?*

But there was no time to think about that; Tallstar had already begun to speak the words that would make him a warrior.

"I, Tallstar, leader of WindClan, call upon my warrior ancestors to look down on this apprentice. He has trained hard to understand the ways of your noble code, and I commend him to you as a warrior in his turn." Facing Onepaw, he continued. "Onepaw, do you promise to uphold the warrior code and to protect and defend this Clan, even at the cost of your life?"

Onepaw's heart was pounding so hard he thought that every cat in the Clan must be able to hear it. "I do," he responded, making his voice ring out clearly.

"Then by the powers of StarClan," Tallstar declared, "I give you your warrior name. Onepaw, from this moment you will be known as Onewhisker. StarClan honors your intelligence and your courage, and we welcome you as a full warrior of WindClan."

Stepping forward, Tallstar rested his muzzle on Onewhisker's head. Onewhisker shivered at the touch as he licked his Clan leader's shoulder in response.

"Onewhisker! Onewhisker!" The Clan acclaimed him by yowling his new name.

As Onewhisker stepped back to join Deadfoot and his mother, Wrenflight, he noticed that Brushpaw was yowling as loudly as any cat. His chest swelled with gratitude for his friend's generosity, and a pang of sadness that Brushpaw wasn't sharing this ceremony with him.

Tallstar continued by making Ashpaw and then Morningpaw warriors in their turn. The Clan welcomed them with loud caterwauls. "Ashfoot! Morningflower! Ashfoot! Morningflower!"

Onewhisker joined in, feeling that he would burst with pride and happiness. Glancing aside, he met Brushpaw's gaze, and saw determination in the eyes of his friend.

I know you'll make it, Brushpaw! he thought. *It won't be long now. And I'll help you train, to make up for all those trips to the Twolegplace. Once we're warriors together, all this will be forgotten.*

CHAPTER 5

✿

Onewhisker crouched beside the fresh-kill pile, sharing a rabbit with Pigeonflight and Ryestalk while he listened to the senior warriors describing how their patrol had scented a fox crossing their territory.

"It went off toward the farms," Pigeonflight mumbled around a mouthful of prey. "And good riddance."

A loud voice coming from the top of the hollow distracted Onewhisker from their talk. Looking up, he saw that Mudclaw had appeared with Brushpaw; they were heading down the slope side by side.

"You're *still* not trying hard enough," Mudclaw was meowing, his voice carrying right across the camp. "Haven't I told you to guard your throat when you're fighting close up? I lost count of the number of times I could have killed you."

"I'm sorry, Mudclaw." Brushpaw sounded thoroughly miserable. "I'll do better tomorrow, I promise."

Mudclaw responded with a grunt. "You'd better. Now go and take some prey to the elders. After that, you can eat."

Brushpaw nodded and trudged wearily over to the fresh-kill pile, where he clawed out a rabbit and began dragging it over to the elders' den.

It must be tough, being the only apprentice in camp, Onewhisker thought.

In the days since his warrior ceremony, he hadn't spent much time with his friend. He wasn't trying to avoid Brushpaw, but they didn't train together anymore, or sleep in the same den. Onewhisker belonged with the other warriors now.

Feeling guilty, he gulped down the last of his own prey and padded over to Brushpaw when he returned. "Are you okay?" he asked as Brushpaw picked out a vole from the pile and settled down to eat.

"I'm having a tough time," Brushpaw confessed. "You must have heard Mudclaw just now. I'm not getting any better at battle moves or hunting. I can't blame him for running out of patience." He paused to take a mouthful of vole, then added, "It's awful, being the only apprentice. There's no other cat to work with, and I'm so lonely and bored."

Onewhisker sat beside him. "It'll get better," he promised, though he wasn't sure that was true. "I'll practice with you if you like."

"Oh, yeah, sure, I've got plenty of free time," Brushpaw retorted sourly. Then he gave his pelt a shake. "Sorry, Onewhisker. But I don't think that would help. Maybe Tallstar has been right this whole time, and kittypets *can't* be warriors. Maybe Melody had the right idea, and I should go back to the Twolegplace and be Leo again."

"What?" Onewhisker could hardly believe what he was hearing. "You can't do that! Honestly, Brushpaw, you're going to be great. Don't you want to prove all those cats wrong, when they said you didn't belong here?"

I have to convince him, he thought, struggling with a pang of guilt. *I was the cat who persuaded him to stay, and I haven't really helped him like I said I would. And he might have had stronger skills if I hadn't given in when he insisted on going to the Twolegplace.* Onewhisker felt he would never shake off that guilt until Brushpaw succeeded as a warrior.

Brushpaw let out a long sigh. "Of course I *want* to," he mewed. "I'm just beginning to doubt that I can. And what will Bailey think if I fail again?"

"Tallstar! Tallstar!" The yowl rang out from Stagleap, who was keeping watch on the Outlook Rock.

The sun was going down, casting a red light across the camp. Onewhisker had been dozing in the last warm patch of sunlight, but he raised his head when he heard Stagleap calling out, his voice taut and urgent.

Now what?

The Clan leader, who had been grooming himself at the entrance to his den behind the Tallrock, sprang to his paws, his black-and-white pelt bristling.

"What is it?" he called out.

"Tornear's patrol is coming back," Stagleap replied. "They're racing across the moor as if a whole family of foxes is on their tail."

He had hardly finished speaking when Tornear burst through the gorse bushes that surrounded the hollow, seeming not to care about the thorns tearing at his fur. The rest of the patrol—Mistmouse and Ashfoot—followed him, and all three cats charged across the camp until they halted in front of Tallstar.

Onewhisker felt his belly lurch with apprehension. He rose to his paws, then eased himself closer to hear what was going on. Barkface emerged from the medicine cat's den, with Bailey anxiously looking over his shoulder. The elders poked their heads out of their den, too, exchanging curious glances. Sorrelshine, who was watching her kits play wrestling outside the nursery, gathered them closer to her with a sweep of her tail.

"What's the rush, Tornear?" The Clan leader's voice was calm. "What happened?"

"ShadowClan happened!" Tornear panted. He took a couple of heartbeats to catch his breath, then continued. "We were patrolling the border not far from Fourtrees, and we picked up those mange-pelts' scent on *our* territory."

Growls of protest broke out among the listening cats. "This isn't the first time," Mudclaw snarled. "They need to be taught a lesson."

"You haven't heard the worst of it yet," Tornear meowed. "We found blood in the grass, and some scraps of rabbit fur," he told Tallstar. "And the whole area reeked of ShadowClan scent. They've been stealing prey."

Even more caterwauls of outrage came from the WindClan warriors. Onewhisker joined in, his claws flexing with fury. He caught sight of Brushpaw, on the other side of the crowd of cats, looking more confused than angry.

Maybe he doesn't realize how important this is.

Deadfoot padded forward and took his place at his leader's side. "We can't let them get away with this, Tallstar," he declared.

"I have no intention of letting them get away with it." Tallstar's voice was still steady, but there was an edge to it, sharp as a claw. "From tomorrow we'll double our patrols along that border. ShadowClan cats have been slipping across it far too often, and they need to be taught to keep to their own territory."

The sun had risen in a clear, pale sky. A brisk wind buffeted Onewhisker's fur, almost carrying him off his paws on the steep slope that led downward to the border beside Fourtrees. Along with Mudclaw, Ashfoot, and Brushpaw, he had been chosen for one of the extra patrols ordered by Tallstar the evening before.

"StarClan-cursed wind," Mudclaw muttered, ruffling up his mottled brown pelt. "It's blowing toward them. If we're not careful, our scent will give them warning."

Onewhisker wasn't sure he was right. The dawn patrol had renewed the scent markers not long before, and the air was filled with WindClan scent. ShadowClan might not be able to distinguish traces of individual cats approaching now.

When they reached the border, Mudclaw led the way along the top of the hollow where the four great oak trees grew. This, Onewhisker knew, was the likeliest place to find ShadowClan trespassers, because they could cross into WindClan territory without risking the big Thunderpath and the monsters that raced along it.

As they left Fourtrees behind, Mudclaw, who was in the lead, suddenly halted, raising his tail for silence. "Smell that?" he whispered.

Onewhisker parted his jaws and let the air flow over his scent glands. Beside him, Ashfoot and Brushpaw were doing the same. Almost at once he understood what Mudclaw meant. He could pick up the ShadowClan scent markers, but there was more: traces of two—no, three—ShadowClan cats, heading away from the border and deeper into WindClan territory.

"Trespassers!" he breathed out.

Mudclaw nodded. "This way, and keep low. We'll give them something they're not expecting."

He flattened himself to the ground and crept forward, following the scent trail as if he were stalking prey. The others followed; Onewhisker could feel the tough moorland grass scraping his belly, and his nose twitched as the scent grew stronger. Now that they had changed direction, the wind was in their favor, carrying the intruders' scent toward them.

The trail led up a gentle slope where here and there boulders thrust their way up out of the turf. At the top of the slope Mudclaw took cover behind one of the biggest rocks and cautiously peered around it.

Copying his Clanmate from the other side of the boulder, Onewhisker gazed down into a narrow gully. A small stream gurgled its way along the bottom. Beside the stream were three ShadowClan cats, all of them hunched over the body of a rabbit.

Mudclaw rose to his paws and emerged into the open. "Amberleaf. Scorchwind. Finchflight. Greetings. How *nice* to see you."

The three ShadowClan cats sprang to their paws and whirled to face the WindClan patrol. None of them spoke as Mudclaw picked his way down to the bottom of the gully to confront them. Onewhisker followed the senior warrior and stood at his side, with Ashfoot and Brushpaw a paw step behind.

Mudclaw abandoned his mock-polite tone. "What do you think you're doing here?" he demanded.

"It's obvious what they're doing," Onewhisker hissed, hardly able to believe what he was seeing. "Stealing prey."

Amberleaf—a dark orange she-cat Onewhisker remembered seeing at Gatherings—took a pace forward and thrust her neck out aggressively. "We are *not* stealing prey."

Mudclaw gave the rabbit a hard stare, then let his gaze travel over the ShadowClan trespassers. "You're here on WindClan territory, stuffing your stupid faces with rabbit, and you say you're not stealing prey?"

"It's a ShadowClan rabbit," Finchflight asserted, his black-and-white shoulder fur beginning to rise.

"And hedgehogs fly!" Ashfoot exclaimed.

"We were chasing it and it crossed your border," Scorch-wind snapped. "So keep your fur on. We're not doing anything wrong."

"If you think that, you're either lying or mouse-brained," Onewhisker meowed. "You know as well as any cat that even if you found that rabbit on ShadowClan territory, as soon as it set paw across the border it became *ours*."

"And if you were a real hunting patrol," Ashfoot added, "you would have taken your prey back to feed your Clan, not shared it among yourselves on another Clan's territory. You're not only stealing from us—you're stealing from your own Clanmates!"

Scorchwind let out a contemptuous snort. "So what are you going to do about it, you miserable rabbit-chasers?"

"*This!*" Without any more warning, Mudclaw leaped forward, his claws extended, and barreled into Scorchwind, knocking the ginger tabby tom off his paws. The two cats wrestled on the ground in a screeching tangle of fur.

Shocked at his Clanmate's sudden attack, Onewhisker hesitated for a heartbeat and found himself staring into Amberleaf's furious eyes. The orange she-cat's paw flashed out and raked him across the nose; Onewhisker could feel the blood bubbling from the wound. Pulling himself together, he lowered his head and dived for Amberleaf's chest, flipping her onto her back, and lashed at her belly with his claws. Amberleaf heaved at him, but she couldn't manage to throw him off.

Risking a swift glance at his Clanmates, Onewhisker spotted Ashfoot grappling with Finchflight, who had Brushpaw pinned down. Finchflight kicked out with his hind paws and forced Ashfoot backward into the stream before slashing his claws down Brushpaw's side. Onewhisker flinched at the sight of Brushpaw's blood flowing into the grass.

He gave Amberleaf one last clawing before thrusting her away from him, desperate to reach Brushpaw. Mudclaw got there before him, and battered Finchflight around the head with both forepaws. Finchflight fled, screeching, with the other ShadowClan warriors hard on his paws.

Panting, Onewhisker glanced around. Every muscle in his body was protesting, but apart from the scratch on his nose he didn't think he was badly hurt. Mudclaw looked uninjured. Ashfoot hauled herself out of the stream and gave her pelt a good shake before staggering over to join them.

Brushpaw was trying to get up, but sank back onto the grass with a groan. He was still bleeding badly. Mudclaw rested a paw on his shoulder. "Lie still." His voice was surprisingly gentle. "We'll get you back to camp."

"I remembered what you said, Mudclaw," Brushpaw mewed feebly. "I gave him a good scratch."

"You did, Brushpaw." Something about Mudclaw's voice made Onewhisker feel cold with fear. "You fought like a warrior."

Mudclaw carried his apprentice on his back across the moor to the WindClan camp, with Onewhisker and Ashfoot steadying him on either side. Then, while Mudclaw went to report to Tallstar, Onewhisker stayed with Brushpaw in Barkface's den, waiting to have his nose treated while the medicine cat examined Brushpaw's wound.

"What happened?" Bailey looked in at the entrance to the den. "Ashfoot told me there was a—" She broke off at the sight of her son lying stretched out under Barkface's skillful paws as the medicine cat cleaned his wounds with moss soaked in water. Brushpaw turned his head, blinking feebly, at the sound of his mother's voice. "Oh, Brushpaw!" Bailey exclaimed, her voice quivering. "Barkface, is he . . ." She couldn't go on.

"It looks worse than it is," Barkface mewed reassuringly. "Bailey, you know where I keep the cobweb. Go and fetch me some, and we'll get this bleeding stopped. Marigold too, while you're back there," he added.

Growing calmer with something to do, Bailey padded to the back of the den to fetch the supplies.

Barkface looked up at Onewhisker and drew him a couple of paces away from Brushpaw before he spoke in a low voice so that no other cat could hear. "I'm concerned that the clawing is very deep," he murmured. "Brushpaw isn't in any danger now, but I'm worried that the wounds might get infected."

When Bailey returned, Barkface patted a poultice of marigold over Brushpaw's scratches and plastered cobweb over it. Then he held out a leaf with a couple of poppy seeds.

"Lick those up," he told Brushpaw. "They'll help with the pain and let you get some sleep."

Brushpaw did as he was told, then reached out a paw to Onewhisker. "I'm sorry I wasn't more help in the fight," he whispered. "I was bleeding so much. I don't think I've ever seen that much blood. . . ."

"You did well," Onewhisker reassured him, resting a paw on his friend's shoulder. "You'll be fine. You just need to rest now."

Brushpaw sighed and his eyes closed, while Bailey settled

down beside him to keep watch over him. Onewhisker looked up to catch Barkface's concerned glance.

I hope I didn't lie to him, he thought. *I hope he will be well soon.*

Good-bye, my friend. May StarClan light your path.

Onewhisker stood at the center of the camp, gazing down at the body of Brushpaw. Half a moon had passed since the fight against the ShadowClan cats, and with every day that passed, Brushpaw had weakened. In spite of all Barkface could do, infection and fever had set in. The last few days had been especially terrible: delirious and in pain, Brushpaw had called for his mother, not seeming to realize that she never left his side. Even she couldn't comfort him.

The last traces of sunlight had left the sky, and the Clan was gathering for Brushpaw's vigil. Barkface sat beside the apprentice's head, with Bailey crouched beside him. Mudclaw, who had been his mentor, found a place nearby.

When all the cats were assembled, Tallstar rose and let his gaze travel around the Clan. "Brushpaw was a cheerful presence around the camp," he began, "and I think I can say that we all liked him. It was brave for a kittypet to try to become a warrior."

Onewhisker looked around defensively, wondering whether any of the cats who hadn't wanted Brushpaw admitted to the Clan were going to speak up now. But every cat was silent; their eyes, glowing in the moonlight, were filled with sorrow. Even the ones who had mocked him, asking "What can you expect from a kittypet?" when he failed his assessment, had nothing to say now.

Wincing at the memory of Brushpaw's failure, Onewhisker felt sick with guilt, as if he had gorged himself on crow-food. *I should have let him go back to being a kittypet,* he told himself. *Why did I convince him to stay? Is it my fault that he's dead?* He rested his nose on his paws and forced himself to gaze at his friend's body all through the long night.

Eventually Onewhisker realized that faint light was creeping over the moor. Barkface rose to his paws and spoke the words over Brushpaw that had been spoken over the bodies of dead warriors for season upon season.

"May StarClan light your path, Brushpaw. May you find good hunting, swift running, and shelter when you sleep."

Onewhisker found a little comfort in the thought that his friend would find his way to StarClan. *He was born a kittypet, but he died a Clan cat.*

The elders stepped forward to carry Brushpaw's body out of the camp for burial. Bailey let out a soft murmur of grief and buried her nose in her son's fur for the last time. Then she moved back, watching the elders bear him away until they vanished through the gorse bushes at the top of the hollow.

When they were gone, Bailey turned to Tallstar. "I will go back to the Twolegplace now," she told him. Her voice was taut with grief, and Onewhisker could tell that it was taking all her strength to cling to her dignity and speak calmly. "There's nothing left here for me, and I want to be with Melody."

Tallstar dipped his head to her in deepest respect. "I understand," he meowed kindly. "I'll send a warrior to escort you back to the Twolegplace. And you mustn't feel guilty about this," he added. "This wasn't your mistake; it was mine. What happened to Brushpaw will always be on my conscience. Kittypets do not belong in the Clans."

Bailey winced, looking down at her paws.

"Onewhisker, go with her," Tallstar ordered. "Make sure she gets safely back to her housefolk."

The sun had risen by the time Onewhisker and Bailey crossed the bridge and headed for the Twolegplace, but there was little warmth in it, and clouds were gathering. Onewhisker guessed that it would rain later.

At first he and Bailey had padded along in silence, but Onewhisker didn't want to say good-bye to her without telling her about his regrets. With every paw step he felt the weight of guilt; he knew it was at least partly his fault that Bailey was grieving now.

"I'm so sorry," he began at last. "I know I should never have persuaded Brushpaw to stay. If I hadn't, he would be alive now, safe in his Twoleg den with you and Melody. I'll never forgive myself."

He was prepared for Bailey to lash out at him, but when she turned to him, her eyes were full of understanding. "It wasn't your fault," she mewed. "No matter what Tallstar says, I know it was mine, because I brought my kits into your Clan. I should have known better, but I wanted them to learn to take care of themselves, and that led directly to Brushpaw's—no, *Leo's*—death."

When they reached the Twolegplace, Onewhisker spotted Smoke sitting on a fence near Bailey's den. As they drew level with her, she leaped down to greet them.

"Hi, Bailey, Onewhisker. Isn't Brushpaw with you? Is he—"

Bailey interrupted her. "Where's Melody?"

"In her den," Smoke replied, blinking in surprise at Bailey's brusque tone.

Bailey brushed past her and disappeared into the gap between two Twoleg nests.

"What's the matter with her?" Smoke asked Onewhisker.

Onewhisker hesitated, hardly able to find the words. "It's bad," he meowed at last. "Brushpaw is dead."

Smoke's eyes stretched wide with shock, and she let out a murmur of grief.

"He thought of leaving WindClan," Onewhisker continued, forcing himself to tell her the worst. "But I talked him out of it. Is it all my fault? I should have known that kittypets can't be warriors, but I just wouldn't accept that."

Smoke padded up to him and gently brushed her cheek against his. "Oh, no," she murmured, her voice full of sympathy. "You can't blame yourself. Brushpaw always did what he wanted, and you were so kind to him. You must have helped him a lot. Besides, Clan life sounds so dangerous. . . ."

Onewhisker breathed in her sweet scent and purred in gratitude for her soothing words. *Smoke understands me.* He knew that what she said wasn't entirely true, but he wanted to believe it so desperately that he crushed his doubts down.

CHAPTER 6

❧

Onewhisker raced across the moor, his gaze fixed on the rabbit fleeing a few paw steps ahead of him. He could already scent the WindClan border markers at the edge of Fourtrees; if he didn't catch his prey within the next few heartbeats, it would cross the border and be lost to him.

Putting on a burst of speed, Onewhisker threw himself onto the rabbit and slashed his claws across its throat. "Thank you, StarClan, for this prey," he panted as the creature went limp.

"Great catch!"

Onewhisker started at the voice, coming from the direction of the hollow where the four oaks grew. Looking up, he spotted Firestar, the leader of ThunderClan. The sun shone on his flame-colored pelt as he padded up to the border and dipped his head to Onewhisker.

"How's the prey running in WindClan?" he asked.

"Not as well as usual," Onewhisker replied, dipping his head respectfully in his turn. "I think the Twolegs might be scaring it away. There are more of them than I've ever seen before, tramping over our territory."

"I've noticed that, too," Firestar agreed. "I'm telling my patrols to keep a lookout. You might advise Tallstar to do the same."

"Good idea, Firestar. Thanks."

Even while he spoke, Onewhisker wondered whether he should have been so candid with Firestar in mentioning the shortage of prey. He didn't want WindClan to seem weak in the ThunderClan leader's eyes.

But Firestar is an old friend, he told himself. *I trust him as much as my own Clanmates.*

Onewhisker had first met Firestar several seasons ago, when he and Graystripe had come to lead the exiled Wind-Clan home from the tunnel beneath the Thunderpath where they'd been sheltering. They had both been young warriors then, and Onewhisker had been shocked to learn that the flame-colored tom had started life as a kittypet.

"I was wrong about Brushpaw," he had confided to Ashfoot when they were settled in their camp again. "A kittypet *can* become a warrior. Look at Fireheart."

Even now, so many seasons after the young cat's death, Onewhisker still felt guilt and grief for Brushpaw, while his admiration for Firestar had grown as the former kittypet advanced through his Clan to become deputy and eventually leader.

"Well, whatever the Twolegs are up to," Firestar continued with a dismissive flick of his tail, "at least we have peace in the forest now. It will be a long time before the Clans produce another Tigerstar."

Onewhisker felt a growl growing in his throat. "I'd like

to have killed him myself," he responded. "He murdered my apprentice Gorsepaw, to try to frighten WindClan into doing what he wanted."

Firestar nodded sympathetically. "Gorsepaw was a promising young cat. He would have made a fine warrior."

Onewhisker felt suddenly chilled, as if a cloud had drifted across the sun. So many cats dead . . . Brushpaw, Gorsepaw, and more recently his old mentor, Deadfoot, who had lived long enough to see his son Crowpaw before his paws led him on the path to StarClan.

But the Clans continue, he thought, trying to push away his dark mood.

"Those were hard times," he murmured. "But you're right, Firestar. Things are better now."

"And they'll stay better, if we all keep alert," Firestar meowed. "It's good to see you, Onewhisker. May StarClan light your path."

"And yours, Firestar."

With a farewell dip of his head, the ThunderClan leader bounded away and disappeared over the lip of the Fourtrees hollow.

Onewhisker watched him go. *Yes, we all keep alert,* he thought. *But if there is to be trouble from Twolegs, it's the Clan leader who will have to make the decisions.*

As he picked up his prey and headed back to camp, Onewhisker was thankful that he had no ambition to be Clan leader. *Not that it's likely to happen,* he comforted himself. *It must be a lonely job.*

* * *

A few days after his encounter with Firestar, Onewhisker was padding across the moor, a rabbit dangling from his jaws. At his side Whitetail was carrying three mice by their tails. Since Twolegs had begun to encroach on the moor, the hunting had rarely been this good, and Onewhisker was looking forward to a nap after he had deposited his prey on the fresh-kill pile.

Early morning sunlight flooded across the moor, so Onewhisker found it hard to believe that leaf-fall was creeping through the forest. He loved the feeling of the moorland breeze flowing through his pelt and the freedom of life under the wide moorland sky.

There's nothing better than being a WindClan cat!

Whitetail had been especially skillful this morning, Onewhisker thought, trapping three mice from a nest she had discovered at the bottom of a rocky bank. He would never have guessed, when he had first seen her as a kit in the nursery all those seasons ago, that she would one day become his apprentice; now, many moons later, she had grown into a clever and capable warrior, and a good friend. She was the first cat he had thought of to come with him on this dawn hunting patrol.

When Onewhisker arrived back at the WindClan camp, he expected to find it almost empty, with most of his Clanmates out on patrol. Instead, as he squeezed his way through the gorse bushes that guarded the hollow, he almost felt as if he had disturbed an ants' nest. Warriors were darting here and there, searching behind boulders and into the dens.

Onewhisker felt every hair on his pelt begin to tingle as he sensed their alarm.

"What in StarClan's name is going on?" he muttered around his mouthful of prey.

He and Whitetail padded down into the hollow and dropped their fresh-kill on the pile. "What's going on?" he repeated to Mudclaw as the mottled brown warrior hurried past him.

Mudclaw halted, his eyes flaring impatience at the question. "Crowpaw is missing," he spat out.

"*Missing?*" Onewhisker echoed.

"That's what I said," Mudclaw replied. He was giving off mingled scents of fear and anger. "He's not in the apprentice den, and he didn't show up for training this morning."

Ashfoot dashed up while Mudclaw was speaking, her eyes wide with anxiety. Onewhisker knew how desperate she must be feeling; Crowpaw was her kit, the only survivor of her litter.

But in spite of her fear, Ashfoot's voice was quiet as she turned to Onewhisker. "Have you seen him?" Onewhisker shook his head. "He didn't tell any cat he was going somewhere," Ashfoot continued. "Oh, StarClan, I'm so worried!"

Onewhisker rested his tail on his sister's shoulder. "We'll find him," he reassured her. "And if he's playing some sort of trick, I'll make sure he wishes he'd never been kitted!"

"You can leave that to me," Mudclaw growled.

Onewhisker and Whitetail joined in the search of the camp, though Onewhisker was fairly sure that the apprentice would have been found already if he were still there. Most cats were already giving up, standing in the center of the hollow as if they didn't know what to do next.

Mudclaw had begun to organize search patrols when Ashfoot let out a joyful yowl from the top of the slope. "I can scent him!"

Onewhisker pelted up to her side with Whitetail a pace behind him. Ashfoot pointed with her tail at a narrow gap between two bushes; putting his nose to the ground, Onewhisker gave it a good long sniff.

Straightening up, he nodded. "That's Crowpaw."

Onewhisker slipped through the gap and located the apprentice's scent trail, leading across the moor in the direction of Fourtrees. Once he was sure, he slipped back to where Ashfoot and Whitetail were waiting.

"He seems to be heading for Fourtrees," he meowed.

Whitetail gave him a puzzled look. "Why would he want to go there?"

"You tell me," Onewhisker mewed, shaking his head. "The scent is starting to grow stale, so he must have left during the night. Why would he do that?"

Tallstar made his way up the slope to join them. "Have you found something?" he asked. "Report." Onewhisker explained what Ashfoot had discovered, and the Clan leader checked the scent for himself.

"You're right," he meowed. "You'd better go after him," he added, his gaze sweeping across all three cats. "And be careful. He may have just decided to try night hunting, but . . ."

His voice trailed off. Onewhisker didn't need him to point out all the dangers that an unwary apprentice might run into on the moor by himself.

"We're on it," he declared, and led the way through the gorse bushes and out into the open.

Crowpaw's scent trail led directly across the moor toward Fourtrees. As he and the two she-cats followed it, Onewhisker felt warm with pride that his leader had chosen him for this task.

Crowpaw is such a promising apprentice. We have to find him!

"You know how hard Crowpaw always works," Ashfoot meowed, seeming to pick up Onewhisker's thoughts. "He would never miss a training session, or do anything to make Mudclaw angry with him. I've been expecting him to have his warrior ceremony soon, but now—" Her voice broke and she turned her head away.

"Try not to worry," Whitetail mewed gently. "You know how apprentices get ideas into their heads. He'll probably turn up with the biggest rabbit on the moor, wondering what all the fuss is about!"

"I hope you're right," Ashfoot murmured, though she didn't look as if she believed it.

Onewhisker gave Whitetail an approving glance, impressed by how kind and sensitive her words had been. "Whitetail is right," he assured his sister. "I'm sure Crowpaw will be fine— though he deserves to have his ears clawed for frightening every cat!"

The scent trail led onward without a break until the patrol

came to a shallow stream winding its way among pebbles. Here, for the first time, the trail ended. Onewhisker headed upstream, nose to the ground, while Ashfoot searched in the other direction.

"It's almost like the stupid furball waded in the water to break his scent," Onewhisker muttered to himself. "But that would mean he doesn't want to be followed. That can't be right, surely?"

Meanwhile Whitetail had leaped the stream and was casting about on the opposite bank. "Over here!" she called, waving her tail. "It's very faint, though; I wonder if he got his paws wet."

Onewhisker stooped to sniff the spot Whitetail had indicated. She was right; the trace was there, though he guessed that most cats would have missed it.

"Well scented," he meowed to Whitetail, who ducked her head in embarrassment at his praise.

The patrol carried on, Crowpaw's trail still leading straight for Fourtrees. They lost it briefly on a stretch of stony ground, and once again it was Whitetail who picked it up. After that, Fourtrees was so close that they hardly needed Crowpaw's scent to guide them; it was obvious where he was going.

At the top of the hollow where the four great oaks grew, Onewhisker halted and tasted the air. The lush growth of ferns on the slopes distracted him briefly, but when he concentrated, he could still detect Crowpaw's scent. Then he stiffened.

Crowpaw isn't the only cat who's been here!

"ThunderClan scent?" he murmured, glancing at Whitetail.

The white warrior nodded. "Yes, and RiverClan, and . . . I'm almost sure, ShadowClan too."

Ashfoot had also picked up the traces, and stood staring into the hollow, mingled anxiety and disbelief in her eyes. "These cats were all here together," she murmured. "What is happening?"

"Ashfoot," Onewhisker began, "you don't know whether Crowpaw was . . . well, padding after a cat from another Clan?"

His sister turned a shocked gaze on him. "Of course not!" she meowed defensively. "How can you even ask that?"

Onewhisker shrugged uneasily. He hadn't meant to upset Ashfoot, especially when she was so worried about her kit. "You know it's not unusual for apprentices to feel that way," he pointed out. "At least until they realize what leaving their Clan would mean."

"Well, Crowpaw would never do that," Ashfoot retorted. "He's far too sensible. . . ."

"I think we can discount that theory," Whitetail put in. "Unless you think that Crowpaw was padding after *three* different cats, all at the same time. Whatever happened, we have to account for *all* the Clans' scents."

Onewhisker nodded, feeling slightly stupid. He led the way down through the ferns until the whole patrol stood on the grass at the foot of the oak trees. Here all the scents seemed to come together, concentrated at the base of the Great Rock.

"They *met* here," he meowed. "What were they doing?"

Ashfoot shook her head, completely bewildered, while

Whitetail sniffed around the rock, alert as if she were searching for prey.

"If you ask me," she mewed after a while," I think there were six cats here."

"*Six?*" Onewhisker found that hard to believe, even though he was well aware of Whitetail's scenting skills.

His Clanmate nodded. "Two from ThunderClan, two from RiverClan, Crowpaw, and a cat from ShadowClan. I don't know them well enough to pick out which ones."

"This doesn't make any sense at all!" Ashfoot exclaimed, with a frustrated lash of her tail.

"They came here, and then they left. . . ." Onewhisker mused.

"Well, obviously!" his sister snapped. "Or they would still be here!"

Onewhisker stroked his tail down Ashfoot's side to calm her. "Yes, of course. But did they split up, back to their own Clans, or did they go somewhere together?"

Whitetail already had her nose to the ground, moving away from the Great Rock in a spiral that grew wider and wider. Soon she raised her head. "Here! And they *did* go together."

With six cats' trails to follow, it was easy to track them up the side of the hollow and out onto WindClan territory again. Though it was sometimes hard to distinguish Crowpaw's scent from the rest of them, there was no doubt about the direction. The cats had headed for the Thunderpath, then followed alongside it.

"Are they going to Highstones?" Onewhisker wondered,

his heart pounding unpleasantly at the thought of what might happen to cats who were heading far away from Clan territory.

"Why would they?" Ashfoot sounded more bewildered still. "What would be the point, unless they're with a Clan leader or a medicine cat?"

"I very much doubt any leader or medicine cat would approve of this little jaunt," Onewhisker responded grimly. "Some cats are going to be in a whole lot of trouble!"

Beside the Thunderpath, the faint scent of fox caught in Onewhisker's throat. He stood, pondering—was it possible that a fox had gotten to Crowpaw and his companions? But there was no blood on the ground. He decided not to worry Ashfoot with the suggestion. Still, he worried that *something* had gotten to the group of cats. Why else would they have disappeared without warning their Clanmates?

Finally the scent trail diminished completely. Even Whitetail had to admit defeat.

"We've lost them!" Ashfoot's voice was almost a wail. "Now what do we do?"

Onewhisker paused briefly, trying to crush his own fears. The fox scent seemed to linger in his nostrils. "We'd better go back to camp and report," he replied.

Ashfoot hesitated for a moment, clearly reluctant, then murmured agreement and turned toward home with Onewhisker and Whitetail.

Onewhisker felt shaken to the tips of his claws, and desperately confused; looking at his Clanmates' twitching whiskers, he could see that they felt the same.

Where would Crowpaw have gone, and why? And what did ThunderClan, ShadowClan, and RiverClan have to do with it all?

"Crowpaw cares about becoming a WindClan warrior more than anything else," Ashfoot meowed when they had been walking for a while. "He knows that Mudclaw will give him his assessment soon. I can't imagine what would be important enough to make him leave."

"Tallstar will have to send patrols to the other Clans," Whitetail responded, her voice crisp and sensible as always. "It looks as though they're missing cats too. Maybe they can give us a hint as to what it's all about."

"Maybe," Ashfoot sighed, though Onewhisker didn't think she believed it.

"Suppose Crowpaw met up with some other apprentices," he suggested, "and they all went off to be kittypets."

Stony silence met his words. Ashfoot glared at him, her lips drawn back in the beginnings of a snarl, then turned her back, obviously offended. Whitetail rolled her eyes as if she couldn't believe Onewhisker had said that.

"Surely such a loyal apprentice would never dream of the life of a kittypet!" she mewed.

Onewhisker didn't dare say so, but privately, he mused that the life of a kittypet wasn't as bad as Clan cats made it out to be. It had been a long time since he had been able to visit the Twolegplace, but ever since Brushpaw and Tansypaw had introduced him to the temptations of kittypet life, he hadn't been able to turn his back on it—not completely. *It's not for me, but I can see the appeal, especially in these lean times.*

"During normal times," he began, "no loyal apprentice would be tempted. But Twolegs are encroaching on the Clans' territories more every day." Ashfoot still looked horrified, and met his explanation in icy silence. "Of course," he added hastily, "you're right. Crowpaw wouldn't ever make that decision."

He quickened his pace a little to draw ahead and let the two she-cats fall into conversation behind him. They were probably telling each other what a stupid furball he was.

All the same, he promised himself, *I'm going to check the Twoleg-place the first chance I get.*

To Onewhisker's relief, clouds covered the sky that night, the moon and stars breaking through only fitfully. Careful not to rouse his Clanmates, he sneaked away from the stretch of ground that formed the warriors' den and crept silently up the slope to slither through the gorse bushes. Once out on the moor, he flattened himself into the grass until he thought he was far enough away to evade Tornear, who was keeping watch on the top of Outlook Rock. Then he rose to his paws and bounded toward the Twolegplace.

Eager anticipation gave speed to his paws. *I would never leave WindClan,* he assured himself, but he had to admit that as Clan life grew worse, with Twolegs encroaching more and more on the territory, it was nice to have something to dream about. If the worst happened and monsters tore up the WindClan camp tomorrow, he was pretty sure that he knew enough about Twolegs to convince one to take him in.

Meow and look pathetic, he thought. *How hard can it be? Though I'm thankful that so far it hasn't come to that.*

Onewhisker reached the den he was aiming for, and stood outside yowling. He was disappointed that the cat he was calling to didn't emerge, but soon he was surrounded by a whole crowd of kittypets from neighboring Twoleg gardens. Melody was one of the first to arrive, with a small orange tom she introduced as Dudley.

"It's great to meet a real warrior!" Dudley exclaimed, his fur fluffing up with excitement. "Melody says you hunt rabbits and fight other cats."

"Tell us about it!" one of the other kittypets begged, and the rest of them chorused, "Yes, please tell us!"

Onewhisker exchanged a glance with Melody. She of all the kittypets would know that Clan life wasn't the exciting adventure that he had described on his previous visits. But she never spoiled the stories for the other kittypets.

"Okay," he began. "I'll tell you how my Clanmates and I fought a fox and chased it off our territory."

The kittypets crouched down to listen, their eyes wide as Onewhisker told them how he and a patrol had tackled the fox and fought a fierce battle before it fled, wounded and whimpering, across the border. He didn't mention that the fox had been old and scrawny, and very easy to convince that life would be easier elsewhere.

"But that isn't why I came," Onewhisker meowed at last, when the story was finished and he had listened to the kittypets' admiring exclamations. "I'm here on an important mission. One of our apprentices is missing, and I wondered whether he might have come here."

The kittypets glanced at one another, shaking their heads.

"We haven't seen any strange cats around here," Melody declared. "But if you tell us what he's like, we can keep a look-out for him."

"His name is Crowpaw," Onewhisker responded. "He's quite small and skinny, and his fur is very dark gray—almost black."

While he was describing the missing apprentice, Smoke appeared from the Twoleg nest and strolled across the garden to his side. "Hi, Onewhisker," she mewed, blinking her huge blue eyes. "It's been so long since I've seen you. I thought you'd forgotten me."

"I wouldn't do that." Faintly embarrassed, Onewhisker repeated what he had already told the kittypets about Crow-paw.

"I haven't seen him." Smoke glanced around at the other kittypets. "What about the rest of you?"

Once again the kittypets put their heads together, discussing the information Onewhisker had given them. But still no cat had seen Crowpaw.

"We haven't seen any Clan cats here," Smoke told him. "Except for you, of course."

Onewhisker had to accept that, though he was slightly disappointed. He had hoped that he could solve the mystery quickly. It had been exciting to imagine that he could have returned to camp as a hero, with Crowpaw at his side.

Ashfoot must be right. He would never come anywhere near Twolegs.

Still, Onewhisker reflected, it had been fun to talk to the kittypets and tell them a story, letting their admiration soak into him like sunlight on his pelt. If he was honest with himself, that was really why he kept coming back.

"I'd better be going," he meowed with a sigh. "If any of you see Crowpaw, tell him to come home."

"Don't go yet," Dudley objected. "You look skinny, and I'd like to share my treats with you."

"Treats?" Onewhisker asked, confused.

"Oh, they're really tasty," Dudley assured him enthusiastically. "My housefolk keep them on a shelf in the garage, but I know how to knock them down."

Garage was another word that confused Onewhisker briefly, until he remembered it was the Twoleg word for a monster den, like the one where he and the other apprentices had sheltered on their first visit to the Twolegplace.

"Okay, thanks," he mewed.

Dudley led the way along the line of Twoleg dens until he reached the corner, where he slid through the fence. Onewhisker and the other kittypets followed.

"Over here!" Dudley called, bounding across the garden to the monster den.

Onewhisker stared after him, his heart beginning to pound and his shoulder fur prickling. The front of the den was open, and inside it crouched the monster.

What if it pounces?

Every muscle in Onewhisker's body was telling him to flee, but he knew he couldn't do that. The kittypets didn't seem at all bothered, and if he ran away, they would know that he wasn't the bold, fearless Clan cat he had always pretended to be. He wouldn't dare show his face in the Twolegplace again.

As casually as he could, Onewhisker strolled up to the mouth of the den. Meanwhile Dudley had leaped up onto the monster's nose and from there onto a flat piece of wood that stuck out from the den wall. He was poking at something brightly colored that lay on the shelf.

While Onewhisker stared, half admiring, half horrified, Dudley managed to knock the brightly colored object onto the ground. It burst open on impact, scattering a shower of small brown pellets.

Rabbit droppings? Onewhisker wondered.

"Help yourself," Dudley invited. "Trust me, they're really good!"

Onewhisker realized he had to at least try one. He sniffed cautiously at one of the pellets, then braced himself and took a taste. *Wow, that's weird!* he thought. *But sort of . . . delicious!* "You're right, Dudley," he meowed. "They are good! Thanks a lot!"

"They're bacon flavored," Dudley informed him. *Whatever that may be.* "Come on," the orange tom called to the other kittypets. "You can share. There's plenty."

The other kittypets crowded around, licking up the remainder of the treats. Some of them even crawled underneath the monster to find the ones that had rolled under there.

As he finished his unexpected snack, Onewhisker realized

that the night was growing darker. Lights were going out in the Twoleg dens, and close by he heard the sound of a Twoleg calling.

"That's my Twoleg," a tabby-and-white kittypet meowed. "I've got to go. Thanks, Dudley." He whipped around and bounded off.

It seemed to Onewhisker that within a couple of heartbeats the air was echoing with Twoleg voices. One by one the kitty-pets headed off, until Onewhisker was left alone with Smoke.

The gray kittypet leaned up against Onewhisker and gave his ear a lick. "Shall I walk you back to Clan territory?" she purred. "We can go the long way around. . . ."

CHAPTER 7

"Ashfoot, you can't go on like this," Onewhisker meowed.

His sister was curled up at the edge of the warriors' den. This was the second morning since Crowpaw had disappeared; when she had returned from following his scent trail, she had gone straight to her nest and stayed there. Onewhisker knew she wasn't eating, and her fur was clumped as if she hadn't groomed herself, either.

Onewhisker found it hard to think of comforting words. He was still shaking inwardly from a terrible dream he'd had the night before. Crowpaw's father, Deadfoot, had appeared to Onewhisker in all the splendor of his starry fur. His gleaming eyes had fixed on Onewhisker, and his voice sounded like a wind blowing over the frozen moor. "You *must* look out for Crowpaw! My son will need you!" Onewhisker had awoken, shivering; the dream had made him feel even worse about his littermate's kit, and all he could do now was try to push it out of his mind.

"Whitetail and I are going hunting," he continued, when Ashfoot didn't respond. "Why don't you come with us? It would be good to take your mind off things."

Ashfoot turned her head toward him, glaring, and let out a furious hiss. "What if I don't *want* to take my mind off my son being missing?"

Onewhisker's head drooped, and wished he could claw his own tail off to punish himself for being so thoughtless.

Bending over, he nuzzled Ashfoot's shoulder. "Crowpaw is a promising young apprentice," he assured her. "And we're pretty sure he's with those other Clan cats. I'm certain he's fine."

Ashfoot sighed. "Do you really believe that?"

"Of course I do."

His sister let out another long sigh and wrapped her tail over her nose.

As Onewhisker turned away to find Whitetail, he wondered whether he had really meant it when he reassured Ashfoot. *After all, Crowpaw hasn't completed his apprenticeship, and there are a lot of dangers out there....*

Clouds hung heavy over the moor, and there was a tang of rain in the air when Onewhisker and Whitetail headed out with Gorsetail and Webfoot. All four of them were keeping a keen eye out for signs of Twolegs. Border patrols had reported seeing more than ever before, and massive monsters had been spotted beside the Thunderpath. Even worse, prey was becoming scarce.

And that's another danger for Crowpaw, Onewhisker told himself. *Unless he's far away from Clan territory by now.*

Gorsetail and Webfoot had drawn some way ahead when Whitetail gave Onewhisker a nudge and pointed with her tail toward where a huge pigeon was pecking at the ground.

"We have to catch it!" Onewhisker whispered, his jaws flooding at the thought of the juicy prey. "It's a pity we can't fly."

"Maybe we can, sort of," Whitetail murmured, her eyes gleaming eagerly. "Look at that boulder, just beyond the pigeon. You climb to the top, and I'll creep up very carefully . . ."

"And when you're in position, I'll leap down and scare the pigeon so it flies toward you, and you can grab it before it gains height," Onewhisker finished.

Whitetail nodded. "I think that should work."

Without delay Onewhisker began working his way around to the back of the boulder. He eyed it doubtfully as it towered way above his head. *Can I really leap up there?* The sides were smooth; there weren't many cracks to drive his claws into in order to scramble to the top.

Onewhisker bunched his hind legs under him and powered upward in a massive leap. His forelegs hit the top of the rock, but his hind legs scrabbled vainly for purchase. Gritting his teeth, he sank his claws into the thin layer of lichen that covered the boulder, and hauled himself up to lie panting at the summit.

From his position Onewhisker had a magnificent view across the moor, but he was more interested in what he could see just below. The pigeon was still pecking, unaware of Whitetail, who was lying flat behind a tussock of grass, her attention fixed firmly on her prey.

Now!

Letting out a yowl, Onewhisker leaped down from the rock. Terrified, the pigeon fluttered upward, and Whitetail sprang to intercept it and claw it out of the air.

She timed that perfectly, Onewhisker thought admiringly. *And she's so graceful!*

The pigeon was still flapping wildly under Whitetail's claws, battering her in the face with its wings. But she didn't let go. Onewhisker pounced on it to hold it down, leaving Whitetail to give the killing bite.

Both cats sat back, panting and gazing triumphantly at their prey.

"We make a good team, don't we?" Whitetail purred, giving Onewhisker a long look from shining eyes.

Onewhisker blinked, slightly shocked. *Does she . . . like me?*

He had never thought of Whitetail as anything but his apprentice and then a good Clanmate, but now he realized that she was a full warrior, very capable . . . and very pretty. It had been a long time since she was an apprentice.

This isn't the time to start thinking like that, he told himself, trying to push the thought away.

As the two cats rose to their paws, the rain that had been threatening all day suddenly came down, as hard as if they had been standing under a waterfall. Carrying the pigeon between them, they dashed for the boulder and sheltered under an overhang. Pressed back against the rock and against each other for warmth, they watched the rain, so heavy that it cut off the view of the moor. It seemed to Onewhisker that he was alone in the world with Whitetail; he was surprised at how good that felt.

Perhaps he could confide in her about his worries. "I have a bad feeling about Crowpaw," he confessed after a moment. "I had a dream about Deadfoot last night—you know he was my mentor. He told me to look out for his kit, the only one of the litter who survived." He shivered. "I want to do what he asks, but how can I, when Crowpaw isn't here?"

Whitetail pressed her nose into Onewhisker's shoulder. "I'm sure Crowpaw will be okay," she meowed. "He's still an apprentice, but he's as intelligent and skilled as most warriors."

"I hope you're right," Onewhisker responded; Whitetail's positive attitude warmed his fur and sent new energy coursing through him. "Come on, the rain's stopping. Let's take this pigeon back to camp."

As he and Whitetail padded down into the hollow, Onewhisker couldn't help noticing how skinny and restless his Clanmates looked. He could almost taste their hunger. *At least Whitetail and I have something to show for our hunt,* he thought, relieved.

Tallstar was sitting close to the meager fresh-kill pile when Onewhisker and Whitetail went to deposit their prey. He examined the pigeon with a pleased expression.

"Great catch," he meowed. "Well done, both of you."

Onewhisker noticed that the Clan leader's voice sounded weak. His eyes were dull and his pelt was thin and had lost its healthy gloss.

"Tallstar, did the other patrols bring you anything?" he asked.

Tallstar gave him a look that told Onewhisker he knew

exactly what he was asking. "No, I haven't eaten," he replied. "And I won't. Fresh-kill is scarce, and the elders and queens need it more."

As much as Onewhisker would have liked to argue, he had to respect his leader's decision. But that didn't stop him from worrying. Tallstar wasn't a young cat anymore, and he was so thin Onewhisker could see his ribs.

He isn't taking care of himself.

Mudclaw was a strong warrior and a good deputy, Onewhisker reflected, but he didn't have the caring side that would see Tallstar's needs. Onewhisker decided to have a word with Barkface, and to look after the Clan leader himself, as much as he could, in the coming days.

If things get worse for WindClan, we'll need our leader's wisdom.

There was a stir of excitement in the camp as Gorsetail and Webfoot returned. To Onewhisker's surprise, each of them was dragging along a huge rabbit.

"You did well!" he exclaimed as they brought their prey to the fresh-kill pile. "How did you ever manage to catch them?"

"They were dozing in their burrow," Webfoot explained. "It's like StarClan led us there."

The Clan gathered around, eating better than they had for many days. Onewhisker and Whitetail shared their pigeon, and insisted on Tallstar taking a portion of it, too.

"I'm so proud of my warriors, and my Clan," he mewed as he swallowed the last bite. "StarClan really is watching over us."

When every cat had eaten their fill, WindClan settled down to sleep. Onewhisker was tired after the hunt, but he felt he had scarcely closed his eyes when something woke him: a groaning sound that he vaguely thought might be the creak of winter branches. He wrapped his tail over his ears and tried to ignore it, but the sound came again. With an exasperated sigh he raised his head and looked around.

The sight that met his gaze drove all thoughts of sleep away. Some of his Clanmates were twitching as they slept, while others had left their nests and were stumbling away from the den into the open area of the camp. All of them were letting out horrific groans of pain, the sound that had awoken One-whisker.

Leaping to his paws, he spotted Whitetail nearby, and thanked StarClan that she seemed to be unaffected. "What's happening?" she called out to him. "Are you okay?"

"I'm fine," he replied.

Webfoot blundered into him in his efforts to leave the den. Onewhisker let the gray tabby tom lean on his shoulder and guided him out into the open. Whitetail was helping Mud-claw, and together the four cats staggered out into the center of the camp.

Onewhisker could hardly believe what he was seeing; it was like something from one of his worst nightmares. *So many of us* . . . His horrified gaze swept over warriors, elders, and apprentices, all lying on the ground and groaning. The sour stink of vomit hung in the air.

Barkface was moving among them, trying to check on them all, feeling their distended bellies and giving each cat a pawful of herbs.

Whitetail hurried over to him, delicately picking her way

among the writhing bodies. "Onewhisker and I are fine," she mewed. "What can we do to help?"

"Fetch more yarrow," Barkface replied at once. "These cats have been poisoned."

"I'll go. I know where it grows." Whitetail took off, her tail streaming out behind her as she sped up the slope and out of the hollow.

Onewhisker began guiding more of the sick cats over to the medicine cat's den. He was relieved to see Tallstar emerge from his den behind the Tallrock; the Clan leader looked shaken by the chaos in the camp, but otherwise fine.

Tallstar . . . Whitetail . . . and me . . . We all ate the pigeon, One-whisker thought. *Not the rabbits. I wonder . . .*

He bounded over to the fresh-kill pile and searched for the uneaten parts of the rabbits. Though they had smelled all right when they were fresh, now there was a distinct horrible reek rising from them.

His lips curled back in disgust, Onewhisker pawed the rabbits away from the remaining prey in the fresh-kill pile, then carried them out of the camp and dug a hole to bury them. His task finished, he headed for the nearest stream and gave his muzzle and his paws a thorough wash.

When he returned to the camp, he went straight to Bark-face with the news. *It's not good. . . . I just hope that we're not too late to save the Clan. . . .*

The days that followed the poisoning were some of the worst of Onewhisker's life. He and Whitetail were the strongest of the healthy cats, and they barely slept. Barkface was on his paws from morning to night, and then all the way through to the following sunrise, in his desperate efforts to save his Clanmates. The experienced medicine cat tried everything he knew, but even giving the cats yarrow to make them throw up didn't help. Some of them were getting better—Onewhisker's father, Stagleap, among them—but every day the row of cats awaiting vigil and burial grew longer. Onewhisker's heart broke to see that the poison had taken so many elders and apprentices.

"Oh, Onewhisker . . ." Whitetail had just helped Barkface carry Runningbrook, the latest victim, from his den. Now she stumbled up to Onewhisker; her voice was shaking, and when she reached his side, she crouched to the ground, wrapping her tail around her head. "I can't bear it anymore. . . . I can't!"

"Whitetail . . . ," Onewhisker whispered.

Through the crisis, the white she-cat had been as steady as a rock, helping wherever she was needed. Both she and Onewhisker had been incredibly busy, especially as Tallstar was too weak to exert himself much. Even when her mother, Sorrelshine, had succumbed to the poison, Whitetail had braced herself and carried on. It terrified Onewhisker to see her break down like this.

With a sudden longing to tell Whitetail how much she meant to him, Onewhisker settled down beside her, rubbing his cheek against hers and resting his tail on her back, trying to let his own strength flow into her.

Whitetail looked up at him, the surprise in her gaze giving

way to love, and then to a profound relief. "I've cared for you for so long . . . ," she murmured. "But I wasn't sure you felt the same."

But I do . . . Onewhisker felt scared and protective and happy, all at once. "You can always count on me," he purred.

Whitetail had proven herself to be such a skillful warrior, but for so many moons Onewhisker's adventures in the Two-legplace had distracted him from truly getting to know the Clanmate she had become. Now he saw her clearly for the remarkable cat she had always been. Relief washed over him that he had found his match, right here in WindClan. *And I never even saw her! How mouse-brained is that?*

Onewhisker guided Whitetail back to the warriors' den and curled up with her in his nest. She was still trembling from the horror of so many deaths, and he lay beside her, keeping watch over her until the shaking gradually died away and she fell asleep.

She was right, he thought, reflecting on how well they had worked together through the poisoning crisis. *We do make a great pair. I'm glad I see it now.*

By the next day, Mudclaw was back on his paws, well enough to lead a patrol across the moor to the burrow where Gorsetail and Webfoot had found the rabbits. Onewhisker was out in the clearing when the deputy came to report to Tallstar.

"We found poison in the rabbit hole." The Clan deputy's voice was rough with anger. "It was obviously put there by Twolegs."

"You didn't touch it?" Tallstar asked anxiously.

Mudclaw shook his head. "No, we were really careful. But it means we can't trust *any* prey from that part of the moor." He lashed his tail. "StarClan-cursed Twolegs!"

Onewhisker felt anger swelling inside him, too. *Why can't the Twolegs leave us in peace?* He could tell how frustrated Mudclaw was. If another Clan had attacked them like this, killing so many of their Clanmates, the deputy would have been the first cat to demand a battle.

But there's nothing we can do against Twolegs. . . .

Onewhisker let one more day pass before he braced himself and headed for the Twolegplace. He had put this off for too long, and he wasn't making up his mind now just because of Whitetail. He had always known that coming to the Twolegplace was wrong. *It isn't safe—it isn't right—for warriors and kittypets to mix. Brushpaw's death should have taught me that.*

As soon as Onewhisker arrived outside Smoke's den, the gray kittypet rushed out through a gap in her garden fence to meet him. "It's so good to see you!" she exclaimed, steering him back through the gap. "I've so much to tell you!"

"Smoke, I—" Onewhisker began.

"I caught a mouse in the Twoleg den today," Smoke interrupted, her blue eyes sparkling with triumph. "I can't show you, because one of my housefolk took it away before I'd finished with it. But I felt so fierce and capable—just like a warrior! I've saved you some food," she went on, as Onewhisker opened his jaws in an attempt to get a word in, "and I can't wait to hear about your latest adventures."

"Smoke, listen," Onewhisker meowed desperately, guilt washing over him for what he was about to say. He really liked Smoke—and he could admit to himself that he especially liked how much she admired him for his bravery and the exaggerated adventures he had recounted to her—but he knew that they couldn't be together anymore. "I've loved being your friend. Our time together has been really special for me. But it has to end. It has to end now."

Smoke halted and stared at him, her blue eyes stretched wide. "Onewhisker? You—you can't mean that!"

It was hard for Onewhisker to see the hurt and indignation in Smoke's face and know that it was his fault. "I'm sorry. I'm so sorry," he mewed. "But yes, I do mean it."

"But it wasn't just friendship!" Smoke protested. "We're in love!"

Onewhisker stood awkwardly, shifting his paws, uncertain what to say, until he realized that Smoke deserved an honest answer.

"Yes, I did have . . . feelings for you," he admitted. "But you have to see that our lives just don't mix. We can't be together; it's not fair to either of us."

"We don't *have* to have different lives," Smoke meowed. "You can't want to live out on that nasty cold moor *forever*! My housefolk would welcome you. Haven't you had enough of adventures? Wouldn't you rather live a comfortable life? Look at Bailey and Melody! *They* came back."

Onewhisker felt worse than ever. He had never realized

until now that Smoke had expected he would eventually come to live with her in the Twolegplace. He hoped he hadn't encouraged her with his own stupid daydreams of becoming a kittypet if the Clans were destroyed. But now that he had Whitetail, he saw that that was all they had ever been: daydreams.

And being a warrior isn't just some adventure. It's who I am. Who I will always be.

Whitetail needed him and Tallstar needed him; Onewhisker knew that now. He could never turn his back on WindClan.

"I'm sorry, Smoke," he murmured. "Truly sorry. But this is good-bye."

He leaned forward to touch noses with her one last time, but Smoke started back with a hiss of fury. "Good-bye, then! But if you change your mind, don't even *think* about sneaking back!"

Onewhisker turned away. As he headed out of the Twolegplace, he still felt guilty, but at the same time somehow lighter. It was hard to leave Smoke behind, but he had no doubt that he had done the right thing.

From now on, I need to focus on my Clan . . . and Whitetail.

CHAPTER 8

Onewhisker padded across the moor, following Stagleap and Tornear. All his senses were stretched to the limit in the desperate search for prey. In the midst of their grief for their poisoned Clanmates, this was the daily task for all the surviving Wind-Clan warriors: to search every mouse-length of the territory for food they could trust to be safe. For all their efforts, though, the Clan was going hungry. The cold weather didn't help; nor did the rain that kept sending whatever prey there was deep into their holes.

Before he left the camp, Onewhisker had tried to persuade Ashfoot to join the patrol, but she had refused, overwhelmed by her sorrow for Crowpaw. Most of the Clan believed that the apprentice must be dead, although no cat would say that out loud.

"Wait!" Stagleap, in the lead, halted and raised his tail. "What's that?"

Onewhisker and Tornear crept up beside him, tasting the air. At once Onewhisker recognized the scent of rats. His belly started churning at the hope of prey, but at the same time he was puzzled. Rats hardly ever ventured onto Wind-Clan territory.

Stagleap gestured with his tail. "This way."

The rat scent grew stronger as the patrol headed cautiously up a gentle swell of moorland. On the far side the hill fell away into a steeper slope, with a narrow stream at the bottom of it. A whole crowd of fat gray rats was scuttling along the waterside.

"Weird," Onewhisker murmured. "Where are they going? They can't have a nest here—if they did, we would know about it."

"Maybe they're running from something," Tornear suggested.

"Whatever." There was a hint of impatience in Stagleap's tone. "Let's just catch the mange-pelts, and discuss them afterward."

He led the way down the slope and along the stream, following the rats. Now that they were closer to the trail, Onewhisker could detect a trace of Twoleg garbage among the rat scent. A shiver passed through him as he realized they must have come from the Carrionplace. Normally, the thought of Twolegs' crowfood rotting in the sun disgusted him, but now his Clan was so hungry, the rats were a welcome sight.

If the rats have been driven from the Carrionplace, he thought, *then maybe we have something to thank the Twolegs for.*

"We're going to be in for a fight," Tornear muttered. "Those rats look strong and healthy. And there are a lot of them."

"So they'll be better prey," Stagleap declared, determination in his tone. "Don't you think it's worth the risk?"

Onewhisker and Tornear both murmured agreement. *I'd risk anything to get food for the Clan,* Onewhisker thought.

Stagleap picked up the pace until the three cats were racing along the bank of the stream. Soon the back of the crowd came into sight. Stagleap signaled with his tail for silence, and the patrol bounded forward until they had almost caught up with the stragglers.

"Now!" Stagleap yowled.

With his Clanmates at his side, Onewhisker leaped in among the rats. Their stink surrounded him; squeals of terror filled the air. He killed one rat almost immediately, sinking his teeth into its throat. *Maybe this will be easy . . .*, he thought.

A heartbeat later, he realized how wrong he was. The first surprise onslaught over, the rats surrounded their attackers, fixing them with small, malignant eyes. A furious chittering noise filled the air. Onewhisker choked on the reek that rose from them, wreathing around him like thick fog. There were so many that he didn't have the space to strike out, and he struggled to stay on his paws.

If I fall now, I'm finished, he thought desperately, imagining the sleek gray bodies swarming all over him, smothering the life out of him.

All Onewhisker could do was keep fighting, but as soon as he threw off one rat, there was another to take its place. He caught a glimpse of Tornear, struggling to stay upright with a rat on his back; Onewhisker fought his way to his Clanmate's side and slashed his claws through the rat's throat.

"Thanks," Tornear gasped, already turning to grapple with another of the vicious creatures.

At the same moment Onewhisker felt teeth meet in his

tail; he spun around sharply and swatted at the rat. It let out a squeal and vanished into the surging throng, but then there was another and another. . . . Onewhisker began to wonder how long his strength would hold out.

After what seemed like seasons of battling, Onewhisker began to realize that the horde was thinning out. He could see farther than his own paws. Then, suddenly, there were no more rats; he could stand still and catch his breath. Gazing around, he spotted a few rats fleeing across the moor and his Clanmates standing nearby. Several rats lay still around their paws.

"Thank you, StarClan, for this prey," Stagleap panted. "And well fought. The Clan will eat well tonight."

Onewhisker thought they had done well just to survive. His whole body burned from rat scratches, and he could still feel the bite on his tail. Tornear's tail was bleeding, too, and Stagleap had a bad rat bite on his face, but none of them looked seriously injured.

Stagleap puffed out a sigh. "Let's get back."

It was a struggle to carry their prey; the rats were big and plump, and each cat had to manage two. Onewhisker felt as if his paws would drop off by the time they reached the camp.

He was aware of a stir of excitement when he and his Clanmates dragged their prey through the gorse bushes and down into the hollow. The rest of the Clan gathered around as they deposited the prey on the fresh-kill pile, yowling their congratulations.

Whitetail bounded up to Onewhisker and touched her

nose to his ear. "Well done," she murmured. "You're a great hunter! But you're injured, all of you," she added, gazing at the hunting patrol with concern in her eyes. "Off you go to Barkface's den, right now!"

Onewhisker gave her ear a lick. "We're fine. But okay, we're going!" he added as Whitetail laid her ears back and bared her teeth in a mock threat.

He led the way across the camp to Barkface's den, only to stop, shocked, in the entrance when he saw Tallstar there with Mudclaw at his side. "Tallstar, what happened?" he asked, panic turning every muscle in his body to ice.

It was Barkface who replied. "Everything is okay—for now. Tallstar lost a life earlier, but now he has returned from Star-Clan. He needs to rest and eat something, that's all."

Onewhisker's panic ebbed, replaced by deep anxiety. Tallstar had lost a life because he had insisted on leaving WindClan's meager prey for the queens and elders. *What's to stop him losing another, if he still refuses to eat?*

Meanwhile, Mudclaw was raking the hunters with a disapproving gaze. "Rat bites!" he exclaimed, turning to Tallstar. "Look how these brave warriors have risked their lives to bring us a few measly rats, and you almost starved to death! This can't go on."

"What do you suggest, Mudclaw?" Tallstar asked.

"We must do everything we can do survive," Mudclaw growled. "If you won't agree to taking territory from another Clan, then we must continue hunting secretly on other Clans' territory, because WindClan can't go on suffering like this any longer."

Onewhisker felt shame at the Clan deputy's words. Though it went against the warrior code, at Mudclaw's direction, he and several other warriors had already participated in a few secret hunts on the other Clans' territories. Each time, he had felt terrible guilt, and told himself it was only to keep WindClan alive until things improved on their own territory. But considering their condition for a couple of heartbeats, he recognized that Mudclaw was right. *Steal from other Clans or die. That's not much of a choice.*

Still, it felt wrong to involve Tallstar in their secret hunting patrols. It was one thing for a few warriors to do what they needed to help the Clan survive; it was entirely another to ask for Tallstar's approval. Mudclaw was forcing a terrible decision on their leader: encourage the Clan to steal, or allow the Clan to wither away. Which was more important, the warrior code or WindClan's survival?

Tallstar let out a long sigh. "I don't want to condone breaking the warrior code. But you're right, Mudclaw—we can't go on like this. Let me consider your advice."

Mudclaw snorted; Onewhisker guessed that he wanted action right away.

"Mudclaw, you need to leave," Barkface meowed, a sharp edge to his tone. "This is no time for you to be bothering Tallstar. Don't you have any duties you should be doing?"

The Clan deputy opened his jaws to reply, then clearly thought better of arguing with a medicine cat and stalked out of the den with an angry whisk of his tail.

Once he had left, Barkface padded up to the hunters and examined their injuries. "Rat bites can be nasty," he murmured, half to himself. "It's a good thing I have plenty of burdock root. I'll trickle some of the juice into your wounds, and then you can go and eat some of your hard-won rats."

The sun was going down. Onewhisker lay stretched out near the fresh-kill pile; he couldn't remember the last time his belly had felt so comfortably full.

Beside him, Whitetail was cleaning up his scratches. "I'm so proud of the three of you," she mewed. "But maybe Mudclaw is right. It's not just that you took a risk fighting the rats—it was pure luck that they were there at all."

Onewhisker sighed, nodding. "I can see why Mudclaw feels the way he does."

He was thinking about withdrawing to the warriors' den when Stagleap padded up and sat down at his side. Anxiety stabbed at Onewhisker when he saw the wound on his father's face. His own rat bite and Tornear's were responding well to Barkface's treatment, but Stagleap's looked puffy, the skin around it showing red under his fur.

"Stagleap, I don't like the look of that bite," he meowed. "You really should go and see Barkface again."

Stagleap dipped his head. "I will," he promised. "But I wanted to say how glad I am that you have Whitetail for a mate."

His warm gaze rested on the white she-cat; Whitetail turned her head away, obviously embarrassed.

"Since your mother, Wrenflight, died," Stagleap continued, "I've been alone, and that's no way for a cat to be. It's good that you have such a reliable and brave cat for a mate. And a great *WindClan* mate, too. Wrenflight would be very proud."

Onewhisker's fur grew warm with happiness that his father approved of Whitetail, but he felt a little awkward, too. Stagleap seemed to be aware that there had been a time when he might have chosen a mate from outside the Clans, and he wanted Onewhisker to know that he thought his son had made the right choice.

Onewhisker glanced at Whitetail. *I certainly did.*

Worry for his father kept Onewhisker awake for most of the night. As soon as the sun rose, he padded over to Barkface's den to make sure that his father had indeed gone to the medicine cat for help.

"Hey, Barkface, did—" Onewhisker called out as he entered the den, then broke off.

His father, Stagleap, lay stretched out in death, the swelling from the rat bite spreading over half his face. Barkface was bending over him, smoothing his fur.

"I'm sorry, Onewhisker," the medicine cat meowed, while Onewhisker stood rigid, stunned by grief. "The rat bite was infected, and he died in the night."

Struggling with shock and pain, Onewhisker wondered whether Stagleap had known the night before, and had been thinking about his mate waiting in StarClan when he came to talk to him and Whitetail.

"Good-bye, Stagleap," he choked out, laying one paw on his father's shoulder. "May StarClan light your path. I promise

I'll keep Whitetail and WindClan safe, no matter what. You can go to be with Wrenflight, and not worry."

When Tallstar heard the news of Stagleap's death, he offered to let Onewhisker off his duties for the day, but Onewhisker told his leader that he preferred to keep busy. Later in the day, he and Whitetail set out on a border patrol.

"We ought to keep a lookout for prey, even though we're not a hunting patrol," he told Whitetail. "The Clan needs every bit we can find."

Whitetail murmured agreement. As they continued along the border, discussing the Clan's crisis in low voices, Onewhisker kept tasting the air. They had almost reached the Twoleg bridge when an all-too-familiar scent drifted into his nose.

Smoke!

The last thing Onewhisker wanted was for Whitetail and Smoke to meet each other. He wondered whether this was why Stagleap had hinted about his interests beyond the Clan the night before. *Had he scented Smoke on our territory?*

Onewhisker pinpointed the scent to a clump of gorse bushes on the riverbank. His heart began to throb with panic as he thought about Smoke emerging into the open and confronting Whitetail.

"I thought I saw prey over there!" he exclaimed, waving his tail wildly to where the ground was broken up with a few boulders poking up through the soil.

Whitetail clearly saw no reason to doubt his words. She shot off in pursuit of the prey while Onewhisker headed in the opposite direction, toward the bushes.

Smoke slid out into the open to meet him. "Hi, One-whisker."

"I've told you before, it's over between us," Onewhisker snapped. "I've chosen a mate from my Clan, and there's no more to say about it." Smoke's eyes widened in disbelief, but he gave her no chance to protest. "Anyway," he went on, "it's not safe for kittypets to wander around here anymore, thanks to your precious Twolegs. You have to go!"

Not waiting to find out why Smoke had come looking for him, he turned his back on her and raced off after Whitetail.

Onewhisker trekked across the moor with sore paws and an aching heart. He had left the camp at dawn with Webfoot and Tornear, and now sunhigh was approaching. In all that time they had caught nothing but a few mice and one scrawny rabbit. In normal times this would have been a pitifully small amount of prey, but life was so tough now that Onewhisker supposed he should be pleased.

They had almost reached the camp when they caught up to another patrol, with Mudclaw in the lead, followed by Rob-inwing and Nightcloud. They too had a meager haul of prey.

"The stink of Twolegs and their monsters is all over the territory," Mudclaw grunted around the single vole he was carrying. "How a cat is supposed to scent for prey with that stench clogging our nostrils? At least it's fairly quiet," he continued, "but there was one odd thing."

"What was that?" Webfoot asked.

"We had to chase off a kittypet—or maybe a rogue, but she was a pretty fluffy gray thing, so I'm guessing kittypet."

"What was a kittypet doing here?" Tornear wondered.

Mudclaw shrugged. "StarClan knows."

StarClan knows, and so do I, Onewhisker thought as the cats continued toward the camp. The kittypet was obviously Smoke. He hoped she hadn't said anything to Mudclaw's patrol. If she had mentioned him, Mudclaw would certainly have told him, but even so, Onewhisker's pads prickled with nervousness all the way back to the hollow.

What was Smoke thinking? he asked himself. *Why would she come here, where there's sickness and no food, and when she knows I've taken another mate?*

Onewhisker knew that he hadn't exactly been kind to Smoke the last time she had come, a couple of days before. His guilt about that had subsided, but now it lodged inside him again, as if he had eaten a tough piece of crow-food.

If I see her again, I'll at least ask her what she wants.

But the problem with that was that Onewhisker would have to see her alone. He didn't want the rest of the Clan to know, and especially not Whitetail.

For the next day or two Onewhisker was on edge, thinking that he spotted Smoke behind every bush or boulder. He half expected that Smoke would try again to see him, and half hoped that she wouldn't. It had been so long since he had stopped visiting the Twolegplace that now it felt strange to be preoccupied with something that had nothing to do with his Clan life.

Whitetail was still the best thing that had ever happened to him, and the Clan was continually in discussion about what to do if there was no end to the shortage of prey. These were the important things, not a kittypet that Onewhisker had vowed not to see again.

But he had begun to realize that if Smoke showed up again, he would have no choice whether or not to see her. He kept offering to patrol by himself, hoping that he could catch Smoke without any of his Clanmates, but with so little prey to be had, Tallstar needed all his strongest warriors out hunting.

Then one evening, when the Clan was crouched beside the fresh-kill pile, sharing out the scanty prey, Tornear came padding up to Onewhisker, beckoning him with a jerk of his head. "I want a word with you in private," he meowed.

Onewhisker rose to his paws and followed the tabby tom into the shadow of the Tallrock. "What's all this about?" he asked.

"Something strange happened when I was on patrol," Tornear replied. "A kittypet came up to me and asked to speak to you. What's going on, Onewhisker?" While Onewhisker was looking for words to explain, Tornear continued. "No, don't tell me. I don't want to know. But it shouldn't be happening."

"Did any other cat hear?" Onewhisker asked; he felt every scrap of his strength drain out of his muscles at the thought that all his secrets were coming into the open.

"No. And I won't tell Tallstar or Whitetail, if that's what's worrying you. But you need to work out your business with this kittypet. She's obviously the same cat Mudclaw spotted the other day—if she won't stop coming onto the territory, the Clan just doesn't have the energy to help you hide from her."

"I'm sorry," Onewhisker responded. "I've told her not to come. I don't know what more I can do. I never meant—"

"I said, I don't want to hear about it," Tornear growled, his tail twitching. "That way, if any cat asks me about her, I won't have to lie to them. But I'll cover for you to go to meet her tomorrow. I told her to wait for you on the edge of our territory, near the Thunderpath. You've got one chance to sort this out, Onewhisker, so don't mess it up." He turned and stalked away toward the warriors' den.

"Thanks, Tornear," Onewhisker meowed to his retreating back.

On the following day, Onewhisker set off on a hunt with Tornear; then, when they reached the Twoleg bridge, he left his Clanmate and hurried toward the Thunderpath. The journey felt eerie; though the sun was shining, there were fewer birds than Onewhisker was used to, and unfamiliar sounds in the distance that set every hair on his pelt rising.

When he reached the edge of the Thunderpath, he spotted the gray kittypet pacing anxiously. As soon as Onewhisker approached, she ran to meet him.

"I'm so relieved you've come!" she exclaimed. "I was afraid you wouldn't. And I really need to talk to you."

"I'm sorry that patrols kept driving you off," Onewhisker began, then launched into the explanation he had been rehearsing in his head. "But our lives are on different paths now, Smoke, and you need to accept—"

"I'm expecting kits," Smoke interrupted, her blue eyes fixed intensely on him. "I've been trying to tell you for some time. So our paths are still intertwined, whether you like it or not."

Onewhisker stared at her, a wild whirl of feelings surging through him: guilt for the way he had treated her, panic in case Whitetail found out, regret that he hadn't told Whitetail the truth before, when it wouldn't have been such a big deal, fear that Smoke would demand something from him, and among it all a little spark of joy.

I'm going to be a father!

"Say something, then!" Smoke prompted him.

"I'm sorry for how you've been treated," Onewhisker told her once again. "I'm happy for you, and I'm glad you told me." *Though both of us might have been happier if you hadn't,* he thought privately. "If you need anything, I'll do what I can," he went on, "but I meant what I said earlier. I can't leave my Clan, and you wouldn't do better in WindClan than here."

"I think the kits might be better off in the Clans than here in the Twolegplace," Smoke told him, staring at him in mingled anger and disbelief. "For one thing, my housefolk will take my kits away and give them to other housefolk. I think you just don't want me to come to WindClan because you don't want your new mate to know about me and the kits."

"That's not true!" Onewhisker reassured her, burying a pang of guilt. "WindClan is starving. Right now it's much safer in the Twolegplace than outside it. You would suffer in WindClan, and your kits might not survive. Remember what happened to Brushpaw—I mean to Leo!"

Onewhisker knew that every word he had spoken was the truth, but deep down he knew it was not the *whole* truth. Smoke was not completely wrong.

Whitetail is not not an issue. And I can't let her find out about this!

CHAPTER 9

Onewhisker's heart was heavy as he padded across the bridge on his way to visit Smoke in the Twolegplace. Since she had told him she was expecting kits, life in WindClan had become worse and worse.

Crowpaw and the other young cats who left with him had still not returned, and by now, few cats expected ever to see them again. The medicine cats had received no word from StarClan to tell them where the missing cats might be, and the Clan leaders argued fiercely about whose fault it was that they left. And Twolegs continued to destroy the Clan territories, their monsters grinding through trees and rocks all day and sometimes into the night.

It was not only WindClan that was suffering. Twolegs were encroaching on the other Clans as well. ThunderClan and ShadowClan were losing territory, and the water level was falling in the river, threatening the fish that were RiverClan's chief prey.

Things are really grim, Onewhisker thought with a sigh.

When he reached Smoke's Twoleg nest, he found her lying on the grass with a tiny white kit by her side. Onewhisker thought that his heart would burst with pride and happiness at the sight of him. *My son!*

He jumped down into the garden and bounded up to Smoke. "Hi," he purred, touching noses with her. "Congratulations! He's so beautiful."

"He's the only one of my litter who survived," Smoke mewed, mingled love and sorrow in her eyes. "After we last spoke, I chased after you and got disoriented on the moor. I started having terrible pains and lay down in the grass, and I gave birth right there. I had no one to help me, even my housefolk. So he's everything to me. I hate the thought of Twolegs taking him from me."

Onestar stared at her. His pelt warmed with shame. "I'm so sorry," he said. "I wish I had known. I would have helped you, of course."

Smoke met his gaze for a moment, hurt in her eyes, but then looked lovingly at the kit. "So far, my housefolk seem charmed by him. But I'm afraid when he gets older, they'll send him away."

"But you might still be able to see him," Onewhisker reassured her. "Besides, he'll have a better life here with Twolegs than anything the Clans can offer him just now."

"Then why don't you bring your Clan here to be kittypets or even rogues, if things are so bad?" Smoke asked.

"Because we're Clan cats," Onewhisker replied, trying to sound more confident than he felt.

Inwardly he had to admit how much it hurt that he didn't have a better answer for her. *We just can't do that, no matter how bad things get in the forest. . . .*

* * *

Once he'd returned to the moor, Onewhisker headed for the new WindClan camp. The senior warriors had decided that the Twoleg monsters were encroaching too close to the old camp, so they were digging out an abandoned rabbit warren, far away from the place where the rabbits had been poisoned. Every cat hoped that they would be more sheltered there from the Twoleg monsters, though privately Onewhisker thought it was a thin hope.

As he bounded across the camp to join Whitetail, he heard Ashfoot muttering into Nightcloud's ear. "I don't know why we're using up energy like this, when we're all so hungry."

Nightcloud only shrugged, but Onewhisker understood why. Tallstar wanted them to do everything they could to survive. He tried not to admit his fear that the Clan *couldn't* survive, that they were facing destruction unless something changed.

He went out with Whitetail to gather moss, and as soon as he returned began dragging bedding into one of the burrows to make a comfortable nest for Tallstar. While inside, he heard a commotion out in the camp, cats' voices raised in a mixture of joy and anger.

What in StarClan's name is going on?

Onewhisker emerged from the burrow to see most of the Clan gathering around as Webfoot walked into the camp, followed by Owlpaw and the rest of the morning border patrol. As they drew closer, Onewhisker spotted a familiar pelt and started. The cat padding along at Webfoot's shoulder was Crowpaw.

His jaws gaping in surprise, Onewhisker halted and stared at the apprentice. The rest of the Clan seemed frozen, too, their exclamations dying away into silence. For a moment the only sound was Ashfoot's purring as she covered her son with frantic licks.

Crowpaw had always been a skinny cat, but he looked better fed now than most of his Clanmates. Onewhisker could see how shocked he was at the state of his Clan as he looked around with wide, disbelieving eyes.

Though Onewhisker was relieved to see him, he could feel anger building up inside him like clouds gathering before a storm. *How dare he vanish like that and then stroll in here as if nothing had happened?*

Webfoot clearly shared the same feeling. "How could you leave your Clan at a time like this?" he demanded.

Before Crowpaw could answer, more cats clustered around him, their eyes shining with welcome. Obviously some of the Clan were so pleased to see Crowpaw that they were ready to forgive him anything. Onewhisker didn't join them. He was still too angry; it took all his self-control to stand still instead of launching himself at Crowpaw with claws extended, as if to drive an intruder out of the camp.

"We're so glad to see you alive and well!" Whitetail exclaimed. "But where have you been?"

"Yes, tell us what happened," Tornear added.

Until now, Crowpaw hadn't spoken, except to greet his mother. Now he glanced around, with something in his face that told Onewhisker that he had serious news to impart.

"Where's Tallstar?" he asked. "I need to talk to him first."

"Here." Tallstar spoke from the back of the crowd, and cats drew back to let him make his way through until he stood in front of Crowpaw, who dipped his head respectfully to his Clan leader. "WindClan welcomes you, Crowpaw, but I hope you have good reason for what you did."

"A very good reason, Tallstar," Crowpaw responded. "May we talk in private?"

The Clan leader gave him a curt nod, and led the way to the burrow Onewhisker had prepared for him.

A buzz of conversation broke out as they disappeared. Seeing Whitetail at his side, Onewhisker let out an irritated hiss. "I'd like to claw the stupid furball's ears off!" he snarled.

"Oh, don't be too hard on him," Whitetail murmured, touching Onewhisker's ear with her nose. "Let's find out what he has to say first."

"It had better be good," Onewhisker snorted, flicking his ears as if he could flick Crowpaw away like a troublesome fly. "I'm going hunting. Coming?"

"Let all cats old enough to catch their own prey join here in the center of the camp for a Clan meeting!"

Onewhisker heard his leader's voice as he was returning to the camp, empty-pawed and frustrated. Whitetail had made one kill: a tiny shrew that was hardly worth the trouble of carrying it back.

Tallstar was standing in the middle of a cluster of their Clanmates, with Crowpaw beside him. Onewhisker and Whitetail slipped into the back of the crowd.

"I have listened to Crowpaw's story," Tallstar began. His

anxiety was clear to Onewhisker, who wondered once again what Crowpaw had told him. "I have decided that I must go to the Moonstone, to ask StarClan what I ought to do."

Onewhisker exchanged a shocked glance with Whitetail, while murmurs of surprise rose up from the cats around them. A Clan leader only made the journey to the Moonstone in times of great need. *Well, the need doesn't get any greater than this*, Onewhisker reflected. *I hope Crowpaw's story was really important, not something he's dreamed up out of thistle-fluff.*

Barkface spoke from the front of the crowd. "Do you want me to come with you, Tallstar?"

The Clan leader shook his head. "In normal times I would, Barkface, but as things are now, I think you will be more use here." Tallstar hesitated, looking around. "Onewhisker. Is Onewhisker here?"

"Here, Tallstar," Onewhisker called.

"I would like you to come, too."

Onewhisker looked around for Mudclaw, wondering why Tallstar hadn't chosen his deputy to accompany him, but there was no sign of the mottled brown tom.

"Mudclaw is out hunting," Tallstar explained, clearly understanding the reason for Onewhisker's hesitation. "And I don't want to wait for him to return."

"Then of course I'll come with you, Tallstar," Onewhisker meowed, pride at being chosen lightening his mood a little.

Onewhisker padded at Tallstar's shoulder as the two cats headed across the moor in the direction of the big Thunderpath. Tallstar's skinny form and unsteady paw steps and the way his breath came fast and shallow when he had to climb a hill made Onewhisker intensely aware of his leader's frailty. *He ought to be resting in camp*, Onewhisker thought uneasily. *Not making this tough journey over something that flea-brained apprentice told him.*

For a long time now, Onewhisker had tried to care for his leader as much as he could: encouraging him to eat and rest, and taking on small tasks for him whenever he had the opportunity. He knew that he would never be deputy or leader. His paws weren't set on that path, and he was glad of it. When he listened to Tallstar making a tough decision, or watched Mudclaw managing the Clan's duties every day, he was relieved that he would never have those responsibilities. But at least he could help the Clan in a small way, by doing his best to keep their leader safe, supporting him in the impossible task of leading his Clan through these hard times.

At first, Tallstar said little, seeming to have lapsed into deep thought. Eventually, when the Thunderpath with its roaring monsters was in sight, he turned to Onewhisker.

"Tell me, what do you think a leader should do with an outlandish story from one of his most trusted cats?" he asked.

He still trusts Crowpaw, after what he did? Onewhisker was shocked. *True, he was trustworthy as an apprentice.* Alarm clawed at him briefly as he wondered what Crowpaw had reported to make Tallstar ask that question.

Tallstar has such a hard job, he reflected. The Clan leader had called Crowpaw's story outlandish, but in these desperate times he seemed prepared to consider it. Onewhisker hesitated to give advice—he wasn't the Clan deputy or the medicine cat—but he comforted himself with the thought that whatever he said, Tallstar would make the final decision, with StarClan's help.

"I'm not sure," he replied at last. "Does the cat have any reason to lie?"

Tallstar fetched a deep sigh, and Onewhisker realized anew how exhausted he was. "No," the Clan leader murmured, shaking his head. "It just doesn't make any sense, that's all."

"Then I suppose you must use your judgment," Onewhisker responded. "After all, your wisdom has always benefited WindClan."

Tallstar met Onewhisker's gaze, seeming touched by his words, then nodded. "You're a good warrior," he mewed. "Will you always use good judgment as well?"

Onewhisker blinked in surprise. *Why would he ask me that?* "Yes, of course," he promised, struggling with a throb of guilt as he remembered the times he hadn't always used his judgment for the good of the Clan. *Does Tallstar know that somehow?* "At least, I'll do my best," he added.

"Thank you," Tallstar breathed out.

Across the Thunderpath the land began to rise, the slope much steeper than the moorland of WindClan territory. Grass gave way to thin, gritty soil and, here and there, patches of heather. Above the cats' heads the rocks were outlined against the sky like a row of jagged teeth.

Onewhisker hadn't traveled to Highstones since he was an apprentice, taking the journey that every cat made before becoming a warrior. He had forgotten quite how tough the climb was, the bare rock hard under their pads and the blustering wind threatening to knock them off their paws. Onewhisker wasn't sure how Tallstar managed it. By the time they reached the yawning gap of Mothermouth, the Clan leader was leaning on his shoulder, every rasping breath an effort.

"Rest for a while before you go in," Onewhisker suggested.

Tallstar shook his head. "This is too urgent, Onewhisker. The Clan's need is too great."

"Then let me come with you," Onewhisker begged, anxiety for his leader growing with every heartbeat.

"This is something I need to do alone," Tallstar responded.

He drew a deep breath, raising his head and tail before stepping fearlessly into the dark tunnel. Onewhisker saw the white parts of his pelt glimmering for a moment; then he was gone.

Onewhisker settled down outside the cave, working his claws impatiently and wishing there were something he could do. He thought of hunting, but there would be no prey among these barren rocks. Besides, it might be disrespectful to Star-Clan, given that no cat was allowed to eat on the journey here. Finally he raised his head and gazed up at the sky, where daylight still hid the warriors of StarClan from his sight.

I'm not a leader or a medicine cat, he prayed, *and I don't understand why this is happening to my Clan, but please, StarClan, show us what to do. It can't be your will for us to be destroyed. Set our paws on the right path.*

Finally, when Onewhisker had begun to wonder whether

his leader had collapsed in the tunnels, Tallstar staggered out into the open and leaned against the nearest rock, drawing in huge, gasping breaths.

"Did StarClan speak to you?" Onewhisker asked anxiously.

It took a couple of heartbeats before Tallstar could reply. "Yes, they granted me visions," he meowed at last. "Awful, terrifying visions of Twoleg monsters breaking down trees and tearing up the moor. There is no way to stop it. We must leave." He took another deep breath. "But where can we go?" he asked, his voice despairing. "Is there really a new home for every cat in the Clans?"

Briefly Onewhisker recalled Smoke's question. *Why not go into the Twolegplace?* But immediately he dismissed the idea. Even if being a kittypet was a better life, it wouldn't work to bring all four Clans. And from Tallstar's words, it seemed as if all of them were in danger.

Tallstar sighed and gave his pelt a shake. "Let's go home," he meowed.

By the time Tallstar and Onewhisker returned to the makeshift camp, the sun had gone down. Mudclaw had returned with prey.

"This is good," Onewhisker commented, sitting beside Whitetail to eat the morsel that was his share. "Really healthy prey."

"Where did Mudclaw find it?" Whitetail asked. "Maybe we can hunt there again tomorrow."

Tallstar shook his head sadly. "Don't ask," he murmured.

Onewhisker looked at Whitetail and saw his own dismay reflected in her eyes. With a swift glance around, Whitetail leaned toward him. "I can tell you're thinking what I'm thinking," she whispered. "Mudclaw has been hunting on another Clan's territory, and Tallstar is letting him do it!"

Onewhisker felt hot beneath his pelt, shame overcoming him. He'd never told Whitetail of his secret hunting patrols with Mudclaw. "I . . . knew that already. I'd hoped we wouldn't make a habit of it," Onewhisker admitted. He knew Tallstar had quietly taken Mudclaw's advice, and ordered his deputy to continue his efforts. Whitetail was right: where else could they have found enough prey to feed the Clan? Still, unable to untangle his own feelings about the patrols, Onewhisker had purposely avoided his leader and deputy when they'd tried to pull him aside to assign him to hunt on other Clans' territories. After a few days, both had stopped seeking him out. Onewhisker couldn't bring himself to tell Whitetail that he had ever been a part of it, not once he saw the disapproval in her eyes. "We have to do *something*," he finished weakly.

"*Not that*." Whitetail lashed her tail emphatically. "There must be another solution. We're warriors with honor, not scrapping rogues out for whatever they can get."

Onewhisker couldn't disagree with her, but mostly he felt sympathy for Tallstar. *There are no good choices here.*

When every cat had finished their scanty meal, Tallstar rose to his paws and beckoned Crowpaw to come and stand beside him. "It's time for you to tell the Clan exactly what happened on your journey."

Crowpaw paused for a moment before beginning to speak. Onewhisker wondered if he was nervous. *He ought to be, after wandering off like that!* Then he saw the intense expression in the apprentice's blue eyes, and realized that what he had to tell was so important, so weighty, that it was hard for him to find the words.

"Four cats were sent a sign by StarClan," Crowpaw began at last. "One cat from each Clan. I was one, and the others were Brambleclaw from ThunderClan, Tawnypelt from Shadow-Clan, and Feathertail from RiverClan."

Onewhisker thought that his voice shook slightly as he named the last cat, but the apprentice recovered himself quickly and went on.

"Deadfoot spoke to me in a dream, and said that I must meet three other cats at the new moon, and listen to what midnight told us. We met at Fourtrees, and waited for midnight, but there was no message."

"Just a moment," Mudclaw growled. "We know *six* cats went on this journey of yours. You've only mentioned four."

"Only four had the message from StarClan," Crowpaw explained. "But Stormfur came from RiverClan because he was Feathertail's brother and he wouldn't let her go alone, and Squirrelpaw came from ThunderClan because—well, because she's Squirrelpaw."

An appreciative murmur rose from the listening Clan. Most of them knew ThunderClan's wayward apprentice; if Squirrelpaw wanted to go somewhere, she wouldn't let Star-Clan itself stand in her way.

"Then Brambleclaw had another dream, about a stretch of water so big that you couldn't see the far side of it," Crowpaw continued. "Every night the sun drowned in it."

"The sun *drowned?*" Nightcloud sounded disbelieving. "Come on, Crowpaw. Even a kit knows that the sun can't drown."

"Drowned, disappeared, whatever," Crowpaw responded with an irritable flick of his tail. "Anyway, Brambleclaw thought StarClan was telling us to go to this sun-drown-water. He found out from Ravenpaw—you know, the ThunderClan apprentice who went to live in the barn with Barley—that it was a real place, and Ravenpaw had some idea of how to find it. Well, in the end, all of us left. We had a really tough time, I can tell you! Dogs, Twolegs, rats . . . But all that isn't impor-tant. What matters is that we found the sun-drown-place. It was awesome. Terrifying. The land ended in steep cliffs with caves, and at the bottom was . . . water. Waves crashing in, sucking at the rocks, on and on without end. Brambleclaw fell into it, and he would have drowned if Squirrelpaw hadn't res-cued him."

"So what happened then?" Robinwing asked.

"Well, after Brambleclaw and Squirrelpaw got out," Crow-paw continued, "we ended up in a cave, wondering what to do next. It was there that we met Midnight."

"You *met* midnight?" Tornear asked. "Crowpaw, is this a tale for kits?"

Crowpaw let out a faint *mrrow* of amusement. "You're mak-ing the same mistake we made. We thought StarClan meant the middle of the night. But we were wrong. Midnight is a badger. That's her name."

The Clan erupted into yowls of astonishment. Onewhisker exchanged a startled glance with Whitetail. "They met a badger called Midnight?" he meowed. "And lived to tell the tale?"

"She scared our fur off," Crowpaw admitted, ignoring the clamor. "But it turned out that Midnight is a friend. She told us—"

"*Told* you?" Mudclaw's shoulder fur bristled as he snarled at his apprentice. "Now I know you're lying. Badgers can't talk— not so we can understand them."

"I'm not lying!" Crowpaw retorted, glaring at his mentor. "Midnight was no ordinary badger. She could talk to us, and she even knew about StarClan."

"She knew *StarClan*?" some cat exclaimed from the crowd.

Ashfoot stretched out her tail and rested it on Mudclaw's shoulder in a calming gesture. "I believe Crowpaw," she mewed, "and not just because he is my son. Ask yourself, Mudclaw, what cat would tell a story like this, and expect to be believed, unless it were true?"

Mudclaw let out a snort, his fur gradually lying flat again. "Fine. Go on," he muttered to Crowpaw.

The young tom took a breath and began again. "Midnight told us that Twolegs would destroy our territories, and that all the Clans would have to leave. She sent us back to our Clans to give them her message."

Onewhisker could see doubt in the faces of his Clanmates, but he felt every hair on his pelt rise in response to a strangeness quite out of his experience. "That's the same vision StarClan sent to Tallstar at the Moonstone," he murmured to Whitetail. "It must be true."

"But how can we leave?" Whitetail asked. "Where would we go?"

"Midnight promised us a place with hills and woods and running streams," Crowpaw replied. "A new home where we could live in peace."

"Oh, if only . . ." Morningflower sighed.

"That's all very well," Oatwhisker grunted, from where he sat at Morningflower's side. "But did this badger of yours tell you how to find it?"

"Yes, before we left, Midnight gave us a sign," Crowpaw nodded at the elder as he explained to his Clanmates. "She said, 'When return, stand on Great Rock when Silverpelt shines above. A dying warrior the way will show.'"

"What does that mean?" Webfoot asked, curling back his lips as if he were faced with a piece of rotting crow-food. "One of us will die if we go to the Great Rock?"

"I doubt it's that simple," Barkface responded; until now the medicine cat had listened without comment, though Onewhisker could see intense interest in his face. "Whatever the 'dying warrior' means, it's some cat or something that *knows* where we have to go."

"No cat has said we're going anywhere yet," Mudclaw growled.

A chorus of comments broke out among the Clan, some agreeing with Mudclaw, some ready to argue with him.

Tallstar listened for a couple of heartbeats, then raised his tail for silence. "Crowpaw, go on with your story," he meowed.

"There's only one more thing I have to tell," the apprentice continued. "We traveled back by a different path, through the mountains, and there we met another Clan of cats, except they called themselves the Tribe. They were being attacked by a huge lion-cat they called Sharptooth. Every day it would pick off one or two of them." He shuddered. "It nearly killed me. They have a StarClan of their own," he went on, "and they sent a prophecy that a silver cat would save them from Sharptooth. That cat was Feathertail. She killed Sharptooth and saved my life, but she died doing it. We kept vigil for her and buried her there in the mountains." His voice choked, and he bowed his head. "Then we came home."

A pang of grief clawed through Onewhisker. He had not known Feathertail well, but she had been a brave and loyal RiverClan warrior. Subdued murmuring all around him told him that his Clanmates felt the same. And she had obviously meant a great deal to Crowpaw. For a moment he was acutely conscious of the warmth of Whitetail next to him, and the way her pelt brushed his.

What would I do if I lost her?

Night was gathering, the cats scarcely visible except for the gleam of their eyes in the darkness. But no cat thought of withdrawing to their den. Crowpaw's story kept them clustered together. *We find strength in one another,* Onewhisker thought. *This is what it means to be a Clan!*

Tallstar stepped forward again and addressed the Clan.

"This is a strange story," he began, "but I must tell you that I believe it. Earlier today I walked with StarClan at the Moonstone, and they showed me exactly what Crowpaw has just told you: Twolegs tearing up all our territory with their vast monsters, leaving no place for us. We must go, and soon."

"What?" Webfoot sprang to his paws. "Cats have lived here for season upon season. Are we going to let a few Twolegs drive us out?"

"Webfoot, if you know how to stop them, then share it with the rest of us." Tallstar's tone was dry. "I don't believe we have any choice."

"But where will we go?" Nightcloud asked.

Whitetail had asked the same question, and Onewhisker wished that he could answer it. Even though Tallstar had told him the same news earlier, he still felt shocked to the tips of his claws by Crowpaw's story. But as he listened to his Clanmates' desperate questions and Tallstar's attempts to answer, his shock ebbed and resignation gradually crept over him.

"If StarClan is telling us the end has truly come for this territory," he declared, "then we should hurry up and leave it, while we still have strength to make it to our new home."

"Onewhisker is right," Tornear agreed. "We believe Crowpaw, don't we?" A murmur of assent came from the Clan. "So we need to decide what happens next."

His words and Onewhisker's seemed to calm the Clan, though many cats still looked doubtful.

"But can we survive a journey like that?" Ashfoot asked. "Look at us! And leaf-bare is coming on."

"And what happens next?" Mudclaw asked. "What if we don't find this so-called sign? What about the other Clans?"

It was Crowpaw who replied. "We—the other cats and I, the ones who traveled . . ." Onewhisker thought the apprentice looked embarrassed at referring to a group of cats from other Clans as *we*. "We agreed to meet at Fourtrees tomorrow night, and to bring our leaders with us if we could. Will you come, Tallstar?" he finished, turning to his leader.

Tallstar dipped his head. "I will. And I believe that if StarClan is telling us to leave, then it must be possible," he meowed, quieting any more objections with a wave of his tail. "Tomorrow I will seek out this sign. Until then, we will sleep on it. And may StarClan send us good dreams."

Another day of fruitless hunting was drawing to an end. Onewhisker watched the last scarlet streaks disappear from the sky and waited for the first warriors of StarClan to pierce the darkness.

What sign will you send us, I wonder?

He had just resigned himself to going to his nest hungry when there was a stir of movement at the top of the hill above the warrens, and four cats came bounding into the camp. In the twilight it took Onewhisker a moment to recognize Mudclaw and Crowpaw, along with Webfoot and his apprentice, Weaselpaw. All of them were carrying prey; Crowpaw in particular was staggering along with a hawk almost as big as he was.

Onewhisker sprang to his paws, and more of his Clanmates

began to gather around, letting out meows of surprise.

"Where did you find all that?" Whitetail exclaimed.

The hunting patrol dropped their prey on the scanty remains of the fresh-kill pile.

"You have Crowpaw to thank," Mudclaw mewed, with an appreciative glance at his apprentice. "I've never seen hunting like it. He even brought down that hawk."

Crowpaw bent his head and gave his chest fur a couple of embarrassed licks. "I learned how to do it when we were with the Tribe," he explained.

Onewhisker found himself warming to the young tom, his earlier anger fading. "Well done!" he meowed. "The Clan will eat well for once, thanks to you."

He could feel a sense of hope in the air as the Clan crouched down to eat—hope that had seemed lost forever as the Twolegs and their monsters gobbled up more and more of the forest. Another expert hunter would help to keep the Clan fed for now. Besides, now they had the prospect of the new, peaceful home that Midnight had spoken of. Onewhisker's paws itched to begin the journey to find it.

At last, when night had fallen and Silverpelt stretched like a river across the sky, Tallstar rose to his paws. "It is time," he meowed. "Crowpaw and I will go to Fourtrees—or at least, where Fourtrees used to be."

"Some cat please tell me . . ." Crowpaw had risen too, and turned to his Clan leader, his eyes wide with concern. "What happened to Fourtrees? Why am I hearing that there's nothing left of it?"

"The Twolegs have destroyed it," Tallstar told him sadly. "They cut down the oaks and overturned the Great Rock."

Crowpaw flinched as if something had struck him a blow, and stood for a moment with his head bowed. Onewhisker shuddered as he remembered the first time he had stood at the top of the hollow and looked down at the devastation: the trees uprooted and sliced into pieces by monster jaws, the Great Rock thrown down as if it were a pebble. None of the WindClan cats had been able to bear returning, once they had seen what the Twolegs had done.

At last Crowpaw raised his head. "We must go," he meowed. "StarClan will send a sign to tell us what to do."

Side by side he and Tallstar padded away from the make-shift camp. With hope in their hearts, Onewhisker and the rest of the Clan watched them go, until they were lost in darkness.

Onewhisker was unable to sleep that night, expecting that Tallstar and Crowpaw would return at any moment. But the first hint of dawn light was seeping into the sky before they reappeared. As soon as he saw them, Onewhisker knew there would be no good news; they trudged along with drooping heads and tails, as if weariness had sunk into their very bones.

The WindClan cats began to emerge from their dens, crowding around the two cats as they reached the center of the camp.

"What happened?" Robinwing called out eagerly.

"Yes, what did StarClan tell you?" Whitetail added.

Tallstar stood still, letting his gaze travel around his Clan. "Nothing," he mewed at last, defeat in his voice. "There was no sign. No warriors died. No StarClan cats appeared. Nothing."

Cries of alarm rose up from the assembled cats.

"That can't be right!" Tornear exclaimed. "Not after what Crowpaw told us."

"*If* he was telling the truth," Oatwhisker grunted.

Onewhisker felt a pang of apprehension deep within his belly. This was no time for the Clan to start doubting Crowpaw, not when his news fit in so well with what Tallstar had seen at the Moonstone.

"I'm as confused as you are," Crowpaw meowed, facing the Clan steadily. "This isn't what I expected."

"What did the other Clan leaders think?" Onewhisker asked. "Do they believe the story their journeying cats told them?"

"As far as I can tell, they don't know what to think," Tallstar replied. "But I can't see any of them setting out on a long, hard journey when they have no idea where to go or what they'll find at the end of it. Blackstar was talking about taking his cats and going to live in the Twolegplace."

What? Onewhisker was startled, remembering how Smoke had suggested the same thing to him, the last time he had seen her. He hadn't believed then that a whole Clan of cats could find homes in her Twolegplace. *But of course, Blackstar must mean the big Twolegplace on the other side of ThunderClan territory, where BloodClan used to live. There would be plenty of room for ShadowClan there.*

"Leopardstar doesn't believe that RiverClan will be much affected by the Twoleg destruction," Tallstar went on. "The river is shrinking, but the Twoleg monsters haven't invaded their territory."

"And ThunderClan?" Onewhisker asked.

Tallstar shook his head. "Firestar wants to leave," he replied, "but he won't go without the others. It has to be all or nothing."

Onewhisker exchanged a dismayed glance with Whitetail. "What are we going to do now?" she asked.

CHAPTER 10

❧

Frustration was roiling in Onewhisker's belly as he padded across the moor beside Tornear. "I should have caught that starling!" he snarled, unable to hold back the fury he felt at himself. "An apprentice could have made that leap. And I missed it!"

"It wasn't your fault," Tornear meowed. His tabby pelt, fluffed up against the cold, hid how skinny he was getting. "We would hunt better if we weren't so hungry all the time. The way the Twolegs are tearing up the territory, there's hardly any prey left."

Onewhisker knew he was right. He had failed to leap high enough because he was too weak; there wasn't enough power in his hind legs to propel him upward.

"I'm sick of this," he growled. "Sick of being hungry, sick of trying to hunt when there is no prey to be caught, sick of the StarClan-cursed Twolegs . . . What's wrong with Firestar?" he asked, not expecting an answer. "If he wants to leave, why doesn't he just leave? We would go with him."

Tornear shrugged. "Well, you know ThunderClan," he mewed. "A paw in every cat's business."

"Then maybe we should just leave on our own," Onewhisker

suggested. "We could go to join this Tribe that Crowpaw told us about. Maybe they would take us in, if it was just us and not all the other Clans."

"Aren't you being a bit optimistic?" Tornear asked, with a doubtful twitch of his whiskers. "From what Crowpaw said, the Tribe doesn't sound particularly welcoming. And their way of life sounds almost as hard as what we're going through now. How would we hunt, up there in the mountains? Then again," he added, "what other choice do we have?"

Before Onewhisker could reply, he was distracted by the all-too-familiar, ominous sound of Twoleg monsters. For many days now they had been everywhere, knocking over trees, digging up the ground, but now the noise was worse than before, seeming terrifyingly close.

"That's coming from the camp!" Onewhisker exclaimed.

Side by side the two warriors raced across the moor. With every paw step the sound grew louder. *StarClan help us!* Onewhisker prayed as he tried to force every scrap of speed from legs made shaky by hunger.

Cresting a rise above the makeshift camp, Onewhisker stumbled to a halt. He was gazing down on a scene of destruction so horrific that he could never have imagined it in his worst nightmares.

Twoleg monsters were advancing, far bigger than the monsters that flashed up and down the Thunderpath. They had huge black paws and shining jaws that sliced into the earth, chomping up the ground where the dens used to be.

What's wrong with Twolegs, that they keep such terrifying creatures?

Onewhisker asked himself as he stood frozen with fear. *And why are they trying to destroy our camp?*

Cats were fleeing in every direction, letting out screeches of terror.

"Whitetail! Whitetail!" Onewhisker yowled, hurling himself down into the chaos as he searched for his mate.

Then he spotted her, struggling up the slope away from the destruction, with the elder Oatwhisker leaning on her shoulder. Tallstar was limping after them, unsteady on his paws, and Tornear hurried to help him.

All Onewhisker's instincts were screaming at him to flee, too, but he hesitated in the midst of the destruction. His legs tingled with the urge to leave the fearful monsters far behind, and he dug his claws into the ground to fix himself in place. He was trying to listen for the cries of cats among the growling of the monsters and the crunching of their shiny jaws. Onewhisker shuddered at the thought of what those gleaming fangs could do to a cat.

Did we all escape?

"Onewhisker!" Whitetail was yowling at him. "Get out! You'll be killed!"

Then Onewhisker heard it: a terrified mewling coming from where one of the tunnels had been. For a heartbeat he froze with horror as a monster reared up above him with earth dripping from between its fangs.

The mewling came again. "That's Owlpaw!" he exclaimed aloud, guessing that the apprentice was too terrified to move. "Owlpaw, I'm coming!"

Onewhisker bounded forward and began to dig at the entrance of one of the collapsed tunnels. Briefly he despaired as the loose earth he scraped out immediately fell back in, tumbling over his paws and clogging his claws.

It's no use. . . .

But then he spotted Owlpaw's small claws frantically trying to scrabble their way up from underneath. Onewhisker plunged his muzzle into the earth and touched fur. He made a wild grab with his teeth, then hauled the apprentice out into the open and bolted away, carrying him by the scruff as if he were a kit, as the shining jaws descended for another bite.

The rest of the Clan was hiding in the shelter of a clump of gorse bushes, trembling with panic and shock. Onewhisker dived in among them and dropped Owlpaw beside his brother, Weaselpaw, where he lay shivering and spitting out earth. His brother huddled closer to him, while his mentor, Tornear, gave him a good sniff, then began scraping earth out of his fur.

"Onewhisker, you stupid furball!" Whitetail crept up beside him; her tone was sharp but her eyes were glowing. "That was the bravest thing I've ever seen!"

Onewhisker puffed out a sigh of exhaustion. His mouth tasted of earth and he couldn't stop shaking. "Are we all here?" he asked.

It was Mudclaw who replied, crouching beside Tallstar nearer the center of the clump of bushes. "Every cat made it," he announced with satisfaction.

"That's a miracle from StarClan!" Onewhisker meowed, overwhelmed by a massive feeling of relief.

"Not so much of a miracle," Mudclaw retorted sourly. "Now we're not just starving; we're homeless too."

Tallstar raised his head; though he looked exhausted, there was authority in his voice. "We must move away from here and try to find somewhere safe."

"Safe!" Webfoot exclaimed. "Good luck with that."

"Safer, then," Tallstar responded. He hauled himself to his paws, with Tornear's shoulder to lean on. "Let's go."

The Clan limped and staggered across the moor, the cats who still had some strength helping those who were too weary or too weak to manage by themselves. Eventually they found a spot not far from the ThunderClan border: a rocky hollow where gorse and bramble grew and where a tiny waterfall spilled out from between a couple of boulders and fell into a pool below.

Onewhisker was enjoying a desperately needed drink when Tornear padded up to him. "Tallstar wants you," he reported.

Shaking the water off his muzzle, Onewhisker followed Tornear and found his Clan leader crouched with Mudclaw in the shelter of a rock.

"Our need is too great for us to ignore it any longer," Tallstar announced. "We know that Firestar is sympathetic to us. We will go to ThunderClan and ask them for prey, and then perhaps StarClan will allow us to recover from this."

Sunhigh was approaching as Tallstar led a patrol across the ThunderClan border and into the forest. Onewhisker was with him, as well as Tornear and Crowpaw, with Mudclaw left in charge of the Clan in the rocky hollow.

Onewhisker felt an unpleasant fluttering in his chest as he and his Clanmates crossed the ThunderClan border. He knew that Tallstar had made the right decision, but he couldn't help wondering what the ThunderClan leader's reaction would be.

"When we were at Fourtrees, Firestar told me that ThunderClan has been driven out of their camp, too," Tallstar announced. "They're at Sunningrocks now."

That meant a long trek almost to the other side of ThunderClan's territory; Onewhisker only hoped that Tallstar had the strength to get there. But the Clan leader kept going until the cluster of flat-topped rocks came in sight, and from somewhere above their heads a startled voice exclaimed, "WindClan!"

Firestar was sitting on a rock about halfway to the summit, his flame-colored pelt gleaming in the pale leaf-fall sun. His daughter Squirrelpaw was with him; when she spotted Crowpaw, she came bounding down to touch noses with him.

"Crowpaw!" she exclaimed, stepping back to take him all in. She was clearly shocked by how much thinner the apprentice was than when he had returned from the sun-drown-place. "Are you okay?"

"I'm as fit as any of my Clan," Crowpaw growled.

Tornear turned to Squirrelpaw, his voice warm with praise. "Crowpaw has been hunting like a whole patrol on his own, finding prey to feed nearly all the Clan," he told her. "He even caught a hawk two sunrises ago."

"I used a trick the Tribe taught us," Crowpaw responded with a shrug.

"Crowpaw!" The exclamation startled Onewhisker, and he turned to see Brambleclaw hurrying up to join them. He looked as shocked as Squirrelpaw to see the change in Crowpaw.

As the WindClan patrol struggled to climb the rock to where Firestar was waiting, hot shame crept through Onewhisker at how scrawny and weak he and his Clanmates were. He hadn't wanted another Clan to see them like this. Part of him was angry, too, to see that although the ThunderClan cats were thinner than they used to be, every one of them was better fed than his own Clanmates.

Of course Firestar wants to wait before leaving. He can afford to.

Finally Tallstar reached Firestar's rock and dipped his head in greeting to the ThunderClan leader. "Firestar, we have come to plead for ThunderClan's help," he rasped. He opened his jaws to say more, but before he could utter a word, his legs gave way and he collapsed onto his side. Onewhisker darted forward to help him, but Tallstar waved him away with a swish of his tail. "The Twolegs have started to destroy the warrens where we have been sheltering," he continued with deep, panting breaths. "We cannot stay a moment longer on the moor, but we are too weak to travel alone. I don't care that we haven't had another sign. I just know we have to leave. Take us to this sun-drown-place, I beg you."

Firestar gazed down at the WindClan leader, and Onewhisker saw grief and sympathy in his eyes. "We have been allies many times," he murmured. "And to watch you starve is more than I can bear."

He paused, raising his head to stare into the forest.

Onewhisker glanced at Tornear and saw a gleam of hope in his Clanmate's eyes, which he knew was reflected his own. Firestar's words surely meant that he would not abandon WindClan to their fate.

Onewhisker couldn't help thinking back to the time, so many seasons ago, when his Clan had been so certain that a kittypet could never become a warrior. *And how wrong we were!* Firestar had begun life as a kittypet, and not only had he learned the skills of a warrior, but he had risen to be leader of his Clan.

Firestar was still gazing into the woods when the bushes rustled and a tortoiseshell she-cat burst into the open. Her pelt was bristling, her ears laid back, and there was terror in her eyes.

That's Tawnypelt from ShadowClan!

"The Twolegs are attacking our camp!" Tawnypelt yowled as she raced to the bottom of the rocks. "They have surrounded us with their monsters! Please come!"

Instantly Firestar bounded down the rocks to join her. To Onewhisker's consternation, Tallstar hauled himself to his paws and stumbled down after him, leaving the WindClan patrol with no choice but to follow.

"Please help us!" Tawnypelt cried out to Firestar as he reached her. "Help us for the sake of the ThunderClan blood that runs in my veins, if nothing else."

Firestar gently silenced her by touching the tip of his tail to her mouth. "We will come for the sake of ShadowClan," he told her. "And for the sake of all the Clans in the forest."

He turned to his warriors, who had begun to gather around, drawn by the sound of Tawnypelt's desperate caterwauling. Swiftly he organized patrols and sent Brambleclaw to see if he could persuade RiverClan to come and help.

Onewhisker lashed his tail; part of him was longing to fight back, every hair on his pelt rising in anticipation. Tornear was pacing restlessly to and fro, while Crowpaw flexed his claws as if he couldn't wait to sink them into a Twoleg.

"We will come with you," Tallstar announced, his voice growing suddenly firmer.

Firestar shook his head. "You are not strong enough."

The WindClan leader met Firestar's gaze steadily. "My warriors and I are coming," he meowed, his voice filled with determination.

Onewhisker felt torn, hearing Tallstar's decision. While his heart swelled with admiration for his leader's courage, he knew that Firestar was right. Tallstar did not have the strength for a battle like this.

"Tallstar, you are on your last life," Tornear meowed urgently as the WindClan patrol merged with the Thunder-Clan warriors and headed for the ShadowClan border. "Please stay here."

Tallstar flicked his ears, as calm as if he were taking a stroll across the moor on a sunny day in greenleaf. Onewhisker was impressed by his resolution. "Whether I'm on my first life or my ninth," he responded, "my duty is to the forest. I will not miss this battle."

He kept pace with the rest of the warriors as Firestar led

them through the trees, picking up speed until they were charging along, their belly fur brushing the grass and their tails streaming out behind them.

When they reached Fourtrees, Firestar raced straight down into the devastated hollow, but before he could climb out on the far side, a commanding yowl halted him. Onewhisker and the others stopped too, and spun around to see Mistyfoot, the RiverClan deputy, standing at the top of the hollow. Brambleclaw was with her, and a patrol of RiverClan warriors.

"Wait!" Mistyfoot called. "RiverClan will join you."

With a nod of acknowledgment Firestar raced on, the mass of cats hard on his paws. He let out a ferocious battle cry as he led them across ShadowClan territory as far as the Thunderpath.

At the edge of the hard black surface they paused. Onewhisker felt a thrill of apprehension, every hair on his pelt rising as he gazed along the Thunderpath in both directions. Instead of the Twoleg monsters racing past, there was nothing but an eerie silence.

"They stopped the other monsters from coming here just before they started destroying our part of the forest," Onewhisker heard Tawnypelt explain to Squirrelpaw. "At least it makes it easier to cross."

As he followed in Firestar's paw steps, Onewhisker could hear the roaring of monsters in the distance. Their acrid scent grew stronger as the cats bounded forward. Onewhisker's belly lurched as he remembered how the huge creatures had torn up the WindClan camp, driving their jaws into the earth with no thought for what they were destroying.

I'm not sure I can go through that again. . . .

But his Clanmates were still pounding along, even Tallstar fighting against his weakness and weariness. Farther ahead Onewhisker caught glimpses of Firestar's flame-colored pelt.

They're such great leaders, he thought, forcing more speed from his aching paws. *I can't let them down.*

They were deep into ShadowClan territory when Onewhisker glimpsed a huge monster among the trees ahead of them. It stretched out massive yellow forepaws, its claws extended to sink into its prey. A deafening sound split the air, louder than anything Onewhisker had heard before, louder than he thought anything *could* sound.

The cats skidded to a halt; most of them flattened themselves to the ground and wrapped their tails or their paws over their ears. Onewhisker looked around for Tallstar and crouched beside him while the terrible noise roared on.

Daring to glance up, Onewhisker could hardly believe what he was seeing. The monster gripped an oak tree in its enormous paws and wrenched it out of the ground as easily as a medicine cat pulling up a plant to get at the root. The branches clattered as the monster tipped the tree over and began chewing up the bark, scattering a hail of scraps over the terrified cats.

Another growling noise broke out behind them; Onewhisker shot a glance over his shoulder to see a second monster steadily advancing, tearing up the ground with shining jaws as it bore down on them.

"They're nearly at the camp!" Tawnypelt yowled.

Straight ahead Onewhisker could see the bramble thicket that surrounded the ShadowClan camp. More monsters were converging on it, and for one horrible moment Onewhisker thought that he and the other Clan cats were too late.

Then Firestar sprang to his paws. "We'll have to go that way!" he cried out, waving his tail toward a gap in the trees the monsters hadn't reached. "Now!"

With the rest of the cats Onewhisker scrambled up and sprang after him, showered with splinters of wood as the tree-eater behind them attacked its next victim.

Firestar halted at the edge of the bramble thicket and began dividing his warriors into separate patrols, each with their own duties.

"What about me?" Onewhisker asked, afraid that he and the other WindClan cats were being overlooked.

"I'll get to you soon," Firestar told him, before turning to Tawnypelt and continuing, "You know this part of the forest better than us. We can't go back the way we came. Which way's the quickest out of here?"

"That way!" the tortoiseshell warrior replied, angling her ears toward a gap in the trees. "If we're quick, we'll get to it before the monsters and pick up a trail that will take us to the tunnel under the Thunderpath."

Tallstar padded up while Tawnypelt was speaking, and Firestar turned back to address him and Onewhisker. "You two must defend our escape route," he meowed.

Onewhisker knew that this task was the least dangerous of all, and for a heartbeat he felt offended, as if Firestar thought they needed protection. But then he realized how stupid he was being, and just felt grateful that his Clan leader wouldn't have to tackle the monsters.

"I wish I could do more," Tallstar murmured as they watched the other cats disappear down the bramble tunnel that led into the ShadowClan camp. Then he shook his head and withdrew with Onewhisker in the direction Tawnypelt had indicated.

They found a spot that was free of monsters, for the moment, and still within sight of the camp entrance. Soon ShadowClan cats began to emerge into the open, their fur bristling and their eyes bulging with terror.

"This way!" Onewhisker called, signaling with his tail. "Follow the trail!" he added as the cats streamed past him. "Wait by the tunnel under the Thunderpath!"

A tortoiseshell queen emerged, one kit dangling from her jaws by its scruff while a second kit tried to cling onto her back. "I can't hold on!" the kit wailed. "Make it stop! I don't *like* it!"

"Stay here," Onewhisker mewed swiftly to Tallstar, then raced toward the queen and grabbed the kit off her back. "Follow me!" he mumbled around his mouthful of fur, and bounded off toward the tunnel, the tortoiseshell she-cat keeping up alongside him.

When they had reached a quieter part of the forest, Onewhisker put the kit down. "You should be safe now," he told the queen. "Just head for the tunnel. The kits should be able to walk that far."

The tortoiseshell nodded. "Thank you," she breathed out. "I won't forget this. Come on, kits."

Onewhisker watched them go, then headed back down the trail to rejoin Tallstar, but before he reached his Clan leader, he was almost knocked off his paws by a panicking Shadow-Clan warrior, blundering into the trees in completely the wrong direction.

Regaining his balance, Onewhisker spotted three or four other warriors, a group beginning to split up, as if they had no idea which way to go. Behind them, Tallstar was standing with his fur bushed out and his tail raised.

"Stop!" he yowled, with all the authority of a Clan leader in his voice.

The ShadowClan warriors halted, huddling together as they gazed back at Tallstar.

"Are you warriors or mice?" the WindClan leader demanded. "Now get your tails down to the tunnel and wait there for your leader!"

Abashed, the warriors turned and raced off, in the right direction this time.

Tallstar rolled his eyes as Onewhisker joined him. "Bees in their brain!" he exclaimed. "Still, I can't blame them for being scared."

More cats came fleeing past: the ShadowClan leader, Blackstar, carrying a kit; the medicine cat, Littlecloud, each of them struggling along with an injured warrior leaning on their shoulder; Russetfur, the deputy, urging on a group of elders. Onewhisker helped a limping apprentice who had a thorn in his paw, managing to pull it out before sending the young cat racing on his way to safety.

All the while Onewhisker's heart was pounding, terrified for the ShadowClan cats, for Tallstar, and for himself. The monsters drew closer and closer, chewing up the forest. Their roaring mingled with the groans of trees torn from the ground and the crash of their trunks hitting the forest floor. The birds were already gone, erupting out of the branches, and small prey creatures scattered in all directions.

Onewhisker slammed a paw down on a mouse as it scurried past him, and tossed the limp body over to Tallstar. "Eat," he meowed.

Tallstar's eyes widened. "That's a ShadowClan mouse!"

"We're risking our lives for them," Onewhisker pointed out. "Don't you think they can spare us one miserable mouse? Besides," he added, "there are no territories anymore. Twolegs are destroying them all. From now on, the Clans will have to pull together if we want to survive."

His Clan leader hesitated a moment longer, then bent his head and devoured the mouse in ravenous gulps.

By now the stream of fleeing cats had dwindled; Firestar and the other rescuers emerged from the bramble tunnel and bounded up to where Tallstar and Onewhisker were waiting.

"Hurry!" Onewhisker meowed. "The others are already heading to the Thunderpath!"

"Did all the queens and kits get out?" Tawnypelt demanded, raising her voice to make herself heard as another oak tree crashed to the ground mere tail-lengths away.

"Blackstar had a kit," Onewhisker replied. "And there was a tortoiseshell with two kits. . . ."

Tawnypelt's eyes flared with alarm. "What about Tall-poppy?"

"I thought Tallpoppy was the tortoiseshell!" Squirrelpaw gasped.

"Tallpoppy's a tabby!" Panic vibrated in Tawnypelt's voice. "She's got three kits, not two!"

The cats exchanged glances of dismay, with Squirrelpaw insisting that no cat was left behind in the camp. *She must be right*, Onewhisker thought. *There is no ShadowClan camp anymore.*

He refused to let himself imagine the queen and her three kits chomped up by the shining jaws of the monsters. *They have to be somewhere!* He raised his head, trying to make out the mewling of frightened kits amid the growls of monsters and the rattling of tree branches. His jaws parted, he tasted the air, trying to shut out the scents of the cats surrounding him to pick out different cat scents at a distance. And at last there was, barely distinguishable, a tiny trace. . . .

"Over there!" he yowled.

He pointed with his nose toward a clearing surrounded by thin, frail saplings, where so far the monsters had not attacked. With Tawnypelt and more of the rescuers racing along behind him, he hurled himself through the trees, only to halt in horror at the sight that met his gaze.

The tabby queen, Tallpoppy, was standing in the middle of the clearing, turning this way and that as she called to her kits and tried to gather them up. But the three kits were so panic-stricken they wouldn't listen to their mother. Instead they darted in all directions; one was trying to climb a tree.

Beyond them, more monsters were already visible, devouring tree after tree and drawing closer with every heartbeat.

Onewhisker only hesitated for a moment. With Firestar hard on his paws, he began trying to round up the kits. "Come here!" he called. "We'll get you out!" But the kits were too terrified to take any notice.

A terrible crunching sound broke out behind Onewhisker, but as he chased a kit toward its mother, he had no time to glance over his shoulder. Somewhere in the chaos Squirrelpaw let out a yowl.

Tallpoppy and Tawnypelt had each managed to grab a kit, but the third was scurrying away, mewling in terror, right into the path of the nearest monster. Onewhisker dived forward and snatched it up by its scruff, then felt something slam hard into his side. He lost his balance and rolled over, the kit still in his jaws. All around him, branches whipped through the air.

For a few heartbeats Onewhisker wasn't sure what had happened. Everything was a confusion of twigs and debris. He still held the kit clamped firmly in his jaws, but he had lost sight of the other cats. He wondered if he had hit his head.

Then he realized that a tree had fallen, right where he had been standing. He was trapped among the outer branches, bruised and scratched but alive, with the kit squirming and squealing in his jaws. *The kit is alive too. That's what matters.*

A moment later Brambleclaw was there, hauling him, still clutching the kit, away from the confining branches that scraped his flanks and legs until he could regain his paws and stumble out into the clearing. More cats were there, with

Tallpoppy and her other kits still safe, but he could see no sign of Firestar.

"Get out of here!" Brambleclaw yowled.

"I'm not leaving without Firestar!" Squirrelpaw cried out.

Then Onewhisker realized what must have happened. Firestar had thrust him away from the falling tree, but the ThunderClan leader himself had been crushed under it. For a moment he felt as cold as if he were standing out on the moor in the middle of a blizzard.

Can even a nine-lived leader survive that?

"We'll find him," Brambleclaw promised Squirrelpaw. Turning to Onewhisker, he added, "Get the others to the Thunderpath."

For a moment Onewhisker was too numb to obey the ThunderClan cat's order. Then a shadow fell across him, and a loud creaking sound snapped him out of his stupor. He pulled himself together as another tree crashed to its ruin. He would rather have stayed to help find Firestar, but there was no time to argue. "We'll wait for you at the tunnel," he managed to gasp out around his mouthful of fur.

Yet it took all the courage and determination he had to turn away and begin leading the others to safety. He wondered whether he would ever see Firestar and the other Thunder-Clan cats again.

The RiverClan patrol and the rest of the ShadowClan cats had made their way through the tunnel that led under the Thunderpath, and flopped down, exhausted, on the grass at the far end. When Onewhisker and Tallstar arrived with Tallpoppy, Tawnypelt, and the kits, they let out cries of relief, while Tallstar rested his tail on Onewhisker's shoulder.

"You did well," he meowed. "I thought you were on your way to StarClan when you leaped after that kit."

Onewhisker felt as if the whole of his body were a single throbbing pain from the scratches where the branches had raked across him. But his warm sense of triumph was worth every bruise, every scrap of hair missing from his pelt. "I thought I might be," he meowed. "But Firestar saved me. I just hope he survives."

Blackstar, the ShadowClan leader, was staring around at his Clan as if he couldn't believe what had happened. His white pelt was smeared with blood; scraps of tree bark and dead leaves were caught up in it.

"What are we going to do now?" Littlecloud asked. "We have injured cats here, and we've lost our store of herbs."

"And where are we going to spend the night, now that our camp is gone?" Tallpoppy was sitting with her kits drawn close to her in the curl of her tail. The tiny creatures were burrowing into her fur, mewling pitifully. "My kits need shelter, somewhere away from these dreadful monsters!"

No cat had any answers. Onewhisker couldn't even try to think about ShadowClan's plight, with their camp destroyed and their territory churned up. His mind was still reeling from the same thing happening to his own Clan. The whole situation was too exhausting, and far bigger than one cat, or even one Clan, could cope with. All Onewhisker could do was focus his attention on the mouth of the tunnel.

Where are the ThunderClan cats? Will they make it out? And where is Firestar?

He found it hard to accept that he might never see the flame-colored tom again: the cat who had proved so triumphantly that a kittypet *could* become a warrior; the cat Onewhisker thought of as his friend, even though he was the leader of a different Clan.

Then he spotted movement in the darkness, and Leafpaw, the ThunderClan medicine-cat apprentice, burst into the open. At first Onewhisker thought she was alone. But Firestar staggered out after her, and trailed his green gaze over the stricken group of cats.

"Is everyone okay?" he croaked.

Relief surged over Onewhisker at the sound of the ThunderClan leader's voice. That was Firestar—always concerned about other cats. *Maybe that means he isn't too badly hurt,* Onewhisker added hopefully to himself.

The sun had gone down by the time all the cats—even Mistyfoot and her RiverClan patrol—had reached Sunning-rocks, the stronger cats helping the weaker and all those who had been injured in the desperate escape from the Shadow-Clan camp. Mistyfoot was there to help Tallstar when he stumbled, while Tornear gently urged on a group of Shadow-Clan apprentices.

It's like we're not separate Clans anymore, Onewhisker thought. There was something comforting in the idea, that now they were all facing disaster together. The problem felt too big for any one Clan, beyond the power of any one leader to solve. *But if we're in it together, maybe we will be okay after all. Especially now that Firestar is with us, perhaps we can start to hope.*

Tallstar was too exhausted to climb the rocks again, so he settled down at their foot. Onewhisker crouched beside him, and a few moments later Tornear limped over to join them.

"Crowpaw is with the other cats who made the journey to the sun-drown-place," he reported. "He might as well stay there for now—unless you want him, Tallstar."

"No, that's fine," the Clan leader murmured.

The cats rested while the last streaks of sunlight faded from the sky and the moon rose in their place. Leafpaw and the other medicine cats were working with the injured, while Blackstar and Russetfur had their heads together with some of the ShadowClan senior warriors.

Eventually Onewhisker realized that the RiverClan cats were gathering together and Mistyfoot was padding over to talk to Firestar. Onewhisker sat up to listen.

"We're returning to our camp," Mistyfoot announced. "But we know that the time has come to make a decision about leaving the forest."

Firestar nodded agreement. Blackstar had also overheard the RiverClan deputy's words, and he left his Clanmates to join her and Firestar. Onewhisker glanced at Tallstar, but his Clan leader was deeply asleep; Tornear too was drowsing. Careful not to disturb them, Onewhisker rose and made his way over to join the leaders.

"I'm sure many of you have noticed that the river is drying up," Mistyfoot continued.

Onewhisker let out a low growl, thinking of the stretches of mud and pebbles where once the water had run clear. "The Twolegs have changed the course of the water," he meowed.

"Our warriors have seen them digging great holes around the gorge to channel the river away."

Mistyfoot shook her head, as if she was simply bewildered by the behavior of Twolegs. Then she turned to Firestar, meeting his gaze steadily. "Leopardstar told me that if the ShadowClan camp was destroyed, then we must accept that the Twolegs are coming," she mewed, her voice firm. "RiverClan will leave the forest with the other Clans."

Onewhisker felt his belly shake with relief; all the strength seemed to drain out of his legs, and he struggled for self-control in front of the Clan leaders.

Firestar rose to his paws, his gaze bright as two green stars. "Onewhisker, tell your Clanmates that ThunderClan and RiverClan will travel with them." Turning to Blackstar, he added, "Will ShadowClan join us?"

Onewhisker felt a shiver of apprehension run through him as Blackstar hesitated. *True, three Clans can leave together,* he thought, *but it won't ever be the same if we leave one Clan behind.*

Firestar gave an irritable twitch of his tail. "You can't still plan to live among the Twolegs after you have seen what they're capable of?" he hissed.

Blackstar hesitated for a heartbeat longer, then nodded slowly. "ShadowClan will travel with you," he responded. "After all, we have no home and no territory now."

Firestar drew a great breath of relief, his gaze seeming to burn even brighter. He raised his head and let out a clear call to reach all the cats on the rocks.

"We will leave at dawn!"

CHAPTER 11

❧

With the decision made, the WindClan cats returned to the hollow on the moor and settled down to get what sleep they could before they met with the other Clans to begin their journey.

We don't even know where we're going, Onewhisker thought. Maybe they would strike out toward the Tribe that Crowpaw and the others had mentioned. *But after that . . . who knows?*

He curled up with Whitetail among the knotty roots of a gorse bush, the best shelter they could find in the moorland hollow. Although he was exhausted from his exertions on ShadowClan territory, his emotions were in such a ferment that he couldn't sleep. For a while he lay still, listening to the trickle of the tiny waterfall. But his paws were itching to be on the move, and finally he eased himself away from the sleeping Whitetail and scrambled up the rocks onto the moor.

He began by padding around the top of the hollow and, when all was quiet there, gradually extended his patrol in a widening spiral. He tasted the air for prey, in the faint hope that he could bring back something to help strengthen his Clanmates for the journey. Instead the air that flowed over his scent glands bore the trace of an approaching cat.

Onewhisker froze, his heart jolting. The scent was all too familiar, even though it was so long since he had smelled it. He felt his shoulders droop under the weight of guilt and apprehension. *Smoke! What does she want now?*

Another cat's scent mingled with that of the gray she-cat, telling Onewhisker that Smoke was not alone. As she padded out of the shadows, shock pulsed through him. The second cat was her kit—his son—now much bigger than the tiny creature he had seen in the Twoleg garden. The kit's white fur almost glowed in the moonlight. At first Onewhisker thought that he had no tail at all, until he realized that it was completely black. There were black blotches around his eyes, too: eyes that were a vivid, unsettling blue.

Though Smoke looked better fed than any of the Wind-Clan cats, she was thinner and much less well groomed than when Onewhisker had last seen her. The kit was sickly-looking, and walked with a limp on one forepaw.

"What happened?" Onewhisker asked as Smoke halted in front of him. "Why have you come here? It's not safe."

There was a piteous look in Smoke's blue eyes as she looked up at Onewhisker. "My Twoleg died," she mewed. "I didn't want to go to animal control—"

"Animal control?" Onewhisker interrupted, confused. "What's that?"

"A place for kittypets who have no Twolegs of their own," Smoke told him. "But I've heard bad things about it. I know they would separate me from my kit. Onewhisker, we need a place to live. Can we come with you to your camp?"

Onewhisker could hardly believe that Smoke was still asking that, after everything he had told her. "I'm sorry, but no," he replied. "Absolutely not. Can't you smell the Twoleg monsters all over the place? Haven't you seen the way they've torn up the ground? We don't even have a camp anymore!"

"But we need—" Smoke began.

"It's just not possible," Onewhisker interrupted, deliberately harsh. He couldn't take kittypets into the Clan when every cat would be moving off at dawn—even supposing that Tallstar would accept them. He remembered Leo, and how joining WindClan had led to his death, in spite of all the time and resources his Clanmates had given to his training. It would be so much harder now, when the Clan was fighting for its very survival.

And how would I explain Smoke and her kit to Whitetail? he wondered, trying to convince himself that that wasn't the reason he was sending his former mate away.

"Anyway, the Clans are leaving the forest in the morning," he continued. "The journey will be dangerous; we can't support inexperienced cats, and especially not kits." As he spoke, the image of Tallpoppy's kit flashed into his mind, its tiny face distorted in a scream as the tree began to fall. *And Smoke thinks her life is difficult!* "Even without a Twoleg, the Twolegplace is safer," he finished.

"Don't you care that this kit is *your son*?" Smoke asked, nudging the kit a little closer to Onewhisker. "His name is Darkkit, after his tail. I named him the way a Clan cat would be named."

"That's a good name." Feeling chastised by Smoke's appeal, Onewhisker spoke more gently as he bent his head and met the kit's gaze.

Darkkit didn't respond, but only stared into Onewhisker's eyes with a strange intensity that sent a shiver of apprehension through Onewhisker's pelt. He gave his pelt a shake. *He has every right to be angry. He's only a kit, and he hasn't had the easiest life so far.* But Onewhisker couldn't quite banish the worm of unease that he felt in his belly.

"What's the matter with his paw?" he asked Smoke, feeling a twist of pity he could not show. At the same time he was still disturbed by Darkkit's anger, averting his eyes from the kit's gaze.

"He stepped on a thorn," Smoke explained. "I got it out, but his paw is still sore."

"He needs a dock leaf for that," Onewhisker meowed. "Wait there, and I'll see if we have one."

Back at the hollow, Onewhisker crept stealthily down to where Barkface was sleeping. He knew that the medicine cat had brought what supplies he could when they'd had to flee the makeshift camp, and stored them in a crevice between two rocks. Careful not to disturb the medicine cat, Onewhisker peered into the gap, then slid one paw inside and snagged a dock leaf in his claws.

When he hurried back to Smoke, he found the gray she-cat standing at the top of the hollow, dangerously close to the other cats. His belly lurched as he realized that she was staring straight at Whitetail.

"Here," he mewed, keeping his voice low as he gave her the dock leaf. "Rub his paw with that."

As Smoke reached out to take the leaf, her paw was quivering with anger, and her blue eyes glittered furiously. "So this is it," she hissed. "You're leaving with the Clans—with *her*—and you'll never see me or your kit again? Well, I won't let that happen. I'll wake the whole Clan and tell them the secret you've been hiding all this time!"

Smoke gathered herself to leap down into the hollow. Panicking, Onewhisker intercepted her and shoved her roughly aside. Smoke caught her claws in a twisting gorse root; stumbling, she knocked Darkkit off his paws and fell on top of him. Darkkit let out a protesting squeal.

"I'm sorry!" Onewhisker helped Smoke to rise and stood watching while she checked her kit, swiping debris from his pelt. "This is just how it has to be," he continued, "but once we find our new camp, I'll come back. I'll find you in the Twolegplace."

As soon as the words were out, he was appalled by what he had said. *Where did that come from? Of course I can't come back for her!*

Smoke was gazing at him with suspicion in her eyes. "I'll believe that when I see it," she meowed. "Onewhisker, you have to promise me that you won't forget us. Your kit needs you."

Onewhisker nodded, feeling trapped into something he had never intended. "I promise," he declared.

Gazing at Darkkit again, he wished with a pang of guilt that he could raise him as a WindClan cat, but it just wasn't possible. *Maybe Smoke and Darkkit will find new Twolegs before I return. If I return,* he added uneasily to himself.

The gray she-cat narrowed her eyes. "If you break that promise," she hissed, "then I'll teach Darkkit to hate you, and to hate all the Clans. Think about that, Onewhisker!"

"I've said I promise," Onewhisker protested, though he had no idea how he would keep his word. *But that's a problem for a future I can't even imagine. One where the Clans are settled in our new home, and WindClan isn't starving. . . .*

As he turned away from Smoke and his kit, he felt as if an ivy tendril were twining around him, trapping him in a prison of his own making. *Whatever I choose,* he thought, *I'm going to betray some cat. Smoke and Darkkit, or my own Clan.*

CHAPTER 12

❧

A blustering wind blew across the field, and frost made the grass spiky underpaw as the Clan cats trekked across it. The mountain peaks ahead looked bare and ominous, yet Onewhisker's heart lifted as he gazed at them. At least their journey had a purpose now; he felt they were making progress.

The morning after the destruction of ShadowClan's camp, they had left the Clan territories in a nightmare of driving rain, the churned-up ground turning to treacherous, slick mud. Yet at the end of it they had found refuge at the farm where the former ThunderClan apprentice Ravenpaw lived with the loner Barley. There had been shelter, warmth, and plentiful prey.

"I'm still thinking about that star," Whitetail meowed.

She was padding along beside Onewhisker, with Tallstar on his other side. Onewhisker had made sure right from the beginning that he stayed close to his Clan leader. And even though he had never wanted to put WindClan's fate in other cats' paws, he was reassured to have the stronger RiverClan and ThunderClan cats walking along with them.

"I know," Onewhisker replied to Whitetail's comment.

"And I keep thinking about when Tallstar and Crowpaw went to Fourtrees, and there was no sign at all. And all the time they were looking for it at the wrong Great Rock!"

Whitetail let out a small purr of amusement. "Midnight meant Highstones all along!"

Leaving Barley and Ravenpaw, the Clans had climbed up to Mothermouth, where the leaders and the medicine cats had gone to meet with StarClan at the Moonstone. Meanwhile the five journeying cats had struggled up to the topmost ridge, where they had seen a star blazing across the sky over Highstones, leaving a shining furrow across the blackness. A warrior of StarClan had sacrificed their life to point the Clans in the right direction.

"So we are going to see the Tribe after all," Onewhisker murmured. "But that can't be the end of our journey. I'm surprised these mountains can support even one Clan; five would be impossible!"

While they'd been talking, the wind had dropped, and up ahead Onewhisker could see a belt of woodland. Enticing scents of prey tickled his nose, and his pads began to tingle with excitement. In spite of everything that had happened, in spite of his foolish and desperate promise to Smoke, the farther they traveled from the Twolegplace, the better he felt.

"We need to hunt," Mudclaw announced, bustling importantly up and down the straggle of WindClan cats. "There's prey up ahead, and we have to get it before any other Clan swipes it from under our noses."

Onewhisker felt hot with embarrassment when he caught

disapproving looks from the cats of other Clans who were walking along with them. He noticed Firestar's ears swiveling in Mudclaw's direction, and his shame deepened as he realized that the Clan leader he admired so much had heard the deputy's words. Even among their own Clanmates, in their weakened and exhausted state, Mudclaw's urging felt more like bullying.

Onewhisker glanced toward Tallstar; his belly cramped with apprehension when he saw how weak his leader was looking.

"Is anything wrong?" he asked. "Do you need to stop for a while? Should the Clan wait for you?"

Tallstar shook his head. "No, I'm fine," he replied with a sigh, staring after Mudclaw, who had bounded off to hunt. "It's just that . . . I don't know if Mudclaw's leadership is quite what WindClan needs, right now."

Onewhisker couldn't suppress a shiver. Tallstar was growing frailer with every day that passed, and the Clan leader clearly knew it. *Is he thinking about what Mudstar will be like?*

"Tallstar," he began hesitantly, his voice a low murmur, "back in the old forest, did you give Mudclaw permission to hunt on other Clans' territory?"

Tallstar paused before replying. "Yes, I did," he sighed eventually. "And I don't regret it, because it might have saved our lives. But I didn't like the way it happened. We should have gone earlier to ask ThunderClan for help." The Clan leader paused again, before confessing, "Mudclaw was going to do it, no matter what I said. And I was too weak to stop him."

Onewhisker drew in a shocked breath. *Would Mudclaw dare to defy his leader like that?* His gaze followed Mudclaw as the mottled tom slid into the undergrowth beneath the trees. *And what will happen to WindClan under Mudstar? Will he really be the leader that we need?* A shiver passed through him, raising the hairs on his pelt. *I've always trusted Tallstar. What will I do if I can't have the same faith in Mudstar?*

Onewhisker's legs trembled as he padded along the narrow mountain ledge. On one side was sheer rock; on the other a massive waterfall roared down, no more than a tail-length from his shrinking body. The rock underpaw was slick with spray, so that Onewhisker found it all too easy to imagine being snatched away by the torrent and broken on the rocks below or lost under the water's churning surface.

If this is the Tribe's home, then I'm glad we're not staying!

Some way ahead, Onewhisker could hear Mudclaw chivvying the cats along. "Come on, best paw forward! There's nothing to be scared of if you keep close to the rock face."

That's all very well, Onewhisker thought. *Mudclaw isn't scared, but he could show a bit more sympathy. He could be encouraging the cats, not barking at them like an angry fox.*

Firestar had done just that as they approached the perilous path, rounding up the stragglers and cheering them up with promises of food and shelter only a few paw steps away. *He's a true leader!* Onewhisker reflected.

Trying to ignore the deputy's harsh tones, Onewhisker concentrated on Tallstar, who was stumbling along just ahead.

Onewhisker was poised to grab him if the Clan leader showed any sign of slipping over the edge. The climb into the mountains had taken almost all of Tallstar's remaining strength, especially when it had started to snow. *I'm surprised he's made it this far.*

At least they had found prey in this beautiful, if strange, landscape, though it was not enough to support one extra Clan, much less all four. On the way, they had met some of the Tribe cats; Onewhisker was thankful that these had recognized Crowpaw and the other cats who had made the first journey.

Otherwise our welcome might not have been so friendly.

As the Tribe cats led them to their cave, the Clan cats watched them bring down a hawk. Onewhisker had been impressed—even more so when he remembered the hawk Crowpaw had caught on the moor. *How did he learn that technique so quickly?*

Now he huffed out a breath of relief as Tallstar, just ahead, disappeared into the cave. Onewhisker rushed to follow him.

"Great StarClan!" he whispered, halting and staring around in wonder.

He stood at one side of a vast cavern. Pale light filtered in through the waterfall, rippling over walls that stretched up for many fox-lengths; in the shadows of the roof Onewhisker could just make out narrow talons of stone pointing down to the cave floor.

Is that what Feathertail used to kill Sharptooth? he wondered, shivering.

At the back of the cave two tunnels led off into darkness; between them and the cave entrance many cats were standing, their eyes gleaming as they watched the exhausted Clan cats stumbling past the waterfall. There were more cats, too, Onewhisker realized, sitting or crouching on ledges, all with their faces turned toward the newcomers.

His pelt began to rise in apprehension at being stared at, but when the Tribe cats recovered from their surprise, they were welcoming, offering food and showing the Clan cats their sleeping hollows, scoops in the cave floor lined with moss and feathers.

Onewhisker shared a rabbit with Tallstar and Whitetail. When they had finished their prey, Tallstar joined a discussion with the other leaders on what their next move should be. Onewhisker was settling nearby to listen when a cat they had not seen before emerged from one of the tunnels and made his way toward them. He was a scrawny brown tabby, his muzzle gray with age, and he had the most intense amber eyes Onewhisker had ever seen.

Leafpaw was escorting him. "This is Stoneteller," she meowed, before dipping her head and drawing back.

Stoneteller! Onewhisker remembered Crowpaw telling him and his Clanmates about this cat, who was the Tribe's leader and their medicine cat too. *That's an awful lot of responsibility resting on one cat's shoulders.*

Almost at once Stoneteller's amber gaze alit on Tallstar, who was half asleep from weariness, paying little attention to the other leaders. "You are not well," Stoneteller meowed.

"We will give you herbs." He turned to the nearest of the Tribe cats. "Bird, bring strengthening herbs."

The gray tabby she-cat raced away and disappeared down one of the tunnels at the back of the cave. Soon she returned with a bunch of herbs in her jaws and set them down in front of Tallstar, who licked them up with a murmur of gratitude.

When the WindClan leader had swallowed the herbs, Onewhisker led him—almost asleep on his paws—to one of the nests, and saw him settled.

"There aren't enough sleeping hollows for every cat," Whitetail mewed, padding up behind him. "But I've found a ledge that looks pretty comfortable."

"I'm so tired I could sleep in a badger's den," Onewhisker responded. "Lead me to it!"

But when he and Whitetail were curled up on their ledge, Onewhisker found that sleep wouldn't come. There was still too much to wonder at in the Tribe's cave, especially now that the daylight was dying and the light from the waterfall sank to a faint glitter.

"We've made it this far," Whitetail murmured after a while. "But this place is too strange for Clan cats, even if there were room for us. Do you think we'll ever find anywhere like the territories we left?"

The territories we left . . . Her words echoed in Onewhisker's mind. He thought of Smoke and Darkkit, and for a moment he wondered whether he ought to tell Whitetail about his former mate and the kit who was his son, both of whom he had also left behind in their old home.

But how can I tell her now? Onewhisker realized that even if Whitetail understood about Smoke, she might blame him for abandoning his kit to the Twolegplace. *I'm sure Smoke and Dark-kit will be safer in the Twolegplace than coming with us on this nightmare journey.* Onewhisker wished he could be sure he had managed to convince himself of that. *All the same, I'm not sure how I would explain it to Whitetail.*

Before he could make a decision, Onewhisker was distracted by a scrabbling sound at the other end of the ledge. Crowpaw appeared; at first he seemed not to notice his Clanmates, but sat with his head bowed, gazing at the endlessly falling water.

"Crowpaw, are you okay?" Whitetail asked gently after a few heartbeats.

The dark gray tom looked up, startled, then relaxed when he saw who had spoken. "I'm fine," he replied awkwardly. "I'm just thinking about Feathertail. This is where she died, on our journey."

Onewhisker nodded sympathetically. He remembered the story Crowpaw had told, about the bravery of the RiverClan she-cat.

"I miss her," Crowpaw continued. "I know she was a River-Clan cat, but all of us on the quest became close. I miss her so much . . . ," he repeated.

A moment later, a soft call rose from the floor of the cave below. "Crowpaw? Is that you up there?"

Looking down, Onewhisker spotted Stormfur, Feathertail's brother, gazing up at the ledge. Beside him was a slender young Tribe she-cat.

"Coming!" Crowpaw called. Glancing at Onewhisker, he explained, "We're going to sit vigil for Feathertail." He leaped down to the ground, and the three cats disappeared along the ledge that led out onto the mountainside.

"Who was that with them?" Onewhisker asked. "Do you know?"

"I met her while we were sorting out the sleeping hollows," Whitetail replied. "Her name is Brook Where Small Fish Swim. I think Stormfur . . . likes her."

Onewhisker's ears flicked up in surprise. "Really? It'll be tough for him when we leave, then."

Whitetail stifled a yawn. "I know. It's tough for any cat who falls in love outside their Clan. I'm glad I've got you, Onewhisker." She curled closer to him and let out a sleepy purr.

Don't I know how tough it is! Onewhisker thought ruefully. "And I'm glad I have you, Whitetail," he meowed.

When Onewhisker awoke, the cavern was already filled with flickering daylight. There didn't seem to be as many cats as he remembered from the night before; he guessed that many of them had already gone out hunting. Spotting Tallstar climbing out of his sleeping hollow, he scrambled down from the ledge to join him, with Whitetail following.

"Good morning, Tallstar," he greeted his Clan leader, dipping his head respectfully. "Did you sleep well?"

"Very well," Tallstar replied, shaking off a few feathers that were clinging to his fur. "Better than I can remember for a long time."

Onewhisker felt a tingle of relief all through his pelt.

Tallstar looked refreshed after his night in the comfortable sleeping hollow; the plentiful prey and the strengthening herbs must have helped too.

"Tallstar, there's something I wanted to ask—" he began, only to break off as Mudclaw came striding across the cave floor from where he had been talking with the other Clan leaders.

"It snowed hard during the night," the Clan deputy reported, "and Stoneteller thinks there's more to come. We decided not to move on today."

"We"? Who's this "we"? Onewhisker thought. *You're not Clan leader yet, Mudclaw.*

There was a flicker of disapproval in Tallstar's eyes, though he responded mildly. "That sounds like a sensible decision. Onewhisker, what was it you wanted to ask?"

"It's about Crowpaw," Onewhisker replied. "If he had never left our territory, he would have been a warrior by now. And since then, he's accomplished more than any apprentice I ever heard of. Don't you think he's earned his warrior name?"

As he spoke, he became aware that Mudclaw was glaring at him, and he realized that since Mudclaw was not only Clan deputy but also Crowpaw's mentor, this suggestion should have been his to make.

Then he should have made it, Onewhisker thought, unrepentant, forcing himself not to glance at the mottled brown tom. Even though he was irritated with Mudclaw, he didn't want to do anything to give the deputy a reason for starting an argument.

But it's hard, when he's being such a stupid furball.

Tallstar turned to his deputy. "What do you think, Mud-claw?"

Mudclaw let out a snort. "I guess so," he muttered grudg-ingly.

"Then we'll hold his warrior ceremony later," Tallstar declared. "Once the hunters come back and I can call the Clan together."

As the daylight died, the Clan cats relaxed together in the cave, thankful for a second night of eating well, after the hard-ships of their journey. The air was filled with the perpetual rushing of the waterfall, and beyond the cascade Onewhisker could make out the fitful glimmer of a full moon.

"We should be Gathering tonight," he murmured, with a pang for everything they had lost.

"But we are," Whitetail pointed out. "Look at us!"

Glancing around the cavern, Onewhisker could see what Whitetail meant. The Clans were mingling, just as they did on the night of the full moon. Dustpelt of ThunderClan was stretched out beside Tallstar; Tallpoppy and Ferncloud, Dustpelt's mate, were sharing tongues. Firestar and his mate, Sandstorm, were deep in conversation with Mistyfoot, the RiverClan deputy. All the kits were playing together, or had collapsed into drowsing, furry heaps.

Onewhisker looked around for Stoneteller, and saw him talking to Leafpaw near the entrance to the cave. As One-whisker watched, he dipped his head to her, then turned to address the rest of the cats.

"Cats of the Clans and of the Tribe," he began, raising his voice to be heard above the roaring of the waterfall, "we have not celebrated our deliverance from Sharptooth. Instead we grieved for Feathertail, who died saving us. But tonight we shall honor the cats who came from far away and killed the terrible creature."

The Tribe cats let out meows of agreement. After rising to their paws, they each took a piece of fresh-kill from the pile and placed it in front of a Clan cat.

What's all this about? Onewhisker asked himself. The enticing scent of the haunch of rabbit he had been given was flowing over his scent glands, but he was reluctant to start eating in case there was more to the ceremony.

When the prey had been distributed, Stoneteller raised his voice again. "We feast in honor of Feathertail," he declared. "Her spirit will live forever in the Tribe of Endless Hunting. We honor too the cats who refused to desert us, and returned to fulfill the prophecy of our ancestors." He dipped his head in turn to each of the journeying cats, who sat with heads high and eyes glowing with pride. "Now let us eat!" Stoneteller finished.

Onewhisker still wasn't sure what to do. Then he noticed Crowpaw taking a bite from his eagle's leg and passing the prey over to the Tribe cat in front of him. The Tribe cat also took a bite and then passed it back to Crowpaw.

Now I get it! Onewhisker thought, relieved. He tore off a mouthful and passed the prey to the Tribe cat who was waiting to share with him.

The Tribe cat blinked amber eyes in approval. "That's right," he meowed. "We always eat together like this."

When he had finished his prey, Onewhisker lay stretched out, enjoying the feel of a full belly. Then he heard Tallstar calling his name, and looked up to see the Clan leader beckoning him with a twitch of his tail.

"Give me your shoulder to lean on," the old cat meowed when Onewhisker padded up to him. "I have something to say."

Onewhisker's paws tingled with excitement; he knew what his Clan leader meant to do.

A stir of anticipation passed through the assembled cats as Tallstar limped into the center of the cave, with Onewhisker supporting him. Glancing around, he called, "Crowpaw?"

The apprentice looked up, blinking in bewilderment.

"Crowpaw has served his Clan with bravery and loyalty," Tallstar rasped. "He should have received his warrior name long ago. But the tragedies of the past moons have prevented this. Tonight, if Stoneteller will do me the kindness of allowing a warrior ceremony in his Tribe's home, I wish to honor Crowpaw's great skill and courage by giving him his warrior name."

Crowpaw's Clanmates broke out into murmurs of agreement that changed to surprise as Crowpaw rose to his paws and stepped forward, dipping his head to Tallstar in deepest respect. "May I ask something, Tallstar?" he mewed.

Tallstar nodded permission.

"I would like to choose my own warrior name," Crowpaw

continued. "If it is all right, I wish to be known as Crow-feather." His voice was so quiet that Onewhisker had to strain to hear him over the rushing of the waterfall. "I wish to keep alive the memory of . . . of the cat who did not return from the first journey."

Tallstar hesitated for a long time, so that Onewhisker wondered if Crowpaw had offended him. Then he responded. "A noble request. Very well, I name you Crowfeather. May Star-Clan protect you and accept you as a WindClan warrior in life as well as after."

A jolt passed through Onewhisker at what Tallstar had said. These weren't the words with which a Clan leader presented a new warrior to StarClan. Then his shock gave way to a chill that crept through his whole body.

Who knows whether StarClan is with us in this strange place? What if we've left them behind along with our old territories?

"Crowfeather! Crowfeather!" All the Clan cats, not only WindClan, yowled Crowfeather's new name, while the friends he had made on his journey gathered around to congratulate him.

But within a few heartbeats Crowfeather moved away from them. "I will sit my vigil tonight beside Feathertail's grave," he announced, then padded across the cave and disappeared down the path behind the waterfall.

As Onewhisker watched him go, he felt a weird prickling in his shoulders, and turned to see that Stoneteller was staring at him. The Tribe's healer beckoned him with a flick of his ears. "Follow," he meowed as Onewhisker picked his way through the crowd of cats to his side.

There was nothing Onewhisker could do but obey, though he couldn't imagine why Stoneteller had chosen him out of all the cats here. *What can he possibly have to say to me?*

He followed Stoneteller across the cavern and down one of the tunnels that led off from the back. For a few paw steps Onewhisker padded forward in utter darkness, the healer's scent leading him on. Then he saw Stoneteller's head outlined against a cold silver light seeping in from somewhere ahead.

"Welcome to the Cave of Pointed Stones," Stoneteller meowed.

Onewhisker stepped forward, and for a moment he could do nothing but stand frozen, with jaws gaping and eyes wide with awe.

The cave where he stood was much smaller than the cavern where the Tribe lived. The light of the full moon poured in through jagged gaps in the roof and was reflected by count-less pools on the cave floor. Stoneteller, who had turned to face him, was standing amid a forest of pointed stones: Some stretched down from the roof, like the ones in the main cav-ern, while others reached up from the floor; here and there the two joined together to form a stone tree. The roar of the waterfall was muted here, so that Onewhisker could hear the perpetual patter of water drops from above.

"Why have you brought me here?" he asked hoarsely.

Stoneteller beckoned him forward to join him among the glimmering pools. "This is where the Tribe of Endless Hunt-ing shows me signs," he replied.

Like our medicine cats talking with StarClan at the Moonstone, One-whisker thought, with a claw-scratch of regret as he realized that they had left the Moonstone far behind.

"I have a message for you," Stoneteller went on, "from the Tribe of Endless Hunting."

Onewhisker felt as if one of the pointed stones had left its place and jabbed him in the chest. "For *me*?" he gasped. "Are you sure that you don't want Tallstar, or maybe Mudclaw?"

Stoneteller shook his head emphatically. "No, this is a message for the cat currently called Onewhisker. You will be crucial to your Clan's survival in your new territory."

Still struggling with confusion, Onewhisker didn't dare ask Stoneteller if the Tribe of Endless Hunting might perhaps have gotten it wrong. He loved his Clan, but he had no wish for the survival of his Clan to depend on him alone. He preferred being an ordinary warrior, not important at all.

"I hope always to do my best for my Clan," he meowed.

Stoneteller dismissed that with an impatient flick of his tail. "There is something that must be done, and only you can do it," he declared. "You will know it, when it comes hunting you."

Onewhisker shuddered at the terrible suggestion behind Stoneteller's words. "What do you mean by 'comes hunting me'?" he asked, trying to keep his voice steady.

"That is all the Tribe of Endless Hunting has to say" was Stoneteller's only response.

That's not particularly helpful, Onewhisker thought as Stoneteller dismissed him and he made his way back to his

Clanmates in the main cave. Overwhelmed by the hugeness of the prediction, he hoped desperately that he could dismiss it. *After all, it came from the Tribe of Endless Hunting, not from StarClan.*

But Onewhisker couldn't manage to do that. The prophecy had the ring of truth about it. Something ominous was hanging over him, and he had a horrible feeling that all too soon the meaning of Stoneteller's words would become clear.

CHAPTER 13

Onewhisker stood a little way above the lake, drinking in the beauty of the vast stretch of water, and the hills and woods around it. His paws itched to explore; there would be plenty of places for the Clans to make their camps, and plenty of prey to be hunted without fear of Twolegs and their monsters. Most important, when they'd arrived the night before, every cat had seen the glory of StarClan spread across the sky and reflected in the clear waters of the lake.

Our warrior ancestors are with us. This is the place they meant for us to find.

After padding down to the lakeshore, Onewhisker soaked his tired paws in the water. For a moment he let go all the troubles he had left behind, and all the possible troubles to come, and just enjoyed the fresh, cool sensation.

If I'm not careful, I'll turn into a RiverClan cat!

Finally Onewhisker bowed his head to lap up a few mouthfuls, then hurried back to join the other cats. The Clan leaders were gathering around the tree stump from where they had addressed the Clans on the previous night, but Onewhisker couldn't see Tallstar among them. Then he spotted him curled up in the grass, with Barkface at his side, giving his fur a worried sniff.

Padding over toward his Clan leader, Onewhisker felt a pang of pity to see how weary Tallstar looked. His muzzle was gray with age, and all his ribs showed through his thin fur. His chest rose and fell convulsively as he struggled to breathe.

At least we reached the lake, Onewhisker thought. *That should make him happy. . . .* He reflected sadly that soon WindClan would have a new leader to go with their new home.

But "soon" isn't "now," he reminded himself. *For now, my job is to care for Tallstar.*

"You did it, Tallstar," he mewed quietly, stooping to touch his leader's ear with his nose. "You brought your Clan to safety."

Tallstar looked up at him, let out a feeble purr, then closed his eyes.

"I'll go and find out what's happening," Onewhisker told Barkface.

When he reached the tree stump, Onewhisker was shocked to see that Mudclaw had leaped onto it, beside Firestar and Blackstar, leaving no space for Leopardstar, who was sitting on a root.

Who does he think he is? Onewhisker asked himself, his anger beginning to rise as he found himself a place to sit a couple of tail-lengths away. The other Clan cats had gathered there, too, waiting to hear what the leaders had to say.

Firestar had begun to make an announcement, but before he could finish what he had to say, Mudclaw shoved him aside, interrupting him.

"Hunting patrols will go out right away," the deputy announced. "WindClan will take the hills and RiverClan can fish in the lake. ThunderClan—"

Onewhisker couldn't stand listening any longer. Springing to his paws, he let out a furious hiss. "Mudclaw, what are you doing, giving orders like this?" he growled. "The last time I looked, Tallstar was still leader of WindClan."

"Not for much longer," Mudclaw retorted, his voice cold. "Some cat has to take charge. Or do you want the other Clans to divide the territory among themselves and leave WindClan out?"

"As if we would!" The indignant protest came from Squirrelpaw.

Onewhisker could feel his shoulder fur begin to bristle. He wanted nothing more than to drag Mudclaw down from the stump and claw his ears until he learned how a deputy should speak of his Clan leader. But he knew he couldn't do that in front of the other Clans.

"Show a bit of respect!" he snarled, glaring at Mudclaw. "Tallstar was the leader of our Clan when you were a kit mewling in the nursery."

"I'm not a kit now," Mudclaw snapped. "I'm the deputy. And Tallstar hasn't done much to lead us since we left the forest."

"That's enough." Firestar waved his tail at Mudclaw, signing him to silence. "Onewhisker, I know you're worried about Tallstar. Mudclaw is only doing his duty."

Onewhisker took a deep breath, through his nostrils and down into his chest, trying to calm himself. "He needn't act like he's leader already," he growled. Half expecting a challenge, he let his gaze travel around the assembled cats, but no cat spoke.

"Onewhisker has a fair point," Firestar went on, turning to face Mudclaw. "It's difficult for a deputy to stand in for their leader—difficult for the rest of the Clan as well as for the deputy."

Onewhisker had seen how arrogantly pleased Mudclaw had looked while Firestar was defending him. Now his eyes widened into a glare of fury. He opened his jaws, but Blackstar spoke before he could get a word out.

"If WindClan has a problem over their leadership," the ShadowClan leader meowed, "let them discuss it in private. We're wasting time."

Mudclaw bared his teeth at Blackstar in an angry hiss, then pointedly turned his back.

Sighing deeply, Onewhisker made himself sit quietly and listen while Firestar held Squirrelpaw's warrior ceremony, naming her Squirrelflight. *That's a sign of hope for our new territory,* he thought as he yowled to welcome her as a warrior, along with the rest of the cats from all four Clans. *Finally we have the chance to live our lives peacefully here.*

Then his gaze rested once again on Mudclaw. *Why is he spoiling for a fight? Can't he defer to Tallstar for just a few more days? Then he'll have all he's ever wanted.*

Onewhisker padded down toward the lake, a bundle of moss in his jaws. Though his paw steps were swift, his heart was heavy. In the days since the Clans had arrived at the lake,

Tallstar had not recovered his strength. Instead he was slowly weakening. Barkface never left his side, and although the medicine cat had not said so, Onewhisker knew that Tallstar was ready to take his last long journey.

He was dipping the moss in the lake when he heard rapid paw steps behind him, and turned to see Barkface racing up to him.

"Tallstar is dying," the medicine cat panted. "He wants you."

There was so much Onewhisker wanted to ask, but time for none of it. Instead he gave Barkface a brief nod, then pelted up the slope from the lakeshore and headed for the gorse bush where they had made a den for Tallstar.

To Onewhisker's surprise, when he approached the gorse bush, he spotted Brambleclaw sitting outside; he rose to his paws as Onewhisker approached.

"Barkface said Tallstar's dying," Onewhisker gasped. "I only went to the lake to get him a drink."

"He wants to see you," Brambleclaw told him.

Onewhisker ducked under the gorse branches and into the space at the center of the bush. He was even more surprised to see that Firestar was there, sitting beside the dying leader.

When Onewhisker placed the dripping moss beside Tallstar's head, the leader roused a little, licked up a few drops, then began to speak.

"Before I go to StarClan, there is something I must do," he mewed, his voice sounding stronger than it had for many days. "Firestar, Onewhisker, listen. Mudclaw is a brave warrior, but he is not the right cat to lead WindClan. In these last moons we have learned that the future of our Clans lies in friendship. I want no rivalry between WindClan and ThunderClan after I am gone. We must have no enemies. But this will not happen if Mudclaw rules the Clan."

Feeling deeply uncomfortable, Onewhisker exchanged a glance with Firestar, reading his own uneasiness in the ThunderClan leader's green eyes. He knew that Tallstar's dream of friendship among the Clans was doomed, whoever WindClan's next leader might be.

We've always been rivals. . . . We always will be.

"I can still choose the cat who will lead WindClan after me." Tallstar's voice rasped in his throat, his strength fading in his effort to get the words out. "From this moment, Mudclaw is no longer deputy of WindClan."

Onewhisker could not suppress a gasp of shock. He had heard of Clan leaders dismissing a deputy before; that was how Firestar had become ThunderClan deputy, when Bluestar had exiled the treacherous Tigerclaw. *But not like this—not moments before the leader dies!*

"I say these words . . . before StarClan." Tallstar was struggling to speak now. "WindClan must have . . . a new deputy. Onewhisker, you must lead the Clan when I am gone."

Onewhisker stared at his Clan leader, appalled by what he had just heard. *Me? Great StarClan, I can't believe this! Why me? I never wanted this.* But he couldn't deny that Tallstar was right to have doubts about Mudclaw.

Stoneteller's prediction, that he would be crucial to his Clan's survival, came back into Onewhisker's mind. It all made sense now. *But I'm not a leader! How can I possibly be up to a task like that?*

He realized too that those were not even the right words to appoint a new deputy. *Will StarClan even accept me now?* Firestar looked just as shocked, his neck fur bristling and his claws flexing, tearing at the ground.

"Tallstar, *no*," Onewhisker protested.

Tallstar ignored him. His eyes seemed full of stars as he gazed from Onewhisker to Firestar and then to Brambleclaw. "I am grateful to have brought the Clan this far," he murmured. "Onewhisker, treat our friends well when you lead our Clan. Remember everything ThunderClan has done for us."

"Tallstar, I'll do my best, but . . . ," Onewhisker meowed.

He crouched, staring at his leader, his mind a chaos of emotion. It was all too easy to imagine what Mudclaw would say about this. *Will I have to fight him? No—I can't fight my Clanmate!* He remembered too what Stoneteller had told him: he would know the threat when it came hunting him. *Could that be Mudclaw?* he wondered. Stoneteller had also said that he would be important to his Clan—but Onewhisker had never imagined that meant he would become leader.

He stretched out a paw, but before he could touch Tallstar's shoulder, the Clan leader's eyes closed and his head slumped into the leaves and bracken of his nest. His breathing had grown fast and shallow.

Onewhisker felt himself surrounded on all sides, as if many other cats were pressing into the den. Then he heard a rustling behind him; he glanced over his shoulder to see Barkface slipping through the gorse branches, a leaf wrap of herbs in his jaws. "Cinderpelt gave me these," the medicine cat meowed, then let the herbs drop as he stared at Tallstar.

"It is too late for herbs," Firestar mewed.

The rapid rise and fall of Tallstar's chest had ceased. Onewhisker pushed his nose into his leader's fur, but Tallstar would not be roused ever again. His spirit had departed.

Onewhisker closed his eyes, struggling with bewilderment and a huge sense of loss, not only for the task ahead of him, but for the great leader who had just departed from WindClan.

"He walks with StarClan now," Barkface murmured.

CHAPTER 14

Onewhisker stood beside Firestar on top of the tree stump and gazed out at the cats crowding around. He wished he were anywhere but there, seeing the shock and sheer disbelief in the eyes of his Clanmates at the announcement Firestar had just made: that Tallstar, before his death, had dismissed Mudclaw and made Onewhisker his deputy. It all felt like a terrible dream.

Am I the right leader for WindClan? he asked himself helplessly. *How can I do this?* How could he convince his Clanmates that he was the right cat, when he wasn't sure himself?

Everything had happened so fast. He had no idea how he was supposed to lead his Clan into their new territory without Tallstar to guide him. He couldn't believe that this was really happening.

At least, Onewhisker reflected, *if I can't have Tallstar, I have Firestar to help me figure out how to be a leader. I couldn't do better than try to be like him.* But even as the thought went through his mind, he knew how hard it would be to become even a pale copy of the great Firestar.

And right there at the base of the stump was Mudclaw, glaring up at him and screeching his fury that the leadership had been snatched out of his claws at the last moment.

"You mean Mudclaw *isn't* our leader?" Webfoot asked, flexing his claws in confusion.

"Mouse dung to that!" Nightcloud snarled with a lash of her tail. "There's no cat better able to lead the Clan."

The last thing Onewhisker wanted was to argue, but he realized that if he didn't take control, this meeting could turn into a fight. His heart raced; he knew that the WindClan cats would never accept his leadership if he couldn't assert his authority now. Already he could see bristling fur and claws extended among the cats surrounding the stump.

Maybe there's a way to satisfy Mudclaw and my Clanmates, and still take leadership, like Tallstar wanted.

"This is as much of a shock to me as it is to you," he announced, looking down at Mudclaw. "And I would like you to carry on being WindClan's deputy. I'll need your support and experience every paw step of the way."

Mudclaw gathered himself as if he were going to leap up at Onewhisker and drag him from the stump. "You don't think I *believe* this load of fox dung, do you?" Every word was spat out. "Every cat knows that Tallstar practically handed our Clan over to Firestar before he left the forest. He's always felt more loyalty to ThunderClan than they ever deserved. And now Firestar tells us that his friend Onewhisker is to be leader! Did any other cat witness this convenient change of mind?"

As Brambleclaw stepped forward to tell what he had heard, panic began to swell inside Onewhisker so that he couldn't pay attention to the argument about what Tallstar said. He wondered once again how he would keep WindClan alive.

Why did Tallstar choose me?

Onewhisker remembered how Tallstar had once praised his judgment, but he knew he had none of Mudclaw's strength and aggression. And WindClan was vulnerable now, in this new place. They had to establish their new territory, and make decisions that would affect the future of the Clan for generations to come. Onewhisker couldn't help wondering if he would be the cat who allowed the great WindClan to falter. Mudclaw was ready for a brawl at the drop of a mousetail, but he certainly would have kept the Clan together.

Will I?

Onewhisker struggled to concentrate on what was happening in front of him: the argument still going on, Firestar hissing in fury beside him on the stump.

"Are you going to sit here and accept this?" Mudclaw demanded, spinning around to face his Clanmates. "Do we let ThunderClan choose our leader for us?" Whipping back to glare at Onewhisker, he added, "How many of our warriors do you think will follow you, you sniveling crow-food-eating traitor?"

Traitor? The word made Onewhisker's fur begin to bush out with anger. He knew he was not a traitor. He had taken better care of their ailing leader than any other warrior, and he had served Tallstar nobly until his dying breath. He opened his mouth to throw the accusation back in Mudclaw's face, but before he could speak, Crowfeather padded forward to stand at the base of the stump.

"I will follow Onewhisker," he announced. "I made the journey to the sun-drown-place with Brambleclaw, and I know he does not lie. If he says that Tallstar made Onewhisker deputy before he went to hunt with StarClan, then I believe him. Onestar, I greet you as the leader of my Clan."

Overcome with gratitude, Onewhisker dipped his head toward the young warrior. Around the stump, several of the Clan began to chant, "Onestar! Onestar!" Some of them sounded doubtful, while others, like Mudclaw and Nightcloud, clamped their jaws together and refused to chant.

Even so, Onewhisker felt himself grow calmer, his fur beginning to lie flat again. *At least some of my Clanmates will accept me.* But after a few moments, he realized that the name sounded wrong. He raised his tail for silence, and the voices died away uncertainly.

"Thank you," Onewhisker mewed to Crowfeather. "But don't call me Onestar yet. I haven't received my nine lives or my name from StarClan."

His ears felt hot with embarrassment as he wondered whether StarClan would accept him, even though Tallstar hadn't spoken the right words to make him deputy. *And how am I going to speak with StarClan at the Moonstone, now that we're so far away?*

"And you never will!" Mudclaw snarled. "You are not our leader! Come down here and fight me if you dare. Then we'll see who'll make the better leader for WindClan."

Onewhisker braced himself, but before he could leap down, he was halted by an outraged cry from Barkface.

"Stop!" the medicine cat yowled. "Sheathe your claws, Mud-claw. Clan leaders have never been chosen by fighting. And do you want to start a fight while Tallstar's spirit is still watching over us? We should be sitting in vigil for him, not bickering over who will take his place. You betray him by behaving like this. He always expected the best from his senior warriors." Barkface paused, gazing at Firestar, then continued, "I believe what the ThunderClan cats tell us. This was Tallstar's choice, and you must accept it."

While Barkface was speaking, Mudclaw's fur gradually flattened and he sheathed his claws. "Very well," he growled. He looked up at Onewhisker, who barely managed not to take a step back, he was so shocked by the hatred in Mudclaw's eyes. "You're brave enough with your ThunderClan friends there to back you up. But if you think I'll serve as your deputy, you're wrong."

Onewhisker felt massively relieved, though he did his best not to show it. He had felt obliged to offer Mudclaw the post of deputy, but he had dreaded having to work with him. "Very well," he meowed, dipping his head. "I'm sorry if that's your decision."

Mudclaw spat, then turned away to join Barkface and some of the other warriors as they went to carry Tallstar's body out for his vigil.

As Onewhisker began to relax, Firestar leaned close to him and mewed quietly into his ear. "Onewhisker, you have to appoint another deputy. *Now*. You can't lead this Clan alone, and you will need all the support you can get if Mudclaw decides to make things difficult."

Onewhisker knew exactly what the ThunderClan leader was saying. *I'm vulnerable now. I don't imagine Mudclaw will let this rest.*

He closed his eyes, thinking deeply. It occurred to him that he could choose Crowfeather, who was an outstanding young cat. But he was *too* young, barely a warrior, and he was too friendly with the cats from the other Clans who had made the first journey with him.

What I need is an experienced warrior, one WindClan will trust.

Onewhisker opened his eyes and let his gaze travel over his waiting Clanmates, wondering who would be most loyal, and who would serve the Clan best. Eventually his gaze fell on his littermate Ashfoot. *She's quiet, sensible, loyal . . . I couldn't do better.*

Pausing for a moment, Onewhisker fixed the right words in his mind before he began to speak. "I say these words before the spirit of Tallstar, and the spirits of all StarClan, that they may hear and approve my choice. Ashfoot will be the new deputy of WindClan."

His sister stared up at him with a look of complete shock on her face, her jaws gaping. She stood like a cat made of stone until Crowfeather let out a joyful yowl and bounded over to press his muzzle to hers.

"Ashfoot! Ashfoot!" the remaining WindClan warriors chanted, sounding really enthusiastic this time.

Onewhisker let out a long sigh. *I've chosen well.*

He leaped down from the stump, and Ashfoot padded up to touch noses with him. "Thank you, Onewhisker," she mewed. "I'll do my best. I never imagined—"

"I know." Onewhisker gave his sister's ear a quick lick. "That's one reason why I chose you. I don't want a cat who thinks they deserve power. I want a cat who will help me make our Clan strong again when we reach our new home."

While he was speaking, Onewhisker saw Barkface and the others returning with Tallstar's body, and became uncomfortably aware that Mudclaw was staring at him. *He must have heard the Clan acclaiming Ashfoot.*

"Then that is what I will do," Ashfoot purred, quietly confident.

Onewhisker felt satisfied that he had made the right choice. There was so much to do; to begin with they would have to mark out WindClan's new territory and find a good place for their camp. He could rely on Ashfoot's help.

The one thing that still worried him was how he would get to the Moonstone to receive his nine lives and his new name. Even if Mudclaw accepted his leadership for the time being, Onewhisker would never feel confident until he was officially made leader by StarClan. *Besides,* he thought, *if I can get back to the forest, I could find Smoke and Darkkit and maybe lead them to the lake.* WindClan couldn't possibly accept them now, not after so much turmoil, but maybe in time they could.

"How will I get my name and my nine lives, Firestar?" Onewhisker asked, turning to the ThunderClan leader. "There's no Moonstone here. Do you think I should take some of my warriors and go back through the mountains to Highstones?"

"I think that's the most mouse-brained thing you could do," Firestar replied with a twitch of his tail. "The journey there and back would take nearly a moon. And Mudclaw wouldn't be sitting on his paws doing nothing while you were away; that's for sure."

Onewhisker knew that Firestar was right. *Maybe it will be possible later, when we're settled.* Meanwhile, until the Clans could find a new Moonstone, he would have to accept that his leadership wouldn't be secure.

The WindClan cats, and some from the other Clans, were gathering around Tallstar's body. It was time for his vigil to begin. Struggling to put aside his worries about his new authority, Onewhisker padded over to join them and took his place crouching beside his dead leader. At the sight of Tallstar's body, looking so small and shrunken in death, an unexpected wave of grief swept over him, leaving him trembling inwardly.

You put me in an impossible position, Tallstar. But oh, great StarClan, I'm going to miss you!

As Onewhisker looked around the new WindClan camp, a sense of satisfaction seeped through his pelt, stronger than the pale sun of leaf-bare. He had hardly dared hope that his Clan would find a place to live that would be just as good as the camp they had left in their old territory. But this shallow scoop in the moorland above the lake was already starting to feel like home.

The hollow was dotted with boulders; his Clanmates were already beginning to call the biggest of them the Tallrock, and Onewhisker had decided it was where he would make announcements. The elders were making their den in an old badger set, long unoccupied. A thick tangle of gorse bushes sheltered the nursery, while the warriors and apprentices had their own places to sleep in the open. Barkface had made his den inside a large crack in a rock at the edge of the camp; there was plenty of space to store his supplies and even to allow one or two sick cats to stay under his eye.

We could have done a good deal worse, Onewhisker thought.

Not far away, Ashfoot was sorting out the day's hunting patrols, as efficient as Onewhisker had known she would be. Already the Clan was getting to know the new territory, and the prey was running well.

But as he watched, Onewhisker became aware of some unfriendly glances cast in his direction. He knew that Mudclaw was still angry with him, but he was disconcerted to find that other cats too were sharing the former deputy's resentment. The day before, he had given some of their territory to ThunderClan, because their medicine-cat apprentice, Leafpaw, had brought healing herbs for WindClan's sick elders; it had not been a popular decision.

If only they could see it was the right thing to do, Onewhisker thought, twitching his tail-tip irritably. *That bit of land is covered in trees and undergrowth; it's far more use to ThunderClan than it would ever be to us.*

Besides, allowing ThunderClan to take that stretch of territory would secure WindClan's friendship with Firestar. The ThunderClan leader had been supportive of Onewhisker's leadership so far, and Onewhisker felt he was learning new things every day about being in charge of his Clan. The only thing that worried him was that no cat had so far found a new Moonstone near the lake. Onewhisker couldn't feel like his Clan's true leader until he had StarClan's blessing.

"Mudclaw, you can lead the last patrol," Ashfoot was meowing when Onewhisker emerged from his thoughts. "Tornear and Owlpaw will go with you. Take them down to the ThunderClan border. There are some tunnel openings down there; it might be a good place for rabbits."

"Just as long as they're not *ThunderClan* rabbits," Mudclaw sneered. "We wouldn't want to steal Firestar's prey, would we?"

Onewhisker took a breath to speak, then clamped his jaws shut. That wasn't an argument he wanted to get into.

A moment later, Mudclaw had swung around toward him, a truculent expression on his face. "When was the last time you hunted for the Clan, Onewhisker?" he demanded, "You're getting out of shape and lazy just hanging around the camp all day. If you're so eager to give away our territory, maybe you need to learn all over again how challenging it is to hunt."

"Mudclaw, that's enough!" Ashfoot snapped, but the former deputy ignored her.

All Onewhisker's instincts told him to throw the insult back in Mudclaw's face, but he knew how stupid that would be. Instead he was determined to show Mudclaw he could be a good leader. He rose calmly to his paws. "It's fine, Ashfoot," he meowed. "It will be my honor to hunt alongside my Clan-mates."

Ashfoot nodded. "Okay."

Onewhisker waved his tail, indicating to Mudclaw that he should take the lead, and the patrol headed off toward the ThunderClan border. As they drew close to the trees, Onewhisker could already pick up the scent of the ThunderClan border markers.

The cats emerged from a gorse thicket to see a stretch of flat ground ahead of them, ending in a steep bank full of the holes Ashfoot had mentioned. Here and there Onewhisker spotted rabbits out to feed, many fox-lengths from their burrows. They were hopping around freely, not a single one of them looking over its shoulder.

They don't know yet that they have to beware of hunting cats!

Onewhisker picked out a plump rabbit and began to creep up on it. There wasn't much cover, so he flattened himself to the ground, trusting that his tabby pelt would blend into the brownish green of the moorland grass. The wind was blowing toward him, carrying the succulent scent of prey.

He had almost reached the right distance for a pounce when he heard a sudden rush of paw steps, and Mudclaw appeared alongside him. The rabbit squealed in terror and bolted for its burrow. Onewhisker let out an annoyed hiss as he saw its white tail disappearing into the darkness.

"What did you do that for?" he demanded, glaring at Mudclaw. "Couldn't you see that I almost had it?"

Mudclaw waved his tail dismissively. "There are other rabbits. I need a talk with you."

Does it have to be right now? Onewhisker thought resentfully. *Mudclaw was blaming me for being too lazy to hunt, and now he's stopping me from catching prey for the Clan.* Then he realized that at least Mudclaw wanted to talk; that was much better than working things out with claws and teeth. He sat up and wrapped his tail around his paws. "Okay. Talk."

Mudclaw paced up and down a few times before crouching to face Onewhisker, a tail-length away. "Now that we're alone," he began, "I want to appeal to your love of your Clan. I've always known you as a loyal WindClan warrior . . . right?"

Onewhisker stared at the former deputy. *What is he getting at?* "Right," he replied at last. "Of course. I care about my Clan more than anything."

"Then do you *truly* believe," Mudclaw continued, narrowing his eyes, "that of the two of us, you're more likely to keep WindClan safe?"

Now Onewhisker understood where this was going. Disappointment wrapped around him like freezing fog. Mudclaw didn't want to talk things out; instead the former deputy was appealing to his conscience in a bid to make him give up the leadership. "Tallstar—" he began.

"I'm not talking about Tallstar," Mudclaw interrupted. "I'm talking about what *we* know, between the two of us. I've been planning to lead WindClan my whole life. Our Clanmates respect me. Even cats from other Clans respect me. And I have no strange . . . associations that might put our Clan in danger."

Onewhisker felt an unpleasant prickling in his pads. "'Associations'?" he asked. *Can Mudclaw possibly know about Smoke and Darkkit?*

"You know what I mean," Mudclaw snarled. "It's obvious that Firestar is very fond of you—too fond, in my opinion."

Onewhisker drew himself up. "Your *opinion* doesn't matter in the slightest," he retorted. "Tallstar made me deputy when he was dying, and Tallstar was chosen by StarClan."

And Firestar gave me much more help than Mudclaw, even though he's from a different Clan, Onewhisker added to himself. *He seems to care more about WindClan's future.*

"But *you* haven't been chosen," Mudclaw pointed out. "How are we to know that you're WindClan's leader when StarClan hasn't approved?"

"When I've been granted my nine lives, every cat will know," Onewhisker replied. "And I know I will be, just as soon as we find another Moonstone." To his annoyance, he couldn't stop his voice from trembling slightly, and he knew Mudclaw must have noticed.

What if we never find another Moonstone? What if we do, and Star-Clan doesn't want me as leader? I never asked for this—unlike Mudclaw, who really has been planning for it his whole life. So how can I be a good leader? How can StarClan give me its blessing? He lay awake at night, worrying about just that, but he knew he had to look confident in front of Mudclaw and the rest of the Clan. *I just wish I knew more about why Tallstar chose me.*

Mudclaw tilted his head, scanning Onewhisker with an insolent gaze. "Are you sure?" he asked. "Because my main concern is WindClan, and whether WindClan will still be around by the time your nine lives come through. *If* they ever do. Until then, Onewhisker, you're not a real leader. Half the

Clan doubts you. In fact, if I challenged you, you might be surprised at how quickly your support would fall apart."

Rage was swelling inside Onewhisker as he listened to the mottled brown tom. As Mudclaw finished speaking, he couldn't control himself any longer. He flung himself at the former deputy, striking out blindly with all four paws.

His claws raked through Mudclaw's pelt, but a moment later he felt his legs hooked out from under him. Mudclaw pinned him to the ground with a paw clamped on his neck. Onewhisker managed to turn his head and saw the gleam of his adversary's amber eyes and his teeth bared in a snarl.

"I won't challenge you now. That would be too easy," Mudclaw hissed into his ear. "But I'll be watching you. I'm willing to do whatever it takes to save the Clan."

He jumped back; Onewhisker stood up and shook out his ruffled pelt. *What now?* he wondered as he watched Mudclaw race away to join Tornear and his apprentice.

He had to believe that Mudclaw was bluffing. Onewhisker had his Clan's support, at least outwardly. *Once I get my nine lives from StarClan, I'll be safe.* Even if Mudclaw was right that he was the cat the Clan wanted, no cat could argue with a leader who had StarClan's blessing. Onewhisker knew he just had to be patient and hope he would get his nine lives soon.

I can work out what to do about Mudclaw then.

Onewhisker was sharing a rabbit with Ashfoot in the center of the WindClan camp. Several days had passed since his confrontation with Mudclaw, and since then the former deputy had kept himself to himself, carrying out his warrior duties as willingly as any cat. But Onewhisker didn't imagine that he had given up the idea of challenging him for the leadership.

He looked up and spotted Mudclaw at the top of the hollow, along with Webfoot and his apprentice, Weaselpaw. They were escorting Leafpaw; there was energy in her paw steps and her eyes were sparkling, sending a quiver of anticipation through Onewhisker.

Swallowing his mouthful of prey, he rose to his paws as the medicine cat apprentice approached him. "What can we do for you, Leafpaw?" he asked.

"I need to speak to Barkface," Leafpaw replied.

Onewhisker felt even more certain that something momentous was about to happen. "A message from Star-Clan?" he asked, pricking his ears. Leafpaw nodded. "That's great news!" Onewhisker continued. "Weaselpaw, go and ask Barkface to come right away."

The apprentice dashed off and reappeared a moment later with the medicine cat. Leafpaw bounded over to him and sat beside him. Onewhisker could see that words were tumbling out of her, but she was too far away for him to hear what she was saying. He flexed his claws impatiently in the ground, aware of Mudclaw standing nearby. He shot a glance at him, but he was unable to read the mottled brown tom's expression.

More cats had begun to gather around; Onewhisker was aware of a buzz of excitement among them as they waited to find out what Leafpaw's message was. He could hear murmurs of speculation passing from one cat to another.

Finally Barkface rose to his paws and padded over to where Onewhisker and Ashfoot were waiting, surrounded by the rest of the Clan.

"Good news," he began. "The best news I've heard for a long time."

"Then tell us," Onewhisker meowed. "Come on, we're all ears!"

"Last night, StarClan guided Leafpaw into the hills," Barkface began. "She found a pool fed by a waterfall, in a hollow guarded by thornbushes. The path down to the pool was dented by the paw steps of other cats who had been there long, long before us. And there, beside the pool, the spirits of our warrior ancestors met with Leafpaw. They told her that this was the place where she and the other medicine cats must come to share tongues with StarClan."

"So there's no Moonstone?" Mudclaw snapped out.

Barkface shook his head. "No, this place has been shown to Leafpaw instead of the Moonstone. Tomorrow night, all the medicine cats will meet at the Moonpool," he continued. "The night after that, Onewhisker, you and I will go together so that you can receive your nine lives and your leader's name."

For a moment Onewhisker felt almost overwhelmed by what Barkface had told him. *We have a place to communicate with StarClan here—now all we need is a place to hold our Gatherings, and this lake will truly feel like home!* The Clans had discussed many places, including the island close to WindClan's lakeshore, but none felt quite right yet. Onewhisker tried to imagine receiving his nine lives. He had been waiting for this moment, but now that it was here, it was daunting to think that so soon, he would have to face up to the question of whether StarClan really would accept him as a leader. Then he shook his head, blinking. *This is no time to start losing my nerve!*

Gradually a warm sensation of confidence and joy spread through his pelt, so that he found he could relax. "From what Leafpaw told you, it's a long journey," he meowed. "You can't travel there twice in two days; you'll be worn out. I've waited this long for my nine lives and my name; I can wait a while longer."

As Leafpaw withdrew, arranging to meet Barkface for the medicine cats' half-moon gathering on the following night, Onewhisker became aware that Mudclaw was watching him. He remembered that only a few days before, a fox had attacked the WindClan camp. Onewhisker had watched it race down into the hollow, heading straight for him; it had taken a sharp tussle, with Ashfoot and Crowfeather to help, to drive it out.

Thinking it over now, Onewhisker was sure that Mudclaw had seen the fox before it attacked. But he had done nothing to warn him. *It could have killed me. Mudclaw was probably hoping it would!* Onewhisker hated to think that Mudclaw would be capable of such disloyalty, but there was no way to ignore the hatred in his eyes.

Yet, for all his suspicions, Onewhisker had to believe that Mudclaw would respect StarClan's authority. Once he had his nine lives, Onewhisker was sure he could work on healing the Clan from within.

When Leafpaw had left, the Clan began to disperse to their

duties. Ashfoot, who had sat quietly by while Barkface passed on Leafpaw's news, rose to her paws. "Walk with me, One-whisker," she mewed. "There's something I need to tell you."

Blinking in surprise, Onewhisker padded beside his deputy as she climbed the slope out of the hollow. She said nothing more until they were out on the moor with the wind blowing through their fur and no other cat in sight.

"There's something you need to know," Ashfoot told him. "Some cats have reported seeing Mudclaw hanging around with Hawkfrost."

Onewhisker would have found that hard to believe, if it hadn't been the sensible, practical Ashfoot telling him. "Whatever could Mudclaw want with him?" he asked.

"I don't know," Ashfoot replied. "But I'm afraid they're up to something,"

Thinking it over, Onewhisker could see that his deputy might well be right. Hawkfrost had once been the RiverClan deputy, when Twolegs had taken Mistyfoot, back in the old forest. But Mistyfoot had returned and reclaimed her old place in the Clan. Onewhisker could imagine that Hawkfrost hadn't been entirely happy about that.

Two cats thwarted in their search for power . . .

"Try not to worry," he reassured Ashfoot. "I know Mud-claw, and I'm prepared for whatever he might try."

Ashfoot gave a doubtful twitch of her ears. Privately, One-whisker was doubtful too. He remembered the time he and Mudclaw had scuffled near the ThunderClan border, and how easily Mudclaw had beaten him. He wondered whether he could ever overcome Mudclaw with teeth and claws. *If I pinned him first? If I attacked him from behind?* He knew he would have no hope at all if Hawkfrost was fighting on Mudclaw's side.

Stoneteller's words echoed in his head. *When it comes hunting you . . .*

"There's something else," Ashfoot meowed.

Onewhisker gave her an inquiring look, but for a few heartbeats his deputy said nothing. She was staring at her paws, and he realized that she was embarrassed.

"Come on, spit it out," he meowed.

"Back in the old territory . . . ," Ashfoot began hesitantly, "there was talk among some of the warriors. A kittypet kept approaching the borders. Some cats said that she was asking for you."

No! Onewhisker cringed inwardly at the memory of how some of his Clanmates had seen Smoke and heard her asking to see him. He remembered too that he still hadn't kept his promise to go back for her and Darkkit. His chest and throat tightened, and he felt he wanted to vomit.

"I saw her once, after she'd been turned away," Ashfoot continued. "She looked so forlorn, I had to go after her. She told me that her name was Smoke, and she had a new kit." She hesitated, then took a breath before she continued, clearly forcing herself to go on. "She said you were the kit's father, Onewhisker."

Onewhisker felt as if all his strength were draining out through his pads. He couldn't meet his sister's eyes.

"It's true, then," Ashfoot mewed.

Ice-cold shivers ran through Onewhisker from ears to tail-tip. "Please don't tell Whitetail," he begged desperately. "It was before we were mates, but still, I could never hurt her like that."

"Neither could I," Ashfoot replied. "But you must realize, a secret like this—it leaves you vulnerable."

Onewhisker knew that his littermate was right. "I don't know why Tallstar chose me," he meowed, the words pouring out of him. "I'm far from the perfect leader for WindClan. I'm no Firestar."

"You're no *Tallstar*," Ashfoot corrected him gently. "Just stop with this Firestar business. Maybe you're not the perfect leader now," she added hastily, "but you will be. You could be."

Onewhisker closed his eyes. "I hope you're right," he sighed. "I feel I have to hang on, to fulfill Tallstar's dying wish. But it's so hard. . . ."

"Come on, Onewhisker—pull yourself together." Ashfoot's tones were vigorous. "You're right about one thing," she continued. "Tallstar chose you to lead WindClan, and soon StarClan will approve you, too. What StarClan decides, no cat can question."

"I hope so," Onewhisker responded. "I don't feel like a leader, though. I never have."

"You *will*." Ashfoot held him compellingly in her gaze. "You *must*. Tallstar was chosen by StarClan, and he saw something in you—something that can make you the right leader for WindClan."

"I know," Onewhisker whispered. He only hoped that he could make it to his nine lives ceremony with his beloved Clan still intact.

The night was dark, the light of moon and stars showing fitfully through thick clouds that shouldered their way across the sky, driven by a blustering wind. Onewhisker could smell the tang of rain, and guessed there would be a storm shortly.

He was crouching in the lee of a rock, eating a lapwing and trying to show a calm and confident demeanor for the sake of his Clan. Inwardly he was anything but calm. His belly was churning with tension as he tried to work out how much time still had to pass before he could go to the Moonpool to be made a leader in the sight of StarClan.

The night before, Barkface had met there with the other medicine cats. *So if I can make it through this night, and the following day . . .* That shouldn't even have been a question, but Onewhisker couldn't forget what Mudclaw had said: that he was willing to do whatever he must to save the Clan. He tried to tell himself that there was no need to worry about the former deputy's threats. *I've tried to prove myself. . . .* But Mudclaw had looked so determined when he had confronted him beside the rabbit burrows. Onewhisker couldn't imagine that he would give up.

A sudden yowl split the darkness, followed instantly by another. Onewhisker shot to his paws. Gazing around wildly, he spotted shadowy shapes pouring over the edge of the hollow. Scuffles were already breaking out with WindClan warriors on the outskirts of the camp.

"No!" Onewhisker screeched.

All his worst nightmares were coming true. He braced himself to leap into the battle, but it was already too late. Mudclaw stood in front of him, his fur bushed out until he looked twice his size, then hurled himself at Onewhisker, bearing him off his paws. Onewhisker struggled to shove Mudclaw off him and stand, only to feel another cat clawing him from behind.

Onewhisker twisted his head around to see Webfoot, and beyond him a muscular gray tom, gathering himself to pounce. *But that's . . . Cedarheart! What is a ShadowClan cat doing here?*

Mudclaw thrust his face next to Onewhisker's. "Are you ready to give up?" he demanded. Raising one paw, he raked his claws across Onewhisker's face; Onewhisker could feel the blood beginning to trickle down. "We both know who's the right leader for WindClan," Mudclaw hissed. "Tallstar might not have realized it, but *we* do!"

Onewhisker snarled defiance at the former deputy, making another massive effort to throw him off. Suddenly Whitetail appeared, a pale blur in the darkness; she leaped onto Mudclaw's back, digging in her claws, and bent her head to sink her teeth into his neck.

Mudclaw let out a shriek that pierced Onewhisker's ears. His weight abruptly vanished as Whitetail dragged him off.

Gasping with relief, Onewhisker leaped to his paws and spun around to tackle Webfoot. "WindClan! To me!" he yowled.

The battle was raging all around him. Onewhisker fought

furiously, too busy trying to stay alive to work out what was happening. He had lost sight of Mudclaw, but Hawkfrost of RiverClan was tackling Ashfoot, while Whitetail faced up to Nightcloud, and Crowfeather was tussling fiercely with a ShadowClan cat.

How can I win this battle? Onewhisker asked himself despairingly. *Mudclaw has brought in so many cats from other Clans!*

Then a fresh chorus of yowling broke out, and more dark shapes leaped down into the hollow. For a heartbeat Onewhisker was ready to surrender, until he glimpsed a flash of flame-colored fur and realized that these cats were not his enemies. Firestar was in the lead, with more ThunderClan cats, including Brambleclaw, and Mistyfoot from RiverClan.

Thank StarClan! They're fighting on our side!

As Onewhisker gazed at his new allies, agony exploded in his shoulder; he let out a screech as he felt the gush of blood. Forcing his head around, he saw that Webfoot had dived in and sunk his claws into his shoulder. *Mouse-brain!* Onewhisker thought ruefully through the haze of pain. *The middle of a battle is no place to get distracted!* Unsteady on his paws, he still spun around and lashed out at his treacherous Clanmate.

At that moment lightning forked down the sky, like a silver branch bathing the moor in a weird pale light. Onewhisker caught a glimpse of Mudclaw and Hawkfrost outlined at the top of the hollow. Then the light was gone; in its place thunder crashed, echoing around the hills, and rain fell like a torrent, plastering Onewhisker's fur to his body within heartbeats.

A yowl rang out from above the camp. Onewhisker looked up to see Mudclaw and Hawkfrost flee, while a couple of

ShadowClan warriors pelted off in the opposite direction.

"Go after them!" Brambleclaw growled at Crowfeather, lashing his tail toward the ShadowClan cats.

As the young warrior dashed away in pursuit, Brambleclaw took off after Mudclaw and Hawkfrost. With the leaders of the rebellion gone, the rest of the fighting began to break up, the cats standing with bowed heads in the driving rain, or tottering about in search of shelter.

Overcome by the pain in his shoulder, Onewhisker sank to the ground. Immediately Whitetail was beside him. "Barkface, come here!" she called. "Quickly!"

"Don't . . . ," Onewhisker gasped. "It doesn't matter. . . . I don't deserve help. I don't deserve you."

Whitetail pressed her muzzle to his face. "You stupid furball, have you got bees in your brain?"

Before Onewhisker could respond, Barkface was there with a pawful of cobwebs. "At least this StarClan-cursed rain will get your wounds clean," he grunted, beginning to plaster the sticky stuff over Onewhisker's injured shoulder.

Onewhisker closed his eyes, but as soon as he did, he saw Mudclaw lunging at him. "I was too blind to see what was right in front of me," he muttered. "I knew Mudclaw was dangerous, but I didn't see the attack coming. . . ."

"Be quiet and let Barkface treat you," Whitetail urged him. "It's over for now."

"I should have chased Mudclaw," Onewhisker mewed, wincing. "I have to stop relying on ThunderClan and be my own leader."

He tried to relax under Barkface's skillful paws, while

around them the storm still raged on. He was half dozing when paw steps splashed up to him, and he looked up to see Firestar.

"Are you okay?" the ThunderClan leader asked.

Onewhisker nodded wearily. "Fine. Thank you for coming to help."

"The least we could do," Firestar responded. "Are you fit to walk as far as the lake? You need to see the end of this."

Onewhisker rose to his paws and, with Ashfoot at his side, followed Firestar down the hill and along the lakeshore toward RiverClan territory. Brambleclaw and Squirrelflight were there; as Onewhisker padded toward them, a blue-white blaze of lightning lit up the sky and outlined another cat standing on the shore near the island.

"That's Mudclaw!" Onewhisker gasped. "But where is Hawkfrost?"

His words were drowned by a deafening crash coming from the island. Flame spurted up briefly from one of the trees there. Slowly it began to topple with a groaning sound as its roots were wrenched out of the ground.

For a heartbeat Mudclaw stared at it, transfixed. Then he whipped around to flee, but he was too late. The tree fell faster and faster; Mudclaw's terrified screech was lost in the rattling of the branches as they thumped down on the shore.

"Mudclaw!" Ashfoot cried. "Is he dead?"

Firestar shook his head. "I'm not sure."

Onewhisker stared at the place where the former deputy had been. *No cat could survive that,* he thought.

As if it was satisfied with the destruction it had caused, the storm grumbled off across the distant hills. The rain gradually eased and the wind tore gaps in the clouds, letting the moon and stars shed a feeble light over the scene.

With Brambleclaw in the lead, Onewhisker and the other cats headed toward the fallen tree. But before they reached it, there was movement among the branches. A tabby warrior was backing out, struggling to stay on his paws as he slipped on the waterlogged ground. For one horrible moment Onewhisker thought it was Mudclaw, surviving to continue this pointless battle. Then he recognized Hawkfrost; the River-Clan warrior was tugging Mudclaw's limp body by the scruff, freeing him from the tree branches and dragging him along, limbs and tail trailing, until he could let him drop at Onewhisker's paws.

"The tree crushed him," Hawkfrost meowed. "Your leadership is safe."

Bending his head, Onewhisker sniffed at his enemy's body. A vast regret swept over him, threatening to overwhelm him. *He could have given so much to his Clan.*

Then he reminded himself that he was a leader, and he needed to set an example. He took a deep breath. "The Clan will grieve for him," he murmured. "He was a fine warrior once."

At his side, Ashfoot let out a hiss. "He betrayed you!"

"As did you!" Onewhisker growled at Hawkfrost while he slid out his claws, ready for the tabby warrior to attack him. "You helped him."

To his surprise, Hawkfrost bowed his head. "I admit it," he confessed, "and I ask your forgiveness. I truly believed that Mudclaw was the rightful leader of WindClan, and because of that, at his request, I brought cats from RiverClan and ShadowClan to help him. But StarClan has given us a clear sign by sending the lightning to destroy Mudclaw. One-whisker, you are WindClan's true leader, chosen by StarClan. Do with me what you will."

Onewhisker was unprepared to have the decision thrown at his paws like Mudclaw's body. He glanced at Firestar, but the ThunderClan leader merely flicked his ears, clearly unwilling to offer advice.

This is your time to be a leader, Onewhisker told himself.

Meanwhile Ashfoot had padded up to investigate the fallen tree, sniffing at its branches. "Hawkfrost is right, One-whisker," she meowed. "You couldn't hope for a better sign than this. StarClan sent lightning to strike the tree and kill the cat who would have taken your place. There's no doubt now that you are the cat StarClan has chosen to lead Wind-Clan."

Hearing the certainty in his deputy's voice, Onewhisker couldn't suppress a flutter of surprise. Right up to the end, he had doubted that he could beat Mudclaw. Now he realized that the last threat to his leadership of WindClan had vanished. The world seemed to tilt, and he dug his claws into the ground.

"Lead!" Onewhisker seemed to hear Tallstar's voice speaking to him from a great distance. "Use your judgment!"

I could tear Hawkfrost to shreds, Onewhisker told himself. *Plenty of cats would back me up. I could punish or exile the WindClan cats who fought on Mudclaw's side. But what would I gain from that? What would WindClan gain?*

He raised his head. "Then I shall be honored to accept my nine lives," he meowed. To Hawkfrost he added, "I can't blame you for having doubts, nor any of the other cats who supported Mudclaw. How can I, when I doubted myself? I forgive you freely, you and all the rest."

Hawkfrost dipped his head in gratitude.

Meanwhile, several more cats had made their way to the lakeside, gathering around Onewhisker and Firestar and investigating the fallen tree. One of them—Onewhisker recognized Brackenfur from ThunderClan—leaped up onto the trunk and padded a few paces toward the island.

"Look at this!" he meowed.

"It's like a Twoleg bridge!" Mistyfoot exclaimed.

Brackenfur returned and sprang down onto the pebbles, his eyes wide with excitement. "We can use the fallen tree to reach the island," he announced. "It's wide enough for all of us to cross safely. We can use it for Gatherings after all!"

More of the cats crowded around, letting out *mrrows* of excitement and approval. One or two leaped up onto the trunk, trying out their balance.

Onewhisker felt a huge sense of satisfaction rising in his chest. Now the Clans had all they needed: a special place to meet with StarClan, and a place, seemingly approved by Star-Clan, where they could meet each other. *This is truly the home our ancestors intended for us.*

Beyond the cats and the tree, Onewhisker could see a rosy

glow on the horizon, and as he watched, the glittering edge of the sun appeared, shedding golden light over the rain-sodden landscape. A new day had begun.

WindClan is still together, Onewhisker reminded himself. *I almost lost it all, but I didn't. Now I must become the leader WindClan needs. And I will.*

He had survived. And he promised himself that WindClan would do the same. Nothing was more important than his Clan.

CHAPTER 15

The sky was clear, with a swelling moon and the whole swath of Silverpelt to shed light over the hills. Onewhisker trudged up a steep moorland slope; the ground felt spongy under his paws after the heavy rain of two nights before.

Barkface padded along at his side. "Are you sure you're up for this, Onewhisker?" he asked. "It's a long way to the Moonpool, and I think that shoulder wound is still giving you trouble."

"I'm fine, Barkface," Onewhisker replied. In fact, the wound Webfoot had given him in the battle was sending deep pulses of pain down his shoulder and into his leg, but he didn't intend to let that stop him. "I've waited too long for my nine lives and my name. I'm not going to wait any longer."

But he couldn't entirely silence the tiny voice at the back of his mind. *What if—in spite of everything—Tallstar made a mistake and StarClan doesn't want me after all?*

He told himself, as he plodded along beside Barkface, that if StarClan really did reject him, he could always go back to the old forest and find Smoke and Darkkit. But if he was being honest with himself, he had to admit that he hadn't thought much about them since the night of the battle. He felt a twinge of shame, as if he had trodden on a thorn, but he tried to convince himself that with all the troubles WindClan had suffered, his former mate and his son must be better off where they were.

With the Clan cats gone, prey must be running well in what was left of the old territories. But Onewhisker expected that Smoke would have found another Twoleg to take in her and her kit. That would be better for every cat. *Kittypets don't do well in the Clans—well, except for Firestar, but he's an exceptional cat in all sorts of ways. Leading ThunderClan was his destiny.*

Finally he and Barkface scrambled up a steep rocky slope and came to a row of thornbushes at the top. Onewhisker could hear the sound of a waterfall, and looked around to see where it was coming from.

"Follow me," Barkface meowed.

The medicine cat thrust his way through the bushes. Onewhisker crouched down and drew his legs under him to slide through carefully, keeping his wounded shoulder well away from the thorns.

Reaching the other side, he halted and straightened up. As he saw what lay in front of him, he drew in a long breath of wonder. He was standing at the top of a deep hollow; opposite, a waterfall tumbled down into a pool. The surface glittered with the reflections of moon and stars. Onewhisker could almost feel the presence of his ancestors in this beautiful spot. It would be a good place for the medicine cats to commune with StarClan.

This feels right.

Barkface led him down the spiral path to the water's edge. "Crouch down and touch your nose to the water," the medicine cat instructed him. "Then StarClan will speak to you."

The touch of the water was colder than Onewhisker could have imagined. It seemed to spread from his nose down into his chest and through his whole body. He closed his eyes, wondering if this was what it felt like to die.

For what seemed like seasons, nothing happened. When he couldn't bear to wait any longer, Onewhisker opened his eyes on utter darkness. Looking up, he could see nothing, not even the moon or a single star. *This can't be the Place of no Stars!* he thought, fighting back panic. *I haven't done anything bad enough to be sent there!*

He had never visited the Dark Forest, but now he remembered the stories he had heard: how no moon or stars broke the blackness of the night, and the forest was illuminated only by a pallid light that seemed to come from everywhere and nowhere. Here, though he could see nothing, he could smell the enticing scents of moorland, and feel a gentle breeze stirring his fur.

So where am I?

Then, so slowly that at first he wasn't sure he could really see it, Onewhisker became aware of his own shadow stretching out in front of him. Gazing beyond it, he saw the wild hills of the moor that WindClan loved, illuminated by a pale, frosty light that seemed to come from somewhere behind him.

The light became stronger and stronger until it was a blaze

of silver, and a warm, familiar voice behind him meowed, "Welcome, Onewhisker."

"Tallstar!" Onewhisker gasped.

He sprang up, spun around, then staggered, blinking at the starry warriors who stood before him in a half circle: row upon row of them, stretching away into the distance until their individual shapes were lost in a fuzz of silver light.

Tallstar was standing in front of him: not the sick, scrawny cat of his last days, but strong and muscular, his black-and-white pelt gleaming. His ears and his paws glimmered with frosty starlight.

"Greetings, Onewhisker," he meowed. "We have been waiting for you."

"Is—is this StarClan?" Onewhisker stammered.

Tallstar inclined his head. "It is. Are you ready to receive your nine lives?"

Onewhisker felt incredibly humbled under the gaze of so many cats with stars in their fur. He had thought that he was prepared for his ceremony, but the astonishing reality had revived all his doubts. "I'm not sure, Tallstar," he replied. "Am I really the right cat to lead WindClan?"

His former leader let out an affectionate *mrrow*. "Of course you are, Onewhisker. You have already been tested as Clan leader, when you didn't even have your nine lives to protect you. Now I'm more certain than ever that I made the right choice."

At his words Onewhisker straightened up, letting his head and tail rise. Finally he could relax completely, feeling at last determined and confident, now that he had heard Tallstar welcome him as Clan leader. "Thank you, Tallstar. Now I'm ready."

Tallstar stepped up to him and stretched out his head to touch Onewhisker's nose with his own. Onewhisker felt as if a shaft of lightning were piercing him; he could imagine flashing into flame like the tree on the island. "I give you a life for judgment," Tallstar meowed. "Use it well to make the right decisions for your Clan."

Onewhisker gasped as the new life jolted through him like a blow from a massive paw. Pain dimmed his sight for a moment, and he clenched his jaws to stop himself from screeching. When his senses cleared, his legs were shaking and every hair on his pelt was prickling.

And I have to do that eight more times!

Tallstar stepped back, and for the first time Onewhisker realized he recognized some of the cats who were standing at the front of the rows of ancestral spirits. His mother and father were there, and Whitetail's mother, Sorrelshine, and—

Leo—no, Brushpaw! It's you! You made it into StarClan!

While he was still gazing in wonder at his old friend, Stagleap padded forward and dipped his head to Onewhisker. "I'm proud of you, my son," he declared. "I give you a life for strength. Use it well to defend and protect your Clan."

This time Onewhisker knew what to expect. When they touched noses, he braced himself for pain, but instead the new life poured into him with a force that recalled the Tribe's waterfall, crashing down from the heights. Its thunder filled his ears; he felt like a leaf caught up in the cascade and hurled into the pool below. As the force ebbed, Onewhisker felt energy and new confidence, as if he could have faced Mudclaw and all his supporters many times over.

Stagleap withdrew, and Wrenflight bounded gracefully up to Onewhisker, giving his ear a lick as she stood close to him. "I'm so happy to see you again," she purred. "I give you a life for love. Use it well for your Clan and for all who depend on you."

Onewhisker stretched forward eagerly to touch noses with his mother, longing to feel the love she had lavished on him when he was a tiny kit in the nursery. He was completely unprepared for the agony that ripped through him, fiercer than a badger's fangs, and he realized that there was nothing more ferocious than a mother's love for her kits. As the pain ebbed, he was trembling, his breath coming in shallow gasps.

Wrenflight gave his ear a final lick, her eyes glowing with love, before she withdrew to stand once again with her starry Clanmates.

The next cat to appear in front of Onewhisker was Sorrelshine, Whitetail's mother, who had died from eating the poisoned rabbit. When he had last seen her, she had been writhing in pain, and then a limp body among so many others at the edge of the camp. "Sorrelshine!" he greeted her. "It's good to see you well and strong again. I'll tell Whitetail—"

"No," Sorrelshine interrupted. "You cannot tell any cat what happens here. But I wish you could tell her how proud of her I am, and how much I love her."

I know exactly how much you love her, Onewhisker thought, still shuddering from the pain of the previous life.

"I give you a life for loyalty," she meowed. "Use it well in the service of your Clan."

Onewhisker made himself stand upright again to receive his next life, and Sorrelshine touched her nose to his. This time the jolt of pain seemed to carry him back to the old territory and brought the images of Smoke and Darkkit into his mind. *Did I betray them?* he asked himself desperately. *I would put it all right if I could!*

Sorrelshine dipped her head to him as if she had heard his thought. She had hardly had time to step away when an excited bundle of ginger fur bounced up to Onewhisker and stood in front of him with eyes shining.

"It's great to see you, Onewhisker!" he exclaimed.

"And you, Brushpaw," Onewhisker responded, all the warmth of his friendship with the former kittypet rekindling inside him. "I'm so sorry you died."

"It was hard," Brushpaw admitted. "And I miss Bailey and Melody, but it's great here in StarClan. I've met so many brilliant cats! There was—"

A cough from Tallstar, who was still standing by, interrupted Brushpaw. "Onewhisker's life?" the previous leader reminded him gently.

"Oh . . . Yeah," Brushpaw mewed. "Sorry. Onewhisker, I give you a life for friendship. Use it well to strengthen the bonds between cat and cat."

And between Clan and Clan? Onewhisker wondered as he

touched noses with his friend.

There was no pain in this life. It flowed into Onewhisker like a bubbling stream, sparkling with the delight each cat found in the bonds of trust with others, the joys of shared duties and relaxation. Images flickered through his mind of bounding across the moor shoulder to shoulder with a Clanmate, of hunting side by side, of sharing tongues in the camp as the sun went down—and of fighting back to back in battle, trusting his friend with his life.

"Did I do okay?" Brushpaw asked anxiously.

"More than okay, Brushpaw," Onewhisker meowed. "My whole Clan thanks you. And I'm so glad to see you again."

Brushpaw let out a final purr before he padded back to the ranks of StarClan warriors.

The next cat to appear was completely unknown to Onewhisker: a thin brown she-cat, her muscles revealing a wiry strength, her yellow eyes burning with intensity as she padded up to him. Radiant starlight clung about her fur, so bright that Onewhisker could hardly bear to look at her. Desperately he searched his memory, but he was sure he had never known her as a living cat, not even as an elder when he was a kit.

"I'm sorry," he murmured, dipping his head respectfully as she padded up to him. "I don't know who you are."

"No reason why you should." There was a glint of humor in the she-cat's yellow eyes. "Though you have heard of me, unless the elders no longer tell stories. I am Windstar, the first leader of your Clan."

Onewhisker could not suppress a gasp; he bowed his head

in awe that this cat should come from a past that stretched back for innumerable seasons, just to give him a life.

"Windstar . . . I—I'm honored . . . ," he stammered.

"You're welcome," Windstar mewed briskly. "Now for StarClan's sake lift your head up. How am I supposed to get at your nose?"

Onewhisker looked up and saw the same humor in the she-cat's eyes, along with wisdom so deep he was afraid he might drown in it.

Windstar stepped up to him and touched her nose to his. "I give you a life for survival," she declared. "Use it well as you settle into your new home."

This life did not bring pain; instead, Onewhisker felt as if his flesh and bones were turning to rock. He was aware of griping hunger, of struggling paw step by paw step across a storm-swept moor, of a red roar as cats lashed out with teeth and claws in battle.

"Thank you, Windstar," Onewhisker mewed as the sensations ebbed. He felt that he had been given a glimpse, however small, of how much courage and strength it must have taken to build a Clan back when there were no Clans, and not even the warrior code for guidance.

The next cat to step out of the rows of starry spirits was another Onewhisker had never seen before: a thin gray tom with a spiky tuft of fur on his head. He and Windstar nodded as they passed each other; Onewhisker could see that they knew each other well, and guessed that this was another cat from the far past.

"I am Gorsestar," the gray tom announced before One-whisker could ask. "I was Windstar's mate and her deputy, and became the second leader of WindClan."

"I am honored to meet you," Onewhisker responded, dipping his head, though he was not quite as overcome as he had been by the appearance of Windstar.

"I give you a life for sense," Gorsestar announced. "Sometimes they call it common sense, but it's not as common as all that, more's the pity. Use it well when you face a crisis in your Clan."

Onewhisker stretched his neck out to touch noses and receive the life. This time, because he was ready, the pang of pain did not seem so sharp. While it lasted, everything seemed clear and sharp-edged, as if he could see the path ahead of him and would always see the way through.

"Thank you, Gorsestar," he mewed as the sensations faded and the ancestral spirit withdrew.

Now that he had received seven lives, Onewhisker began to feel so full that he was afraid if he even twitched a whisker, the lives would begin spilling out of him, as if he were a moorland pool about to overflow in heavy rain.

And there are still two more, he thought, taking a deep breath.

The cat padding toward him now was small and young, clearly an apprentice. Onewhisker felt a stab of joy as he recognized his lean body and short thick fur.

"Gorsepaw!" he exclaimed, as the cat he had mentored halted in front of him. "I thought I'd never see you again."

Gorsepaw let out a loud purr. "I know. Isn't it great? I was so pleased to be chosen to give you a life."

Onewhisker brushed his muzzle against Gorsepaw's shoulder, his delight in meeting the young cat darkened by memory. His apprentice had been brutally murdered by Tigerstar to threaten WindClan with destruction if they refused to join him in his monstrous attempt to take over the forest.

"I give you a life for compassion," Gorsepaw declared, touching his nose to Onewhisker's. "Use it well to care for the weakest in your Clan."

This time Onewhisker felt no pain, but the sorrow that enfolded him was even harder to bear. He wanted to wail aloud in grief for all the kits and young cats dead before they had a chance to live, all the cats who died in battle or from Twoleg poison. He felt as if he were drowning in a dark, icy pool of love and loss.

I will care for them all, he resolved.

As the stress of receiving this life ebbed away, Onewhisker realized that Gorsepaw had already rejoined his starry Clanmates. Instead, the last cat Onewhisker would have expected to see was standing in front of him. Onewhisker gaped as he took in the mottled brown pelt, dusted over now with starlight, and the challenging look in the cat's amber eyes.

"Mudclaw!" he exclaimed. "What are you doing here?"

Mudclaw's mouth twisted. "What—you thought I would end up in the Dark Forest?"

"No!" Onewhisker protested. "I mean, what are you doing *here*? Waiting to give me a life?"

The former deputy gave his pelt a shake. Onewhisker could

hardly believe it, but Mudclaw looked embarrassed. "It was Tallstar's idea," he muttered, then added aloud, "I give you a life for determination. You must protect WindClan in the way you think is best. And please believe me . . . I'm sorry for everything. I hope you can forgive me."

Onewhisker stared at his former rival and Clanmate in wonder. *He sounded so different from the Mudclaw who'd teamed up with Hawkfrost to try to wrest power from him. Then all his wondering* was swallowed up in agony as Mudclaw stepped forward and touched noses with him.

The pain of this life was worse than any of the others. Onewhisker felt himself whirled into darkness, a roaring in his ears like the huge monsters that had torn up the old territory. By the time it was over, he was trembling and gasping for breath.

Tallstar was at his side; the other eight cats who had given him lives stood in the front of the mass of StarClan warriors, who had moved to surround him in a tight circle.

"Onestar, I greet you with your new name," Tallstar declared. "You have received your nine lives, and StarClan gives WindClan into your keeping." Onestar bent his head in wordless gratitude. "Now WindClan has a new leader, in a new territory," Tallstar continued. "You must put the Clan first; ensuring its survival is your life's work now. Are you prepared?"

"I am, Tallstar," Onestar responded. For the first time he really meant his words; his doubts and lack of confidence had faded. "I promise you, nothing matters to me more than my Clan."

"Onestar! Onestar!" The spirits of StarClan greeted him with his new name, just as living cats would greet a new warrior. Their voices rose into the sky in a chorus so beautiful Onestar thought his heart would break.

As the acclamation continued, Onestar realized that the voices were beginning to fade. The glitter of stars on the spirits' pelts was fading too, becoming a frosty glimmer in the moorland grass until they had all completely vanished. Their voices continued for a heartbeat longer, impossibly distant; then silence fell, and Silverpelt blazed out across the sky in a glory of starlight.

Onestar woke, stiff and chilly on the stone at the edge of the Moonpool, with the sky paling toward dawn and Barkface drowsing by his side.

The full moon floated high above the lake as Onestar led his Clan down the hill toward the Gathering with his deputy, Ashfoot, by his side. This was the second Gathering on the lake island, his second as WindClan leader.

At the previous meeting the other Clans had congratulated Onestar on becoming leader of his Clan, and he had announced that Owlwhisker and Weaselfur had received their warrior names. He had been the first to suggest the limit of two fox-lengths from the water's edge when cats needed to cross another Clan's territory to attend Gatherings. *It couldn't have gone better,* he told himself, with a spark of satisfaction.

In other ways, too, he felt his leadership was going well. He had forgiven the cats who'd supported Mudclaw and allowed them to remain in the Clan, though for the first moon he had given them extra tasks to atone for their disloyalty. They were all working as hard as they could to prove themselves.

In spite of that, and in spite of StarClan's acceptance, it still gnawed at his mind, like a mouse gnawing at a nut, that his own Clanmates had so distrusted his leadership that they had plotted against him. If he was to keep his promise to Tallstar, and ensure WindClan's survival, he knew he had to focus all his energy on becoming the strongest leader he could possibly be.

As they reached the lake and began padding along the waterside, Onestar flicked his ears at Ashfoot, signaling to her to draw a little way ahead with him. "Tell me honestly," he began when he thought they were out of earshot of the others, "what do our Clanmates think? Are they happy?"

Ashfoot hesitated for a moment, blinking thoughtfully, before she answered. "I think so, on the whole. You've really stepped up since you got your nine lives."

"But?" Onestar prompted her, sensing a certain doubt in her voice.

"Some of them are still worried about how friendly you were to Firestar, and ThunderClan in general," Ashfoot admitted. "Look at the way you gave them that bit of woodland territory after Leafpool brought us those healing herbs."

"But Firestar gave that back," Onestar argued.

"Yes, *Firestar gave* it back," Ashfoot pointed out with an irritated flick of her ears. "Like it was his decision whether we had it or not. Sure, he's a noble cat, Onestar, but we're WindClan cats, and we don't want him to be our leader."

"You don't need to worry," Onestar reassured her. "*I'm* your leader, and I understand that now. Don't you remember how I sent Firestar away when he came to warn us about the fox?" When Ashfoot didn't respond, he added, "There's nothing more important to me than WindClan. Not friendships, or my own private concerns."

"I'm glad to hear it," Ashfoot meowed, though there was a dubious note in her voice. "But I suspect you'll still have to prove it, to some of the cats."

Onestar felt his pelt begin to ruffle up, and consciously forced it to lie flat again. The cats he had chosen for the Gathering were a mixture of his own supporters and those who had supported Mudclaw. He guessed Ashfoot was right: he would need a show of strength to make sure they all believed he was the right leader for WindClan. "That won't be a problem," he declared. Bracing himself, he added silently, *I'll make sure it's not.*

Onestar crouched in the Great Oak, between a thick branch and the trunk. A couple of tail-lengths away, Blackstar was standing on a jutting branch, with Leopardstar and Firestar just above him. At the foot of the tree, Ashfoot and Mistyfoot had taken their places on the tree roots, while the clearing was a shifting mass of cats, greeting friends from other Clans or finding a place to sit. The formal part of the Gathering had yet to begin.

While he waited, Onestar kept his gaze fixed on the cats below. He was especially careful not to look at Firestar, in case the ThunderClan leader thought that he wanted to talk.

I wouldn't mind talking, he reflected sadly. *Just not here, in front of every cat. I miss the old days, when Firestar and I were friends.*

As well as Firestar himself, Onestar missed the time when he had considered ThunderClan a loyal ally rather than a possible threat. Deep down, he knew they were a threat only in his own imagination. But he had to put his Clan first, just as Tallstar said, and convince his Clanmates that he would never defer to Firestar or ask for his help.

Onestar's drifting gaze alighted on Crowfeather, who was exchanging news with Brambleclaw and Squirrelflight. *Now there's a cat who's a bit too close to ThunderClan,* he thought.

Yet Onestar didn't seriously doubt Crowfeather's loyalty. The gray-black tom was one of WindClan's strongest warriors, and had after all been chosen by StarClan to find their new territory, but Onestar still suspected that he was hiding something. Recently he had often gone missing, and no cat knew where he was, though he was always around for the dawn and evening patrols, and did his fair share of hunting.

Maybe I should give him a talking-to, Onestar thought. *But no—it's too soon for that. For now, I'll just keep an eye on him.*

While Onestar had been studying Crowfeather, Blackstar had begun the Gathering, and Firestar was reporting how ThunderClan had taken in a she-cat and her three kits from the horseplace. *Typical,* Onestar thought. The she-cat had crossed WindClan territory first, and his warriors had made it clear that she and her kits weren't welcome. *I wonder if that was the right decision.* He pushed the thought away. *Too late now.*

Leopardstar spoke next, thanking Firestar for Leafpool's

help in caring for her cats who had been poisoned by some Twoleg stuff abandoned on RiverClan territory. She was followed by Blackstar, giving yet more thanks to ThunderClan for helping his warriors fight off a couple of vicious kittypets whose Twoleg den was on ShadowClan territory.

Onestar felt anger rising inside him. *ThunderClan wants a paw in every Clan,* he thought. *And no cat is blaming Blackstar or Leopardstar for accepting Firestar's help.*

He leaped to his paws, his shoulder fur bristling and his lips drawn back into a snarl. "What sort of a Clan leader are you?" he challenged Blackstar. "Aren't you ashamed that you needed help from another Clan? You too," he added, whipping around to face Leopardstar. "RiverClan has its own medicine cat. Why do you have to go crawling to ThunderClan?"

An angry muttering had broken out in the clearing below. Onestar flashed one glance downward to see RiverClan and ShadowClan warriors, and most of ThunderClan, glaring up at him. He paid them no more attention, swiveling his head around to fix Firestar with a ferocious stare.

"It's time ThunderClan stopped paying so much attention to what's happening in the other Clans," he growled. "Your warriors ignore our boundaries and think they can tell every cat what to do. We all made the journey here together, and ThunderClan is no stronger than any other."

As he spat out the words, Onestar could see shock and hurt in Firestar's green gaze, but he couldn't let himself react to it. *This isn't exactly easy for me, either.*

Before Firestar could reply, an outraged yowl came from

the clearing below. Looking down, Onestar spotted the ThunderClan warrior Cloudtail, standing with his white pelt bushed out until he looked twice his size. "You were glad enough of ThunderClan's help when WindClan was starving," he snarled.

"That was different," Onestar retorted.

"Exactly." It was Firestar who spoke, his voice calm but with all the authority of a leader. "Back then, we had to join together to survive what the Twolegs were doing to the forest. I don't believe StarClan would want us to stop helping each other now."

Onestar yearned to agree with him, but he knew that he could not. His own Clan would be hanging on his every word, waiting to see if he would give way to ThunderClan.

"They would," he retorted, "if it meant keeping the Clans separate. There have always been four Clans; every kit knows that."

More caterwauls of protest rose up from the cats in the clearing. Dustpelt let out an earsplitting yowl to make himself heard. "WindClan would have been destroyed without us!"

Onestar took a pace forward on his branch, feeling the bark rough beneath his claws. "Look up at the moon!" he snapped. "Do you see clouds covering it? No, it's shining brightly—and that means StarClan agrees with what I'm saying."

"No cat has ever claimed there shouldn't be four Clans," Firestar meowed defensively. "But that doesn't mean Star-Clan want us to turn our backs on each other when trouble comes."

Onestar felt rage and regret—and with it all an admiration for Firestar that he couldn't shake off—roiling together in his chest, so that he hardly knew what he was saying anymore.

"I can see why you would say that," he hissed at Firestar. "You'll use any excuse for ThunderClan to take charge and weaken the other Clans."

Firestar only shook his head helplessly, as if he couldn't agree with Onestar but he had given up trying to convince him.

The Gathering rumbled on for a little longer, with more wrangling among the Clans, but soon Blackstar put an end to it. Onestar leaped down from the Great Oak and began to gather his warriors together.

He led them through the bushes and down to the shore, where ShadowClan was already crossing the tree-bridge. As Onestar stood waiting with his Clan, he realized that Firestar was standing a little way away, apart from the ThunderClan cats.

The ThunderClan leader beckoned him with a tilt of his head, and after a moment's hesitation Onestar padded over to him.

"You're proving yourself a worthy leader, Onestar," Firestar meowed. "Of course I understand that WindClan must come first, but I hope we can still be friends."

More than anything, Onestar wanted to agree, but he could feel the eyes of his warriors on him. "A leader can have no real friends in other Clans," he responded.

Firestar's whiskers drooped in disappointment. "Whatever

I've done to help you in the past," he began, "it was done out of concern for you and the many fine cats in WindClan. Not out of a desire to control you. Onestar, do you really believe I'm that selfish?"

Onestar didn't know how to answer. He didn't believe Firestar was selfish, but whether he did or not was irrelevant now. *I have to run my own Clan.*

"Surely we can put our own Clans first, but still be cordial?" Firestar's voice and the look in his eyes showed how upset he was by Onestar's silence. "There are four Clans beside the lake, but we are meant to work together. StarClan has made that clear."

Onestar still didn't know what to say. By this time Shadow-Clan had cleared the tree-bridge, so with a dip of his head to Firestar he padded up to the tree roots and leaped up onto the trunk to lead his Clan across.

Halfway to the shore, Onestar paused and looked back. Firestar was sitting at the water's edge, still a little way apart from his Clan. Deep regret pierced Onestar like a claw. Firestar had done so much for him, and maybe one day they could be friends again.

But right now Onestar had a higher priority: to keep his Clan safe.

CHAPTER 16

Onestar crouched in the nursery, drinking in the sweet milky scents and gazing down at the tiny kit curled up in the shelter of Whitetail's belly. His heart was throbbing painfully; he would never have thought he could feel such love for every hair on his daughter's brown tabby pelt.

In the seasons since the Clans had come to live beside the lake, Onestar had settled comfortably into the position of leader. He and his deputy, Ashfoot, were working well together to keep the fresh-kill pile stocked and the Clan running smoothly. He regretted that he had lost his closeness to Firestar, but he had accepted that his old friend was a great leader—for *ThunderClan*. Onestar was creating his own leadership, and under his guidance WindClan was thriving.

And now, with the birth of his kit, he had everything that he could wish for.

"She's perfect!" he breathed out.

Whitetail gazed up at him, her eyes brimming with joy. "She's wonderful! I spent so many moons in the nursery, helping raise other warriors' kits. It feels amazing to be nursing my own. And I just know she's going to grow up to be a great warrior."

"Yes," Onestar agreed. "I know she'll be important to her Clan. I must find a good mentor for her. I'll make sure her life in WindClan is as perfect as she is."

Whitetail let out a little *mrrow* of laughter. "She's only a few days old, and here we are talking about when she's a warrior!" She bent her head to nuzzle her sleeping kit. "You have a lot of growing to do yet, Heatherkit."

Onestar didn't respond. He knew his expression must have darkened, because Whitetail stretched out her tail to touch him on his shoulder.

"I know you're thinking about Galekit," she murmured. Heatherkit's littermate hadn't even drawn a single breath. "But she's surely being cared for in StarClan, and we must be grateful for the healthy kit we have."

Onestar nodded, but he still couldn't find words to express what he felt; the loss of Galekit still hurt terribly. "I have to talk to Ashfoot about the border patrols," he mewed, and slipped quickly out of the nursery.

But as he thrust his way through the branches of the gorse bush, Onestar was not thinking about Galekit. It was Darkkit and Smoke who occupied his mind. Seeing how helpless Heatherkit was, he felt the deep grip of guilt that he hadn't done more for Smoke when she gave birth. Now he understood why she had come so often to WindClan territory, trying to speak to him.

His mind recoiled from imagining what Darkkit might think of him now. *Maybe I could have truly been his father, if only I'd been able to welcome him and Smoke into the Clan.*

Onestar sat at the foot of the Tallrock and gazed out over the camp. It was hard to see Smoke and Darkkit fitting in here. Surely they would have found themselves a Twoleg nest and settled down long ago. They must have given up hope that he would come back for them; maybe they had forgotten him entirely.

Could I go back to the forest for them now? he wondered.

As soon as the thought crossed Onestar's mind, he shook his head. It would be even harder now to explain who they were to Whitetail and the rest of the Clan. Besides, he would always remember Brushpaw and Tansypaw, and how difficult they had found it to become true Clanmates. Not every cat could adapt as well as Firestar.

WindClan is strong now . . . , Onestar thought. *I can't risk weakening it.*

He comforted himself with the thought that both cats were safe and doing well; perhaps the greatest gift he could give to Darkkit was to leave him and his mother in peace.

Ashfoot's voice was a welcome distraction from his thoughts. "Onestar, you have a visitor."

Onestar looked up to see his deputy padding across the camp. To his surprise, Firestar and Leafpool were following her; the young medicine cat was carrying a leaf wrap of herbs. Several WindClan warriors watched them curiously as they approached.

Rising to his paws, Onestar dipped his head to the newcomers. "Greetings, Firestar. Leafpool. What can I do for you?"

"We came to congratulate you on the birth of Heatherkit." There was warmth in Firestar's voice and his green gaze. "I wouldn't surprise you in your own camp," he added hastily, "but you weren't at the last Gathering. Of course, I understand why. I'm terribly sorry that Galekit died."

Onestar found himself overwhelmed with emotion at the mention of his lost kit; he only managed to nod in response to the ThunderClan leader.

"The birth of my kits was the happiest day of my life," Firestar continued. "I can't imagine what you must have experienced—such joy and such heartache, all at once."

It was hard for Onestar to reveal his true emotions now; so many of his Clanmates were watching. But it touched him to the heart to have Firestar understand him so well.

"Thank you," he choked out.

Since he had rejected Firestar's help when he'd first received his nine lives, Onestar had never regained the closeness he'd once had with the ThunderClan leader. But he still recognized the kind friend who had helped him so much in the early days of his leadership.

I miss him so much, he thought, struggling with another pang of regret. *But I understand now: being a leader is a lonely job, and it's one I never asked for.*

Meanwhile, Ashfoot was scanning Leafpool with a critical gaze. "What's that you've brought?" she asked.

Leafpool set the leaf wrap down at Ashfoot's paws. "It's just a few herbs for Whitetail," Leafpool explained. "Borage to help her with nursing, a few poppy seeds if she's in pain, and thyme leaves to calm her."

As Onestar thanked the medicine cat, Ashfoot nosed the leaf wrap open and gave the contents a suspicious sniff.

"Do they smell like the wrong herbs?" Leafpool asked, a hint of humor in her voice.

"No," Ashfoot replied. "It's just a bit odd that Thunder-Clan would assume that we *need* their herbs."

Onestar was aware of Firestar and Leafpool both glancing at him with identical looks of surprise, their tails twitching as if they were offended.

"Kestrelpaw mentioned at our last half-moon meeting that the WindClan herb store was low," Leafpool responded smoothly. "I only wanted to help make Whitetail comfortable, after all she's been through."

Ashfoot gave her an icy stare, while Onestar, embarrassed by his deputy's suspicion, looked briefly down at his paws.

"Is there a problem?" Firestar asked.

The WindClan deputy faced him with narrowed eyes. "Will you expect some territory in exchange for these herbs?" she challenged him. "Isn't that how it works, with you bringing Leafpool here?"

"Ashfoot, that's enough!" Onestar snapped, appalled at his deputy's suggestion.

The gray she-cat said no more, but swung around and fixed Onestar with such a fierce glare that he knew she was annoyed *he* wasn't the cat questioning Firestar, or treating him with equal suspicion.

Onestar gave Firestar an awkward glance, wishing that he

knew what to say. To his relief, Firestar seemed unwilling to retaliate.

"I brought the herbs because you're still my friend, Onestar," the flame-colored tom declared calmly. "I wanted to make Whitetail and the kit stronger, because when one Clan thrives, all Clans thrive. We may not share the same territory, but our needs are the same, and we all respect the same code."

Onestar took a deep breath before responding. "Thank you for your kind words," he meowed at last. "But the herbs will not be necessary. WindClan can manage for itself, and Barkface is taking very good care of Whitetail, whatever Kestrelpaw may have told the other medicine cats."

And I must have a word with him about that, he added to himself silently.

Firestar nodded in acknowledgment of Onestar's words. "I'm glad to hear it. Come on, Leafpool. It's time for us to go."

Hastily Leafpool gathered up the scattered herbs while Firestar said his farewells. The two ThunderClan cats left, followed by unfriendly gazes from many of the WindClan warriors, including Ashfoot, who stalked off with an annoyed hiss.

Watching them leave, Onestar realized that Firestar had been surprised by his refusal of the herbs. Part of him was sorry he had rejected the friendly gesture, but he remembered what Tallstar had told him: *Put WindClan first.*

His Clan had been lucky, he reflected, in the seasons since he became leader. His cats were healthy and thriving. Prey was running well, and they had been spared any serious outbreaks of illness. He had a mate he loved dearly, and a kit he would do anything for, even give his life.

I just wish I still had friends.

A blustering wind swept across the moor, stirring up the sandy floor of the WindClan camp. Onestar fluffed out his pelt as he emerged from the nursery, where he had just taken fresh-kill to Whitetail. Heatherkit's eyes were open now; when Onestar stooped to give her a lick, she stood on three tottery legs and batted him on the nose with her soft, tiny paw.

"I told you she'll be a brilliant warrior!" Whitetail mewed lovingly, her eyes glimmering with amusement.

The sun was well up over the hills, and most cats were out of camp on border patrols or hunting. Onestar sat down and had just begun to give himself a good grooming when he was distracted by a stir of movement at the top of the hollow. He rose to his paws again, his shoulder fur beginning to rise in mingled surprise and apprehension at the sight of Owl-whisker and Tornear escorting the ThunderClan warriors Brambleclaw and Thornclaw. They in their turn were flanking Crowfeather, who padded along with his gaze fixed on his paws and his tail drooping.

What has he done now? Onestar wondered.

A few seasons ago, not long after Onestar had received his nine lives, he had finally learned the reason for Crowfeather's mysterious absences. The gray-black warrior had been padding after Leafpool; even though she was a medicine cat, she had returned his love, and the two of them had even fled the

Clans to be together. However, they had returned almost at once, when Leafpool had realized that her calling as a medicine cat would always be closest to her heart. Onestar had been furious; it had taken a long time for him to forgive Crowfeather and think of him again as a loyal WindClan cat.

Warily, Onestar approached the ThunderClan warriors, signaling to his own cats to stand back. "Well?" he rasped. "What's all this about?"

Thornclaw faced the WindClan leader, his eyes blazing with fury. "We found Crowfeather hanging around on our territory, near one of our best herb-gathering places," he hissed. "We think he was stealing herbs, or trying to."

"That's mouse-brained!" Crowfeather spat back. "I was doing no such thing!"

"Then why were you on their territory?" Onestar demanded.

Crowfeather clamped his jaws shut, a mutinous look in his eyes. Onestar took a deep breath. He would have liked to give his warrior a good clawing around the ears, but he wasn't going to do it in front of the ThunderClan cats.

"Crowfeather—" he began.

"Firestar made it quite clear that he expects Crowfeather to be punished," Brambleclaw interrupted. "Trespassing on ThunderClan territory isn't something we can just let go."

The tabby warrior's words had the opposite effect from the one he meant. Onestar had no intention of letting Thunder-Clan cats—not even Firestar—tell him how to discipline his warriors.

"I will deal with it," he replied, making his voice sound

chilly. "I can handle WindClan's affairs, thank you very much."

Brambleclaw exchanged a glance with his Clanmate, clearly dissatisfied. "What am I going to tell Firestar?" he demanded.

"Tell him what you like." Onestar flicked his tail dismissively. "Tell him that Crowfeather will be dealt with appropriately."

"Yeah, you'll probably give him the first choice of fresh-kill," Thornclaw snapped, drawing his lips back in a snarl. "How do we know this isn't some kind of WindClan plot?"

The accusation made Onestar's shoulder fur bristle. He bit back a growl. "Brambleclaw," he meowed, deliberately ignoring Thornclaw, "it's time for you to leave." With a wave of his tail he beckoned to Tornear and Owlwhisker. "Escort these warriors to the border," he ordered. "And make sure they cross."

With no more than a brusque nod in farewell, the two ThunderClan warriors turned away, Tornear and Owlwhisker close by their side. Onestar watched them go, then turned to Crowfeather. "Well?"

Crowfeather hesitated, looking more troubled than defiant now that the ThunderClan cats had gone. "Can I talk to you where we won't be overheard?" he asked.

Onestar glanced around to see that several of their Clanmates were still watching them. "Very well," he agreed with a twitch of his whiskers.

He led the way out of the camp and a few fox-lengths away, to a small hollow sheltered by a twisted thorn tree. "Okay," he meowed when he and Crowfeather were settled side by side.

"This is about Leafpool, isn't it?"

"Yes," Crowfeather admitted. "But it's not what you think."

"I *really* hope it isn't," Onestar told him. "Go on, then. Spit it out."

Crowfeather hunched his shoulders, a defeated look on his face. "I did trespass on ThunderClan territory," he began. "I was waiting by the herb place; Leafpool and I used to meet there, when . . . you know. I wanted to talk to her."

"To ask her to be with you again?"

Crowfeather's eyes flew open in shock. "No! I swear, I never meant to do that. That prey was eaten long ago. Great StarClan, Onestar, I'm with Nightcloud now. We have Breezekit! And I would never disrespect Leafpool by asking her to change her mind once she made her decision."

"Then what did you want?"

"I . . . I'm not sure. I only know that when she came to the camp with Firestar the other day, it stirred everything up inside me. I *had* to talk to her. I think I just wanted to make sure that she's happy now. I never meant any harm to Wind-Clan."

He lapsed into silence, and for a long time Onestar did not respond. He couldn't ignore the fact that one of his strongest warriors had done something mind-numbingly mouse-brained, treading very close to the edge of betraying their Clan. But even so . . .

"I can understand something of what you're feeling," he admitted to Crowfeather at last. "I too have had my loyal-ties . . . split. And tested."

Crowfeather shot him a stunned look, clearly wondering if Onestar was confessing to loving a cat outside his Clan. He opened his jaws to speak, but no words came out.

"Crowfeather, you can never do this again," Onestar meowed. "I believe you, but I'm not sure if there is any other cat, in WindClan or ThunderClan, who wouldn't assume you were padding after Leafpool again, if they ever found out that you tried to see her. So you will *never* speak in private to her again, and you will not even *think* of setting paw over the ThunderClan border. Do you understand?"

Crowfeather examined his paws. "Yes, Onestar, I understand," he murmured.

"Good." Onestar nodded in satisfaction. "I see no need to punish you further. The way you're tying yourself in knots is punishment enough."

"Thank you, Onestar. Er . . ." Crowfeather gazed at him, blinking in embarrassment. "Will you tell the rest of the Clan why I trespassed on ThunderClan territory? Will you tell Nightcloud?"

"No," Onestar replied, rising to his paws and preparing to leap out of the hollow. Smoke and Darkkit were trying to claw their way into his thoughts, but he resolutely pushed them away. "Some secrets are better kept."

Onestar stretched out on a branch of the Great Oak, gazing down at the cats in the clearing below while he listened to Leopardstar meowing on about a couple of dogs that had come dangerously close to the RiverClan border. So far the

Gathering had been peaceful, with only routine news to report. He had very proudly announced the births of Heatherkit and Breezekit, then let himself relax and enjoy the brilliant light of the full moon.

Leopardstar had taken a step back, and Blackstar was about to announce the end of the Gathering, when Firestar sprang to his paws. "Crowfeather!" he called out, staring down into the crowd of cats. "I'm surprised to see you here, after that incident the other day."

"What do you mean?" Leopardstar asked.

"Crowfeather was found lurking on our territory," Firestar explained, his voice raised so that every cat in the clearing could hear him. "He was close to one of our best herb-gathering places. I sent a patrol to escort him back to Onestar, who agreed to punish him." He turned to Onestar. "Is that how WindClan punishes wrongdoers?" he demanded. "Allowing them to attend the next Gathering?"

Onestar glanced down and spotted Crowfeather in the crowd, sitting next to Webfoot and Weaselfur. He was gazing up at Firestar, his expression a mixture of anger and embarrassment.

Firestar didn't wait for an answer to his question. "Kestrelpaw told the other medicine cats that WindClan's herb stocks were running low," he continued. "But when I offered to give them some, Onestar refused. Onestar, maybe you prefer your warriors to trespass on another Clan's territory, stealing herbs, just to protect your pride. Why else would you allow a disgraced warrior to come to a Gathering?"

Onestar couldn't believe that Firestar was attacking him; it was like being struck by lightning when the sky was clear and blue. Regretfully he realized that he had pushed Firestar away too many times, insisting that they couldn't be friends while they led rival Clans. *So I can't blame Firestar for finally behaving like a rival.*

"Crowfeather was not stealing anything," he retorted, drawing himself up on his branch and hoping he looked dignified. "Knowing the whole story, I decided there was no need to punish him."

Blackstar let out a snort of disbelief. "Maybe that's because you sent him, Onestar," he suggested. "To spy, or to steal herbs? I dare you to try it with ShadowClan! Your warriors would return bleeding, if they returned at all."

"Stop that now!" Onestar growled, offended to the tips of his claws. "Of course I would never condone spying. But I am leader of WindClan, *not* Firestar, despite what Firestar might think. I dealt with my own warrior as I saw fit, and I have no regrets." Fixing Firestar with a furious glare, he continued, "Are you looking for a fight? WindClan and ThunderClan have been at peace for many seasons, but that can change at any time."

The air thrilled with tension for the next few heartbeats as Firestar returned Onestar's challenging gaze. Onestar realized that something had irrevocably changed between them. They had not been friends—true friends—since he'd received his nine lives, but now he felt as if a deep cleft were opening up at their paws, dividing them. He knew they would never recover their earlier friendship.

Firestar was the first cat to look away. "No," he meowed. "This isn't worth lives. But if a WindClan warrior is caught trespassing on my territory again, I may adopt Blackstar's methods."

Some warriors let out *mrrows* of amusement, and the tension relaxed a little. With the argument over, Blackstar continued speaking the words that would bring the Gathering to an end.

When Onestar led his cats down to the tree-bridge, he saw that the last of the ThunderClan cats were crossing, but Firestar was waiting beside the tree roots. *Waiting for me,* Onestar realized.

Warily Onestar approached him, with a twitch of his ears at Barkface, who was padding alongside him, signaling him to stay back. "Well?" he mewed. "What do you want now?"

"I can't understand why you didn't punish Crowfeather," Firestar replied. "I admire him just as much as you do. He's an outstanding warrior. But this isn't about how much he has done in the past; it's about the warrior code."

Onestar's anger had calmed down since their exchange during the Gathering, but now it swelled inside him again like a storm cloud about to release a deluge. "I will not punish Crowfeather," he growled, with a lash of his tail.

"But Onestar . . ." It was clear that Firestar was making an effort to sound reasonable. "As ThunderClan's ally, you must understand—"

"ThunderClan's ally?" Onestar interrupted, flexing his claws in the gritty soil. "I don't know anything about that.

What I do know is that I'm WindClan's leader, and I decide what to do with my warriors. Prick your ears, Firestar, because you obviously didn't hear me the first time: I will not punish Crowfeather. And instead of meddling in our affairs, you would do well to pay better attention to what your own cats are doing—even your own kin."

Firestar looked puzzled, then nodded. "So this is how it is," he murmured. "Very well. I hope you'll remember this conversation the next time WindClan needs ThunderClan's help."

"That will be never," Onestar retorted, and led his cats across the bridge to go home.

CHAPTER 17

❧

"*You know, I just wanted to* mention again," Harespring suggested. "Perhaps we could ask ThunderClan for help when we meet at the Gathering?"

Onestar had called his deputy to his den, intending to discuss the arrangements for that night. Instead, his fur began to bristle as Harespring insisted on talking about WindClan's latest crisis. Stoats had infested the tunnels that led between WindClan and ThunderClan. In an attempt to drive them out, Nightcloud had disappeared and Breezepelt had been injured; he was overwhelmed with grief at what seemed to be his mother's death.

Earlier, Harespring had suggested that they should ask for ThunderClan's help to get rid of the stoats, but Onestar had refused. And now here he was, bringing the idea up again. Onestar had to admit to himself that Harespring was doing the duty of a good deputy, but his belly roiled with fury at the thought of going back on his word of so many seasons ago, and admitting to ThunderClan that WindClan couldn't cope alone.

That promise had been made to Firestar, but the

ThunderClan leader had given up his last life in the Great Battle when the cats of the Dark Forest had erupted into the living world and tried to destroy the Clans. The forest was still shaken by the loss of so many cats. The survivors were struggling to forgive the Clanmates who had taken the side of the Dark Forest. Those warriors had not really understood what the cat spirits intended until it was almost too late, but many survivors still saw their actions as a betrayal.

"This is the first Gathering since the Great Battle," he meowed curtly. "And the first time we'll meet Bramblestar as ThunderClan leader. There'll be more important things to discuss than our difficulty with the stoats."

In spite of Onestar's refusal, Harespring went on trying to persuade him. "If nothing else," he pointed out, "more cats in the tunnels would mean more stoats would be chased off, right?"

"I thought I made myself clear," Onestar growled. "This is WindClan's problem to solve, and none of ThunderClan's business."

Harespring blinked unhappily. "I know you chose me as deputy to make a point," he mewed. "That the cats who trained in the Dark Forest before the Great Battle are trustworthy and have been accepted back into the Clan. But I remember how much you admired Ashfoot, and relied on her, and how often you took her advice."

Onestar felt darkness enveloping him at the memory of Ashfoot, who had been his littermate and his confidante, not to mention Crowfeather's mother. He tried not to think about the Great Battle, but Ashfoot's death still haunted him. He respected Harespring, but he couldn't rely on him the way he had relied on Ashfoot.

He bared his teeth at Harespring, lips drawn back in the beginning of a snarl. "If you had a fraction of Ashfoot's knowledge, of course I would listen to you. But you don't!"

Harespring flinched at his anger, not even trying to defend himself, and Onestar realized that he had gone too far.

"You will have to *earn* my trust," he continued, "just like every deputy, before and after the Great Battle. Now accept this: I have given you my final answer about the stoats."

Harespring looked disappointed, but he didn't try to argue further. "Which cats do you want to take with you to the Gathering?" he asked resignedly.

"We need our strongest warriors," Onestar mewed thoughtfully. "The other Clans need to see that we've made a good recovery from the Great Battle. You will come, of course," he continued to his deputy, "and Kestrelflight, and Crowfeather. And I think—yes, I think we'll take Breezepelt. He—"

"Breezepelt?" Harespring interrupted, his eyes widening in shock. "Onestar, are you sure? Is he ready?"

"Ready or not, he needs to be there," Onestar replied. "Otherwise it will look as if I'm ashamed of him, hiding him away because he sided with the Dark Forest. Breezepelt comes with us."

Harespring gave a tiny shrug but didn't protest anymore.

"Larkwing," Onestar continued, naming another Dark Forest ally, "Heathertail, Sedgewhisker, and Gorsetail. And the two apprentices can come too. Oh, and Weaselfur. That should be enough."

Harespring frowned. "Do you really want to reward Weaselfur?" he asked. "After the spiteful way he accused Breezepelt at Nightcloud's vigil? He wanted to make us believe that Breezepelt had killed his mother!"

Irritation prickled every hair on Onestar's pelt. He was sick of Harespring questioning him, even though with the fairer part of his mind he recognized that questioning the Clan leader was an important part of a deputy's duties.

He's actually right about Weaselfur, he admitted to himself. *He's a strong warrior, but he's a troublemaker. But I'll seem weak if I back down now.*

"Yes, Weaselfur," he growled. "Now go and round them up."

Blackstar opened the Gathering by reciting the names of all the cats who had died in the Great Battle. The list seemed to stretch out for seasons, until every cat had been honored.

When it was over, Onestar rose to his paws to make his report. "Thank you, Blackstar," he began. "I'm afraid I must continue this Gathering by sharing some sad news with the Clans. Nightcloud is dead."

The cats in the clearing gazed up at Onestar with dismay in their eyes, letting out yowls of shock. Onestar felt a twinge of pride that his warrior clearly commanded respect from all the Clans.

"How did it happen?" Mistystar asked, her voice full of concern.

"She fought so well in the Great Battle," Blackstar added. "It's hard to lose her now, after she survived that."

Onestar was reluctant to explain, but he realized that there was no way of hiding the trouble that WindClan faced. "Stoats have come to live in the tunnels between WindClan and ThunderClan," he meowed. "Nightcloud—"

Bramblestar interrupted before Onestar could continue. "And of course it never occurred to you to warn ThunderClan about the stoats."

"I understood that ThunderClan already knew about them," Onestar retorted. *In fact, I know very well you did, because your warriors caught mine emerging from the tunnels on your territory.* "I trust you've been able to cope?"

"We're coping very well." There was the hint of a snarl in Bramblestar's voice, and his shoulder fur began to rise. "We've doubled the patrols in that area, and—"

"Bramblestar, this isn't the time," Mistystar mewed; her voice was quiet, but filled with the authority of a Clan leader. "Onestar was speaking."

Onestar couldn't help enjoying the ThunderClan leader's discomfited expression as he clamped his jaws shut. "As I said," he continued, "stoats are living in the tunnels, and Nightcloud was part of a patrol that tried to clear them out. She never came home."

His report made, Onestar was about to step back, so that another leader could speak. But at the same moment Weaselfur, down in the clearing, sprang to his paws. "Yeah, ask Breezepelt why not!" he yowled.

Onestar drew in a breath of pure fury. He realized Harespring had been right. He had been mouse-brained to choose Weaselfur to attend the Gathering, after his wild accusations at Nightcloud's vigil the night before. He was paying for that now.

"Weaselfur, keep your mouth shut!" Harespring called out from where he sat on the roots of the Great Oak with the other deputies.

"Why should I?" Weaselfur swung around to face him. "We all know that Breezepelt was with Nightcloud in the tunnels when the stoats attacked. Why was *he* the only one who got out alive?"

For a few moments Onestar was uncertain what to do. He was afraid that if he commanded Weaselfur to be quiet, his warrior might not obey. Besides, it was too late. WindClan's most private affairs were being revealed to the other Clans like maggots in a piece of crow-food.

Wait until we get back to camp, Weaselfur, he thought. *You'll be on dawn patrol for a moon. At least.*

While he hesitated, cats of all the other Clans were turning to stare at Breezepelt, making comments to one another. Up in the Great Oak, Onestar couldn't hear what was being said, but he could see that it wasn't kind. The ThunderClan cats in particular were involved, and Bramblestar was making no attempt to stop them.

Eventually Breezepelt sprang to his paws, and to Onestar's horror charged straight at Spiderleg of ThunderClan.

No! Breezepelt, you mustn't break the Gathering truce!

To his relief, Breezepelt halted in front of the Thunder-Clan tom, his teeth bared in a furious snarl. "If so many cats have a problem with me, they should say so directly, not prowl around it like little mouse-hearts!"

"Breezepelt, stop now!" Onestar ordered, but Breezepelt either didn't hear him or chose to ignore him. He had been goaded too far.

The argument with Spiderleg continued, with Spiderleg's Clanmate Berrynose sticking a paw in, accusing Breezepelt and other WindClan cats of spying. This time it took Crow-feather standing between the hostile warriors, glaring at each of them in turn, to prevent a skirmish. Onestar stood on his branch, appalled, with no idea what he could do.

Finally Jayfeather, the ThunderClan medicine cat, made himself heard. "Spying or not, why did Nightcloud and Breeze-pelt go into the tunnels in the first place?"

Onestar drew a huge breath of relief. Finally some cat had asked a sensible question, instead of flinging accusations. "I can answer that," he meowed. "It was because of the stoats. And because Kestrelflight had a vision. Kestrelflight, tell them about it."

The young medicine cat rose to his paws, glancing around nervously as every cat turned toward him. "I saw a great wave of water," he responded. "It swept out of the tunnels and drowned WindClan's territory. Clearly it was a warning."

For a few heartbeats silence fell on the clearing, as cats exchanged puzzled or dismayed glances. In the sudden quiet, Bramblestar padded forward to the end of his branch and fixed Onestar with his amber gaze. "Does WindClan intend to share *any* information with ThunderClan?" he demanded. "This vision wasn't just a warning for you. It affects Thunder-Clan too, because some of the tunnels lead into our territory. Why wasn't I told about this?"

With a massive effort Onestar held on to his rapidly fraying patience. "It was a WindClan vision to warn WindClan. Does ThunderClan need to stick its nose into everything?"

"I'm not trying to meddle." Bramblestar too was clearly making an effort to stay calm. "But we need to work together to take care of the threat before any more cats get hurt."

And so we still argue, Onestar thought despondently as Bramblestar continued to insist that their Clans should cooperate. He began to wonder whether Harespring had been right, and he should be prepared for WindClan to work with ThunderClan. It would be a way of honoring Firestar's memory, and creating a good relationship with the new ThunderClan leader.

Anything would be better than this continual bickering.

But before he could speak, Lionblaze ended the discussion by charging Breezepelt with disloyalty. Their skirmish—*with words alone, not claws,* Onestar thought thankfully—ended with Breezepelt storming out of the clearing. The remaining cats were so disturbed that the other leaders made their reports quickly and the Gathering came to an end.

It couldn't end soon enough for Onestar. All Wind-Clan's difficulties had been made public: the problem with the stoats, the question of Breezepelt's loyalty, the meaning of Kestrelflight's vision. *It sounds as if our Clan is in complete chaos,* Onestar thought. *But that's not true at all . . . is it?*

He was preparing to leap down from the Great Oak when he realized that Bramblestar was still standing on the branch beside him, watching him with head tilted and a sympathetic look in his eyes.

"What?" Onestar growled.

"Crowfeather and Breezepelt seem to be having difficulties," Bramblestar commented.

Onestar felt his shoulder fur beginning to rise, though the ThunderClan leader's tone was friendly, not critical. Remembering the two toms glaring at each other in the midst of the upheaval, Onestar had to agree. "They're hardly the first father and son to argue," he pointed out.

Bramblestar let out a small *mrrow* of amusement. "Yes, raising kits teaches you humility," he mewed. "Sometimes it shows you parts of yourself you never knew were there, right, Onestar?"

"It certainly does." Onestar forced his voice to remain calm even as he responded to the younger cat's comment. He had never struggled with Heathertail; they had always been friends as well as kin. So what exactly was Bramblestar referring to?

A pang of worry griped deep in Onestar's belly. *Could Bramblestar know about Smoke and Darkkit?*

It was unlikely, but not impossible, Onestar realized. A few WindClan warriors knew his secret, and word could have spread, especially during the Great Journey, when the Clans were so close to one another. What if Bramblestar's comment was his way of telling Onestar that he knew, that he had power over him? And what would it mean, for another Clan's leader to have a secret to hold over him?

What a fool I was, to think that Bramblestar would be just like Firestar! Ashfoot was right: you can't trust other Clans! I should have listened to her, not that naive Harespring. He has as much sense as a kit still in the nursery.

"You know, Onestar," Bramblestar continued, "if you're having problems, ThunderClan is ready to help."

Panic battered inside Onestar's chest, making it hard to breathe, let alone form words. "WindClan has everything under control," he managed at last. "We don't need Thunder-Clan sticking their paws in!"

Bramblestar's widened in shock at Onestar's harsh rejection. "If that's how you feel," he meowed, dipping his head in acceptance. "If you change your mind, you know where to find us."

He leaped down from the Great Oak and bounded across the clearing to disappear into the bushes.

Onestar followed more slowly. He hadn't thought about Smoke and Darkkit in moons . . . but suddenly he could think of nothing else.

Flames wreathed around Onestar. Though he couldn't see more than a tail-length in any direction, he somehow knew that he was back in the old territory. Fire raged across the moor, scorching his pads and singeing his whiskers if he got too close.

"Smoke! Darkkit!" he called desperately, only to break off, coughing, as smoke burned his lungs.

Onestar kept on searching, growing more and more frantic, until a white shape flashed out of the flames and barreled into him, knocking him off his paws. He looked up into the face of a fully grown Darkkit, his powerful body completely white except for the black blotches around his eyes and a black tail. His massive paws pinned Onestar down by his shoulders.

"What's happening?" Onestar gasped. "Darkkit, are you okay?"

Darkkit's lips moved into an unpleasant smirk; he raised a paw with his claws unsheathed. "Did you think you'd gotten away with it?" he asked, and brought his paw sweeping down to slash at Onestar's throat.

Onestar jolted awake and for a few heartbeats lay panting in his nest as the dream gradually lost its grip on him. Then he became aware of a commotion outside his den: yowls of terror or defiance; the screeching of cats in pain.

As he stumbled into the open, a white shape leaped at him, trying to carry him off his paws. *Darkkit—here?* Onestar wondered, bewildered. *Am I still dreaming?*

A sudden flash of memory came to him, of Stoneteller's prophecy. *You'll know it when it comes hunting you.*

Could this be it?

Trying to battle with the creature that was attacking him, Onestar gazed around and saw a whole crowd of Darkkits tussling with his warriors. *How can that be?* he asked himself. *There's only one Darkkit.*

Then the last shreds of his dream fell away and he realized that the creatures were stoats; he had been confused by their white bodies and black tails.

No! They're attacking the camp!

CHAPTER 18

Fully awake now, Onestar threw himself into the fight. The sleek, wiry stoats seemed to be everywhere, their white pelts gleaming in the moonlight, their eyes glittering with malice. More of them were pouring in over the edge of the hollow. They were smaller than the cats, but they were fast and vicious; Onestar realized that his Clan could soon be overwhelmed.

He lashed out to rake his claws down the side of the nearest stoat, then whirled to strike out at another with his hind legs; his blow landed on its belly as it sprang at him.

"Breezepelt! Harespring!" he yowled, calling to two of his strongest warriors, hoping that they might drive out the stoats if they worked together.

He spotted Harespring, almost buried under a writhing heap of stoats, with Weaselfur clawing at them in a frantic effort to help his Clanmate. But there was no sign of Breezepelt. Onestar's belly lurched as he realized that he couldn't see Heathertail, either.

Have they gone off together somewhere? Onestar asked himself as he struck out at yet another of the malignant creatures. *Or is Heathertail . . .* He couldn't bring himself to use the word *dead*, even to himself.

A few days before, Onestar had sent Crowfeather into exile when the dark gray warrior had refused to obey his order to block up the tunnels where the stoats were living. He had begun to believe that Nightcloud was still alive, and he had wanted to go and look for her.

We could use Crowfeather now, Onestar thought ruefully. Three of WindClan's best warriors were missing, leaving their Clan vulnerable when they were most needed.

Onestar let his fury build and flow out through his body in a ferocious attack on the invaders. He slashed his way through the thick of the battle, shrieks echoing in his ears, blood clogging his claws and trickling through his pelt.

In the middle of the turmoil he caught glimpses of his Clanmates: Leaftail shoving his apprentice, Oatpaw, into a bush and spinning around to strike out and protect the young cat; Kestrelflight tugging a fallen warrior—Onestar thought it was Crouchfoot—away from the battle toward the medicine cat's den; Furzepelt and Larkwing fighting back to back. Through his rage Onestar felt a warm touch of pride at their courage and their skill.

Then he spotted two stoats wriggling their way through the crowd and heading straight for the elders' den, where Whitetail was sleeping.

"No!" he yowled, hurling himself after them. "Turn and fight, mange-pelts!"

He didn't think the stoats had heard him, but he caught them before they reached the gorse bush, and leaped onto the back of the one in the rear, digging his claws in and trying to get a grip on the creature's neck. It went limp underneath him, but as he let it drop, it squirmed around and sank its fangs into his shoulder. At the same time, the second stoat slashed its claws all the way down Onestar's side.

Onestar's vision blurred. He heard Emberfoot screech, "Hold on! I'm coming!"

Too late . . . Onestar thought. Blinking painfully, he just made out the wedge-shaped head of the stoat looming over him, vicious triumph in its eyes. Then everything went dark.

Onestar opened his eyes in brilliant sunlight. He was lying on the springy moorland grass, and he could hear the gentle trickling of a small stream somewhere nearby. He took a deep breath and struggled to sit up.

Tallstar was standing a couple of tail-lengths away, with Mudclaw, Wrenflight, and Stagleap. Onestar felt a pulse of pure delight at seeing them, yet he knew why he was here.

"I've lost a life, haven't I?" he rasped. Tallstar dipped his head, but when no cat spoke, Onestar continued, "I have to hurry back! I'm needed in the battle!"

"There's time enough," Tallstar assured him. "Before you go, we need to warn you of something. The dream you were having before the battle is just a taste of what's to come."

Onestar bit back a gasp of shock. "You know about the dream?"

"We're StarClan. We know everything," Mudclaw mewed drily; then, with a sidelong glance at Tallstar, he added hastily, "Almost everything."

"You have unfinished business," Tallstar told Onestar.

Mudclaw nodded agreement. "Yes. The past catches up with us."

Onestar blinked uncomfortably. His dream had been about Darkkit; that must be the unfinished business Tallstar and Mudclaw were referring to. When Mudclaw was alive, Onestar had been afraid that he knew the secret of his relationship with Smoke. Now their leadership struggle was over; Onestar had won, and Mudclaw walked with StarClan.

That means he certainly knows my secret! Shame warmed Onestar's pelt, and he found it hard to meet Mudclaw's gaze. *But I don't know what I can do for Darkkit or Smoke now.*

"It's not too late," Tallstar told him, almost as if he could read Onestar's thoughts. "You must return."

His last few words faded away, and the sunlit moorland vanished, leaving Onestar in darkness again. He could hear the groans and whimpers of injured cats, but none of the furious screeches that had filled the hollow during the battle.

He opened his eyes to find himself lying stretched out in his own den. He could smell the clean scent of marigold and realized that the wound on his side had been poulticed. From where he lay, he could see his warriors chasing the last few stoats out of the hollow; the floor of the camp was littered with their white bodies—and the bodies of WindClan cats.

He let out a gasp and tried to sit up. Immediately Whitetail appeared above him, pressing him gently back with a paw on his shoulder. "Lie still," she murmured. "It's all over."

There was a patch of fur missing from Whitetail's neck, and her pelt around it was matted with dried blood, but she didn't seem to be seriously injured.

"How many dead?" Onestar asked hoarsely, dreading the reply.

"One," Whitetail replied. "You. Some of the others have serious wounds, but Kestrelflight thinks that they'll all recover, with care."

Onestar drew a breath of relief; then his heart gave a jolt as he remembered. "Heathertail?" he asked.

Whitetail shook her head. "I don't know, Onestar. She isn't here, and neither is Breezepelt. Gorsetail and Hootpaw are missing, too."

Onestar stared at her, hardly able to take in her news. His heart was fluttering uncomfortably like a bird trying to escape out of his throat. He knew Heathertail had wanted him to do more about the stoats, to join with ThunderClan to drive them out. But Onestar had refused, because he'd suspected Bramblestar of knowing his secret.

Have I sacrificed one kit because I hid the truth about the other? Or is something going on that I know nothing about?

While he was still confused, he heard Emberfoot's voice raised from the far side of the camp. "Onestar! They're back!"

This time Onestar insisted on getting up and emerging into the camp, Whitetail anxiously padding alongside him.

Approaching down the slope, with Crowfeather in the lead, were all the missing cats: Gorsetail and her apprentice, Hootpaw; Breezepelt; and Heathertail. And another cat with them that Onestar had never expected to see again.

Nightcloud! She's alive! And Heathertail is safe.

For a moment Onestar couldn't accept what was in front of him, his relief at seeing his daughter was so great. But as he stalked forward to meet the returning cats, he felt a sudden surge of optimism.

I'm alive. Whitetail and Heathertail are alive. And believe me, I will bring Crowfeather into line. Onestar thought back to what Tallstar had told him. *Things will soon be right again in WindClan, so I'll have time to turn to things I should have dealt with long ago. It's not too late to do right by Smoke and Darkkit.*

CHAPTER 19

🍀

"Let all cats old enough to catch their own prey join here beneath the Tallrock for a Clan meeting!"

Onestar's voice rang out across the camp. As he stood on the Tallrock, watching the Clan assemble, he reflected that on the whole, WindClan had been very lucky to get rid of the stoats with so few casualties. The wounds from that battle in the camp, and the later battle beside the tunnels with Thunder-Clan as their ally, had almost all healed. A moon later, life in the camp was returning to normal.

But Onestar knew that he still had work to do. His concern about Bramblestar maybe knowing his secret about Darkkit had almost cost the lives of his Clanmates, because he hadn't been able to bring himself to accept ThunderClan's help until it was almost too late.

It's time to face my past, once and for all.

"Cats of WindClan," he began when the cats were all sitting around the base of the Tallrock, "I'm troubled by Kestrelflight's vision about the flooded tunnels. I'm not sure it was entirely about the stoats."

So far what Onestar had said was true; he paused to take a

breath, because what he was about to say was not true at all.

"I am going to travel to the Moonpool," he announced. "I want to reflect on our future and commune with StarClan. I may stay away for several days, to find out whether our warrior ancestors can advise me about how to protect WindClan in the moons to come."

Murmurs of surprise rose from the crowd of cats, but Onestar was pleased to see that most of them were nodding agreement. *They might not be so approving if they knew what I'm really going to do,* he thought wryly.

"Would you like me to go with you?" Kestrelflight asked.

Onestar shook his head. "No, you will surely be needed in the Clan. But I'd appreciate some traveling herbs."

"Of course, Onestar." The medicine cat headed for his den.

Onestar leaped down from the Tallrock and followed Kestrelflight to collect the herbs. The cats began to disperse, except for Heathertail and Breezepelt, who padded over to him side by side.

"Please be careful up there on the moor," Heathertail meowed. "You never know what might be lurking outside Clan territories."

That's truer than she realizes, Onestar thought, knowing that he was about to undertake a journey far more perilous than his daughter imagined. Anxiety welled up inside him, not for himself, but for his kin and the Clan that he was abandoning. "And you take care, here at home," he responded.

Heathertail glanced at Breezepelt, her eyes shining. "Breezepelt and I are mates now. We'll take care of each other."

"Breezepelt? Hmm . . ." Onestar flicked his ears at Breezepelt, who was looking smug and embarrassed, all at once. He wasn't sure how he felt about his daughter taking up with a cat who had fought for the Dark Forest, and who until recently had seemed perpetually angry. *But all that is over now,* Onestar told himself. *Many cats were deceived by the Dark Forest, and that's all forgiven and forgotten. And Breezepelt is doing his best to deal with his anger.*

"That's good news," he meowed at last, seeing a look of relief in Breezepelt's eyes at his words. *At least he's a WindClan cat,* he added to himself. *He and Heathertail aren't repeating their fathers' mistakes.*

When he had said his farewells, and licked up the bitter bunch of herbs Kestrelflight had prepared for him, Onestar left the camp and headed across the moor to the stream that formed the border with ThunderClan. He followed the stream up into the hills, the route he would have taken if he had really intended to go to the Moonpool. But once he had crossed the WindClan border markers, and was sure that he was well out of the way of border patrols, he veered around until he could leave Clan territories past the horseplace, retracing the route that the Clans had taken long ago on the Great Journey.

The old territories were far away, and Onestar was acutely aware of how long he would be absent. Forcing himself into a fast pace, thankful for the extra strength the traveling herbs gave him, he spent as little time as possible hunting and sleeping, but every paw step of his journey recalled his decision to abandon Smoke and Darkkit.

In such a hard time for the Clans, Onestar still believed that the kittypets would never have survived if they had joined WindClan on the Great Journey. They had been terribly upset to be left behind, but he knew he had been right to make them stay. It was harder to accept his decision not to go back for them as he had promised. He had convinced himself that they were better off in their Twolegplace, but now he could see that he had deceived himself. He had abandoned them so that he could move forward with his new life without feeling guilty.

Onestar still thought it was likely that Smoke and Darkkit had found new Twolegs and ended up as kittypets again, but now he admitted to himself that he had a duty to make sure. He hoped that if he could find them and see that they were safe and happy, then they could all part as friends.

And I'd really like to see Darkkit grown up. I want to know how my first kit turned out.

Onestar's path led him into the mountains, a hard and grueling climb where prey was scarce and the sharp rocks tore his pads. Eventually he began to recognize his surroundings, and realized that he was traveling through the Tribe's hunting grounds. Unsure whether to approach their cave, he found himself a spot behind a rock, sheltered from the icy wind, and gazed down into a narrow valley. Faintly in the distance he could hear the thunder of the waterfall.

A patrol of cats was making its way along the valley bottom; Onestar picked out the lithe bodies of the prey-hunters and the sturdier ones of the cave-guards keeping a close watch on the sky. The cat in the lead, a powerful gray tom, was familiar to him.

Stormfur!

The former RiverClan warrior looked healthy and strong, suggesting that the Tribe was doing well. Onestar remembered his stupid idea, seasons ago, that WindClan might move in with the Tribe after they were driven out of the forest. Shocking himself, he felt a sudden ache of longing to join them now.

What if I did? What if I never returned to WindClan, never faced Smoke or Darkkit?

Onestar had never wanted to be Clan leader. *And how right I was!* He had guided his Clan through some difficult times, and his earlier fears had come true: being leader had separated him from the rest of his Clan, and it was almost impossible to have any friends.

It would be great to be a Tribe cat and have no responsibilities, other than helping to keep my Tribemates fed. Then Onestar remembered Whitetail and Heathertail. *Maybe they would join me. But then there's Breezepelt, and sooner or later there will be kits. . . .*

Onestar shook his head, trying to push aside these mouse-brained ideas. He decided it would be best if he stayed away from the Tribe altogether.

A clump of twisted thornbushes yielded up a mouse, and when he had eaten, Onestar scraped together a makeshift nest under their branches. The climb had tired him so much that he soon slipped into a deep sleep.

* * *

"Get up. I have a message."

A paw in his side prodded Onestar awake. Blinking, he sat up. Through the branches of the thorn trees he could see the moon riding high; it was the middle of the night. A familiar-looking muscular dark gray tom was crouched beside him, a serious, urgent look in his eyes. "I am the new Stoneteller," he meowed. "Before that, my name was Crag Where Eagles Nest. I must speak to you."

"We've met, haven't we?" Onestar murmured, only half-awake. "But you weren't Stoneteller then."

"This is important," Stoneteller told him. "I have received a message for you from our ancestors, the Tribe of Endless Hunting."

Icy dread washed over Onestar. *Oh no—another message from the Tribe?* The last one hadn't been good news. . . .

Stoneteller led Onestar down into the valley, then up another slope, which led to the path behind the waterfall. On the way, Onestar remembered Crowfeather telling him that Stoneteller never left the cavern, and the thought only increased his dread.

This must be really important, if he came out to find me.

The cave was dimly lit by flickering moonlight, the falling water a screen of liquid silver, as Onestar entered in Stone-teller's paw steps. The Tribe's healer led him past the cats curled up in their sleeping hollows and down the tunnel into the Cave of Pointed Stones.

"Sit down," he ordered Onestar, gesturing with his tail

toward the edge of one of the pools, then sat beside him and stared into the falling water.

Onestar sat shivering, partly from the cold that struck up through his pads, partly from the sight of the weird stone trees and the endless patter of water drops into pools silver with reflected moonlight. He was aware that Stoneteller was caught up in communion with the unseen spirits of his ancestors.

Eventually Stoneteller turned to him and spoke. "I see darkness approaching the Clans, and I am afraid the darkness might win. Onestar, you are pulling this darkness like a dog being pulled by a vine."

Onestar let out a gasp of horror. "*I'm* bringing danger to the Clans? Maybe I should leave—exile myself!"

"That's no good," Stoneteller declared, his eyes grave. "It has already begun, and only you can stop it, when it comes hunting you."

An even more deathly cold crept over Onestar as he remembered the words of the previous Stoneteller. But then he realized that there was good news mingled with the bad.

"I can stop it!" he exclaimed. "How? I'm on my way to the old forest now—will that solve it?"

Stoneteller narrowed his eyes in a critical glance. "You have the power within you, Onestar," he pronounced, "but it will cost you dearly."

CHAPTER 20

Onestar paused, staring at the sight in front of him. He was sure
he had come the right way; this should be the edge of the old
WindClan territory. But instead of the open moorland, the
small streams and gorse thickets, all he could see were rows
and rows of Twoleg dens, crisscrossed by Thunderpaths.
Instead of the scents of wind and water, the air was filled with
the acrid tang of monsters.

Longing for the old territory gripped Onestar like the jaws
of a badger; he felt old and tired. *I should never have come. I should
never have seen this.*

Then Onestar pushed the feeling away. He knew it was
important for him to have returned, even more so after the
ominous prophecy he had received from Stoneteller.

At least the river was still here, and the wooden bridge he
had crossed when he went to visit Smoke and the other kittypets, though now it was built of stone, with a Thunderpath
running over it. Onestar had to wait a long time, crouched
beside it, before a gap opened up in the never-ending lines of
monsters.

As he raced across, hating the feel of the hard, black surface under his pads, he heard a loud roaring noise coming from behind him. Glancing over his shoulder, he saw a monster bearing down on him. The end of the bridge was too distant; Onestar knew he would be crushed long before he could reach it. Desperately he scrambled onto the flat stones that edged the Thunderpath, and crouched as far away from the monster as he could. He was convinced he would be crushed under its huge black paws. For a moment his whole world was filled with its roaring and the gusty stinking wind it brought with it. Then it was gone, growling off into the distance while Onestar forced himself to his paws and fled the rest of the way to collapse, panting, on a stretch of grass at the far end of the bridge.

That was close! And I'll never get this StarClan-cursed stink out of my fur!

The small Twolegplace on the other side of the river was much bigger than Onestar remembered. He had no idea how to find his way among the new Twoleg dens; all he could do was wander on and hope that eventually he would find a familiar sight.

Twolegs were everywhere: some of them pushing small, noisy monsters across the grass in their gardens, some digging in new plants, while others were pulling them up.

Why do they plant stuff if they're only going to pull it out again? Onestar wondered. *Twolegs are weird!*

Outside one of the dens was a pile of Twoleg trash; Onestar wrinkled his nose at the stink. As he approached, he spotted three rats feasting on the garbage: huge creatures with scabby pelts and long thin tails. Onestar crept past, keeping his belly close to the ground, wondering why Twolegs never seemed to learn to keep their territory clean.

He was beginning to grow tired when he spotted a couple of kittypets sunning themselves on a stretch of flat stone outside a Twoleg den. Warily he slipped through the fence and padded up to them.

"Hi," he mewed. "Don't be scared; I'm not here to make trouble. I'm just trying to find a couple of cats. They're called Smoke and Darkkit. Do you know them?"

Both kittypets looked up at him, blinking sleepily. Neither of them looked afraid; Onestar reflected that he needn't have bothered reassuring them. The bigger of the two, a plump, sleek ginger tom, stretched his jaws in a massive yawn, then asked, "What? What are you meowing about?"

"Smoke and Darkkit," Onestar repeated patiently. "Do you know them?"

The second kittypet, a pure white, long-haired she-cat, opened beautiful blue eyes and stared at Onestar. "Smoke and Darkkit?" she mewed.

Hope started to spring up inside Onestar. "Yes!"

The white kittypet shook her head. "No."

"No, never heard of them," the ginger tom confirmed.

Frustrated, Onestar scraped his claws on the hard stone. "What about Melody, then?" he asked desperately. "Do you know her? Is she still living around here?"

The white kittypet blinked thoughtfully. "Yes, I think I know the cat you mean," she replied. "But if I'm going to get up and show you the way to her garden, you'll have to give me something first." She tilted her head coaxingly. "Do you have any toys? Any nice jingly things?"

Onestar stopped himself from rolling his eyes. *Is she mouse-brained?* He knew he would have to be polite to her if he wanted her help.

Meanwhile the ginger tom was batting playfully at his denmate's ear. "He won't have any toys," he meowed. "Just take a whiff of him—he's clearly a stray."

All Onestar's thoughts about being polite fled out of his brain. He drew himself up and slid out his claws. "I am *not* a stray," he asserted. "I am a *warrior!*"

To his dismay both kittypets collapsed into *mrrow*s of laughter. "Yes, sure you are," the white she-cat purred. "Sometimes I pretend I'm a princess."

It took all Onestar's self-control to hang on to his patience. He had no idea what a princess was, and he didn't want to know. "If one of you will lead me to Melody," he mewed, "I'll catch you some fresh-kill, and the taste of it will *blow your minds!*"

He thought that was a pretty good offer, and he couldn't imagine why the kittypets burst out into *mrrow*s of laughter again.

"Fresh-kill?" the white kittypet asked. "You mean mice and stuff like that? Oh, no." She bent her head and gave a few licks to her luxuriant chest fur. "The blood would get all over my pelt." Then, when Onestar was beginning to despair, she reluctantly rose to her paws. "Okay, I'll be nice and take you for free this time. But if you come across anything jingly, you know where to bring it."

She led the way out of the garden and padded alongside Onestar beside the Twoleg dens. "My name is Snowflake," she meowed. "What's yours?"

"Onestar."

Snowflake's eyes stretched wide in surprise. "That's . . . a bit odd."

Onestar thought of telling her it was the name of a Clan leader, then reflected that it wouldn't mean anything to Snowflake, who clearly had snowflakes for brains. *Besides, I've had enough of boasting to kittypets!*

"Tell me about those other cats you asked about," Snowflake continued after a few moments. "What did they look like?"

"Smoke is a she-cat," Onestar replied. "Very pretty, with long gray fur. Darkkit—well, he won't be a kit any longer—is white with black splotches around his eyes, and a black tail."

Snowflake shuddered. "I don't remember ever seeing Smoke, but I think I did have a run-in with Darkkit—though the cat I met was called Dark*tail*. And . . . *wow*. That cat is not nice." She halted and leaned over to whisper into Onestar's ear. "I heard that he *killed* a cat who lived a few streets away. Dudley was his name."

Onestar gulped uncomfortably. He remembered Dudley, the kind, friendly ginger tom who had shared his treats in the monster den.

"Surely that's not true," he meowed.

I hope it isn't, he mused silently. *Or at least that Darktail had a good reason.*

Snowflake merely shook her head, and led him on until she slipped into a garden that seemed familiar to Onestar.

Padding up to the den, Snowflake flung back her head and yowled, "Melody! Melody! There's someone to see you!"

A few moments passed, and then a small door in the big Twoleg door opened and Melody slipped into the garden. When she spotted Onestar, she halted, her eyes wide with shock. "Onewhisker!" she exclaimed, racing across the garden to rub her muzzle against his. "I thought you left. Where have you been?"

Before Onestar could reply, Snowflake dipped her head to him and took a step back. "I'll be going then," she mewed. "I have my sleep to catch up on. Don't forget the jingly thing!"

Onestar dipped his head in return. "Thank you, Snowflake," he responded. "You've been a great help."

"Come over here," Melody urged him when the white kittypet had gone. She led him across the garden into the shade of a flourishing bush with huge flat leaves. "Now we can talk. What happened to you, Onewhisker? Where did you go?"

"I'm Onestar now," Onestar told her, and was pleased to see her eyes grow wide. The cat who had been Tansypaw would know exactly what it meant to be Clan leader.

"I'm so impressed!" she declared. "But if any cat deserves it, it's you, Onestar." She tucked her paws comfortably underneath her. "Tell me all about it."

Onestar gave her a quick account of the Great Journey,

and how the Clans had found their new home beside the lake. Melody listened with her gaze fixed on him and her jaws slightly gaping as if she were drinking in every word.

"You almost make me wish I'd stayed," she mewed wistfully when he had finished. "But I would never have made it as a warrior. Not like you—and Brushpaw."

Onestar hesitated. *I know I can't speak of this to my Clan, but it can't do any harm to tell this kittypet.* "I've seen Brushpaw," he told her. "He's in StarClan. He's happy."

Melody took a huge breath, joy flooding into her eyes. "Oh, thank you, Onestar! It makes me so glad to hear that. I've missed him so much, but I can bear it, if he's happy." She paused for a moment, then gave her pelt a shake. "Bailey died a few moons ago, too, when it was cold. I wish I could tell her Brushpaw is okay. But maybe she knows, wherever she is."

Onestar nodded. He couldn't imagine where kittypets went when they died, but he hoped that Bailey did know, and was at peace.

"Anyway, tell me why you're here," Melody continued. "Why have you come all this way?"

"I wanted to see if I could find Smoke and Darktail," Onestar explained.

Melody's expression darkened, and a few heartbeats passed before she responded. "I'm sorry, Onestar. It isn't good news."

"Why?" Onestar's belly cramped with anxiety. "What happened?"

"Smoke and Darktail were taken in by a Twoleg down the street, when Darktail was still quite young," Melody began.

"But as Darktail grew, he developed a mean streak. He got into a fight about territory with another kittypet who lived nearby, and killed him. But the worst thing was when he attacked the Twoleg's kit. That made the Twoleg furious. You won't know this, Onestar, but . . ." Melody hesitated, blinking unhappily. "There's a place where Twolegs sometimes take cats—cats they don't like. I don't know what happens there, but the cats never come back."

"Are you telling me Darktail is dead?" Onestar asked.

Melody shook her head. "Smoke realized her kit was in trouble, and the two of them escaped before the Twoleg could catch him."

"So they went back to being strays?"

"Yes. Darktail liked to call himself a warrior, but he was a terrible hunter. He'd never had the proper training, and both of them were used to being fed by Twolegs. I tried to help, and so did some of the other kittypets, sharing our food, but it was never enough. They both got so skinny, and Darktail picked fights with every cat, even the ones who were trying to help. Then . . ." Melody paused, squeezing her eyes tight shut, then took a breath and went on. "Smoke was killed at the end of this street. A monster got her just as she was running across to join Darktail."

Deep sadness crept over Onestar, as if a fog were gathering around him. Even though he knew that he could never be mates again with the pretty gray she-cat, he had looked forward to meeting her once more, and doing what he could to make up for abandoning her.

She'll never know that I kept my promise, he thought, *because I'm too late. She said she'd believe I'd come back when she saw it, and now she never will.*

"What happened to Darktail?" he asked hoarsely.

Melody shook her head. "I don't know. I never saw him again. I don't want to see him."

Onestar was still trying to make sense of what he had heard. He had cared deeply for Smoke, back when he'd lived in the old territory, and he had always thought she would do well for herself without him. Now she was dead, and partly because of the actions of the kit they shared.

I didn't mean it to end like this.

Melody leaned over and gave his ear a gentle, comforting lick. "I know you were . . . close," she murmured.

"Did Smoke tell you?" Onestar asked.

"Not exactly," Melody replied. "But she always said that Darktail's father was a Clan cat. And it was pretty obvious *which* Clan cat. They didn't all come visiting, you know."

She sat beside Onestar in silence while, just for a few moments, he gave himself up to his fog of grief. He had loved Smoke for her soft fur, her shining eyes, and her sweet scent—and, if he was honest with himself, for her admiration of him. She hadn't meant as much to him as Whitetail, who shared his warrior's life, but it was still devastating to hear of her death.

"Smoke's Twoleg found her body," Melody mewed eventually, her voice soft and sympathetic. "She was terribly upset, too. I'm sure she would have kept Smoke if it hadn't been for

Darktail. She buried her in her garden—would you like me to take you there?"

Onestar turned to her with a purr of gratitude. "Yes, please."

Melody led the way out of the garden and alongside the Thunderpath until they reached a large, comfortable-looking Twoleg den. Onestar could imagine that Smoke would have been well looked after there. Melody sneaked through a gap in the fence and Onestar followed her.

The grass in front of the den was strewn with bits of brightly colored Twoleg kit stuff. Skirting it, Melody led Onestar to a small tree with bright red leaves and gestured with her tail.

"That's where Smoke is buried," she meowed.

It was a beautiful place, but a shiver passed through Onestar at the thought of his bright, active Smoke lying there in the cold ground. *She was a kittypet. She won't even make it to StarClan.*

Melody brushed her pelt against his. "I'll leave you alone now," she murmured. "If you need anything more, you know where to find me. It was lovely to see you again."

"It was great to see you," Onestar responded. "Thank you, Melody."

He rubbed his cheek against hers, and watched her as she slipped out of the garden.

Left alone, Onestar sat quietly beside Smoke's grave, pondering all the decisions he had made since they met. *Where did it go so wrong?* He had always told himself that he'd had no choice but to leave her, but he had always believed that someday he would have the chance to tell her how sorry he was that he had never come back, and find a way to make it up to her. But now, here, guilt was swamping him as if he were sinking into mud. *Smoke didn't deserve to die like this. She didn't deserve to be treated like I treated her.*

"Smoke, I'll never forgive myself," he meowed aloud. "I should never have left you, but I'm here now. I'm so, so sorry."

The sun was going down as Onestar finally rose to leave. He knew he had to go home, to the lake. His Clanmates would be wondering what had happened to him.

But Onestar couldn't help mulling over what Stoneteller had told him, about the darkness that was coming to the Clans. The Tribe cat had told him that he had the power to solve the problem, but it would cost him.

What will it cost? he asked himself. *What will I lose?*

Even though those were important questions, there was one that was more important still—a question that nagged at Onestar's mind like a burr in his pelt.

Where is Darktail now?

CHAPTER 21

The last red streaks of sunlight were fading from the sky as Onestar trekked across the moor toward the WindClan camp. Every muscle in his body was groaning with weariness, but even worse was the weight of turmoil in his own mind.

With every paw step of the long journey, he had been unable to shake off his memories of Smoke: her beautiful soft fur, her playfulness, and the admiration in her eyes when she gazed at him. Her look of hurt and betrayal when he had refused to take her into the Clan and be a father to their kit. And now she was dead.

"I'm sorry, Smoke," he murmured aloud. "I never meant for it to end like this."

Onestar hoped that somewhere—wherever Smoke's spirit resided now—she could hear him, and maybe even find it in her heart to forgive him.

Eventually Onestar's regret and guilt over Smoke gave way to the dread about Darktail, which was growing like a malignant worm in his belly. He wished he could have seen his son while he was in the Twolegplace, and found out whether what the kittypets had told him was true.

Where is Darktail now? And what is he thinking? Does he feel guilty about Smoke's death? Does he resent me? Onestar wondered.

The worm of dread began to swell inside him as he worried that Darktail was still angry with him, and might try to find him. He remembered how Snowflake had told him that Darktail had killed Dudley, and asked himself if he should fear for his own safety, or that of his Clan.

Could he have followed me all the way here to the Clan territories?

Onestar let out a snort, dismissing his fears as absurd. He had never seen Darktail in the Twolegplace, and he had no reason to suppose that Darktail had seen him. Besides, he wasn't a new apprentice, just out of the nursery. He didn't think that any cat—much less an untrained rogue—could have followed him all the way back to the moor without being spotted.

Yet the vision of his destiny, padding along his trail on inexorable paws, wouldn't leave him. He cast a nervous glance over his shoulder, but he could see nothing except the empty sweep of the twilit moor.

Where are you, Darktail? Are we fated to meet again?

Deep in thought, Onestar didn't realize how close he was to the camp until a rush of paw steps startled him out of his musing. Three cats were racing toward him out of the near-darkness; Harespring was in the lead, closely followed by Whitetail and Emberfoot.

"Where have you *been?*" Whitetail demanded, her eyes frantic. "What took you so long? We thought something must have happened to you."

"Yes, I was beginning to think I ought to go to the Moonpool to ask StarClan for my nine lives and my name," Harespring declared. There was a hint of humor in the deputy's tone, contradicting the worry in his eyes. "I hope the journey was worth it."

I hope so, too, Onestar thought, reflecting on his real journey. He was touched by his Clanmates' concern, but he couldn't tell them the truth about why he had been away for so long.

"Yes, my visit to the Moonpool was helpful," he responded, stroking his tail across Whitetail's shoulder. "But on my way back, I spotted some stoats heading for the camp, so I chased them off, right out of the territory. When the stoats were gone, I found myself in some woodland that I'd never seen before, and the whole place reeked of fox."

"Did you meet them? Are you hurt?" Whitetail asked, scanning him anxiously.

"No, I didn't see the foxes," Onestar reassured her. "I got out of there pretty quickly, I can tell you! I was on the edge of a Twolegplace—I think it must have been near where Crowfeather and the others found Nightcloud. I crossed the Thunderpath and took refuge from the foxes in a Twoleg garden. It started to rain, so I sheltered in a small Twoleg den. And would you believe it, the next morning, just as I was waking up, the Twoleg came and shut me in!"

Emberfoot shook his head "Twolegs!"

"I yowled and yowled," Onestar continued. He had thought up this story on the way back, and he had to admit that he was getting unexpected enjoyment out of telling it. "But the flea-brained Twoleg took no notice. I must have been trapped for *days!* If there hadn't been a mouse or two in there, I could have starved."

Suppose they notice that I haven't lost weight? he asked himself worriedly. *Maybe if I just keep talking . . .*

"And there was no way out?" Harespring asked.

Onestar shook his head. He was almost starting to believe in the small, dark Twoleg den himself. "Eventually the Twoleg opened up the den again, and I escaped. I don't think the daft furball even realized I was there. And after that I came back, but it took me two or three days to find the way. And here I am. I'm sorry for worrying you," he added, "but making sure the stoats were gone was my first priority."

"It's great that you protected the Clan," Emberfoot meowed.

"And mouse-brained that you did it by yourself!" Whitetail hissed.

"Yes, she's right," Harespring agreed with an irritated flick of his tail. "The Clan leader shouldn't be facing off with dangerous stoats alone. You're much too important."

Onestar nodded, letting out a sigh. "Thank you, Harespring. I promise that if the vicious creatures are spotted again, I'll organize a patrol and take care of them once and for all."

He headed toward the camp, escorted by his Clanmates, with Whitetail so close to his side that their pelts brushed. Onestar felt an extra pang of guilt that he had upset and worried her so much.

But it had to be done, he reflected. *And I seem to have gotten away with it.*

As he padded into his den and flopped down gratefully

into his nest, Onestar was still thinking about the real danger that might be on the horizon. He could only hope that it would be as easy to face, and that he didn't need to go on worrying about it—or lying to his Clan.

Snow lay thickly on the forest floor as Onestar padded through the trees, feeling the icy cold strike up through his pads. Icicles glimmered in the moonlight as they hung from the leafless branches. He thought he must be in the small stretch of woodland on the WindClan border, though he didn't exactly recognize the place.

Just ahead, Onestar heard the crunch of paw steps heading his way. Still, he couldn't see any creature in the stark white expanse. Then suddenly two startlingly blue eyes opened up in front of him, rimmed by black fur. With a gasp of horror he recognized the cat he had last seen as a tiny kit. *Darktail!*

Darktail barreled into him and pinned him down, hissing in his ear as he raised a paw to slash his sharp claws through Onestar's throat.

Onestar startled awake to find himself in his own den. He lay there for a moment, his chest heaving, thankful that his encounter with the fearsome cat had been only a dream. Rising to his paws, he gave a long stretch, then padded out into the open, thinking that he would eat a piece of prey and look up at the stars until his mind settled again and he could go back to sleep.

But on his way to the fresh-kill pile he spotted a white cat crouched at the top of the hollow, gazing out across the moor.

All he could see were its haunches and rounded shoulders; the moon was hidden behind cloud, so it was hard to make out details, but something about the cat made him suddenly sure it was Darktail.

But that's mouse-brained! Onestar tried to reassure himself. *How could Darktail possibly find me here?*

His heart thudding in his throat, Onestar almost called out, then stopped himself just in time. He didn't want to rouse the whole Clan. If his son really had followed him to the new territories, he needed time to think before he introduced him to his Clanmates.

Onestar padded silently across the camp and began to climb the slope toward the white cat. "Darktail, is that you?" he murmured as he drew closer. "I'm sorry—I never meant for things to turn out like this."

At the sound of his voice the cat sat up and turned toward him. Onestar halted, shock and relief wrestling inside him. The cat was not Darktail; she was Whitetail. Onestar realized that it must be her turn to guard the camp. Seeing only her back view and in a poor light, he hadn't recognized her.

How much did she hear?

"Onestar?" His mate gave him a puzzled look. "What are you doing here? And what were you meowing about? Something about being sorry?"

"Sorry . . . yes, sorry you were upset." Onestar was thankful that she clearly hadn't heard everything he had said, and especially not the name of Darktail. "I didn't mean to stay away so long."

"Well, it wasn't your fault." Whitetail tilted her head, inviting him to sit at her side. "And you're back safe. That's all that matters."

Settling down close to her, Onestar enjoyed the feel of her soft fur and her sweet, familiar scent. *The moor is peaceful,* he thought, gazing out across the hills. *The Clan is safe, and I have Whitetail by my side. Life is good.*

Onestar told himself that he needed to stop worrying about Darktail, and enjoy what he had. There was no way that Darktail could possibly find him.

But he couldn't quite forget about Darktail and the thought that sometime in the future, their paths must converge again.

If so, I'll have to deal with him. But not now. There's plenty of time.

CHAPTER 22

Onestar padded across the moor, a rabbit dangling from his jaws. Prey was running well; Oatclaw, Gorsetail, and Furzepelt, who made up the rest of the hunting patrol, were also carrying fresh-kill. The Clan would feast tonight.

The ground was spongy underpaw from heavy rain the night before, the moorland dotted with tiny pools reflecting the gray of the sky. The sun must have risen by now, but the clouds threatened more rain. Onestar was reminded of the recent Great Storm, when it had seemed as if the whole forest would be swallowed up in the flood. He and many other cats had assumed that that was the meaning of the second wave of water in Kestrelflight's vision, the threat to the Clans that would be even worse than the stoats.

But it's over now, Onestar thought, the rich juices of the rabbit in his nose. *It's over, and the Clans survived.*

Once, Onestar had believed that the medicine cat's vision must have referred to Darktail, but he had heard nothing of his son since his visit to the old territories. As the seasons passed, he convinced himself that there was no way Darktail could have discovered where the Clans were living now. *He might even be dead,* Onestar reflected—hardly knowing how he felt about that—if Darktail had gone on picking fights until he met a cat bigger and tougher than himself. Onestar thought about him now and again, with a twinge of the old regret, but he was sure that his secret must be buried forever.

Now there was a new prophecy, and all the medicine cats were busy working out what it might mean. *Embrace what you find in the shadows, for only they can clear the sky.* Many cats thought it must refer to the two abandoned kits Alderpaw and Needlepaw had found. But Alderpaw was training to be a medicine cat in ThunderClan, and Needlepaw was a ShadowClan apprentice, so those two Clans had each taken a kit. Onestar felt like shrugging off the whole affair. It didn't seem to have much to do with WindClan.

As soon as Onestar and his patrol reached the camp and looked down into the hollow, he could see that something was wrong. Cats were dashing about anxiously, like ants if some other creature accidentally stumbled over their anthill. A wailing sound of a cat in deep distress rose from the nursery.

Onestar's heart began to pound. *That must be Heathertail!* His daughter had recently given birth to Breezepelt's kits, and Onestar couldn't have been prouder. His pelt rose in horror at the thought that something might have happened to one of them.

As he began to race down into the hollow, Harespring came rushing up to meet him. "It's Smokekit!" the deputy gasped. "She's missing. We're searching the camp."

Onestar's belly cramped when Harespring named the kit.

He knew that Heathertail and Breezepelt had named her because of the color of her fur, and not after the cat Onestar had secretly mated with. But he wished they could have chosen any other name.

He pushed the thought aside as he bounded into the camp and followed Harespring into the nursery. Heathertail was there, curled around Smokekit's sister, Brindlekit; her eyes were distraught, and when she saw her father, she let out another heart-rending wail.

"It's Smokekit! She's gone!"

Beside her, Breezepelt pressed closer to her and bared his teeth. "If some cat took her, I'll tear his pelt into tiny bits!"

"Try to be calm," Onestar meowed, though his own thoughts were in a turmoil. "We *will* find her. I promise."

Harespring slipped out of the nursery, and returned a moment later to stand at Onestar's shoulder. "I'm sure she's not in the camp," he reported. "But Crowfeather is here. He says he might have information."

"Bring him in," Onestar ordered.

The gray-black warrior padded in through the gorse branches and dipped his head. He was clearly tense, his claws sliding in and out. *Smokekit is his kin too,* Onestar told himself.

"I've been on the dawn patrol," Crowfeather told Onestar and the others. "All the scents are faint because of the rain, but we picked up something in the air."

"Rogues?" Onestar asked.

"We couldn't be sure," Crowfeather replied. "But it might have been."

Fear griped deep inside Onestar's belly. He couldn't imagine why a passing group of rogues would have risked sneaking into the camp by night to steal a kit.

Unless they had a reason to hurt us. His old fears reawakened, a shiver passing through him from ears to tail-tip. He wondered whether it was possible that Darktail, after all this time, *had* found the Clans and come seeking his revenge. *What better way than to steal—and maybe kill—my kin?*

Onestar took a deep breath, telling himself not to imagine the worst. "If you're not sure about the rogue scent," he meowed to Crowfeather, "then maybe Smokekit just wandered off. In that case, she might not be far away."

"She would never do that," Breezepelt objected.

Who knows what a kit might do? It's more likely that Smokekit would wander off than that a rogue would take her. But Onestar had enough sense not to disagree out loud with the worried father. "I'll organize a patrol," he declared. "Crowfeather, you can come and show us where you thought you scented the rogues."

"I'm coming too," Breezepelt growled.

Onestar could tell from the anger in the black warrior's voice that if he found a rogue anywhere near his kit, that cat would wish they had never been kitted, let alone dared to enter WindClan's camp.

"Put more cats on guard outside the camp," he instructed Harespring as he left the nursery. "And a couple of the strongest warriors on guard here. Just to be on the safe side."

Harespring gave a brisk nod. "I'm on it, Onestar."

With Breezepelt and Crowfeather alongside him, Onestar

headed out of the camp, calling to Oatclaw and Sedgewhisker to join them.

"Where did you scent these rogues?" he asked Crowfeather.

"In the woods near the ThunderClan border," the gray-black warrior replied.

"Then we'll go that way."

The patrol padded across the moor, spreading out in a long line to search as wide an area as they could. Onestar tasted the air at every paw step, but he couldn't scent anything except for moorland soil and water, and traces of prey. There was no sign of Smokekit, or of any rogues. The recent rain had washed most of the scents away.

Onestar felt his chest tighten with panic, though outwardly he fought to stay calm. *Maybe Breezepelt was right when he said Smokekit would never wander away. But then—what happened to her?*

As the patrol reached the outskirts of the woodland, Onestar thought that he could detect something unusual flowing over his scent glands. It was very faint, nowhere near strong enough to identify as rogues.

"Was that what you picked up?" he asked Crowfeather.

The gray-black warrior gave a curt nod. "Yes, but what does it tell us? This StarClan-cursed rain . . ."

If some cat was looking to steal a kit, Onestar thought uneasily, *they might have planned to strike in the rain.* But he didn't want to believe that, and quickly pushed the thought away.

Once inside the wood, the patrol split up, with orders to check under every bush and bramble thicket. Onestar's pelt was soon soaked as he brushed through the long grass; more water dripped on him from the tree branches, and from thrusting his head beneath roots and into clumps of fern.

"Smokekit! Smokekit!" he called, but there was no reply except for the echoes of his Clanmates' voices.

Onestar was ready to despair when he heard Crowfeather's voice raised from the direction of the stream that marked the ThunderClan border. "Over here!"

Onestar raced through the trees to his side; Breezepelt dashed up from farther downstream. Oatclaw and Sedge-whisker joined them a moment later.

Crowfeather was standing beside an elder bush that leaned out over the stream. As he drew closer, Onestar spotted Smokekit lying among the roots. Her gray fur was darkened by rain, plastered to her body so that she looked heartbreak-ingly tiny and vulnerable. At first, Onestar was afraid she was dead, his heart thumping painfully, until he saw the steady rise and fall of her chest.

"Smokekit! Smokekit!" Breezepelt bounded up to her and bent over her, covering her ears with frantic licks and stroking her with a paw that shook with relief. "Smokekit, wake up!"

Onestar bent his head to give the sleeping kit a thorough sniff, but the ThunderClan border markers on the far side of the stream—clearly renewed that morning after the rain—were strong enough to swamp anything else.

Smokekit's eyes opened and she let out a tiny gasp. "Breeze-pelt!" she exclaimed, gazing up happily into Breezepelt's eyes. "You found me!"

Breezepelt let out a long breath. "Yes, we found you. Every-thing's okay now, Smokekit."

"But what are you doing out here?" Onestar asked.

Smokekit blinked, bewildered; it took a few moments before she could wake up completely and tell her story. "I was asleep in the nursery," she began, "but something woke me . . . a sound like a cat was hurt. I thought maybe it needed help, so I went out and followed the sound. I thought it was coming from outside the camp, so I climbed the slope. . . ."

"Oh, Smokekit!" Breezepelt breathed out.

"Maybe I shouldn't have," Smokekit admitted. "I guess I should have woken up an older cat."

"So what happened next?" Crowfeather asked.

"I'd just gotten to the top of the slope when something clamped its mouth around my neck and squeezed. I tried to call out, but I couldn't."

Onestar felt his heart jolt painfully. At first Smokekit's story had sounded as if she might have just wandered off, but now it was obvious that something—or some *cat*—really had attacked her. *Oh StarClan, that's not good!*

"A fox?" Sedgewhisker asked.

Smokekit shook her head. "I saw a flash of white fur, and then everything went dark. And I don't remember anything else until I woke up here, with all of you around me."

The kit's story filled Onestar with apprehension. Her mention of white fur instantly brought Darktail back to his mind. There were no white predators in the forest; even the stoats had been gone for seasons—and in any case, their pelts wouldn't have been white now, in early leaf-fall. And no other cat, not even a rogue, had any reason to steal a kit.

Could it have been Darktail? he wondered. *He might have asked* wandering rogues until he found someone who could tell him where to find the Clans . . . and find me.

Then, somehow, Darktail must have entered the Wind-Clan camp, avoiding the warrior on guard, and managed to get so close to the nursery that he could lure one of the Clan's most vulnerable members off into the forest.

If it was Darktail, why didn't he kill Smokekit? Onestar asked himself. Then the answer came, even more chilling.

He hadn't killed her, but he had choked her into unconsciousness to show how easily he could have killed her. Then he had left her for Onestar to find.

A deep shudder passed through Onestar from his ears to the tips of his claws. He could hardly bear to think about the horror that could have befallen his young kin—the horror she had already suffered—all to send him a message. His belly began to roil with apprehension as he thought about the questions his Clanmates were sure to ask.

Some of them met Smoke, and Darktail when he was a kit. Will any of them connect this white predator with the kit I left behind so long ago?

Onestar realized that he had been wrong when he'd assumed that his son would never be able to find WindClan. He was beginning to believe that Darktail had done just that.

Will my past go on stalking me forever, until at last it traps me?

"It could have been rogues," Crowfeather mused. "We were here very early, before ThunderClan renewed their scent markers, and I'm sure I picked up that weird scent near this elder tree."

"But the scent could be old," Oatclaw argued. "Rogues pass

by our borders all the time, after all."

"That's true," Sedgewhisker agreed. "If rogues were responsible, we ought to be able to scent them on Smokekit, rain or no rain." She bent her head and gave the kit a thorough sniff, then straightened up, shaking her head. "There's something there, but I can't say what. Smokekit is probably confused, and no cat can blame her for that. Maybe the stoats are back, and it was one of them that attacked her."

"Yes, that must be it!" Onestar exclaimed, desperately wanting to believe Sedgewhisker's words. *But how could a stoat lure Smokekit out of camp?* he wondered. And he had already realized that a stoat wouldn't be white at this season. "They tried to take Smokekit as prey," he asserted, "but something must have scared them off."

Sedgewhisker and Oatclaw murmured agreement, and even Breezepelt seemed to accept the explanation, though Onestar noticed that Crowfeather was giving him a doubtful look.

"Breezepelt, you take Smokekit back to camp and have Kestrelflight check her out," he meowed. "The rest of you can go with them. I'll check the tunnels. If we do have stoats on the territory again, that's probably where they're hiding."

"I'll go with you, Onestar." There was a sarcastic edge to Crowfeather's voice. "With dangerous stoats on the loose, you shouldn't go into the tunnels alone."

Crowfeather must suspect me of something, Onestar thought, fighting panic. *Could he know about Darktail? Others in the Clan did—Crowfeather's mother did—so it's possible.*

But arguing with Crowfeather, Onestar knew, would just make him more suspicious. "Very well," he mewed curtly, and led the way to the tunnels while Breezepelt and the others headed back to the camp.

When WindClan had first moved into the territory, the tunnels had been home to rabbits, but when the stoats invaded, they had either been killed or scared off. Even when the stoats were driven out, the rabbits had not returned, and now the tunnels were empty. When Onestar entered, with Crowfeather hard on his paws, there were no scents to pick up except for the sandy soil and the moorland vegetation drifting in from outside.

It's obvious there are no stoats here, Onestar thought.

Even so, he kept on searching in side tunnels and the dens where rabbits, and then stoats, had cared for their young. He was desperately hoping that they might find a stoat or two, or recent traces of them, because that would be easier to deal with than the reappearance of Darktail.

Crowfeather padded after him in disapproving silence until they reached the place where the last light from the entrance faded away and the tunnel led on into darkness.

Here, Crowfeather halted. "What's going on, Onestar?" he demanded. "If there were stoats here, the smell would have struck us by now. And I don't think it was a stoat who took Smokekit. I'm not sure what it was, but I have a feeling that *you* know. Smokekit is safe, but you're behaving like ants are crawling through your pelt. Is there anything you want to tell me?" The look he gave pierced Onestar to his depths. "I know some secrets are better off kept," he continued, repeating the words Onestar had spoken to him so many seasons ago. "But if one becomes a burden, it might be easier to bear when it's shared. And if your secret might endanger Wind-Clan, shouldn't you tell some cat the truth?"

How did that difficult young cat become so wise? Onestar wondered. For a moment he considered confiding in Crowfeather. Being Clan leader was lonely work, and he could use a friend, a cat he could trust. He hadn't experienced that since his friendship with Firestar, before he ever became Clan leader. *Maybe I would feel better. Crowfeather might even have an idea about how to deal with Darktail.*

Then Onestar realized all over again that Smokekit could have died. If he told the truth, the Clan might blame him for keeping such a dangerous secret from them—a secret that put the safety of their kits at risk. *No,* he decided, *I have to deal with this on my own. For now, I have to stick to my story.*

"I don't know what you're meowing on about," he told Crowfeather with an irritated twitch of his tail. "It must have been a stoat, and we should go on through the tunnels to ThunderClan so that we can warn them."

Crowfeather let out a long sigh, clearly showing Onestar that he thought doing that would be pointless. "If that's how you want to play it, fine," he mumbled. "But some secrets have a way of revealing themselves."

A chill crept over Onestar as he led the way into the darkness. He didn't want to admit, even to himself, that Crowfeather was right. And if it turned out that Darktail *had* stolen Smokekit, he had no idea what his next move should be.

Emerging from the tunnels on the ThunderClan side, Onestar immediately picked up a strong, fresh scent. A moment later, Poppyfrost and Rosepetal padded into view from around a clump of ferns. Both she-cats were carrying prey. They approached warily when they spotted the WindClan cats; Onestar hoped they wouldn't think he and Crowfeather were trespassing.

"Hi," Onestar meowed, careful not to move away from the opening of the tunnel. "We're just here to give you a message."

Rosepetal set down the vole she was carrying. "Okay, spit it out," she meowed.

"We have evidence that stoats might be moving back into our territory," Onestar informed the ThunderClan warriors. "You should tell Bramblestar to keep a lookout."

Rosepetal and Poppyfrost exchanged a surprised glance. "It's a long time since we've seen any stoats," Poppyfrost mewed. "But we'll pass your message on."

Onestar dipped his head. "Thank you."

The two ThunderClan cats hurried on, while Onestar and Crowfeather turned back in to the tunnels. As they made their way toward their own territory, Onestar was aware of annoyance coming off Crowfeather in waves, like the scent of nearby prey. He knew that the younger warrior didn't believe him, knew that he was only inventing the stoats' return for some reason of his own.

Well, that's just too bad, Onestar thought. *Stoats or no stoats, WindClan's safety is at stake, and I'll do whatever it takes to protect them.*

As soon as he arrived back in camp, Onestar called Harespring to him. "We'll keep an extra guard on the camp, and on the nursery, for the next couple of nights at least," he instructed his deputy. "Something is going on, and until we know what it is, we can't be too careful."

Seeing Breezepelt sitting outside Kestrelflight's den, Onestar padded over to him. "How is Smokekit?" he asked.

"Okay, I think," Breezepelt replied, and added with a touch of his old resentment, "Kestrelflight threw me out so he would have enough room to work."

Onestar touched the black warrior on his shoulder with the tip of his tail. "I'm sure that means there's nothing to worry about." *I hope that's true.*

Slipping through the crack in the rock that led to Kestrelflight's den, Onestar picked up the clean tang of marigold and saw the medicine cat trickling the juice into Smokekit's scratches. Heathertail was crouching beside her kit, covering Smokekit's ears with gentle licks.

"Is she badly hurt?" Onestar asked, with an uncomfortable squirming in his belly.

"No, she'll be fine," Kestrelflight assured him. "She has a few scratches and bruises, but that's all. I'll keep her here overnight, just to be sure."

"Do I have to?" Smokekit complained. "I want to go and play with Brindlekit. I thought up this really cool game! I'm going to be a rogue sneaking into camp, and Brindlekit—"

"That's enough!" Onestar interrupted. "A rogue sneaking into camp isn't something to make a game of. But I don't think you should keep her here, Kestrelflight," he added to the medicine cat. "I'm going to have her spend the night in my den. If any stray stoat wants to get at her, it'll have to go through me first."

"Sleep in the leader's den?" Smokekit's eyes stretched wide, and she gave an ecstatic little wriggle. "Wait till I tell Brindlekit! She'll be *so* jealous!"

Meanwhile, Heathertail and Kestrelflight were exchanging a puzzled glance. "That's a bit unusual," Kestrelflight commented, "for a kit to sleep in the leader's den. Smokekit will be safe here in my den for tonight."

"No, she stays with me," Onestar insisted. "She will be safe—because I'm going to make sure of it!"

CHAPTER 23

❧

Onestar kept up the extra guards around the camp for the next few days. He also sent out more patrols around the territory to look out for anything strange and to make sure that the border markers were always fresh and strong, offering a message to any rogues who might be wandering near the moor: *This is WindClan territory, and you cannot enter uninvited.* Every time he sent out a patrol, he noticed Crowfeather's growing curiosity and frustration. Onestar didn't dare confide in him; all he could do was ignore his penetrating gaze and the flexing of his claws.

He had also taken to hunting alone. "I need to clear my head," he had explained to Whitetail when she wondered why he wouldn't join a patrol, or at least go with another cat. "And I want to see if there are any changes to how the prey is running."

But his real reason was his hope that if Darktail was stalking him, his son would approach while he was by himself, so Onestar could confront him without any of his Clanmates around. More than that, he hoped that Darktail *didn't* approach him, so that he could convince himself that it was some unknown threat that had taken Smokekit.

A couple of days after Smokekit's disappearance, Onestar was out on the moor before sunrise, the boggy scent of water filling his nostrils. It was quiet, and the prey was running well. To begin with, Onestar lost himself in tracking small creatures through the gorse and heather, until he ended up on the outskirts of the stretch of woodland where he and his Clanmates had found the missing kit.

Scratching at the earth underneath a tree to bury the mouse he had just killed, Onestar heard the crack of a branch above his head. He looked up to see the branch falling, rustling the leaves as it plunged through them, plummeting straight for his head. With only a heartbeat to spare, Onestar sprang aside and rolled clear, while the branch fell with a sickening thud right beside him.

While he was still on his back, Onestar glimpsed a flash of white darting through the upper branches of the tree. "Darktail!" he exclaimed, his voice a hoarse croak.

The flash was gone too quickly for him to be sure it was his son, but Onestar knew it would be mouse-brained to assume that what had happened was an accident. The branch was dead, easy enough for a powerful cat to tear away from the tree, and solid enough to have injured him badly or even killed him if he hadn't been quick enough to dodge.

Could it really be Darktail? he asked himself. It was so unlikely that his son would ever find him. And if he had, why wouldn't he confront Onestar, instead of playing these sickening games? *Have I got bees in my brain? If it isn't Darktail, what is it?*

Onestar knew that if this was Darktail, his son was toying with him, just as if he were a mouse. What kind of cat would torment a cat he resented, instead of having it out face-to-face? *Is that the sort of cat Darktail is?*

Whoever it was, they wanted to terrify him, and Onestar had to admit to himself that so far the plan was working. He shivered as he scrambled up and shook debris out of his pelt, Stoneteller's long-ago words rising to the surface of his mind. *Only you can stop it, when it comes hunting you. . . .* Clearly, something was hunting him now.

The Tribe's healer had also told Onestar that solving the problem would come with a cost. *But what if that cost is one I cannot pay?* Onestar asked himself. *My life? My kin's?*

Standing underneath the tree, his heart still pounding from his narrow escape, Onestar accepted that he needed help—more help than his Clanmates would be able to provide. *I need StarClan.*

Ordinarily, Onestar would have turned to his medicine cat to speak to StarClan for him and ask for guidance. But this wasn't an ordinary problem, and Onestar wasn't sure he could trust Kestrelflight with it. He remembered the medicine cat's puzzled look when he'd said that Smokekit would sleep in the leader's den. Kestrelflight clearly suspected that something was going on. *If I told him the whole story, would he feel he had to tell the rest of the Clan?* Onestar didn't think so, but it was a risk he wasn't prepared to take. He would have to embark on this mission alone.

Sunhigh was still a long way off. Immediately, Onestar

plunged deeper into the woodland, until he reached the WindClan border markers. His pads prickled briefly with anxiety at the thought that once again his Clanmates might wonder where he had gone, but he knew he had to take the risk. Glancing swiftly around to make sure that no cat saw him, he headed upstream and crossed out of his Clan's territory, on his way to the Moonpool.

At the end of the long trek into the hills it was a relief for Onestar to pad down the spiral path and settle himself on a flat stone at the water's edge.

"I'm not a medicine cat," he mewed aloud. "But my need is very great. Please, warriors of StarClan, help me and tell me what to do."

Then he leaned over and touched his nose to the water. At once darkness gathered around him and a chill crept into the depths of his fur. The gentle splash of the waterfall died away; he couldn't see or hear anything or even feel the stone where he crouched in the living world.

Gradually, Onestar began to sense the presence of another cat, though still nothing penetrated the darkness. A voice spoke in his mind. "Tell me what is troubling you."

Onestar poured out his explanation: all about how Smoke had been his secret mate, how they had had a kit together, and how he had left both of them behind when the Clans made the Great Journey. He described his return to the Twolegplace, the news of Smoke's death, and what he had learned about Darktail. He admitted that he had kept the whole disastrous episode from his mate and the rest of his Clan.

When he reached the point in his story when he returned from the old territories, Onestar hesitated. But he realized that this would be all for nothing if he was not completely honest now.

I'll never stop feeling guilty about what happened to my daughter's kit. But there's no point in hiding it from StarClan. They see it all anyway.

Taking a deep breath, he began again. "Some creature crept into our camp and took away a kit. From what she tells us, I think it was Darktail. And earlier today I was almost killed when a branch fell on me. I saw a flash of white in the tree, and I think that was Darktail, too. He has come to take revenge; I'm afraid for my own safety and that of my Clan. Please, tell me what to do."

As Onestar finished speaking, light began to grow in front of him, revealing a black-and-white cat with a long tail and the glitter of stars in his fur.

"Tallstar!" Onestar exclaimed, dipping his head in deepest respect and awe.

"Onestar, you know what you must do," Tallstar informed him calmly.

Onestar stared at him, bewildered. *Did I come all this way just to be told I didn't have to?* "Truly, Tallstar, I don't," he responded.

The former WindClan leader tilted his head to one side. "A mother bird will sometimes leave her nest to draw a hunter's eyes away from her young," he meowed.

His words made Onestar even more confused. *The medicine cats always say that StarClan cats never give you a straight answer.* "Tallstar, I don't know what you mean," he meowed desperately.

But Tallstar's figure had already begun to change, the stars in his pelt beginning to grow and melt into one another until he became a cat made of pure light.

"No!" Onestar cried. "Please don't go!"

The light grew brighter and brighter until it was so dazzling that Onestar had to turn his eyes away. Then Tallstar was gone, leaving him in darkness again. He opened his eyes to find himself beside the Moonpool with the sun going down behind the hills.

Onestar headed back to camp with Tallstar's message still ringing in his ears. Surely his former leader couldn't really mean that he should flee and leave his Clan unprotected? He could see the logic behind it, but it still didn't feel right. But then, he told himself, StarClan wouldn't have given him that advice if they didn't know it was the best plan.

A hollow space seemed to open up inside Onestar as he accepted what he must do. As soon as he arrived back in camp, he would step down as WindClan's leader and announce that he was leaving the Clan. He knew there would be questions, and he had no idea how he would explain his decision to Whitetail.

But if it saves them from the menace that is Darktail, it will be worth it.

Onestar resolved that he would tell Kestrelflight first; at least the medicine cat would understand that he was acting under StarClan's guidance. After all, it was Kestrelflight who had received the vision about the engulfing wave sweeping out of the tunnels. Onestar had assumed that the vision had referred to the Great Storm, but now he saw that he could have been wrong.

Maybe Darktail is bringing that wave.

* * *

Night had fallen by the time Onestar arrived back at the WindClan camp. He had collected the prey from his morning hunt, so no cat questioned him when he padded into the hollow and dropped his catch on the fresh-kill pile.

Bracing himself, Onestar headed for Kestrelflight's den. But when he arrived there, he saw Fernpaw sprawled on one side, her eyes filled with pain as Kestrelflight fixed a poultice to her shoulder with cobweb.

"What happened?" Onestar asked.

"While you were away, Fernpaw went out on a hunting patrol with Crowfeather and a couple of others," Kestrelflight replied. "Somehow they got separated, and Fernpaw was attacked from behind. She got some fairly deep wounds."

Onestar felt every muscle in his body cramp with apprehension. "Fernpaw, I'm sorry," he meowed. "Did you see who or what attacked you?"

Fernpaw shook her head, wincing with pain. "No, Onestar. I hit my head on a rock, and I didn't see anything until Furzepelt found me."

"Whatever it was, it must have disappeared quickly afterward," the medicine cat declared. "Maybe it was a hawk . . ."

"Maybe," Onestar murmured. But inwardly he knew it was no hawk that had injured the apprentice. *This was the work of Darktail.*

He took a breath, bracing himself to tell Kestrelflight about his decision to leave his Clan. But before he spoke, he began to wonder what would happen if Darktail went on attacking WindClan, even after he had left. His Clanmates would be defenseless, because they would have no idea what they were dealing with. And Darktail had already shown that he was willing to hurt Onestar's kin to take his revenge on the cat he believed had ruined his life.

Suppose I tell them the truth before I leave? The idea shocked Onestar to the tips of his claws. He had always felt nothing was more important than protecting his secret. He knew how his Clan would despise him if they knew the truth. But if he was gone, he reflected, it wouldn't matter what they thought of him.

I know the cat who is doing this. . . . Onestar wanted to speak, but the words choked in his throat. He couldn't bear to see the way that the faces of his Clanmates would change. And even if they knew the truth about Darktail, the evil cat might be too powerful for them to defeat.

No, I have to stay and protect them. It's the only way!

Though he still struggled with guilt, he gave up the idea of renouncing his leadership and abandoning his Clan. It was clear that it made no difference whether he was here or not: Darktail's plan was to wreak havoc on WindClan.

Onestar thought back to the time when he had received his nine lives. Tallstar had advised him that he must always put WindClan first, no matter what his private wishes might be. Now, at the Moonpool, the former leader had seemed to be saying that to put WindClan first, he would have to leave it.

But that can't be right.

Tallstar couldn't expect him to leave WindClan vulnerable, without its leader to protect it, or to leave his kin behind, too, just as he did with Smoke and Darktail.

I won't make that same mistake twice.

His guilt vanished as Onestar realized that he hadn't understood what Tallstar was telling him. Not until now. When the mother bird left her nest, she didn't abandon her young ones. She went to face her predator head-on, away from her nestlings.

It was time for him to deal with his past, face-to-face.

CHAPTER 24

❧

Onestar was sick of being Darktail's prey. It was time to turn the hunt around onto Darktail himself. But even though his paws itched with impatience, he knew there was nothing he could do that night, except for ordering an extra guard on the nursery. Then he retreated to his den, but sleep stayed far away from him.

As soon as the first light of dawn seeped through the entrance to his den, Onestar emerged into the camp. Harespring was already there, rousing warriors for the dawn patrol.

I have to tell them something, Onestar thought. *Maybe I don't have to mention Darktail directly.*

His mind made up, Onestar strode over to join his deputy. "I think rogues are sneaking onto our territory," he announced brusquely to the assembled warriors. *No point any longer in mentioning stoats or birds.* "I want you to keep a lookout," he continued. "And report back straight away if you find anything."

Furzepelt, who was leading the patrol, nodded understanding. "If they're here, we'll find them," she promised. "Come on, Oatclaw, Emberfoot."

The three cats bounded up the slope and disappeared into

the gray mists of early morning. Harespring watched them go, then turned to Onestar. "You think we have a rogue problem?" he asked.

"Smokekit was taken, and yesterday Fernpaw was attacked," Onestar replied. Still not mentioning Darktail, he added, "We have some kind of problem, and I'm not going to stop until I find out what it is."

"But it might have been a fox that attacked Fernpaw," Harespring objected. "Smokekit too, though that doesn't explain why she wasn't killed."

"No, there's something going on that we know nothing about," Onestar insisted. "Some rogue, or some . . . creature is attacking WindClan."

Harespring stared at him, disbelief evident in his eyes. "Why would they?" he asked.

"I'm not sure," Onestar lied, "but I mean to find out."

Harespring didn't object anymore, only shook his head with a completely bemused expression. "Okay, Onestar, whatever you say," he mewed.

Nodding farewell to his deputy, Onestar checked the elders' den and made sure Whitetail had a guard, too. After that, all he could do was pace the camp, his pelt bristling and his claws digging into the ground, ignoring the weird looks he was getting from the cats who still remained in the hollow.

The sun had risen, shining red through the mist, by the time Furzepelt dashed back into the camp. "Rogues!" she gasped. "A whole group of them. We spotted them at the ThunderClan border, on our side of the stream."

Onestar's heart began to pound with anticipation at the thought of confronting Darktail face-to-face—if he really was one of the rogues who were intruding on WindClan territory. He couldn't deny that he felt a tingle of fear all through his pelt, especially when he remembered Stoneteller's words: . . . *when it comes hunting you.*

But this is a good thing, Onestar assured himself. *WindClan can beat this bunch of mange-pelts, and then all this will be over.*

"Show me where," he growled.

He took off after Furzepelt, energy surging through him as he raced across the moor. *Action at last! Watch out, Darktail—I'm coming for you!*

Plunging through the woodland, Onestar reached the border stream to see Oatclaw and Emberfoot hissing defiance at several rogues who stood clustered together on the bank. In their midst was a powerful white tom with black splotches around his eyes and a black tail.

Darktail!

A pulse of fear throbbed through Onestar at the sight of his enemy. Now that he knew that Darktail truly was hunting him and WindClan, he had to ask himself what kind of cat his son had become.

But along with the fear, a fierce satisfaction filled Onestar from ears to tail-tip. *I was right—I'm not crazy!* At least his son wasn't a shadow in his mind any longer, or a flash of white among trees.

Darktail narrowed his eyes at Onestar as he approached. "Is this how Clan cats treat visitors?" he sneered.

"No, it's how we treat trespassers," Onestar hissed.

Darktail drew his lips back in a humorless grin. "What's the matter?" he asked Onestar. "Do I remind you of some cat or something? Maybe one you knew a long time ago?"

"Maybe," Onestar responded warily. He realized that Darktail could reveal his secret, here and now, in front of his Clanmates. Drawing a deep breath, he accepted it. He couldn't bring himself to admit the truth on his own, but he was powerless to stop Darktail telling it. Maybe it was worth having his Clan know what was behind the attacks, as long as they were kept safe.

"You remind me of a cat I knew once, too," Darktail continued. "A worthless warrior who thought his Clan was more important than his kin."

Onestar winced, aware of curious looks from his own Clanmates. Then, bracing himself, he stepped aside, gesturing with his tail for his cats to stay where they were.

"A word with you," he snapped to Darktail.

His son hesitated for a moment, his eyes widening briefly before narrowing them in suspicion. He was clearly wondering whether it was worth his while to talk. Then he too signaled to his companions to keep back, and padded up to Onestar, who eased a little farther away, well out of earshot of the others.

Maybe we can settle this without claws, Onestar thought, though he recognized that it was a faint hope.

For the first time since Darktail was a kit, Onestar had a real chance to look at him. He had grown so much since then.

His fur was sleek, his muscles rippling beneath it, and he held his head and tail up with confidence. Onestar could almost have been proud of him, if it weren't for the anger that burned in his blue eyes, the same anger Onestar had sensed in him when he was a kit. *Is that my fault?* he asked himself. *Did I feed it when I abandoned him and his mother?* He had to assume it was that anger that had led to Darktail snatching Smokekit away and almost killing her, and attacking and wounding Fernpaw.

Even though it was hard to keep his claws sheathed, the memory prompted Onestar to whisper, "What is it you want?"

"I want my mother back," Darktail replied instantly.

Onestar hadn't expected that. "I'm sorry about what happened to Smoke," he mewed, bowing his head. "I never wanted that, and it must have been terrible for you to be left alone that way." He paused, but when Darktail didn't respond, he went on, "I know you feel like I wronged you. I'm sorry for that, too. But enough is enough. This has to end now."

"You can save your sympathy," Darktail snarled. "I don't need it. I have a family now." He waved his tail toward the group of rogues. "These are my Kin."

Guilt throbbed in Onestar's belly. He had denied Darktail his rightful kin, and now the rogue had created a family of his own—however rough and threatening they might be,

"I'll decide what's enough," Darktail continued. "Maybe next time I'll show your mate how bad you are at protecting your Clan. Maybe WindClan should be run by a *real* leader, like me. . . ."

Onestar almost let out a *mrrow* of laughter at the thought

of Darktail taking his place as leader of WindClan, receiving nine lives at the Moonpool, and standing on the Tallrock to issue orders to the Clan. *I made sacrifices to be a leader. Darktail wasn't even raised as a Clan cat.*

But Onestar's amusement was short-lived. The threat to Whitetail and to his own leadership stripped away the last of his patience.

"This is no place for you!" he yowled, sliding out his claws and baring his teeth. "Get out of here now and never come back!"

Darktail remained calm in the face of Onestar's show of strength. "Oh, no, it won't be that easy for you to leave me behind this time." His blue eyes glittered cruelly. "You took away the only cat I ever cared for with your selfish, cowardly choices."

"*I* took Smoke away?" Onestar couldn't let that accusation go unchallenged. "I heard it was because of *your* behavior that your Twoleg kicked you and Smoke out of her den. *That's* what led to Smoke's death, not anything I did!"

"Lies, mange-pelt!" Darktail hissed, pure fury in his eyes and his bristling fur. "It was *your* fault Smoke died. And now I'm going to do the same to you. Before I'm through, every cat you've ever loved will know pain."

"Not if you're dead!" The screech came from behind Onestar; Furzepelt flashed past him and pounced on Darktail, her claws swiping at his white fur.

For a moment Onestar stood rigid with shock. *How long was Furzepelt standing there? How much did she hear?*

Darktail sprang back so that Furzepelt's swipe caused only a surface wound. But Furzepelt's attack, the sudden reek of blood in the air, was enough to rouse the rogues. A long-furred gray tom and a she-cat with a dirty white pelt moved in to attack Furzepelt from both sides. Emberfoot and Oatclaw leaped forward to ram the two rogues from behind and reach their Clanmate's side. But then a long-furred black she-cat and a silver-gray tom let out loud yowls and leaped onto the backs of the WindClan warriors. Within a heartbeat, the encounter had become an all-out battle, the cats rolling around on the forest floor in a furious tangle of legs and tails.

The rogues' ferocity, their fighting skills, dismayed Onestar. He hadn't expected them to be a match for Clan cats. For the first time he realized that he and his Clanmates were outmatched—that they could easily lose this battle.

I didn't want this, Onestar thought. *I hoped Darktail would see reason.*

But he knew that it was much too late for that. He circled Darktail, whose muscular body looked even more formidable now that they faced each other, perhaps because of the malice glittering in his eyes.

Taking Onestar by surprise, Darktail lunged for him, ramming his weight into his shoulder. Onestar tumbled backward, pain flaring beneath his pelt. From where he lay on the ground, he could see Oatclaw struggling to reach his side, but the black she-cat and the silver tom were blocking his path. Oatclaw was fighting them both off, while Emberfoot was bravely battling the huge gray tom, trying to avoid the white she-cat's teeth at the same time. A brown tabby tom had his claws dug deep into Furzepelt's back, and for all her efforts Furzepelt couldn't get him off.

Even while Darktail moved in for a second attack, Onestar's mind was suddenly clear. He had believed that he was confronting Darktail to end their conflict. A flash of memory showed him the truth. Stoneteller, the Tribe's healer, had prophesied that there would be a cost to pay. On the verge of despair, Onestar was ready to accept that the time to pay it had come. *We're all going to die.*

The WindClan cats were badly outnumbered, but they were too far away from their camp for any of their Clanmates to notice what was happening. Then, at the last moment, hope surged into Onestar's mind: he had to move the fight to somewhere he knew Clan cats would hear it.

Just before Darktail could reach him, Onestar struggled to his paws and took off, leaping the stream and racing deeper into ThunderClan territory.

"Come back, coward!" Darktail screeched. "We aren't finished with you!"

Onestar glanced over his shoulder and saw that Darktail was charging in pursuit, with the rest of the cats, rogues and WindClan warriors, streaming after them. By the time Darktail caught up, pulling Onestar down with sharp claws, they were well on the way to ThunderClan's camp.

Darktail slashed at Onestar's neck; screeching in pain, Onestar felt a rush of blood dampen his fur. He battered at Darktail with his hind paws, but he knew he was tiring. His

Clanmates were battling bravely, but the fight could only have
one conclusion.

*Come on, ThunderClan. You're always offering help, and now I'm
ready to take it. Where are you?*

Then a gust of fresh ThunderClan scent reached Onestar,
for a moment overwhelming the reek of blood. Turning his
head, Onestar spotted Cloudtail and Mousewhisker, appearing from behind a bramble thicket several fox-lengths away.
Both cats halted, staring at the struggling cats with eyes and
jaws wide in shock.

Onestar's gaze locked with Mousewhisker's. He jerked his
head to one side, trying to tell the ThunderClan cats that they
needed to fetch Bramblestar.

Massive relief shook Onestar as the two cats raced off,
heading for their camp. Onestar was sure ThunderClan would
come; all he and his Clanmates needed to do was hold on. But
he knew that would not be easy. Writhing under Darktail's
claws, he could catch glimpses of Emberfoot and Furzepelt,
struggling in the grip of the rogues, and hear their anguished
cries. Tufts of their fur were scattered on the ground, and
their pelts were matted with blood.

Hurry, ThunderClan, Onestar urged silently.

He could feel himself weakening under Darktail's relent-
less blows when at last he heard the thrumming of many paw
steps, and a group of cats—warriors *and* medicine cats, he realized—burst out of the undergrowth.

Bramblestar was in the lead. "Help them!" he ordered.

Behind Bramblestar were Cloudtail, Birchfall, Lionblaze,
and Rosepetal; their paws seemed to fly over the ground as

they raced toward the intruders. Jayfeather and Alderpaw, both carrying leaf wraps of herbs, withdrew to the shelter of a holly bush.

For a couple of heartbeats Darktail froze in shock at the sight of them. Then he dug his claws deeper into Onestar's neck, thrusting his muzzle into Onestar's face. "Coward!" he snapped. "What pathetic excuse for a leader are you, needing ThunderClan to fight your battles?"

Onestar was stunned to silence. Darktail knew that this was ThunderClan territory, and that the newcomers were ThunderClan cats. He must have been studying the Clans for some time. When he had revealed his presence through the attacks on Smokekit and Fernpaw, and Onestar himself, it was only because he wanted to issue his challenge.

Tossing Onestar aside, Darktail threw himself at Bramble-star, who was wrestling the big gray tom off Oatclaw. But even Darktail must have realized that the tide of battle had turned. Onestar managed to sit up and saw Cloudtail thrusting himself between Furzepelt and the brown tabby tom; the tom hissed defiance and lunged at Cloudtail, knocking him off his paws. Then Birchfall was there, grabbing the tabby tom by the scruff and tossing him aside. Rosepetal had her forelegs clamped around the white she-cat's neck, rolling with her on the ground, while Emberfoot and Bramblestar together were driving back the silver gray tom.

The rogues were clearly defeated, but they still fought on. At last, Bramblestar leaped onto a tree stump and yowled, "Stop!"

The authority in his voice was enough to make warrior and

rogue alike freeze as if they had been turned to ice, each cat's face turned toward him. Onestar was affected just as much as the others, hating to admit that even he found the Thunder-Clan leader intimidating.

Bramblestar stared straight at Darktail, compelling the rogue's gaze. "Leave," he snarled. "Before we rip the pelts off your back."

An involuntary shudder rippled through Darktail's body; when he spoke, it was Onestar he addressed, his eyes filled with hatred. "This won't be the last you see of us," he hissed. "We came here for a reason, and we don't intend to leave until we're good and ready. We have a mission here, and we know more about your so-called Clans than you think."

Onestar couldn't help feeling grateful when Darktail turned to leave without another word. As he watched the other rogues limp after him into the ferns, and heard Bramblestar call Jayfeather forward to help the wounded, he wondered how close they had come to a massacre.

The ThunderClan cats had only minor injuries; they stepped back to allow the medicine cats to treat the more severely wounded WindClan warriors.

"Alderpaw, find some cobwebs," Jayfeather ordered, sniffing at a long gash down Oatclaw's side.

As the ThunderClan apprentice darted away, Onestar heard a strangled groan coming from beside a nearby tree. Furzepelt staggered into the clearing. She exchanged one glance with Onestar: a glance filled with regret, sorrow, and questions. Questions that would never be answered. She collapsed to the ground with another drawn-out groan, and the light died from her eyes.

Onestar struggled to get up, to go to his Clanmate's side. Sorrow surged over him at the thought that Furzepelt had been willing to attack Darktail and his rogues, not even knowing who he was or what he wanted from WindClan.

And now she'll never know.

But Onestar had been too badly weakened by the wound in his neck where Darktail had slashed at him. Sinking to the ground again, he heard Alderpaw and Jayfeather arguing about what they could do for him; their voices echoed strangely, as if they came from a great distance.

Letting out a final gasp, Onestar followed Furzepelt into the dark.

CHAPTER 25

Rain set in as the cats trekked back to the ThunderClan camp. When they arrived, Onestar crouched outside the medicine cats' den, his shoulders hunched against the downpour. Inside the den, Oatclaw and Emberfoot were resting after Jayfeather and Alderpaw had treated their wounds.

Even though only a few moments had passed before Onestar returned to his body, the ravages of the battle completely healed, he hadn't yet recovered from the jarring experience of losing a life. Even worse, it sickened him that it was Darktail who had stolen it.

Is this what Stoneteller meant? he wondered. *Is this the sacrifice that I had to make, to be rid of Darktail?*

He hoped that he was right, and that the price had already been paid, so that now he could concentrate on driving Darktail out of the Clan territories for good. He hadn't expected that his nine lives would slip away so quickly. *I lost a life in the stoat battle, one to greencough, one when I drove a fox off our territory . . . So many lives. Will it be Darktail who takes my last one?*

Bramblestar had called a Clan meeting, and the Thunder-Clan cats were gathered beneath the Highledge to discuss what they should do about the rogues. But Onestar's paws were itching to return to his own Clan. He was deeply grateful for what the ThunderClan cats had done, but his gratitude felt like a whole nestful of ants crawling through his pelt. He remembered the warnings Ashfoot had given him when he first became leader, about being too dependent on Thunder-Clan. *Am I in debt to Bramblestar now?* Onestar trusted the powerful tabby tom—Tigerstar's son—far less than he had trusted Firestar.

Darktail had lost the battle, but Onestar knew one defeat wouldn't be enough to stop him from haunting WindClan. His hatred ran too deep; besides, he and his rogues had killed a WindClan warrior and taken a life from their leader. With that success on his tongue like a tasty piece of fresh-kill, why wouldn't Darktail redouble his efforts?

Our conflict is not over. And we need to bury our dead.

Rising to his paws, Onestar splashed his way across the camp until he stood just below the Highledge. "I want to take Furzepelt back to our camp so we can sit vigil," he announced.

"Before you do, I'd like a quick word with you," Bramblestar meowed. "I was wondering whether these rogues could have something to do with the prophecy."

Onestar stared at him. The thought had never crossed his mind. "I doubt it," he murmured, with a dismissive flick of his ears. "What could rogues have to do with clearing the sky?"

Bramblestar's amber gaze rested on him a moment longer. "You could well be right," he admitted. "But it might be worth bearing in mind."

Onestar couldn't agree, but the ThunderClan leader's words woke a worm of uneasiness in his belly. *Could Darktail be planning something that would disrupt all the Clans? No!* He tried to push the thought away. *Surely this is our own private quarrel?*

Before Onestar could respond to Bramblestar, Jayfeather stepped forward. "Oatclaw and Emberfoot are too badly wounded to help carry Furzepelt," he objected. "Movement will reopen their wounds. They should stay here for a few days."

Onestar glared at him, even though he knew that the blind medicine cat couldn't see his hostile expression. "They are warriors. They are strong. They will travel with me."

Jayfeather turned in his direction, his blue gaze calm and unyielding. "I have an apprentice," he meowed. "Kestrelflight has none. Let him save his herbs and his energy for his Clanmates on the moor. We can take care of Oatclaw and Emberfoot until they are fit to travel."

Onestar transferred his glare to Bramblestar, opening his jaws to protest.

But the ThunderClan leader forestalled him. "I will send a patrol home with you, Onestar," he declared, his voice quiet and persuasive. "They can help carry Furzepelt's body."

Onestar gave an angry twitch of his tail, though he was beginning to accept that this was an argument he wasn't going to win.

"You've lost one Clanmate today," Jayfeather pointed out. "Don't risk another."

The patrol isn't only meant to carry Furzepelt home, Onestar guessed, *but to protect me too, from rogues that might be lurking.* He was thoroughly embarrassed, in front of the whole of Thunder-Clan, to admit that he needed their aid, but he knew that turning it down could mean his Clanmates might die, and he might be robbed of yet another life. "Very well," he snorted.

Bramblestar summoned Snowbush, Blossomfall, and Berrynose, who took up Furzepelt's body as respectfully as if she had been their own Clanmate. Onestar looked into the medicine cats' den, intending to say farewell to Emberfoot and Oatclaw, but they were both sleeping from the poppy seed Jayfeather had given them for their pain. With grudging thanks to the medicine cats, he trudged out of the camp, the ThunderClan patrol following him.

Trekking across the moor, with the ground boggy from the rain, took a long time, especially as the cats were slowed down by carrying Furzepelt. Onestar breathed a sigh of relief as the gorse bushes around the top of the hollow came into sight.

Before they reached the camp, a patrol emerged from the bushes; Harespring was in the lead, followed by Sedgewhisker and Slightfoot. They bounded forward as soon as they spotted Onestar and the ThunderClan cats.

"What happened?" Harespring demanded, halting in front of Onestar. "Where have you been?"

"Furzepelt!" Sedgewhisker exclaimed, her eyes wide with horror. "Oh, StarClan, no!"

"Let's get back to camp," Onestar replied to his deputy. "Then I'll tell you everything."

He said no more while Slightfoot and Sedgewhisker took

Furzepelt's body from the ThunderClan cats and bore her off into the camp for her vigil. The ThunderClan cats turned away with respectful dips of their heads, heading back across the moor to their own territory.

"Thank you for your help," Onestar muttered, every word an effort. "We need to step up our patrols," he continued to Harespring as he and his deputy padded back to the hollow side by side. "Starting now, WindClan is on high alert."

Over the next quarter moon, Onestar did everything he could think of to guard his camp. The border patrols were increased from two or three cats to five. The nursery and the elders' den had a guard day and night. Apprentices were barely allowed to move without permission from their mentors. Onestar even ordered a warrior to accompany Kestrelflight if he needed to visit another Clan's medicine cats, in case Darktail should ambush him on the way.

It's going well, he thought, gazing around the camp with an inward purr of satisfaction. *I know the Clan isn't too keen about the changes, but sooner or later they'll know it's for the best.*

Then Onestar noticed Fernpaw, Crowfeather's apprentice, pushing her way through the gorse bushes at the top of the hollow, a mouse dangling from her jaws. She bounded down the slope to drop her prey on the fresh-kill pile.

Onestar padded up to her. "Where have you been?" he demanded. "Where's your mentor?"

Fernpaw flinched at his harsh tone but answered him readily. "Crowfeather's on a border patrol, Onestar. I'm not allowed to go with him."

That was a rule Onestar had made, because of the danger from Darktail. "You're not allowed out of camp without him, either," he meowed. "So why did you think it was okay to go off hunting?"

"I didn't, Onestar," Fernpaw protested, her gray tabby pelt beginning to bristle up with indignation. "I spotted the mouse in the bushes. It seemed mouse-brained not to catch it. I only went a couple of paw steps out of the hollow."

"And that was a couple of paw steps too many," Onestar snapped. "Go and report to Kestrelflight and tell him I said you were to do the elders' ticks until the next Gathering."

Fernpaw stared at him, disbelief in her eyes, as if she thought that he might be joking. But Onestar saw nothing amusing about having his orders disobeyed. The silence between them stretched out until Fernpaw's disbelief faded, giving way to shock.

Her head and tail drooped. "Okay, Onestar. I'm really sorry." Her voice shook a little; Onestar gave her a curt nod, acknowledging that at least she was brave enough not to complain. She trudged off toward the medicine cat's den.

Onestar turned away and noticed for the first time that Whitetail was standing a couple of tail-lengths from him, gazing at him with disapproval in her eyes.

"Why are you doing this?" she asked plaintively. "Poor Fernpaw didn't really do anything wrong. You're making every cat miserable with all these extra rules."

"I'm doing it for the good of our Clan," Onestar responded. "I'm trying to keep us safe. There are rogues lurking about."

"I know that," Whitetail mewed. "But is there some reason

you think WindClan is more at risk than any other Clan?"

Once again, Onestar wished that he could tell his mate the whole truth. *But that's just too difficult.* "Their leader, Darktail, is a very dangerous cat," he declared. "And his fellow rogues are no better. Look what they did to Furzepelt. And how Smokekit was taken away. . . ."

"Smokekit was fine," Whitetail pointed out. "If it was Darktail who took her, and not a stoat, and he intends to destroy WindClan, why wouldn't he have killed her?"

He just wanted to show me he could have, Onestar thought. *He was sending me a message.*

"I don't pretend to know all the thoughts of an unstable cat," he meowed aloud, shaking his head. "But I don't intend to leave my Clan vulnerable to another attack. I'll do what I feel is necessary, and if the rest of the Clan doesn't like it, too bad."

Whitetail sighed, seeming bemused by his concern, but she didn't argue any further. And even though Onestar knew that his Clanmates felt stifled under the new restrictions, no other cat spoke out against him.

That night, Onestar fell into restless sleep. He saw once more Furzepelt's body staggering toward him, the pain and questioning in her eyes; he relived his death, his brief journey into StarClan, and his return to his body. Above all, he heard Darktail's parting words, repeated over and over.

This won't be the last you see of us. Only, in Onestar's dream, the last word turned into the hiss of a snake.

Onestar's eyes flew open. He was in his own den, with Whitetail sleeping beside him, his heart pounding uncomfortably with the memory of his dream. Then through the darkness he was sure he could see two gleaming blue eyes watching him intently from the entrance to the den, and the white fur of a cat glowing in the moonlight.

He leaped to his paws, ready to confront the intruder, but within a heartbeat whatever he had seen had disappeared. He poked his head out of the den, but all he could see was the empty expanse of the camp, and the stars gazing down at him.

For a few moments, Onestar stood in the entrance, his chest heaving as he struggled to catch his breath. *What is happening to me?* he wondered. *Was Darktail really here, or am I losing my mind?*

"What's wrong?" Onestar heard Whitetail calling out sleepily behind him. She stumbled to her paws and reached out to nuzzle his cheek with her nose.

"He's here for me," Onestar muttered grimly.

But Whitetail was too drowsy to hear what he said, and settled back into their nest.

For a little longer, Onestar stayed looking out across the camp. It was clear to him now that Darktail wouldn't rest until he had his revenge.

From now on, I won't rest either.

CHAPTER 26

Onestar sat on a branch of the Great Oak and gazed around at the cats clustered below him on the Gathering island. Bright moonlight shone on their fur and gleamed in their eyes, yet the leaders looked worried. Even though moments before the Clans had been cheering for new warriors, the mood in the clearing had become somber.

Rowanstar stepped forward to the end of his branch and surveyed the cats in the clearing gravely. "The rogues that attacked Onestar's patrol are living on the edge of our territory, near the border with ThunderClan," he announced.

At the ShadowClan leader's announcement Onestar stiffened, as shocked exclamations rose from the cats below. *ThunderClan helped us to drive them out, and now ShadowClan is letting them live on their territory?*

"Why don't you chase them off?" Brackenfur of Thunder-Clan called out.

Rising from a group of WindClan cats, Breezepelt showed his teeth. "They're murderers!" he yowled.

Crowfeather, sitting beside his son, lifted his muzzle. "We should join forces and drive them away."

Before Crowfeather had finished speaking, Rowanstar raised his voice to make himself heard. "They asked to join ShadowClan. They came with gifts of prey, but I turned them away."

"How dare they?" Oatclaw lashed his tail in fury; the shoulder wound the rogues had given him in the battle was still visible.

"They could never be Clan cats!" Sparkpelt of Thunder-Clan put in.

"I turned them away!" Rowanstar repeated, his fur beginning to bristle. He hesitated a moment before adding, "Some of our apprentices have chosen to join them."

What? Onestar couldn't believe what he had heard. Did Rowanstar have so little control over his Clan that his apprentices felt free to wander off and do as they pleased?

Shocked silence greeted the ShadowClan leader's words. Onestar thought that Rowanstar was struggling with something, as if he had more to say, even worse than the news he had already revealed.

But what could be worse than that?

Rowanstar took a deep breath. His voice quivered with shame and sorrow as he confessed, "They took Violetkit with them."

Mistystar, the RiverClan leader, snapped her head around to stare at him. "The kit from the prophecy?"

Embrace what you find in the shadows, for only they can clear the sky. The words of the prophecy echoed in Onestar's mind. He had dismissed it as having little to do with WindClan, but he felt a pang of mingled grief and anger at the thought of a kit—whether or not she was important —abandoned to the mercy of Darktail and his rogues.

Rowanstar nodded.

"You let them take her?" Bramblestar, his ears flattened and his tail lashing, looked as if he was about to spring on the ShadowClan leader, truce or no truce.

"We were wrong about the prophecy, Bramblestar," Rowanstar meowed with a scowl. "Violetkit is just an ordinary kit. Twigkit is probably ordinary, too. And Needlepaw found her. Why shouldn't she take her?"

Onestar listened, stunned, as the argument raged on about the prophecy and the fate of Violetkit. Rowanstar tried to defend himself, but there was little he could say to justify letting a vulnerable kit leave her Clan to live with cats who had already shown that they couldn't be trusted.

ShadowClan had allowed Darktail and his rogues to stay on their territory, and some of their cats had willingly joined him. *Why would any Clan cat do something so opposed to everything the warrior code stands for?*

Onestar wondered what would happen the next time they had to face Darktail in battle. Would they have to fight Clan cats as well as rogues?

"It's unthinkable," Onestar muttered aloud. "I can't believe Rowanstar would be so reckless."

Eventually Bramblestar's voice, raised in a commanding yowl, cut through the wrangling of the other cats. "What are you going to do about this, Rowanstar?" he demanded.

There was guilt and fear in Rowanstar's eyes as he replied. "We attacked them last night. We hoped that when they saw us fighting for them, our apprentices would come back to us. But they didn't." Now Rowanstar's voice was trembling. "In fact, one more apprentice and two of our warriors joined them and fought against us."

Onestar couldn't control his outrage any longer. "Who?" he asked, letting his shoulder fur spike up with fury.

He knew that he was responsible for Darktail's arrival in Clan territories, but he had hoped that he could rely on his fellow leaders to drive his son and the rogues he led out. Now, glaring at Rowanstar, his hope died. Was this cowering cat supposed to be a Clan leader? What hope would there be for ShadowClan with this pathetic excuse for a cat in charge?

Rowanstar's head drooped and he stared at his paws. "Beepaw, Berryheart, and Cloverfoot," he admitted.

Onestar took a pace forward on his branch to thrust his muzzle close to the ginger tom. "How dare you call yourself a leader?" he snarled. "You can't even control your own Clan!"

"They'll come back," Rowanstar choked out. "They're young and wrongheaded, but they'll realize their mistake and come back."

"Perhaps you're right." Bramblestar's meow had softened.

Ha! When hedgehogs fly!

"Meanwhile, we have rogues on the edge of Clan territory," Onestar rasped, unable to believe that Rowanstar could deceive himself so completely. "If they steal Clanmates, you can be sure they'll steal prey."

Or worse, he added silently to himself, remembering what had happened to Smokekit. He remembered too Darktail's threat to him at the beginning of the battle: that *he* was the rightful leader of WindClan. If Darktail had swayed a few ShadowClan warriors and apprentices, what if he began recruiting WindClan warriors next? Soon he could be powerful enough to destroy all the Clans.

And he would probably enjoy it, given how much he hates me. A shiver passed through Onestar. The thought that Darktail might threaten every Clan made him seem more terrifying than ever.

Onestar was distracted from his thoughts as he realized that Mistystar was glaring at him. "They're as far from your borders as they can be," she snapped. "There's no need for you to worry about your precious rabbits."

"Or you to defend your fish," Onestar retorted, then regretted the words as soon as they were out. He couldn't afford to antagonize Mistystar when he needed her cooperation. "I'm sorry—" he began, but the RiverClan leader had already let out a furious hiss and turned away.

The other leaders were discussing an attack on the rogues, but with far too little enthusiasm, in Onestar's view. *Can't they see how dangerous Darktail is?*

Finally they agreed to wait, afraid that if they attacked Darktail's camp, he might kill Violetkit.

"So we're going to do nothing?" Onestar demanded, feeling his hackles rise. "These cats killed my Clanmate." *And took one of my lives.* "We should attack now," he added, "and drive them as far from the lake as we can."

Please, he added silently to himself. He had never before needed the Clans to back him up as much as he did now. Except perhaps the time when Firestar had helped him to become a real leader.

Onestar's heart ached at the memory of Firestar. Surely the previous ThunderClan leader would have seen how dangerous Darktail was, and done what was needed to drive him out.

But Rowanstar shook his head, his eyes still fearful. "I don't want to fight my Clanmates, even if they've made a terrible decision," he meowed. "They still might change their minds and return to the Clan."

Onestar couldn't believe what he was hearing. He knew he was to blame for abandoning Darktail and Smoke, and he felt thoroughly guilty that he hadn't tried to do more to help them. But his pelt bristled with anger that Darktail held him responsible for the bloodthirsty cat he had become.

Should I confess everything? he wondered. Darktail had more motive than the other leaders knew, and he was more dangerous than they could imagine in their worst nightmares. Onestar knew that Rowanstar was valuing the lives of a few ShadowClan warriors now against countless lives that would be lost when Darktail closed his grip on the forest. *But he can hardly be blamed for that, when he doesn't know the truth.*

Onestar took a breath to speak, but the words wouldn't come. He dug his claws into the branch in frustration, feeling as trapped as if he were struggling in the middle of a bramble thicket. He wanted to explain everything, and he knew that Rowanstar and the others wouldn't understand unless he did.

But I can't. Oh, StarClan, I'm sorry, but I can't.

"Then WindClan has no more to say," he growled.

He leaped down from the Great Oak and beckoned his Clanmates with his tail as he stalked across the clearing and through the bushes.

As he crossed the tree-bridge and led the way along the lakeshore to WindClan territory, Onestar felt his anger building until he felt it must burst out of him. *Will no cat help me to defeat Darktail?*

At first he had worried that WindClan was Darktail's only target. But with what he had just learned about the threat to ShadowClan, he had hoped that the other leaders would see that Darktail and his rogues threatened the whole of the forest, not just WindClan. Now he understood that WindClan stood alone. *And we can't beat him on our own, especially now that ShadowClan warriors have joined him.*

Yet much of Onestar's anger was directed at himself. He had been given the chance, at the Gathering, to tell the truth and make the other leaders see why Darktail had to be defeated. *And you backed out!* he berated himself. *Coward!*

Onestar had a sudden memory of an earlier Gathering, when he had told Firestar that WindClan would never need ThunderClan's help. At first he had rejected Bramblestar's help against the stoats. *And yet here we are.* He wondered whether this was his punishment for putting WindClan first, for refusing to work with ThunderClan or see them as an ally. Now he couldn't count on help from any of the other leaders.

But isn't that what Tallstar told me to do—always put WindClan first?

By the time he returned to camp, the worst of Onestar's

anger had faded, and he was able to think clearly again. He reminded himself that he could still protect WindClan, and if that meant more extreme restrictions, it was just too bad. Even though he couldn't tell his Clan the truth about Darktail, he could still do everything he could to keep them safe.

Could that be the "cost" that Stoneteller warned me about? he wondered. *My Clanmates' respect? Their understanding?* Onestar took a breath, bracing himself. If that was true, it was a cost he was willing to pay.

"Harespring," he meowed, summoning his deputy with a jerk of his head.

Harespring, who was on his way to the warriors' den, halted and turned back. "Yes, Onestar?"

"We're stepping up our patrols again," Onestar told him. "See to it."

"But Onestar," Harespring protested. "Every cat is stretched to breaking point already."

"Then they must stretch a bit more," Onestar retorted. "Every able-bodied warrior needs to prove their loyalty to WindClan now. No cat rests, no cat sleeps, until the threat that is Darktail has been dealt with."

Harespring shook his head, not arguing anymore, only confused. "If you say so, Onestar." He padded off, discouragement in the line of his shoulders and his drooping tail.

Onestar didn't care whether his deputy agreed with him or not, as long as he carried out his orders.

They'll thank me when Darktail is gone, and WindClan is still standing.

CHAPTER 27

❧

More than a half-moon passed after the Gathering, and nothing happened, except that Harespring, following Onestar's orders, increased the patrols around WindClan territory. From dawn to nightfall the camp was almost empty; the whole Clan was out on patrol, hunting or guarding the borders. Even at night, guards encircled the camp; every cat snatched food and sleep where and when they could.

Onestar was sitting on a wide, flat rock at one end of the hollow, his shoulders hunched against the rain that swept across the moor, driven by an icy wind. His mind had flown back to the time when Darktail and his rogues had invaded WindClan, to the battle that had killed Furzepelt and stolen one of his nine lives.

I'm on my last one now.

Movement among the gorse bushes at the top of the hollow pulled Onestar out of these dark thoughts. His muscles tensed and his fur began to bristle at the thought of an attack, only to relax as Crowfeather led his patrol back into camp. They were escorting Puddleshine, the ShadowClan medicine cat, along with Tigerheart, Scorchfur, and Violetkit.

Onestar sprang to his paws and leaped down onto the grass, watching the cats as they approached. Glaring at Violetkit, he demanded, "What is *she* doing on my territory?"

Crowfeather halted in front of his Clan leader, confusion in his eyes. "Er—we caught them inside our border."

Like that answers my question! Fury crackled through Onestar as if he had been struck by lightning. Glaring at Violetkit, he lashed his tail toward her. "This one is a *rogue*," he snarled. "She lived among the same cats who killed Furzepelt! How dare you? Get her off my territory before I take my revenge!"

The young she-cat stiffened, her ears flattening with fear, but she faced Onestar steadily, not letting herself flinch. He couldn't help feeling a reluctant respect for her.

Meanwhile Tigerheart had stepped backward, and Onestar spotted his claws flexing as if he was ready to leap into battle. But when he spoke, his voice was even. "Hear me out, Onestar. Violetpaw is a ShadowClan cat now. She poses no threat."

So she's an apprentice now, and accepted back into ShadowClan, Onestar thought. He decided there was no point in objecting further. It was more important to find out what these cats were doing on his territory.

"Make it quick," he snarled.

"Three of our Clanmates are ill with a sickness we've never seen before," Tigerheart explained, with a glance at Puddleshine. "StarClan sent Puddleshine a dream telling him which herb would cure it. They told him that he must gather it on the moor."

Onestar narrowed his eyes, letting his gaze flicker from Tigerheart to Puddleshine and back again. Tigerstar's account was completely normal, but Onestar couldn't suppress a twinge of apprehension, as if something wasn't right about ShadowClan being here.

Are they up to something?

"I don't care what StarClan told him," he responded. "No ShadowClan cat crosses onto WindClan land."

Tigerheart's tail twitched, but his voice remained calm. "We mean no harm. But we can't let our Clanmates die."

Onestar let out a snort, glaring once more at Violetpaw. "And yet you shelter rogues who killed *my* Clanmate."

The hair on Scorchfur's shoulders began to bush up. "Violetpaw is one of us! We're not sheltering them!"

"Even if she is loyal to ShadowClan," Onestar snarled, thrusting his muzzle close to the dark gray warrior, "you let the others live on the edge of your territory, despite the fact that they are murderers. Half your apprentices left to join them. It just proves what I've always thought: ThunderClan cats are no better than rogues. You will not gather herbs on my land."

Movement at his shoulder made Onestar turn, and he saw that Kestrelflight had padded up, unnoticed until now.

"Surely Puddleshine can gather herbs?" he pleaded, blinking nervously. "The Clans have always allowed medicine cats to gather herbs when lives are at stake."

Onestar whipped around to face him, trying not to let his voice or his expression betray his apprehension. "No!" he snapped.

"But our Clanmates need—"

Onestar cut off Kestrelflight's attempt to protest. "They will gather no herbs here," he growled. Turning to Tigerheart, he added, "Get off my land."

Tigerheart returned his gaze, but made no move to leave. Puddleshine looked simply bewildered, and the WindClan warriors were gazing at their paws in embarrassment that they would have to enforce Onestar's refusal.

Seeing every cat ignoring his order made fury swell inside Onestar. "Go!" he screeched. "Head for the border and don't stop. The moment you leave the camp, I'm sending a patrol after you. If they catch up with you, they'll tear the pelts from your backs."

Even then, Tigerheart didn't move, except to shift his paws. "Please . . . ," he begged, his voice soft and his gaze imploring.

A stab of guilt clawed through Onestar's chest as he heard how desperate the younger warrior sounded. He knew that Tigerheart was a strong, powerful ShadowClan cat, who must *hate* having to come into another Clan's camp and ask for help. At any other time, Onestar would have wanted to help, but he knew that if Darktail and his rogues took over ShadowClan, helping them now would only have strengthened WindClan's enemies. He had to follow Tallstar's instructions and put WindClan first.

Sickness roiled in Onestar's belly, and the sour taste of vomit was on his tongue. But while Darktail still lurked out there, he could take no chances with his Clan's safety.

"Leave!" he yowled.

Tigerheart gave Onestar a single last reproachful look, then turned and signaled with a jerk of his head for his patrol to follow. Onestar watched them go, then flicked his tail at Crowfeather.

"Get after them," he ordered, then added, "but don't attack them unless you really can't avoid it."

As the WindClan patrol headed out after the visitors, Onestar was aware that the few warriors remaining in the hollow had turned toward him, their eyes filled with questions. He said nothing, but only whipped around and stalked off to his den.

When he reached it, he realized that Kestrelflight had followed him and entered uninvited. "What do you want?" he demanded.

The young medicine cat wasn't intimidated by his harsh tone. "Why would you refuse the medicine cat—*any* medicine cat?" he asked. "Remember the new addition to the warrior code—that the Clans would help each other in time of need. What happens the next time WindClan is really in need, and ShadowClan refuses *us*?"

Onestar hesitated, wondering whether to give voice to the concern that had struck him as he spoke to the ShadowClan cats: if Darktail was recruiting their Clanmates, then it was only a matter of time before he controlled the whole Clan. *And if I'm Darktail's ultimate target, then by giving the herbs, I would only be strengthening my enemies.*

But as Onestar had this thought, he realized how terrible a reason that was for refusing help now. He knew he couldn't explain it to Kestrelflight. Without understanding that Dark-tail's purpose here was to destroy him, the medicine cat would think he had bees in his brain.

"Kestrelflight," he began, "I understand that a medicine cat would be confused, even upset, at not giving ShadowClan leave to gather the herb, but I have much bigger concerns than Clan customs at the moment."

Kestrelflight let out an annoyed sigh, but at least he showed no hostility as he backed out of the den and disappeared.

Onestar could sense the confusion from the cats in the camp, and could feel the weight of their furtive glances looking toward his den, like a giant paw pressing down on his back and head. He deliberately didn't poke his head out to see them.

Letting himself sink into his nest, Onestar took deep breaths, trying to calm the chaos inside him. A few heart-beats later, a shadow passed over him, and he looked up to see Whitetail slipping into the den.

"Seriously, Onestar, what was all that about?" she asked, sitting at his side.

"Keep your voice down," Onestar murmured, greeting her by touching his nose to her ear. "I don't want to upset any of our Clanmates. I'm trying to keep us all safe from a danger-ous rogue."

Whitetail gave him a puzzled look. "Why are you so worried about a few rogues? The other leaders aren't that concerned. We're warriors; we can defend ourselves."

Onestar's heart began to thump in panic; he was so tired of lying, so tired of hiding the truth from cats who had the right to know. With his mate's questioning gaze still pinning him down, he sought urgently for some answer he could give her.

"There are things I've never told you . . . ," he began, forcing out the words.

"You mean you got into a fight when you were wandering our territory, or out on patrol, and now you have conflict with some random rogue?" Whitetail asked. "There's no shame in that. You're protecting your territory and your Clan, like any good leader would."

Onestar felt deeply ashamed that Whitetail was trying to comfort him, even more that she never suspected the "random rogue" might be Darktail or one of his group.

"Onestar, I would gladly go into battle at your side against this rogue," she mewed, twining her tail with his. "Whoever or whatever they are."

Struggling to meet her loving gaze, Onestar knew that he would soon run out of excuses, run out of the half-truths he could use to satisfy her without telling her the full, awful story.

The story that would cause her to reject him. He was in no hurry for that to happen. Breathing in her sweet scent, he just wanted to enjoy what he thought might be these last moments of togetherness with his mate.

What has become of ShadowClan?

Onestar gazed up through the leafless branches of the Great Oak and watched the silver circle of the moon as it drifted across the sky. Time was passing, the other three Clans were assembled, but as yet there was no sign of ShadowClan.

Well, I for one can do without them!

Bramblestar had begun the Gathering, but so far all the discussion had been about the prophecy, and how Violetpaw had abandoned the rogues to return to ShadowClan. Onestar still had his doubts that she could be trusted, and he couldn't believe how the other three leaders were missing what was really important, unaware of the danger that lurked among them.

He listened to the discussion, his claws kneading the branch. *Prophecy, prophecy, prophecy . . . Who cares about the cursed prophecy? Can't they see that the Clans are in danger of being destroyed?*

Finally, Onestar's anger became too much for him. He rose and padded to the end of his branch, glaring around at the cats in the clearing. "Why are we wasting time when there are more important matters to discuss?" he demanded. "A few days ago, a ShadowClan patrol invaded our land—with one of the former rogues!"

Dovewing of ThunderClan raised her head to fix him with a challenging gaze, "It wasn't an invasion!" she protested. "I saw the patrol. It was Puddleshine and Violetpaw, who is a ShadowClan apprentice now. They wanted herbs, not a battle!"

"Then why send two warriors with them?" Onestar drew his lips back in the beginnings of a snarl. "Why send a cat who has aligned herself with those who killed *my* warrior?"

"Two warriors and an apprentice don't make an invasion," Bramblestar retorted with a contemptuous snort.

Furious at how the younger leader was dismissing his

concerns, Onestar lashed his tail. "They were *ShadowClan!*" he hissed. "For all we know, that apprentice was scouting for her rogue friends."

"Traitors!" Emberfoot yowled from where he sat with his Clanmates near the edge of the clearing.

"Rogue lovers!" Crowfeather hissed.

"ShadowClan has forgotten what it is to be a Clan," Oatclaw added, flattening his ears in anger.

Onestar felt warmed by his Clan's support, even more so when Harespring sprang to his paws from where he sat on the oak roots with the other deputies.

"Half their apprentices live with the rogues," he meowed.

Onestar gave him a nod of approval. "They don't even come to Gatherings anymore."

To his surprise, Leafpool stood up and padded forward to the foot of the Great Oak, glaring up at him. He had always thought of her as a peaceful and reasonable cat, and he wasn't prepared for the hostility in her voice.

"Stop yowling about ShadowClan's mistakes and think about your own!"

Onestar's first reaction was a jolt of fear. *What does she know?* Then he calmed himself. There was no way that Leafpool could have discovered anything about his history with Darktail.

He narrowed his eyes and leaned down toward the medicine cat. "I have made no mistakes!" he hissed.

"You denied a valuable herb to a Clan in need!" Leafpool retorted, not at all intimidated by Onestar's hostility.

Onestar's shame at the truth of her accusation kept him

silent for a moment. While he hesitated, there came a rustling in the bushes, and the ShadowClan cats appeared, led by the Clan deputy, Crowfrost. He thrust his way through the crowd of cats and clambered into the Great Oak to join the other leaders.

"Rowanstar has the sickness that has stricken our Clan," he announced. "I will take his place tonight."

Bramblestar and Mistystar dipped their heads in greeting, but Onestar let out a low growl from the depths of his throat.

Crowfrost seemed to ignore him, though Onestar saw his claws digging hard into the branch where he stood. "Rowanstar would be well by now," he meowed, "if Onestar had allowed us to gather herbs on his land."

"Gather your herbs somewhere else," Onestar hissed, baring his teeth. "No ShadowClan cat will ever set paw on WindClan land again."

He sat still, inwardly seething, while the other leaders and the medicine cats discussed the herb they were seeking, lungwort. Eventually Mothwing asked, "May I pick the herb on your land? I'm not a ShadowClan cat."

Onestar hesitated, sensing that his Clanmates were looking toward him, waiting for his answer. He knew that by denying the sick cats the herb, he was going against the spirit of the warrior code. And Mothwing had suggested a sensible compromise. But he couldn't bring himself to back down, making himself and his Clan seem weak. And even if Mothwing picked it, the herb would ultimately help to strengthen the rogues.

"Not if the herb is for ShadowClan," he snarled.

Crowfrost whipped around to glare at him, his pelt bristling. "Two of our elders are sick," he snapped. "They can't last much longer without the herb. Are you determined to see innocent cats die?"

"No ShadowClan cat is innocent," Onestar spat. "You are all sheltering the rogues!"

The argument swirled around him. Alderpaw even tried asking Kestrelflight for help, putting pressure on him to disobey his Clan leader. That made Onestar even more furious.

"If ShadowClan drives the rogues away, they can have the herb," he meowed. Then he leaped down from the Great Oak and gathered his Clan together with a whisk of his tail. But even as they rose and followed him, he sensed that not all of them were happy with his decision.

I can't help that. We're leaving. There's nothing more for WindClan here.

Onestar crouched in his den, thinking back to the Gathering. He felt soaked with misery, like filthy water, that he had denied help to sick cats, but he felt as trapped as prey before the hunter's paw descended.

Too restless to stay doing nothing for long, Onestar emerged into the open and gazed around the camp. The first cats he spotted were Emberfoot and Gorsetail, standing outside Kestrelflight's den.

He bounded over to them. "What are you doing here?" he demanded. "You're supposed to be on patrol."

"We were," Emberfoot explained. "We met Leafpool and Alderpaw at the border, and they asked to speak to Kestrelflight."

"They're in there with him now," Gorsetail added.

Onestar's pelt prickled with hostility. He knew exactly why the ThunderClan medicine cats had come. But there was no point in blaming his warriors; it was only ShadowClan cats he had forbidden from setting paw on his territory.

Onestar paced the hollow as he waited for the visitors to emerge. Eventually Alderpaw appeared through the crack in the rock, followed by Leafpool and Kestrelflight. Onestar flexed his claws as they approached, pondering how Shadow-Clan must be using ThunderClan to put pressure on him.

"You've brought Bramblestar's kit," he snarled at Leafpool. "Was Bramblestar too mouse-hearted to come himself?"

Alderpaw answered, his voice quivering with outrage. "Nothing scares Bramblestar!"

"Perhaps he's just too proud," Onestar mewed scornfully. "I assume you've come to beg for lungwort. Has ShadowClan been whining in his ear?"

Now Alderpaw's anger gave way to nervousness, his claws flexing spasmodically. "ShadowClan is holding Twigpaw hostage until you give it to them."

Onestar drew himself up, fury slicing through him like a massive claw. "Typical ShadowClan. If they can't get what they want fairly, they resort to sly tricks."

"They've promised not to hurt her," Alderpaw told him.

"Then why are you worried?" Onestar asked with a

contemptuous sniff. "Let her stay with them. She has a sister in their Clan, doesn't she? Perhaps she'll enjoy living there."

Before he had finished speaking, Leafpool stepped forward, authority in the angle of her head and the way she held her tail. "Twigpaw is not the issue," she meowed. "We miss her, of course, but if Rowanstar has promised not to hurt her, he will not hurt her. He will keep his promise."

Onestar's ears flattened. He was beginning to see a way of maybe guiding other Clans to the decision of taking on Darktail and driving him out. If he could stress the size of the threat, and Rowanstar's weakness, he might be able to ensure that every Clan would turn on Darktail, and few if any Wind-Clan cats would be hurt in the upcoming battles.

"Just as he kept his promise to the rogues," he spat.

"He's promised nothing to the rogues!" Alderpaw retorted, his tail twitching in anger.

"Then why are they still here?" Onestar demanded, glaring at the young medicine cat. "ShadowClan allowed them to stay near their territory." His mew rose to an angry yowl. "They paid for this foolishness by losing some of their best apprentices. When the so-called 'special' kit returned, they took her back in, and now she lives among them—giving who knows what information to her rogue friends! They are weak and foolish!" he went on, letting all his suppressed fear and anger surge out of him. "They deserve no help. They don't even deserve the name of Clan cats. They are no more than rogues themselves. Let them keep Twigpaw. Let them die of sickness. I will not be tricked or bullied into helping traitors.

They deserve everything StarClan has brought upon them."

Alderpaw and Leafpool just stared at him in disbelief. "Come on," Leafpool meowed; the scorn in her tone made Onestar feel his fur was shriveling. "We're wasting our time here."

She gave one last, pleading look to Kestrelflight, but he had backed away, his gaze firmly fixed on his paws as though shame washed his pelt.

Leafpool headed for the bushes that surrounded the camp, Alderpaw hurrying after her.

Once the ShadowClan cats were gone, Kestrelflight padded up to Onestar, his eyes distraught. "How could you do this?" he asked, his voice shaking.

"I am WindClan's leader," Onestar replied brusquely. "My word is the code."

Privately he was as shaken as his medicine cat by the encounter. *I need a way to pressure ShadowClan to do what they must, since I can't convince them with words,* he thought. He didn't know how to explain to Kestrelflight that the lives lost to this illness might be nothing compared to the lives that Darktail would take. *He wants to see every cat I care about suffer. I know I'm doing something terrible . . . but it's to save you all.*

"You need to decide where your loyalties lie," he told Kestrelflight. "Because I speak for WindClan. Are you loyal to WindClan, or to ShadowClan?"

He didn't wait for Kestrelflight's response; instead he stormed away toward his den. Briefly he caught Nightcloud's gaze where she crouched by the fresh-kill pile, gulping down a vole. She looked confused, disappointed, and frustrated, all at once. Onestar felt a new stab of shame in his heart, remembering how the black she-cat had fought in Mudclaw's rebellion.

Yes, she once supported Mudclaw, but she was still prepared to suffer for WindClan—for my Clan.

Onestar could feel his Clanmates' respect for him slipping, and he could never tell them the truth, never explain the reason for his harsh refusal of help to the sick cats.

Please, StarClan, he begged silently as he settled down in his den, *let Rowanstar come to his senses and work with the other Clans to drive Darktail out. To kill him,* he added.

He knew there was only one way for this terror to end: with Darktail's death. But even as fearsome as his kit had proven himself to be, Onestar still couldn't imagine being the cat who killed him. He let out a faint murmur of pain, his heart aching for the son Darktail could have been.

CHAPTER 28

❧

Onestar lay curled up in his den, drowsing uneasily. The wails of sick and dying cats rose all around him, accusing him and pleading with him.

It's not my fault! he wanted to yowl. *Go and make Rowanstar see reason!*

A voice at the entrance to his den roused him from his dark imaginings. "Can I come in?"

Onestar rose up to see his daughter, Heathertail, peering in at him. "Yes, of course," he replied, rising to his paws and giving himself a long stretch. "What can I do for you?"

"Oh, I just wanted a chat." Heathertail seemed uneasy— even embarrassed— as she advanced into the den, sitting a tail-length away from Onestar and wrapping her tail around her paws. "You're so busy, being leader, I hardly ever get to see you."

Onestar let out a grunt; he was convinced that his daughter was hiding something. Only a couple of days before, he and Heathertail had gone hunting with Gorsetail and Crowfeather. Now she was talking as if they hadn't met for moons. He began to groom scraps of moss and bracken out of his pelt, and waited for her to continue.

"It's such a responsibility being leader," Heathertail went on. "It must be so hard for you, and you're doing such a brilliant job. . . ."

Onestar narrowed his eyes. *Brilliant? With everything that's going wrong?* "You're either trying to flatter me, or you're mousebrained," he snapped. "And I know you're not mouse-brained. So what do you really want? Spit it out!"

Heathertail took a deep breath. "It's the herbs," she confessed, distress flooding into her eyes. "Please, give them to ShadowClan! How would you feel if I were dying of a sickness that our medicine cat could heal, if he had the right herbs? Or if it were our kits, mine and Breezepelt's? I can't bear to think about it. What would *you* think of the cat who denied you the cure?"

His daughter's words tore through Heathertail like claws. His horror at the thought of losing those who were most dear to him made him want to give in to her at once. But he felt an even deeper horror at the thought of what Darktail might do, not only to WindClan but to all the Clans, if he were allowed to roam the territories unchecked.

"I can't—" he began.

"But you could!" Heathertail interrupted him, her eyes shining in the dimness of the den. "You said your word is the code—"

"*What?*" Onestar sprang to his paws. "That's what I said to Kestrelflight, but you weren't there. Have you been discussing this with him? Did he send you?"

Without waiting for his daughter's reply, Onestar barreled past her and erupted out into the camp. Kestrelflight was standing a fox-length from the entrance, close enough to hear everything that was said in the den. He stepped back nervously as Onestar confronted him.

"How dare you!" Onestar snarled, his belly shaking with anger. "Using my own daughter against me! Cats have been banished for less."

"I'm sorry, Onestar," Kestrelflight responded, recovering himself. "But the situation is so desperate. *Please* change your mind. Cats are dying who don't need to die."

"And whose fault is that?" Onestar demanded. "Rowanstar knows what to do if he wants the herb. Let me remind you, Kestrelflight, this is *my* Clan. For better or worse, I make the decisions, and I'll take the consequences."

"But you're *not* taking the consequence." Heathertail spoke quietly from behind Onestar. "The sick cats are doing that."

"I'm disappointed in you, Onestar," the medicine cat continued, his shoulders drooping. "I never thought you were this sort of leader."

"Tough," Onestar snapped. "You don't have to agree with me, or even like me, but you have to do what I say. My word is the code, remember?" Whirling around, he added to Heathertail, "If you ever try to fool me again, I'll never forgive you."

He stalked past her into his den and curled up in his bedding with his tail over his face. But sleep wouldn't come. All he could see, behind his closed eyelids, was the shock and hurt in his daughter's expression.

* * *

As Onestar leaped up into the Great Oak, he saw that ThunderClan and RiverClan were already assembled in the clearing, but there was no sign of ShadowClan. He heard Bramblestar mutter irritably, "We're wasting moonlight."

Maybe they won't come at all.

Eventually the bushes rustled and Rowanstar thrust his way into the clearing. Tawnypelt and Tigerheart followed him. Onestar and the rest of the cats waited, their faces turned in ShadowClan's direction, but no other cats emerged.

Rowanstar halted at the edge of the crowd. "We come alone," he announced.

Onestar felt his fur begin lifting in shock as he gazed at the ShadowClan leader. Rowanstar's pelt had been raked into tufts, and here and there skin showed through the fur. His muzzle was covered with dried blood. Tawnypelt and Tigerheart looked ruffled but uninjured.

What in StarClan's name happened? Onestar asked himself.

It was something serious, he was sure. Rowanstar's tail trailed behind him as he made his way through the crowd to the Great Oak. His Clanmates were carefully avoiding the gaze of other cats.

"You have recovered from the sickness," Bramblestar called out, his voice full of relief.

Rowanstar leaped up onto a low branch of the Great Oak. "The whole Clan has recovered."

A murmur of surprise passed through all the cats in the clearing. Mistystar, her head tilted to one side, gave voice to the question that Onestar, for one, wanted to ask.

"Then why haven't you brought them?"

The ShadowClan leader lifted his head, raking the assembled cats with an angry gaze. "They believe you betrayed them by allowing Onestar to withhold the herb we needed so desperately."

Onestar let out a snort of contempt. "You recovered, didn't you?" he growled. "You never really needed it."

At that, Rowanstar turned on him, his lips drawn back in a fearsome snarl. It took all Onestar's self-control not to flinch.

"We only recovered because Harespring and Kestrelflight have more compassion than you!" Rowanstar spat out every word. "They gave us the herb!"

Shock pierced Onestar like a bolt of lightning; it was echoed in the exclamations of the cats in the clearing below. Looking down, he spotted Kestrelflight among the other medicine cats, earnestly studying his paws. Harespring, sitting on the oak roots with his fellow deputies, was staring straight ahead; Onestar couldn't see his expression.

As Onestar's shock ebbed, it was replaced by a pure, throbbing rage. He had known that Kestrelflight didn't agree with him, but he had never expected this. *They betrayed me! My own deputy! My medicine cat! The cats who are bound by the code to follow my orders. Is there no cat I can trust?*

"Is this true?" he snarled, glaring down at Harespring.

His deputy turned to meet his gaze steadily. "I could not let a Clan die."

Kestrelflight rose to his paws and padded up to the foot of

the Great Oak. "I consulted StarClan," he meowed, his voice even. "They told me that it was the right thing to do."

Onestar felt his pelt begin to bristle; he slid out his claws, digging them deep into the branch. For a few heartbeats he felt utterly alone. He wanted to punish Harespring and Kestrelflight for disobeying him and undermining what he was trying to do. *I'll exile them from the Clan! See how they like that!*

But how can I? he asked himself a heartbeat later. *WindClan needs its medicine cat, and no cat in the Clan is more loyal to me than my deputy.* Suppressing a sigh, he reflected that even Whitetail and Heathertail, who loved him, didn't understand why he was doing this. *This is my battle, mine alone. I can't trust any cat.*

His secret about Darktail had turned his own Clan against him. He had endured the contempt of every cat in his attempt to force ShadowClan to drive out the evil rogue, and now he had failed because of what his own Clanmates had done.

Should I have told them the truth? he asked himself. *How could I? They would only despise me more.*

He turned to Rowanstar, but before he could speak, the ShadowClan leader flicked his tail and dipped his head to Onestar, who was surprised to see respect in his expression. "You were right about the rogues, though, Onestar," he mewed.

Onestar could only stare at him.

"We should have driven them from our territory moons ago," the ShadowClan leader confessed. He heaved a deep sigh, the sound of defeat. "They have taken over my Clan."

More shocked yowling rose from the cats in the clearing. Bramblestar padded along his branch until he stood close to

Rowanstar, thrusting out his muzzle. "What do you mean?" he asked.

Rowanstar looked up; Onestar could see it was an effort for him to meet Bramblestar's gaze. "Before we left for the Gathering, the rogues entered our camp."

Mistystar drew in a sharp breath, her blue-gray fur beginning to rise. "Was there a battle? Are many hurt?"

The ShadowClan leader shook his head, deep shame in his eyes. "There was no battle," he choked out. "My Clan chose them over me."

"They *chose* them?" Bramblestar blinked, puzzled. "What do you mean?" he repeated.

Rowanstar's paws were shaking and there was fear in his voice as he replied, "They said that any ShadowClan cat who came here tonight would not be allowed to return to the Clan."

Onestar felt a stab of sympathy for the ShadowClan leader. For the first time he noticed that while Rowanstar might have recovered from the sickness, he hadn't recovered his full strength; his pelt was mangy, his ribs clearly visible beneath it. There was a lost air about him, as if he had no idea what to do now that his Clan had turned against him.

Briefly Onestar felt a kinship with the ShadowClan leader. Rowanstar's Clan had driven him out. WindClan still survived, but in a way they had abandoned him by refusing to follow his orders. *It's hard to be a leader!*

But Onestar's sympathy didn't last long. All he wanted was to keep his Clan safe, while Rowanstar had failed as a leader. *He brought this on himself!*

"I always said that ShadowClan was no better than rogues," Onestar meowed contemptuously.

Rowanstar whipped around to face him, glaring at him with a sudden rush of energy. "That's not true! They have just made a mistake!"

"The real ShadowClan cats will come to their senses before long and drive the invaders out!" That was Tigerheart, calling out from below in a clear voice. His amber eyes glowed in defense of Rowanstar, and Onestar remembered that the ShadowClan leader was his father.

His mother, Tawnypelt, was standing beside him, her head held high. "The sickness scared them," she meowed. "They are like frightened kits looking for someone strong to protect them!"

Onestar flicked his tail dismissively. "And why didn't they look to Rowanstar?" he demanded. "Isn't he strong?"

Suddenly Rowanstar straightened up, steadying himself and meeting Onestar's gaze. "I have been sick," he responded. "Crowfrost has died. For days, ShadowClan had no leadership, thanks to you. If you'd given us the herb earlier, this might never have happened."

Onestar heard murmurs of agreement rising from the cats below. RiverClan and ThunderClan were nodding their heads, and, to Onestar's dismay, so were many of his own Clan.

Bramblestar raised his tail. "What's done is done," he mewed calmly. "For now Rowanstar, Tawnypelt, and Tigerheart will be welcome in ThunderClan. They can stay until their Clanmates realize their mistake."

"*If* they realize their mistake," Tawnypelt hissed, misery in her eyes and the droop of her whiskers.

"I know you feel betrayed." Sympathy vibrated in Bramblestar's voice. "But it takes more than sickness and rogues to destroy the bonds of Clanship."

"Not in ShadowClan," Onestar snapped.

Rowanstar swung around on him, his teeth bared as he let out a hiss of defiance. Once again, Onestar was afraid that the ShadowClan leader might attack him, breaking the Gathering truce. With a massive effort, he squared his shoulders and met Rowanstar's furious gaze.

The ShadowClan leader hesitated for a long moment, then turned back to Bramblestar. "Thank you for your offer," he meowed. "We will be honored to stay with ThunderClan."

"Tawnypelt and I thank you, too," Tigerheart called once more from the clearing. "It's a generous offer, but it's not enough. What are you—what are *all* the leaders—going to do, to put this right?"

Mistystar looked down at him with disapproval in her blue eyes. "I understand how you feel, Tigerheart," she mewed, "but this is ShadowClan's problem. The other Clans don't owe you anything."

"*WindClan* owes me something," Rowanstar retorted. "Onestar, I've said this before. If you had given us the herb when we first asked for it, Darktail would never have been strong enough to take ShadowClan."

Onestar's shoulder fur bristled at the accusation. "I offered you a deal, right here at the last Gathering," he snarled. "Drive out Darktail, and you could have the herb. You chose to refuse. So don't start blaming me, Rowanstar. This was *your* fault."

"Rowanstar, you should never have let Darktail stay in the first place," Jayfeather called out from where he sat with the other medicine cats. "It was obvious he was trouble, right from that first skirmish on the WindClan border."

At his words, a chorus of yowls broke out in the clearing.

"Onestar did this!"

"Rowanstar is no leader!"

Bramblestar let the clamor continue for a few heartbeats, then stepped forward, raising his tail for silence.

"We could argue all night about which cat is responsible," he began when he could make himself heard. "But what good would that do? We have to decide what to do *now*. Does any cat think that Darktail will settle down peacefully on Shadow-Clan territory? Does any cat think the rest of us are safe?"

In the hush that followed his words, Onestar could have heard a mousetail drop. Moonlight reflected in the eyes of the crowd of cats as they looked up at their leaders. He could smell the fear-scent.

Eventually it was Mistystar who broke the silence. "You're right, Bramblestar," she sighed. "As much as I wish that you weren't. What do you think we should do?"

There was the heaviness of regret in Bramblestar's voice as he replied, "We must fight. Darktail has his own rogues and most of the ShadowClan warriors, but if all four Clans join together, we should be able to drive him out."

"All *four* Clans?" Mistystar twitched her ears. "Shadow-Clan is reduced to only three cats."

"You would expect us to fight against our own Clanmates?" Rowanstar asked, his eyes troubled.

"You mean those Clanmates who abandoned you and chose to follow Darktail?" Crowfeather challenged him from the clearing, his voice heavily sarcastic. "Yeah, I can see how that would be really difficult."

"Rowanstar," Bramblestar began, turning toward the ShadowClan leader, "I think it's safe to say that no other cats will help you if ShadowClan does *not* fight."

"And we will!" Tigerheart called out. His amber eyes were blazing, and he worked his claws rhythmically into the ground.

Rowanstar sighed, then nodded. "I understand."

"RiverClan will join you," Mistystar meowed. "Even though other cats"—her gaze flickered from Rowanstar to Onestar and back again—"have brought this danger on us. We will follow the new addition to the warrior code." She dipped her head to Bramblestar, reminding every cat that the code had changed at his suggestion. "In dire need we will give our help so that no Clan will fall."

All this while Onestar had remained silent, his mind a whirl of conflicting fears and desires. Right from the beginning he had wanted to get rid of Darktail, and here was a good chance of doing it. And how could WindClan stand aside when every other Clan was prepared to face the evil cat and his followers? He felt a stab of guilt, too, that the Clans' danger now was the result of mistakes he had made in the past. But at the same time he shrank from the thought of his Clanmates being wounded or maybe killed, and he still did not want to be the cat who put an end to his son's life.

Tallstar told me to put WindClan first, he thought. *But now it seems as if we lose either way.*

He was aware that all the leaders had turned toward him, and knew there was no putting off his decision. "WindClan will join you," he declared brusquely.

Bramblestar nodded to him in acknowledgment. "Then I suggest we—the Clan leaders and deputies—meet to discuss tactics," he meowed. "I will send messengers to arrange a time and place."

With that the Gathering came to an end. As he crossed the tree-bridge and led his Clan home along the shoreline, Onestar felt the prospect of the oncoming battle wreathing around him like thick fog. He wanted nothing more than to return to the camp and curl up in his den, well away from any cat.

But before they had passed the horseplace, he realized that Crowfeather was padding alongside him. At first Onestar tried to pretend he wasn't there, but Crowfeather wasn't an easy cat to ignore.

"Are you up for this, Onestar?" the gray-black tom asked. "WindClan needs you to be strong and focused."

So it's come to this, Onestar thought. *A warrior has to ask his Clan leader if he's strong enough.*

"I will fight to the death to protect WindClan," he replied, his brusque tone giving Crowfeather no encouragement to question him further.

But as soon as he had spoken, he had to clench his teeth against the shudder that ran right through him. Stoneteller's words echoed in his mind: that Darktail would demand a cost that he would have to pay.

Onestar couldn't believe any longer that the cost would be something unimportant, or something he could replace.

He was afraid that he would have to pay with his life. *My last life.* But perhaps that was the only way to save the cats he loved.

CHAPTER 29

Cats *from all four Clans were* gathered in a shifting mass along
the ShadowClan border. Onestar drew in their mingled
scents, carried on the cool dawn breeze that ruffled his fur
and stirred the branches of the trees above his head. Across
the stream, the dark pines of ShadowClan territory, where
light had scarcely penetrated, grew thickly enough to hide an
enemy.

Onestar sniffed. *I'd rather fight in the open, where I can see what's
coming at me.*

Almost a moon had passed since the decision at the Gathering that all the Clans would join together to drive out
Darktail and his rogues. Time had been needed to make
their battle plans, and to give the renegade ShadowClan cats
a chance to change their minds. The delay had also allowed
Rowanstar to regain his full strength.

Onestar would have preferred to move faster, once the
decision had been made. *Don't they realize we've given the sick
ShadowClan traitors time to regain their full strength, too?*

But for all the danger that he faced, Onestar's mind was
calm. He had accepted that he would die in this battle, and he

wasn't afraid of death. He would go to StarClan, to be with Wrenflight and Stagleap, Tallstar, and all the other cats he had loved and lost. He would be at peace.

"Cats of all Clans!" Bramblestar spoke commandingly, his voice ringing out over the crowd of warriors. "The time has come to take the rogues by surprise and force them out of ShadowClan territory."

"Yes," Rowanstar agreed. He looked strong and powerful again, his ginger pelt a flame in the growing light. "We must get rid of the rogues *once and for all*. The future of the Clans depends on it!"

Hearing the ShadowClan leader speak so confidently to the other Clans about a crisis *he* had created made Onestar's shoulder fur begin to rise in anger. "That's an interesting order," he snapped, "coming from the cat who allowed the rogues to live on his territory for moons, until finally most of his Clan decided they would rather follow Darktail! Maybe, Rowanstar, you could stop issuing orders to cats who are cleaning up *your* mess."

Rowanstar glared at him. "And just maybe, WindClan cats could mind their own business," he snarled.

"You made it our business!"

"Enough!" Mistystar thrust herself between Onestar and Rowanstar. "What hope do we have if we fight among ourselves?" the RiverClan leader continued, authority in her blue eyes. "Rowanstar is right about one thing: the rogues must be driven out. They killed Furzepelt, they enticed Shadow-Clan warriors away from their Clan, and now they've stolen

ShadowClan's territory. It's time to get rid of these fiends once and for all."

"Exactly." Bramblestar's voice was calm. "So please, can we stop blaming one another, and work together to drive out these rogues?"

Onestar dipped his head in agreement, remembering that this was his best chance of expelling Darktail from Clan territory. He hoped with every hair on his pelt that the combined strength of the Clans would be enough to drive every rogue out of the forest for good.

Rowanstar made no response, only turned aside and gave his pelt a furious shake.

Bramblestar paused for a few moments more, then raised his tail as a signal for the cats to move. Silently, moving as one, the cats leaped the stream or waded through it, then headed deeper into ShadowClan territory. The thick layer of pine needles that covered the ground swallowed up the sound of their paw steps.

As they drew closer to the ShadowClan camp, the cats spread out on both sides of the leaders, ready to encircle the camp and attack it from all directions. But before the bushes surrounding the camp came into sight, a patrol emerged from the trees: four of the ShadowClan cats who had decided to stay with the rogues.

Sleekwhisker was in the lead. She halted, staring at the advancing warriors, her pelt bushing out with shock. The rest of her patrol clustered around her, their eyes wide as if they couldn't believe what was advancing toward them.

"Intruders!" Sleekwhisker screeched. "We're under attack! All cats—back to camp, now!" She whipped around and raced into the trees, her patrol pelting after her.

Onestar felt his paws grow heavy and his tail droop with disappointment. Harespring, padding at his shoulder, let out a hiss of annoyance. "There goes our chance of surprising them," he muttered, shaking his head.

"Into your groups!" Bramblestar ordered.

Before they'd left ThunderClan territory, each cat had been assigned to a group: Onestar raced forward now with Crowfeather, Heathertail, and Breezepelt hard on his paws, while Harespring led more WindClan warriors alongside.

Almost before Onestar realized it, the mingled scents of ShadowClan cats and rogues washed over him. He could see the line of bushes that marked the edge of the camp. Yowls of shock and fury split the silence of the forest.

Then the bushes parted as cats thrust their way through and hurled themselves toward the advancing Clans. Onestar found himself in the midst of a tussling mass of cats. To begin with, the crowd was so thick that he could hardly free a paw to strike a blow.

The big gray rogue loomed over him. Since Onestar had last seen the fearsome cat, he had lost an eye, and he looked all the more menacing for that. Onestar struggled to his hind paws, aiming for the gray tom's throat, but his teeth only met in fur, while the rogue dealt him a blow on the side of his head, so hard that he was knocked off his paws. He scrabbled frantically with his hind legs while the gray rogue fastened his claws in his shoulder. Onestar knew he was going to die.

StarClan, not like this! he prayed. *Not before I've even set eyes on Darktail!*

Then suddenly the gray tom's weight vanished. Onestar staggered to his paws as Crowfeather slashed his claws down his attacker's flank and blood gushed out. Crowfeather let out a furious snarl and the gray rogue backed off, disappearing into the heaving crowd of warriors.

"Thanks!" Onestar gasped.

"Anytime," Crowfeather responded, and flung himself back into the battle.

Onestar scrambled up and took a moment to catch his breath. The air was heavy with the reek of blood. Already the first throng of battling cats was beginning to break up into separate skirmishess, two or three cats grappling together, rolling around on the forest floor in spitting, clawing bundles.

None of them was Darktail.

Intent on finding his son, Onestar forced a path through the battling cats, fighting his way toward the camp. Scorchfur, a former ShadowClan cat, rose up against him, but Onestar raked a paw over his nose and he fled screeching. He dodged around Rowanstar and a black rogue, locked together in a furious tussle, and fought off another rogue with a blow to his throat.

Darktail, where are you?

Tawnypelt raced past him, also heading for the camp, letting out a fearsome caterwauling challenge. As she reached the bushes ahead of Onestar, a cream-furred she-cat broke out into the open, and crouched to leap on Tawnypelt.

Tawnypelt halted, a screech dying in her throat. The cream-colored she-cat scrabbled backward, disappearing into the bushes again. Instead of following her, Tawnypelt veered aside; Onestar caught a look of horror on her face before she bounded toward Ivypool of ThunderClan, who was battling two of the rogues.

That was Dawnpelt! Onestar realized, a shiver passing through him from ears to tail-tip. *Tawnypelt is her mother. Oh, StarClan, what have we come to?*

While Onestar hesitated, two rogues rushed at him, yowling defiance. Onestar spun around to face them, slashing one across the face while he barreled into the second, knocking him off his paws and raking one hind paw across his belly. Both cats staggered away, and beyond them, Onestar saw his son.

Darktail was standing just outside the bushes that encircled the ShadowClan camp, at the top of a rise so that he could look down on the chaos of the battle. His fur was torn in a few places and there was a trickle of blood coming from one ear, but he had no serious wounds.

He'd rather watch the rest of us fight than risk his own life, Onestar thought. *Well, that ends here!*

His gaze locked with Darktail's as the battle raged around them. Onestar felt as if the harsh tang of blood and the screeches of pain and defiance were all fading away, leaving him alone with his son. There was a malicious glint in Darktail's eyes, as if he was almost proud of the devastation he had caused, and not at all worried that he and his Kin might be driven off or killed.

That makes him difficult to truly defeat.

Onestar let out all his fear, all his tension, in an earsplitting yowl. He charged toward Darktail, dodging from side to side to avoid the clawing knots of fighting cats. Darktail bounded down to meet him; Onestar felt the shock run right through him as they collided in a furious tangle of teeth and claws.

He released everything, all the fury that he had clamped down inside him for moons, ever since Smokekit had been taken and he had first suspected that Darktail had found the Clans. Now that he and his son were finally joined in combat, Onestar felt the weight of everything Darktail wanted to take from him, all that he faced losing because of this evil cat's lust for vengeance.

I will not let Darktail take my Clan, or the cats I love.

Onestar could feel the strength in Darktail's powerful body, and was alert for the trickery he knew lay beneath the surface of his twisted mind. But he was a seasoned Clan leader, whose warrior training had never left him. He soon realized that Darktail had few fighting moves that he had never seen before, no tactics that Onestar couldn't counter by adapting his own skills. As the two toms writhed together, clawing and battering at each other, Onestar began to see that this was a fight he could win.

A faint voice—a father's voice—seemed to speak at the back of Onestar's mind: *Darktail could have been a strong, capable warrior if he had been trained in a Clan.*

But Onestar fought to ignore the voice. He wasn't sure that even warrior training could have fixed the dark heart in this tom's chest.

With a final screech of rage, Onestar slammed his forepaws down on Darktail's neck and pinned the rogue to the ground. He struck out, over and over again, his claws leaving blood-stained tracks across his son's white fur. Darktail struggled feebly, gasping for breath. His throat was exposed; Onestar bent his head for the bite that would end the evil cat's life.

But before Onestar's teeth could meet in his son's throat, Darktail somehow found a new burst of strength and threw him off, dealing a couple of hard blows to Onestar's head. Onestar thumped down on the ground; for a heartbeat, he was too dazed to move.

By the time he recovered, Darktail was staggering over to him, his white fur matted with blood. Onestar stiffened. He braced himself for a killing blow, but he was determined to take Darktail with him into the darkness.

But it wasn't a claw Darktail lowered toward him. It was his head, as he bent down to whisper in his ear. "I will destroy you, and all the Clans, for what you did to me. What do you think will happen to a cat who rejected, and then killed, his own son? Surely that cat would end up in the Dark Forest. Think of that when you are on your last life!"

A chill of utter horror thrilled through Onestar. He remembered once more what Stoneteller had mentioned: the cost that he must pay. He was prepared to lose his final life . . . but to be exiled forever in the Place of No Stars? Never to have the chance to explain his secret to the cats he loved when they all met together in StarClan, and perhaps be forgiven for all his mistakes? *Is that how I must pay? I'm willing . . . but not eternally.*

More than that, Onestar knew that he *was* on his last life. Terror shook him right down to the tips of his claws. He didn't think he could pay that price, even if it would save the Clans from Darktail. He doubted that he was strong enough.

Onestar remembered how he had reacted when Tallstar made him leader: *I never asked for this.* And he had never asked to be responsible for this ruthless, bloodthirsty cat. *Was it truly what I did that created this evil?*

Everything that was in Onestar rejected the thought. *I can't believe it. I can't accept it.*

As Darktail sagged to the ground, Onestar rose to his paws and slowly backed away from the rogue. Raising his head, he let out a loud yowl.

"Cats of WindClan! Retreat! Back to the camp! Wind-Clan! Retreat!"

Then he spun around and fled, shame burning like fire in his blood as he led his Clan away from the battle.

CHAPTER 30

☙

Onestar didn't stop until he burst through the gorse bushes at the top of the hollow and raced down into the WindClan camp. His Clanmates followed, gathering around him in a ragged circle. Onestar couldn't meet their confused gazes. They had followed his order to retreat, but once they had left the battle behind, they had begun to question him.

Why are we retreating?

Onestar had no answer he could give them. He just kept on running.

But it wasn't that easy to avoid their questions. They surrounded him now, silently waiting for him to explain. Instead Onestar thrust his way out of the circle and slipped into his den.

He half expected that Whitetail would come to talk to him, once some cat had told her what had happened, but he really hoped she wouldn't. He wasn't sure how he could explain, and if she knew he had been fighting Darktail, only to let him go and give the cowardly order to retreat, would she ever respect him again?

Paw steps sounded outside, but it wasn't Onestar's mate

who entered the den; it was his deputy. Harespring's brown-and-white pelt was streaked with blood, and he was limping on one forepaw. His eyes smoldered with fury as he faced his Clan leader.

"Onestar, why did you order us to retreat?" he demanded. "Why did we abandon the other three Clans like that? That's not the warrior way; it's not the way of WindClan!"

I didn't ask for this! I didn't ask for any of this!

Onestar knew that he couldn't explain to his deputy that he'd never wanted to be in charge of his Clan; he'd never wanted to lose his friends because he was a leader; he'd never wanted his stupid, youthful mistake to endanger not only WindClan but all the Clans. He had no idea how to answer Harespring's question, so he tried to talk his way around it.

"My first duty is to WindClan, and my Clanmates' safety," he meowed stiffly. "Leaders have to make difficult decisions sometimes. You'll understand this when . . ."

Onestar let his voice trail off. He was about to tell Harespring that he would understand when he was leader of WindClan, but that thought reminded him that he might have to pay a price much higher than his own life.

What if Darktail doesn't only destroy me . . . what if he destroys my whole Clan? What if he doesn't stop even after I'm dead?

That was what Onestar had promised Tallstar would never happen, and yet . . . He realized that he had no reason to believe that Darktail would give up his destruction once he had killed his father. Just the opposite: Darktail would delight in destroying anything he knew Onestar loved.

And I love nothing more than my Clan.

Onestar's heart lurched with regret and dread: regret at not killing Darktail when he had the chance, and dread of what would happen because of it. His only hope was that Darktail had died in the battle, even though WindClan had fled, and even though Onestar had not struck the killing blow. The rogue had been seriously wounded; if some strong warrior like Bramblestar or Tigerheart took him on, surely they would finish the job that Onestar couldn't.

Could that really have happened? Onestar wondered. *Maybe it's already over.*

He drew a long breath, waiting for his heart to grow lighter, for optimism to replace the weight of dread he had felt ever since Darktail had discovered the Clans' territories. But renewed hope did not come. In his heart, Onestar knew that it was not over. In his heart, he feared that something much worse was looming over him, and there was no escape from what had come—determined, inexorable—to hunt him down.

The other Clans were already in the clearing when Onestar led his cats across the tree-bridge and onto the Gathering island. He was aware of every cat's head swiveling toward him as they pushed their way through the bushes, and the accusing stares that were leveled at him and WindClan. He sensed his Clanmates' embarrassment as they saw how battered and ragged the other cats were—the ones who had stayed and fought. In contrast, his own cats had few wounds, none of them serious.

Mistystar was one of the most severely wounded, with a gash running the whole length of her body. She was standing at the foot of the Great Oak as Onestar approached, and turned to glare at him, her blue eyes blazing with fury. Onestar struggled not to flinch or avert his gaze as he sprang up into the branches and found a position well away from the other leaders. Mistystar struggled up after him.

When Bramblestar declared the Gathering open, the RiverClan leader was the first cat to rise to her paws. "I think we all know what we need to discuss tonight," she growled. "Onestar, what got into you this morning? You cost us the battle when you fled and took your cats with you. And RiverClan took the worst of the damage."

"So you say," Onestar snapped, hiding his guilt under a show of anger.

"And how would you know?" Mistystar retorted. "You weren't there, you coward! Perchwing was *killed*, and many more of my warriors were injured. All to solve a problem we did nothing to cause!"

Onestar's belly tensed at the RiverClan leader's words. He hadn't known until then that any cat had died in the battle. *Mistystar has every right to despise me,* he thought, hardly able to meet the scathing contempt in her eyes.

"Perhaps I should do the same as you," Mistystar continued, "and just close my borders when I don't agree with other Clans. It would certainly be easier than fighting their battles for them!"

"Mistystar, no cat wants you to do that," Bramblestar

meowed with a calming gesture of his tail. "But we certainly don't blame you for feeling as you do. Onestar, in StarClan's name, *why* did you order your cats to retreat?"

That was the question Onestar had expected, the question he feared above all others. *There's no way I can answer it! It's all gone too far now.* His whole body felt heavy with regret as he wished he had been open and truthful from the beginning, but it was too late for that. "I don't have to tell you anything," he responded, his neck fur bristling up defensively. "I had my reasons."

"Yes," Rowanstar snarled, "that you're a coward."

"I am *not*!" Despairingly, Onestar knew that it looked that way. Yet he hadn't been afraid to die, only that after his death he would be condemned to spend uncounted seasons in the Dark Forest. "But I shouldn't have to see my Clan destroyed rescuing ShadowClan from its own incompetence. My only responsibility is to WindClan."

"You gave your word that you would help us drive out the rogues," Rowanstar pointed out. "And then you broke that word. How can any cat trust you again?"

Anger flared inside Onestar. *I'm not the only cat who broke my word!* He wanted to question whether Rowanstar deserved his place in the Great Oak, but bit the words back. That was an accusation that could too easily be turned back on himself. "You're a fine one to talk!" he snarled instead. "You and the ShadowClan cats with you were trying to protect your *former* Clanmates, the cats you were supposed to be fighting! Don't blame *me* for losing the battle!"

He had seen Tawnypelt and Dawnpelt draw back from fighting each other, and he could understand that, but Harespring had told him later that Tigerheart had actually *rescued* Yarrowleaf from Ivypool. There was no way he would stand silent under Rowanstar's accusations.

"That is true, Onestar," Rowanstar responded. His tail drooped wretchedly, but there was still pride in his voice as he continued, "But I do not believe that we lost our honor because we could not bring ourselves to attack our true Clanmates. Once the rogues are driven out, ShadowClan—"

"Thanks to you and Onestar," Mistystar interrupted bitterly, "right now the rogues don't seem anywhere close to being driven out."

The discussion, hostile to begin with, descended into a full-blown argument, with cats in the clearing yowling out their opinions, drowning the voices of the Clan leaders. Onestar sat silent on his branch, a hollow feeling inside him as he looked down to see cats with their fur bushed out, their ears flattened, and their claws extended as if they were ready to start fighting one another. Despairingly, he realized that the other Clans couldn't agree enough to drive out Darktail without WindClan's help. He felt as if he were standing on the edge of a dark pit as he accepted that he would have to be involved.

How can we recover from this? he asked himself. *Will we ever have peace in the forest again?*

Gradually he became aware that the light in the clearing was growing dim, and looked up to see clouds drifting over the full moon. Every hair on his pelt rose in apprehension.

At the same moment Bramblestar's voice rang out across the clearing. "Look at the moon! StarClan is angry! This Gathering is at an end."

Instantly silence fell over the clearing as every cat gazed anxiously up at the sky. Onestar and the other leaders leaped down from the Great Oak and signaled to their Clans to follow, crowding together on the shore of the island as they waited to cross the tree-bridge.

While he stood there, Onestar wondered whether the darkening sky was an omen especially for him, a warning that soon he would enter the Place of No Stars, as Darktail had predicted.

It will cost you.

The ominous words passed through Onestar's mind once again. He had always believed that ridding the Clans of Darktail would cost him one single thing, but now the fear grew inside him that it would cost him everything. His life, his Clan, the happiness that would have been his forever as one of the warriors of StarClan. All lost, over one stupid mistake, and Onestar had no idea how to stop it.

All I can do is keep Darktail away from me for as long as I can.

The journey back to the WindClan camp was silent, each of his warriors wrapped in their own thoughts. Onestar guessed that none of them knew what to think about how the Gathering had ended, nor what it meant that clouds had passed over the moon.

"Kestrelflight." Onestar called his medicine cat to him as

he led the way down into the hollow. Mistystar's words about closing her borders were echoing in his mind. *And maybe she had the right idea.* "Tomorrow morning, gather any herbs you need off other territories. After that, the WindClan borders will be closed to all outsiders."

Kestrelflight gave him a bewildered look. "But we haven't asked permission . . . ," he objected.

Onestar let out a contemptuous snort. "We don't need to ask permission from those mange-pelts! Just do it!"

Kestrelflight nodded, though he didn't look happy about it. Some of his other Clanmates, who had heard Onestar give the order, didn't look happy either, exchanging shocked glances.

"Does this mean that *we* can't cross our own border, either?" Crowfeather asked.

Onestar ignored the question. He couldn't tell any cat the reason why he was doing this. His only hope was to let out all the outrage he felt, convincing his Clanmates that he was in the right. "Did no cat *hear* some of the accusations that were flung at me during the Gathering? I was called a coward; I was called dishonorable. ShadowClan was too weak to turn away the Kin, so Rowanstar tried to get the other leaders angry at WindClan." He let out a furious hiss. "I will not stand for that. From now on, WindClan will look after itself, first and foremost."

CHAPTER 31

☙

Onestar crouched in his den. A shaft of sunlight angled in through the entrance, but he felt no temptation to go outside and enjoy the warmth. The light outside could do nothing to lift the darkness in his mind and heart.

How long before Darktail comes for me, and I'm forced to pay the price Stoneteller foretold?

A shadow cut off the sunlight, and Onestar looked up to see Oatclaw nervously peering into the den. "What do you want?" he snapped.

The pale brown tabby flinched. "A ThunderClan patrol is here to see you, Onestar," he mewed.

Onestar surged to his paws. "What did I say last night?" he growled. "The borders are closed! Which cat brought them here?"

Oatclaw took a pace back. "Crowfeather's patrol tried to drive the ThunderClan cats away," he explained. "But Gorsetail insisted on letting them in."

"I'll have a few words to say to Gorsetail," Onestar muttered. "She—"

"She thought you'd want to speak to Bramblestar," Oatclaw interrupted.

Shock drove all thoughts of punishing Gorsetail out of Onestar's mind. "The ThunderClan leader is here?" he asked.

Oatclaw nodded.

Onestar let out a long sigh, swallowing his irritation. He didn't want conflict with Bramblestar, especially not with Darktail still out there, still plotting his destruction. Besides, Bramblestar had behaved reasonably at the Gathering, not flinging accusations like the other leaders. A faint hope crept into Onestar's mind that he might convince Bramblestar to deal with Darktail. He wasn't Firestar, but their two Clans still had a long history together. Onestar even wondered whether he could confess to Bramblestar about his connection to the evil rogue.

But then he remembered that Bramblestar wasn't alone. Onestar had no intention of revealing his deepest secrets to a whole ThunderClan patrol.

"Tell them they can come in," he ordered Oatclaw.

When his Clanmate had left, Onestar gave his pelt a good shake to get rid of any scraps of bedding, then emerged into the open and positioned himself just outside his den.

Gorsetail and Featherpelt led five ThunderClan cats into the camp, with Bramblestar in the lead. His deputy, Squirrelflight, padded along at his shoulder, with the young medicine cat, Alderheart, on his other side. Lionblaze and Dovewing brought up the rear.

Apprehension gathered in Onestar's belly, like a huge bunch of worms writhing around each other. Once again he felt disappointed that Bramblestar wasn't alone. He didn't want the rest of the ThunderClan cats intruding into his camp. To cover his frustration, to show his Clan that he was in control, he let his shoulder fur fluff up, and his voice was hostile as he spoke.

"Well, Bramblestar?" he demanded as the ThunderClan cats approached. "What is it that you want? If it's about the battle, you can turn around right now and get off my territory."

The fur along Lionblaze's spine began to rise, but Bramblestar was calm as he responded.

"This has nothing to do with the battle. There's something important that you ought to know." He hesitated with a glance at Alderheart before he continued. "Do you remember, seasons ago, back in the old forest, when Firestar left ThunderClan for a while . . . ?"

Onestar listened, hardly able to believe that the ThunderClan cats were here to talk about something in the past, so many seasons ago, when all their resources should be focused on Darktail. The story they were telling was just as unbelievable: how there had once been a fifth Clan—SkyClan—in the forest. They had been forced to leave when Twolegs built the Twolegplace on their territory. Seasons later, Firestar had been guided by a SkyClan ancestor to find the gorge where they had settled.

"What few cats know," Bramblestar told him, "is that Star-Clan charged Firestar with renewing the lost Clan."

Onestar vaguely remembered something weird going on in ThunderClan at that time; no cat had seen Firestar for over a moon, and the ThunderClan cats were keeping very quiet about why. Graystripe had even lied that Firestar was sick, to explain his absence from Gatherings. *The sickness went on for a suspiciously long time,* he thought. *I'm not surprised something else was going on.*

Now that Onestar heard the explanation, outrage was swelling in his belly. He had always believed that the other Clans were trustworthy, and that Firestar in particular had always told him the truth. *Was I wrong? Can no cat be trusted?*

"So ThunderClan has been lying all this time?" The words burst out of Onestar. "I should have known you couldn't be trusted, Bramblestar—you or Firestar before you!"

For a brief moment Onestar had hoped that Bramblestar might be able to help him with his own secret. Now he realized that was impossible. Bramblestar had been keeping secrets too. Every cat had to look out for himself and his Clan first. Now he knew that he had been right to cut WindClan off from the others.

Even as he reviled ThunderClan for keeping secrets, Onestar was acutely aware of his own hypocrisy, but he couldn't help himself. He had been wallowing in his own mistakes for so long, and yet he couldn't bear to think that others had hidden information that surely they should have shared with the other Clans.

"No cat has lied to any cat!" Squirrelflight retorted, a glint of indignation in her green eyes. "But Firestar saw no need to spread the story around, and neither did Bramblestar—until now."

"So what has changed?" Onestar asked with a snort of disgust.

It was Alderheart who replied, stepping forward to Bramblestar's side and dipping his head to Onestar. His whiskers were twitching nervously, but his voice was steady as he replied.

"I have been having visions," he explained. "Visions I interpreted as messages from StarClan, urging us to bring SkyClan back, to live with the other Clans as once they did. I'm sure that the prophecy is StarClan's way of telling us that we need to help SkyClan."

Onestar was barely listening. Until now, he had thought very little about the prophecy. *Embrace what you find in the shadows, for only they can clear the sky.* Darktail had given him quite enough to think about. But now it seemed that Bramblestar wanted to ignore the threat from the rogues in favor of welcoming this new, unknown Clan.

"So you want my support," he rasped, with a furious lash of his tail, "to help some strange Clan that only ThunderClan has ever heard of? Are you planning to bring them here and give them WindClan territory? You won't get the chance!"

At his words, Lionblaze and Dovewing slid out their claws. The WindClan warriors who had gathered around to listen had begun to let out threatening growls. Onestar knew that if he gave the order, they would attack the visitors without hesitation.

"We don't intend that at all," Bramblestar responded; Onestar found his calm demeanor more persuasive than his actual words. "Alderheart, tell Onestar about your quest."

Onestar listened, his tail-tip twitching impatiently, while Alderheart told the story of how he and his Clanmates, and Needlepaw from ShadowClan, had made the long journey to the gorge where SkyClan had their camp.

"When we arrived, we found cats living there," he explained, "and we thought they were SkyClan. But it was weird—worrying. They didn't behave like a Clan. They fought over fresh-kill, and the stronger cats pushed the weaker cats around."

"And this is the Clan you want to bring back here?" Onestar asked.

"No, because they *weren't* SkyClan," Alderheart continued. "They were rogues, and they'd driven the real SkyClan out of their territory and killed many of their cats. We never saw *SkyClan* at all."

"And these rogues . . . ," Onestar began, a terrible uneasiness beginning to grow in his belly.

"They were the same rogues who attacked you here in WindClan," Alderheart explained. "The same who have taken over ShadowClan territory."

Onestar felt a pain in his heart, as if a huge paw were crushing it. All the air seemed to rush from his body, and he felt as dazed as if some cat had fetched him a massive blow on his head.

Darktail has even attacked SkyClan? he asked himself. For some time Onestar had wondered how Darktail had managed to find him. He had assumed that kittypets or other rogues must have given him the information he needed. Now he guessed that discovering SkyClan—cats who organized their lives like WindClan and the others from the old forest—had given Darktail a clue, and when Alderheart and the rest of the questing cats had arrived, he had been able to follow them back to the Clan territories by the lake.

And I never even knew that SkyClan existed!

A deep shudder passed through Onestar that he strove to hide from the other cats. *What else am I responsible for? Caused by my foolish mistakes, so long ago?*

Desperately, Onestar tried to pull himself together. "So Darktail was to blame for SkyClan being driven from the gorge?" he asked. "And nearly destroyed?"

Alderheart nodded.

Onestar fell silent for a few moments, wondering how this vicious tom could be his kin. Had the evil been inside him from the beginning? *Or did I put it there,* Onestar mused, *by leaving him and Smoke behind?*

Mingled terror and anger swelled up inside Onestar. A chill spread through his whole body, as if his blood had turned to ice. Horror gripped him at the thought that all this was his fault, and even worse, that every cat would find out what he had done. He couldn't bear the thought any longer, and he turned on the ThunderClan cats to hide his dread and guilt. "WindClan owes SkyClan nothing!" he screeched. "And you ThunderClan cats need to get out! Go on—get off my territory! WindClan's borders are closed!"

He saw Bramblestar exchange bewildered looks with the

rest of his patrol, as if he couldn't understand what had made Onestar so furious. "There's no need for this," the Thunder-Clan leader protested. "SkyClan—"

"Enough about SkyClan!" Onestar yowled, quivering on the brink of losing all control. "I've told you to get out—so go!"

As he spoke, he saw his warriors loyally gathering around the ThunderClan patrol. If the visitors delayed any longer, blood would be shed.

Bramblestar dipped his head. "Very well, Onestar," he sighed. "Send a patrol to me if you change your mind."

Onestar clamped his jaws shut, refusing even to answer.

Then Gorsetail stepped forward, beckoning more cats to join her with a sweep of her tail. "I'll escort you to the border," she meowed, an edge to her tone that left a clear threat unsaid.

When the ThunderClan patrol was gone, Onestar retreated to his den, keeping his back to the entrance and to the camp beyond. He didn't want his Clanmates to see the fear and dread that must be obvious on his face.

Only a few moments passed before Kestrelflight's scent drifted into his nose. Before he could snarl, "Go away!" the medicine cat spoke softly. "Onestar, you shouldn't fear losing your last life, if that's where all this is coming from."

Onestar turned, making sure that Kestrelflight was alone, and that no other cats were lurking around outside. "How do you know this is my last life?" he demanded.

"It's a medicine cat's job to know," Kestrelflight responded, still in the same soft voice. "And I can tell that you know it's your last life, too. Your behavior has changed."

Onestar didn't know whether to panic or to be relieved that his medicine cat had observed that. "I know I'm on edge," he admitted. "And it's not just because I'm on my last life. I think . . ." It was hard to force the words out. "I think I might go to the Dark Forest when I lose it."

Kestrelflight stared at him, surprised. "Why would you think that, Onestar?" he asked. "Every cat makes mistakes, but you have done your best to lead WindClan honorably—what could you have done that would make that not matter?"

If you only knew . . .

For a few heartbeats, Onestar was tempted to tell the medicine cat everything. He hadn't been able to confide in Bramblestar, but maybe it wasn't too late to trust a cat from his own Clan. The need to unburden himself of the secret that had weighed him down for so long was so great that the words came bubbling up into his throat.

But Onestar thrust them down again. He felt too much shame, and dwelling on it made him more certain than ever that he was bound for the Dark Forest. Besides, there was nothing Kestrelflight could do. If Onestar could have told Bramblestar, perhaps the ThunderClan leader would have fought harder to get rid of Darktail. As a medicine cat, Kestrelflight would only worry, and that wouldn't help WindClan.

"Oh, don't listen to me, Kestrelflight," he meowed, flicking his tail dismissively. "It's probably just my fear of dying, making me imagine stupid things."

Kestrelflight held his gaze for a moment, clearly unconvinced. Then he dipped his head. "If you need me, Onestar," he murmured as he left the den, "you know where to find me."

When he had left, Onestar collapsed into his nest and lay there. Anxious, dark thoughts whirled around in his head like froth on a whirlpool, and however hard he tried, he could not put them to rest.

Death would have held no fears for him, if it were not for the ominous shadow of the Dark Forest, ready to engulf him. Terror throbbed through him at the very thought of it. *Is that the sacrifice I must make to save my Clan?*

But now his earlier realization, even more horrifying, crept back into his mind. *Suppose I die, and go to the Dark Forest—and WindClan is still destroyed?* A shudder shook Onestar to the tips of his claws. *Oh, StarClan, no! You couldn't let that happen!*

But no starry warrior came to reassure him.

Onestar padded along a narrow path through the forest. Tall pines lined his route, seeming to crowd closer together with every paw step that he took. He wondered if he was on ShadowClan territory, though he couldn't believe that even ShadowClan would live in a place so dark and forbidding.

His paws fell softly on the thick covering of pine needles, but every so often Onestar thought that he could hear some creature padding just as softly behind him. He kept glancing over his shoulder, but he could see nothing.

At last the thought of his invisible pursuer spooked him so badly that he began to run, his paws flying down the narrow path until he burst out into sunlight. The dens of a Twolegplace confronted him, and when he gazed around wildly, Onestar realized that the pine forest had vanished.

As he caught his breath, Onestar recognized the place where he was standing. This was the Twolegplace near the old forest, where he used to visit Smoke. And Smoke herself was sitting on a nearby fence, gazing at him with wide, sorrowful eyes. For the first time, Onestar realized that he was dreaming.

Just looking at the pretty gray she-cat gave Onestar a feeling of shame like claws hooked into his heart. It was as if all his guilt, for all his mistakes, came crashing down on him all at once.

"Smoke, I'm so sorry," he meowed, bounding up to her. "I know it's all my fault—my fault for being weak, and for letting down cats who cared for me. I've spent so many moons trying to cover up my previous mistakes, trying to do something to make me feel like I've atoned for them, but now—after so long—I'm beginning to think that I can't do it." Gazing up at Smoke, drinking in her scent, he added humbly, "I don't expect forgiveness—or want it, or deserve it—but I do want to say that to you."

Smoke looked down at him, arching her whiskers. "You have to help," she told him.

"But . . . Darktail is beyond help, surely?" Onestar asked, thoroughly confused.

"You have to help," Smoke repeated. "You *can* help. . . . But it's up to you, whether you do or not. . . ."

Smoke's voice began to fade on the last few words, and Smoke herself began to recede, getting smaller and smaller as though an invisible wind were carrying her away.

"Help who?" Onestar called urgently. "Help *how*? Smoke, you have to tell me!"

But Smoke didn't answer.

Onestar jerked awake to find himself in his den. The chilly nip of early morning seemed to claw right through his pelt, and a new heavy guilt weighed down his chest and throat as he glanced aside and saw Whitetail curled up in peaceful sleep.

Later that day, Onestar was picking at a vole near the fresh-kill pile when Kestrelflight came bounding over to him.

"Onestar, will you allow me to bring Curlfeather and Duskfur into camp?" he asked. "They're injured."

"Injured?" Onestar sat up, between annoyance and surprise. "It's about half a moon since the battle. They can't *still* be injured. What are their medicine cats doing?"

"This has nothing to do with the battle," Kestrelflight explained, his claws working tensely. "Darktail and his Kin have taken over RiverClan. These two warriors escaped, but they're badly hurt."

A heavy weight of weariness descended on Onestar as he heard the news. He wasn't even shocked. *Of course Darktail wouldn't be satisfied with taking over ShadowClan!* This thought was followed by another, even darker one: *Will he work his way through every other Clan before he comes for WindClan?*

Kestrelflight was waiting for his answer, an anxious expression in his eyes, as if he expected Onestar to refuse. Several of the WindClan warriors had gathered around to listen, looking equally expectant.

Onestar nodded. "Yes, bring them in," he responded.

As the medicine cat turned and raced out of the hollow,

Onestar heard a murmur of relief pass among his Clanmates. Their faces had brightened; they were happy he was helping, acknowledging the bonds between Clan and Clan.

Onestar reflected that his warriors had probably been confused by some of the orders he had given recently, and perhaps disappointed that they weren't joining the other Clans in fighting off the rogues and driving them out.

If only I could explain the reason why . . .

Kestrelflight returned, with the two RiverClan cats limping after him. Duskfur, a small brown tabby she-cat, had a torn ear and a face covered with scratches. Curlfeather's pale brown pelt had been ripped off in several places, and she tottered along on three legs, with one forepaw held off the ground. They headed straight for the medicine cat's den and disappeared inside.

A jolt of pity shook Onestar as he saw their injuries. Darktail's evil was truly reaching out for the other Clans, not just WindClan. *Can I really keep my Clan apart, and not do anything to help? Could Darktail really destroy all the Clans?*

Onestar gave Kestrelflight enough time to treat the injuries, then crossed the camp to the den and slipped inside. The air was full of the clean tang of marigold. Curlfeather was lying on one side, her pelt matted with marigold juice and a poultice plastered with cobweb over her wounded paw. Duskfur was sitting beside her with her face cleaned up and more marigold poultice applied to her ear.

"Thank you, Onestar," she meowed. "We really appreciate this."

Onestar hardly knew how to reply; it was so unusual these days for a cat to praise him for anything. "You're welcome," he mumbled.

"These cats have been telling me what Darktail did," Kestrelflight meowed.

"Oh, it was terrible!" Curlfeather exclaimed. "He attacked us on our border—Darktail and his Kin, and the ShadowClan cats who joined him. There were too many for us, especially when some of us hadn't recovered from the battle."

"And that's not the worst of it," Duskfur added, her eyes dark with memory. "Four of us *died*. And Darktail took the wounded cats prisoner; he starved us, and wouldn't allow us healing herbs unless we took an oath of loyalty to him and his Kin. Curlfeather and I managed to escape, but some of our Clanmates are still there."

Onestar shuddered to hear the RiverClan cats' news. He had known that Darktail was evil, and would do anything to destroy his father, but he hadn't realized that he would torture other cats or leave them to die under his leadership.

"He's out of control!" Curlfeather raised her head, then let it drop back onto the soft bedding. "Some cat needs to do something about him," she finished.

"I wonder why Darktail is doing this," Kestrelflight murmured. "What can be driving him?" He let out a bewildered sigh. "We've never seen any cat like him—*can* he even be stopped?"

Onestar could have answered some of his questions, but he didn't dare. The burden of what he knew, of what he regretted, was growing heavier and heavier within him. He realized that he had deceived himself when he believed he could ever keep WindClan out of the conflict. Whatever he did, Darktail would come for him. By delaying, he was just robbing more cats of their lives.

Some cat needs to do something about him. Curlfeather's words came back into his mind. "She's right," he muttered under his breath. "And that cat has to be me!"

CHAPTER 32

☙

Onestar woke from a fitful sleep to see the first dim light of dawn
seeping through his den entrance. He rose to his paws, careful
not to disturb Whitetail, who was curled up asleep at his side.
Briefly he looked down at her, grateful for her support. Even
when she hadn't understood his decisions, she had believed in
him, and had stayed beside him, urging him to be better. She
couldn't possibly know what her love meant to him. Purring
softly, he padded out into the camp.

It was so early that even the dawn patrol wasn't yet stirring.
Onestar shook out his pelt, then arched his back in a good
long stretch. As he relaxed, he froze. He gave a deep sniff,
then opened his jaws to let the air flow over his scent glands,
desperately hoping that he was wrong.

He wasn't wrong. The scent he detected had become all too
familiar. Onestar blinked away the blurriness of sleep to see a
line of cats standing around the top of the hollow, inside the
barrier of gorse bushes. Darktail and his Kin, standing still, as
if they were cats made of ice, their faces eerily expressionless.
Darktail's white pelt seemed to glow in the half-light.

For a moment Onestar wondered if this was another
dream. But he soon realized that Darktail had come for him,

before he could seek out Darktail. *It ends now. I must protect my Clanmates!*

Now that the crisis was upon him, Onestar even felt relief. No matter what this battle would cost him, the long struggle with secrets and lies would be over.

Onestar opened his jaws to yowl a warning to his Clanmates, but before he could get a word out, Darktail let out a fearsome screech to his followers. "Finish this!"

The Kin bounded down into the camp, with Darktail in the lead. The WindClan warriors, taken by surprise, blundered out into the open, easy prey for the vicious attackers—rogues and former Clan cats—who pounced on them, their claws slashing and their teeth biting. Shrieks of pain and fury split the dawn silence.

Onestar headed toward Darktail, so focused on reaching the evil cat that he didn't notice the two rogues charging forward until they barreled into him from both sides. Onestar let himself fall to the ground, lashing out at his attackers with all four paws. The two rogues obviously hadn't expected such a fierce defense. One of them fled; Onestar battered the other around the ears until he too backed off. Onestar struggled back onto his paws, gasping for breath and looking around for Darktail.

"Fight hard, WindClan!" he yowled. "You're warriors, better than rogues. . . . We *will* win! StarClan will make sure—"

The breath was knocked out of him as a pair of fierce paws struck him from behind. A crushing weight landed on his ribs; twisting his head to one side, Onestar saw the hate-filled eyes of his son.

All the fear, all the dread, all the foolish wishing that the other Clans would take care of Darktail, had led up to this moment. Onestar no longer believed that he would be able to save his own life, and he wasn't sure what would happen to him when he died. Now he had only one hope: to put Wind-Clan first and save it from the claws of this evil cat.

Onestar writhed to get free, threw Darktail off, and sprang to his paws. As soon as he regained his balance, he aimed a vicious swipe at Darktail's head; Darktail staggered backward and fell, his paws flailing at the air. Quicker than Onestar would have thought possible, he rolled over and leaped up, hurling himself at his father once again.

Even without a warrior's training, Darktail was a strong opponent, filled with viciousness and determination to win. Onestar pulled out every battle move he had ever learned, every trick from his warrior's training, but he was still only just holding his own. Onestar threw his son to the ground, over and over, slashing at the rogue's pelt until his white fur was streaked with blood.

And still Darktail kept on coming.

I'm sure I could have beaten any other cat. . . . But Darktail won't give up!

Each time the rogue rose to his paws, Onestar felt more and more weary, while there seemed no end to the vicious rogue's strength. Beginning to despair, he wondered whether his secret son might be right after all. Was his tireless fighting a sign that he had StarClan's favor?

Is this how my life was always meant to end? Onestar asked himself, panting with exhaustion. *Were my mistakes always meant to catch up with me?*

There had been so much more to his life, he mused, than his doomed relationship with Smoke. He had loved Whitetail and Heathertail; he had led WindClan successfully beside the lake; he had won Firestar's friendship; he had respected and cared for Tallstar. And yet in the end what he had done to Smoke seemed to be all that mattered.

Would things have been different if I'd admitted my mistake as soon as Darktail appeared?

Wrestling on the ground with Darktail, Onestar managed to glance around at the combat in the rest of the camp. To his amazement, the strengthening light showed more cats pouring through the bushes and down into the hollow. A sturdy dark gray tabby tom that Onestar had never set eyes on before was fighting side by side with Harespring, gradually driving back a long-furred, brown rogue. Twigpaw, the ThunderClan apprentice, was grappling with a black she-cat, while Violetpaw, who had once been one of the Kin, was now crouching to spring on a silver-gray tom.

What in StarClan's name is going on?

"Stop!"

The earsplitting yowl came from Darktail. He thrust Onestar off and scrambled to his paws, while Onestar staggered upright and stood facing him, nose to nose. Around them the sounds of battle sank into silence as every cat drew back from their opponent.

Darktail let his gaze travel over Onestar, filled with contempt. "You mouse-hearted excuse for a cat!" he meowed, a mocking edge to his voice. "Is that the best you can do? A kittypet fights better! But then . . . you always were a *coward.*"

Onestar heard his Clan murmuring together in bewilderment. His belly cramped as he waited for his secret to be revealed. To his surprise, he still felt a trickle of apprehension: as bad as things were, he still didn't want every cat to know the truth.

"Darktail, you're talking like . . . like you *know* Onestar. How can that be?" Harespring asked.

Onestar kept the rogue leader pinned by his gaze. "This cat's word is not to be trusted," he declared, desperation roiling in his belly. For a moment he felt a frantic hope that Darktail would go on keeping the secret. *But I don't really believe it.* "Look at what he's done," he continued. "Raided camps, kept prisoners, killed more Clan cats than we can count. He'll clearly do or say anything in his efforts to steal territory. And that's what this is all about, isn't it?"

An evil glitter kindled in his son's dark-furred eyes. "Of course it's about territory," he sneered. "It's always about territory. And I think you handing some of WindClan's territory over to me would only be fair." His eyes narrowed, his expression grew more malignant, and Onestar's head began to swim with stress and panic, because he knew, just a moment before Darktail spoke, what he would say next. "Especially after what you did to me!"

Onestar opened his jaws to respond, but before he could say a word, his rogue son had turned to address the other Clan cats.

"You all think of Onestar as an honorable leader, don't

you?" he challenged them. "Well, I know things about him that would make every WindClan cat's fur stand on end."

Onestar was aware of the crowd's gaze piercing him like thorns. He held his tail straight in the air, while his claws flexed and dug into the ground. *My secret . . . my precious secret . . . It's all out in the open. All that effort I put into hiding it, all wasted. . . .*

"What is he talking about?" Harespring asked.

"Why would you listen to him?" Onestar snarled. "You've all seen the kind of cat he is!" But even while he was speaking, he knew that his denial would not convince any cat.

Darktail spun around to face Onestar again. "And they should know what kind of cat *you* are," he retorted, his voice full of defiance. "The Onestar they think they know could not have done what you did to *me*!"

His last words rose into a frenzied yowl, and he flung himself once more at Onestar.

Onestar leaped back, his claws at the ready, but he did not need to strike a blow. Squirrelflight grabbed Darktail and thrust him away, aiming her claws at his throat.

Darktail twisted himself free and tottered upright. "Retreat!" he screeched.

His followers broke away and fled up the slope, plunging through the gorse bushes, until the last of them had left the camp.

Only Darktail remained. At the top of the hollow he turned, raking the camp with a hate-filled gaze. "We're leaving now," he yowled. "But we'll be back! You can count on that, Onestar!"

Watching the departing rogues, Onestar could hardly

believe that Darktail and his Kin were retreating. He felt a huge weight of weariness descend on him: he had been ready to die, here in his camp, and now he had to face it all again.

When Darktail was gone, a heavy silence fell over the camp. It was hard for Onestar to muster the strength to look up at the cats who surrounded him. He straightened up, with a massive effort to appear dignified.

Even though moments ago he had been trying to cast doubt on Darktail and cling to his secret, he began to realize that he had to put an end to his lying and deceiving. Otherwise the Clans would have no idea what they were up against. *And no other cat can do this. It's time.*

"Now I must tell the truth," he meowed. "But I will not speak until the Clan leaders are here. This is a matter for them . . . and I can only bear to explain once."

"Okay," Squirrelflight agreed. "Bramblestar, Rowanstar, and Leafstar are—"

"Leafstar?" Onestar interrupted, mystified.

"Oh, of course, you don't know," Squirrelflight continued. "Leafstar is the leader of SkyClan. They have returned!" In the midst of wondering exclamations from the WindClan warriors, the ThunderClan deputy nodded toward the sturdy gray tom Onestar had noticed earlier. "This cat is the Sky-Clan deputy, Hawkwing."

Onestar couldn't suppress a pang of guilt when he remembered the story Alderheart and the others had told him about SkyClan. They had suffered so much because of his son, and he wasn't sure that he would survive long enough to make it up to them.

Hawkwing dipped his head respectfully. "It's an honor to meet you, Onestar."

"You might not say that when you've heard my story," Onestar grunted.

"I'll fetch the leaders from ThunderClan's camp," Squirrelflight meowed, bounding up the slope and disappearing through the bushes.

"And I'll fetch Mistystar—she and her warriors are rebuilding RiverClan's camp," Tigerheart added, racing away in the other direction.

Once they had left, Onestar headed back to his den. He could sense curiosity flowing from his Clanmates, as strong as a river, and avoided the glances directed his way. Behind him, he could hear Harespring arranging hunting and border patrols, though he told them not to leave camp until they had heard what their leader had to say.

"Keep a sharp lookout for Darktail and his Kin," the deputy ordered. "But don't fight unless it's a last resort."

Onestar settled down in his nest, waiting for the Clan leaders to arrive. Part of him wanted to spring to his paws and run right out of camp and over the hills, never to come back. Instead he crouched motionless. Every muscle in his body, every nerve, was braced for their reaction to the tale he was about to tell. . . .

Movement out in the camp signaled to Onestar that the leaders were arriving. He caught Squirrelflight's scent, mingled with Bramblestar's, Rowanstar's, and a scent that was completely unfamiliar to him.

That must be Leafstar, the SkyClan leader.

"He won't see you until all the leaders have arrived." Harespring's voice drifted into the den. "We must wait for Mistystar."

It was not long before the RiverClan leader's scent joined the others, along with Tigerheart's. Onestar knew that he couldn't put off the time he was dreading for any longer.

Harespring ducked his head as he slipped into the den. "All the leaders are here, Onestar," he mewed.

Onestar felt as though he couldn't move, not even a single claw.

But I must face up to them.

The future of all the Clans depended on it.

Onestar rose to his paws and headed out into the camp, waving his tail to beckon the other leaders closer.

"Maybe we should leave the leaders to it," Hawkwing suggested, rising to his paws.

Onestar shook his head. "No," he responded, trying not to let his weariness show in his voice. "The way you fought today proves that you're a worthy warrior—and besides, every cat should probably hear this."

He stood still as the other four leaders found places around him, while the remaining cats withdrew a fox-length or so, exchanging anxious or mystified glances, and settled down in a rough semicircle.

Onestar took a deep breath and began to speak, amazed to hear his voice emerging clear and steady as he began the confession he had avoided for so long. "*I* am the reason the Clans have been blighted by Darktail and his rogues. And the story goes back many seasons, to when we lived in the old forest, when I was called Onewhisker and Tallstar was the leader of WindClan."

He was aware of the WindClan cats glancing at one another in bewilderment, murmuring to one another, only to fall silent again as he continued.

"You all know that I never expected to be chosen as deputy, or to become your leader. Tallstar appointed me in the last moments of his life, and no cat was more astonished than I was. I felt I was unworthy. . . ." He paused, bowing his head, his shame burning in his heart and throat. "And events have proved that I was right."

"No!" Crowfeather sat erect, protesting vehemently. "You've been a noble leader, Onestar."

There was some comfort in his Clanmate's words. *We've had our differences, but if even Crowfeather sees me as noble, maybe there is hope for me,* Onestar thought wryly with a sad shake of his head.

"When I was a young cat, back in the old forest," he went on, "I carried out my warrior duties, but I also liked to sneak off to explore the little Twolegplace beyond the farm where Barley and Ravenpaw lived. It was fun to spend time with the kittypets there, and tell them stories about what it was like to live in a Clan."

"I never knew that!" Whitetail's voice was shot through with anger and hurt. Onestar didn't dare look at her face.

Onestar continued, telling the assembled cats how he had enjoyed impressing the kittypets in the Twolegplace with stories of hunting and battle training. His swelling shame made it harder to force out the words, especially when he had to admit that he'd exaggerated to make himself look good.

"But what does this have to do with Darktail?" Bramblestar asked.

"I was coming to that," Onestar replied, wishing with every hair on his pelt that he didn't have to. "There was one kitty-pet . . . a young she-cat called Smoke. She had such soft gray fur, and such brilliant blue eyes . . . It was like I was staring into pools of pure water."

He spotted Squirrelflight rolling her eyes, and heard her murmur, "I see." For the first time he dared to glance at Whitetail, and saw her sitting with her head bowed, her gaze fixed firmly on her paws. Every word Onestar had to speak pierced him like a claw, knowing how much he must be hurting her.

"Smoke and I became . . . more than friends," Onestar continued. "She loved to hear my stories of Clan life; she couldn't get enough of them. She was happy to be my mate, but of course I only ever saw her in the Twolegplace. There was no way I could have brought her into camp."

Rowanstar exchanged a glance with Mistystar. "You can say that again," he muttered. "What was the mouse-brain thinking?"

"Obviously he *wasn't* thinking," Mistystar responded.

Shame washed over Onestar once more as he continued with his story: how Smoke had told him she was expecting kits, and how she wanted to join WindClan. He admitted he had given her a completely false idea of Clan life, telling of adventure and abundant prey, without mentioning the hazards of dogs or Twolegs, or the harsh days of leaf-bare.

"What did you say to her?" Violetpaw asked, then started back with a squeak of embarrassment at her boldness in speaking up.

"What *could* I say to her? I knew there was no way I could bring a kittypet into WindClan."

Onestar found that the story was coming more easily now. He recounted the birth of Smoke's kits, how only one of them had survived, and how she had begged that he might have a place in the Clan. He told how he had refused, and how finally Smoke had threatened to teach her kit to hate him, and to hate the Clans.

"Wait," Bramblestar put in. "This kit—are you saying that he grew up to be Darktail? That Darktail is *your son?*"

Onestar nodded, bracing himself to continue, raising his voice over the shocked muttering of his listeners. "I tried to tell myself that I was protecting Smoke and her kit. I thought that whatever she'd said when she was angry, she would take him and go back to being a kittypet, and their lives would be better that way."

"So Darktail knew that you rejected him," Mistystar mewed thoughtfully.

"Yes, he was old enough to understand," Onestar told her, struggling against growing weariness. "StarClan knows where he went for so long, but wherever it was, he grew into a bitter and resentful cat, full of grief for a father he never knew, and hatred for a way of life he never got the chance to understand."

Tigerheart puffed out a long breath. "You can say that again!"

What if I'd accepted him? Onestar wondered. An image passed into his mind of the warrior Darktail could have been: strong and powerful, a skilled fighter, but using his talents for the good of his Clan. *He could have been such a splendid warrior! I would have been so proud....* A pang of grief shook Onestar, as piercing as if he were mourning a dead son. *But that son never had the chance to live.*

After a deep breath, Onestar began again. "He must have gathered rogues to him as his followers, and not long ago he wandered upriver and found SkyClan. He attacked them and drove them out. When Alderheart arrived on his quest, Darktail got the information he had been seeking for so long: where I and the other Clans had gone after we left the forest territories. And just like that, he got the chance he'd always craved: to wreak revenge on me—the father who had rejected him—and our whole way of life."

"I'm beginning to understand why you behaved as you did," Mistystar remarked.

Her tone and her expression gave nothing away; Onestar wasn't sure whether she was sympathizing with him or mocking him. He also hesitated to tell the other leaders the full story, of how long he had been keeping this terrible secret.

"When the rogues attacked us here, in WindClan territory," he continued, "and the fighting spilled over into ThunderClan—that was the first hint I got that Darktail was my own kit."

The lie stuck in his throat, and shame licked at his heart like flames. *If I tell them about Smokekit, and Fernpaw, and all the other times, they could lose their focus,* he thought. *And that mustn't happen. When all this is over, if I survive, I'll tell them the truth,* he promised himself.

"When he attacked me," he went on, "he whispered, 'I will destroy you, and all the Clans, for what you did to me.' At once I understood the threat that Darktail posed to all of us, and to WindClan in particular. That's why I wanted you, Rowanstar, to drive him out of your territory."

"It would have helped if you'd told the truth from the start," Rowanstar grunted. "I might have understood why you were so furious when I hesitated."

"I know," Onestar admitted. *So much suffering could have been avoided, if only I'd been brave enough.* "But I couldn't. All I could do was close my borders. And then Bramblestar convinced me to join with the other Clans to expel the rogues from Shadow-Clan. But in that battle . . ."

Onestar hunched his shoulders and let his tail droop. This was it, the moment when he had to confess his greatest deed of cowardice, the decision that had lost the battle. He imagined cold condemnation in the eyes of all the leaders, and even his own Clan turning away from him.

"What happened?" Mistystar demanded with an impatient flick of her tail. "You wanted the rogues off Clan territory so badly, but suddenly you retreated with all your warriors. Why?"

"I'm not proud of what I did," Onestar replied, struggling to find the words. "But when I was grappling with

Darktail—and I've never battled an enemy with strength so vicious—this cat who was my son leaned into me and whispered something. . . ."

"What?" Squirrelflight asked, her whiskers quivering with tension.

"He said . . . 'What do you think will happen to a cat who rejected, and then killed, his own son? Surely that cat would end up in the Dark Forest. Think of that when you're on your last life!' But what Darktail didn't know was that I *am* on my last life. He made me so afraid. . . ."

Onestar cringed inwardly as it seemed that every cat let out a gasp of shock. He saw Kestrelflight wince and close his eyes briefly.

Rowanstar stared at Onestar for a heartbeat, jaws gaping. "You must be joking!" he meowed. "The Dark Forest is not for a leader who saves his Clan from a terror such as Darktail—no matter whose kin he is!"

"That's true," Kestrelflight agreed. There was deep understanding in his eyes as he gazed at Onestar. "The Dark Forest is for cats who have given themselves to evil. That isn't you, Onestar. I could have told you that long ago, if you'd trusted me enough to be honest with me."

If only . . . "Maybe," Onestar sighed, looking down at his paws. "I admit it was a selfish fear. But . . . well, things look a bit different when a leader is on his final life. I started to worry that StarClan would judge me harshly for my mistakes—and StarClan knows, I have made many of those."

Silence fell as Onestar ended his confession. Along with

the shame he still felt was a lighter sensation, new strength flowing through his body now that he had unburdened himself of his terrible secret. He raised his head again to face his listeners, holding them in a steady gaze.

"We all have the same problem," he began. "The rogues go on attacking us, stealing territory, threatening vulnerable cats and kits. I know this problem is of *my* making, and I'm very sorry that I've turned away from my friends. I won't do that again. I'm no longer afraid," he told them, suddenly full of joy that he could speak those words truthfully. "Darktail and his rogues need to be dealt with, no matter what happens to me—otherwise they will keep on coming back, and more good cats will perish."

"Then—" Bramblestar began.

"Yes," Onestar declared, full of resolve as he met the ThunderClan leader's gaze. "WindClan will fight with the other Clans, to drive Darktail off our territory once and for all."

CHAPTER 33

Onestar let himself sink into his nest, giving way at last to exhaustion. When the Clan leaders and their Clanmates had left, his first thought had been to talk to Whitetail, but she had gone with Crowfeather and Gorsetail on a hunting patrol. Onestar wondered whether she would ever want to talk to him again. He loved her so much, and he knew how much he had hurt her, especially since she had learned the truth with the whole Clan around her, when he could have spoken to her privately.

He was struggling with his regrets, sharp and clinging as bramble tendrils, when Harespring appeared at the entrance to his den.

"Come in," he mewed with a weary sigh. "I suppose we have to talk."

"I thought you were really brave to admit your mistakes," Harespring told him, sitting near the entrance to the den and wrapping his tail around his paws. "And the way you vowed to put them right. That can't have been easy, when you didn't know how the other Clans would react."

"It wasn't," Onestar admitted, warmed by his deputy's praise. "But you know—though I hope you never have to experience this yourself—there's something very freeing about unburdening yourself of your secrets."

Harespring shifted uncomfortably. Onestar guessed he had sounded as if he expected his deputy to have to worry about that pretty soon.

Now that the other Clans were joining together to defeat Darktail, Onestar wondered briefly if he might survive after all. But he couldn't make himself believe it. Stoneteller had spoken of a cost; until he had paid it, Onestar knew he would have no peace.

He said nothing to reassure Harespring. He *did* expect that his deputy would soon be getting his nine lives. But he also had no intention of saying that out loud. WindClan, would need all its warriors focused on tomorrow's fight. All the Clans would.

Onestar slept, and woke to see that twilight was falling. A cat's head was outlined against the den entrance; in the dim light it was scent rather than sight that told him it was Heathertail. And another cat with her . . .

"Can we come in?" Heathertail meowed.

Onestar sat up and invited them with a gesture of his tail. Heathertail padded in; the cat who followed her was, of course, Whitetail. Relief swept over him that his mate was ready to talk, yet the shame he had felt leaving him when he had finally told his secret threatened to return. "There's nothing I can do to take back the hurt you feel right now," he began, trying not to let his voice shake. "And there's nothing

I can do to atone for what I've done. But I—"

"Oh, you stupid, *stupid* furball!" Whitetail interrupted. She rushed up to him and rubbed her muzzle against his face.

Onestar sat rigid with shock. For a moment he had no words, only letting himself enjoy her sweet scent and the soft touch of her fur. He had expected words of anger and bitterness, not the kind of scolding you might give to a reckless but beloved kit.

"Don't you mind about Smoke?" he asked eventually.

"Of course I *mind*," Whitetail replied, "but not for the reason you think. You were never her mate while you were mine. But I wish you could have trusted me enough to tell me the truth from the first—or at least when she turned up with her kit. It sounds like she needed your help, and we might have been able to work something out."

Onestar hung his head. "I was so afraid of losing you," he confessed.

"Onestar, I love you. We share a kit, and you have been my closest companion for so many moons. I haven't always understood the decisions you made, especially lately, but I would never give up on you for a mistake like this. Our lives are too short."

There was sorrow in Whitetail's eyes as she spoke, and Onestar knew why. *I might not lose her, but she knows that she will lose me, very soon now.*

"You're going to give your last life tomorrow, aren't you?" she asked.

"If that's what it takes," Onestar responded. "I have to do

everything I can to remove the threat of Darktail. Too many cats have suffered and died because of him—because of *me*. That needs to be put right, one way or another."

Heathertail's smoky blue eyes shimmered with sadness. "You are going to *fight*, though? You're not going into tomorrow's battle *intent* on dying, because you think you have to? Because you think you deserve to?" She padded closer to Onestar and touched her nose to his ear. "I'm having a new litter of kits soon," she told him, "and I can't imagine them not knowing my father, the Clan's leader. . . . It just feels *wrong*."

Onestar twined his tail around his daughter's, while he leaned his head against Whitetail's. "Of course I'm not," he responded. "But I am prepared to. For so long, I've been scared of losing my last life, and it's only now that I know why. My guilt and shame were like a trail leading to the Dark Forest. And now that I'm at peace with what I've done, I'm not afraid anymore. My fate is in the paws of StarClan."

The sun was setting, and clouds were massing above the lake. Onestar led WindClan to join the others as they approached ShadowClan territory, ready to reclaim it from Darktail and his rogues.

In their battle practice earlier that day, Onestar had felt that his Clan was truly united. They had clearly forgiven him and were prepared to fight hard against Darktail. Hope was welling up inside him that WindClan would survive and thrive, whether or not he returned alive from the battle.

Onestar also felt more confident after he learned that

the living Clans had the support of StarClan. Their warrior ancestors had sent a message to the medicine cats: that each Clan should fight using their own unique skills.

Let's hope it works, Onestar thought.

The Clans crossed the border stream and drew close together as they headed into ShadowClan territory. Their paw steps were almost silent as they padded over the thick layer of pine needles on the forest floor. Wherever he looked, Onestar could see whiskers twitching and eyes gleaming with eagerness. Only RiverClan was absent; they had a special part to play.

When the cats were drawing close to the ShadowClan camp, Bramblestar signaled for a halt and turned to Leafstar. "Are you ready?" he asked her.

The SkyClan leader nodded and sprang into the nearest pine tree, gesturing with her tail for her Clanmates to follow. SkyClan would use their special leaping skills to attack the rogues from above.

Onestar could see how Bramblestar's battle plan would work, with the other Clans using their special skills, too. WindClan would dart in to strike a blow, then dart away with their extra speed. ThunderClan would attack head-on with all the force of a storm, while ShadowClan would lurk in the darkness, so familiar with their own territory that no rogue would escape them.

And RiverClan would put *their* skills to use, for sure. One-star felt a grim amusement as he thought of their part in the plan. *Darktail won't be expecting that!*

By now the last of the sun was gone, and shadows clotted in the hollows under the pine trees. Every hair on Onestar's pelt prickled warily as he stayed alert for any sign of Darktail's rogues.

The invading cats spread out into a line as they drew closer to the camp. Now they crept forward as if they were stalking prey, belly fur brushing the pine needles, ears angled forward to pick up the least sound of movement from the rogues. Every so often, Onestar caught a flash of movement in the trees above, where the SkyClan warriors were keeping pace with them.

Finally, the invading Clans reached the bottom of the slope that led up to the ShadowClan camp. For a heartbeat Bramblestar paused; then he let out a ferocious yowl. "Now!"

Flowing like water, the attacking cats charged up the slope and thrust their way through the bushes and brambles that encircled the camp. Onestar plunged forward, ignoring the thorns that tore at his pelt.

Shocked caterwauling came from the dens as Darktail's Kin staggered into the open. Before they knew what was happening, Bramblestar and the ThunderClan cats were upon them, clawing and biting, buffeting them like a storm wind.

In the last of the light, Onestar spotted WindClan around the edges of the battle, attacking any rogue who tried to escape the camp and driving them back into the thick of the fighting. He couldn't see the ShadowClan cats, but he knew they would be hovering in the shadows at the top of the slope, ready to jump out at any rogues who managed to get past WindClan.

SkyClan leaped from the branches and joined in the fray.

Within heartbeats, the camp was filled with screeching, tussling cats. Onestar caught a glimpse of Darktail's pale pelt and heard his voice snarling orders, though it wasn't clear if any cat was listening to him. The rogues were hugely outnumbered, and Onestar could pick up the scent of their growing panic.

He had thrown himself into the midst of the fight, lashing out at any rogue who came up against him. All his instincts were telling him to ignore Bramblestar's battle plan; he wanted instead to seek out Darktail and cut a path to him, finishing their conflict once and for all. But he kept his rage under control.

StarClan will send him to me when the time is right.

Above the camp, the sky grew darker still. The air shook with the sound of thunder, rolling on and on, almost drowning out the screeches of the battling cats. A fat drop of rain fell on Onestar's head.

That's all we need! he thought irritably. *Fighting will be even trickier now.*

A rogue swiped at him with claws extended; Onestar ducked under the outstretched foreleg and spun around on his hind legs, clawing at his adversary's ears. The rogue let out a screech of pain and fled, vanishing into a tangle of fur.

At the same moment, a flash of lightning split the sky and lit up the entire forest, so that for a heartbeat Onestar could see every cat, and every pine tree that surrounded the clearing.

But that was not all he saw. His focus was on the figure of Darktail, charging straight for him from across the camp.

Then the light was gone. Weird shapes swam across Onestar's vision and he wasn't aware of Darktail until his son reared up right in front of him and swiped at his face, knocking him off balance. As he struggled to get up, another peal of thunder rolled across the camp.

Darktail's voice rose above it. "Kin! Follow me! If you're smart enough, retreat with me—you deserve to survive!"

At their leader's command, the rogue cats tore themselves away from battling with the Clans and raced out of the camp, hard on his paws. Onestar spotted Sleekwhisker and some of the other young ShadowClan warriors actually fleeing with him. The sight shocked him to the tips of his claws. Then he asked himself what else they could do, when they had abandoned and betrayed the Clan of their birth?

"Follow the rogues!" Bramblestar yowled, racing up the slope and through the brambles after the vanishing Kin. The Clan cats followed him, with no special tasks now, only an overwhelming urge to drive the rogues from Clan territory.

Onestar sprang to his paws and joined in the pursuit. "Bramblestar!" he screeched. "Darktail is mine!"

The warriors surged through the pine trees in the paw steps of the fleeing rogues. By now the rain was thrumming down, plastering Onestar's pelt to his sides while his paws splashed across ground churned up to mud. But he could ignore all of it, cheered by the sight of the rogues as they pelted desperately toward the lake, intent on escaping from the *real* warriors.

Then he remembered the next part of Bramblestar's plan. Victory for the Clans might come at the cost of him truly making amends for his mistake.

As the rogue cats burst out of the trees onto the open lakeshore, dark shapes rose up out of the shallow water. RiverClan! Stunned, the rogue cats skidded to a halt, staring in utter disbelief at the RiverClan warriors who had been lying there in wait. Now they advanced, their eyes gleaming menacingly as they emerged onto dry land, cutting off the rogues' retreat.

The rogues spun around and fled back toward the forest, only to be confronted by Bramblestar and Onestar, with the rest of the Clan cats beside them, ranged in a line along the edge of the trees.

Onestar's gaze caught his secret son's. He felt frustration, almost sadness, at seeing the look in Darktail's eyes: defiant, enraged, malicious. There was not a trace of fear, even though he and his group were outnumbered, and on terrain they surely did not know well enough. Onestar saw once again that there was true madness in those eyes: madness that reflected the darkness in the rogue tom's heart.

He had once wondered where Darktail's evil had come from, blaming himself. But now he knew that he didn't have that kind of evil inside him. Maybe nothing could have prevented the cat Darktail had become, even if Onestar had welcomed him into WindClan.

There is nothing to be done for him. He cannot be saved now. If he ever could . . . Maybe my only purpose is to stop him.

The thought lightened Onestar's heart, driving out the last traces of regret. He leaped forward, the other Clan cats hard on his paws. Most of the rogues broke away with panic-stricken shrieks, dodging here and there and diving under outstretched claws as they tried to escape. But Darktail stood still, confronting his father.

Onestar approached warily, determined not to throw away the fight by striking out in uncontrolled rage. He and Darktail circled each other while the rain pelted down, the drops bouncing up again as they hit the ground, drenching both cats until water streamed off their pelts.

Lightning flashed once again above their heads, glittering on the surface of the lake. The rumble of thunder followed it, like a growl from the throat of an enormous cat.

"You would never have made it as a warrior," Onestar taunted his son. "You were better off as a kittypet."

Darktail let out a furious shriek and hurled himself at Onestar. But Onestar was ready for him, and dragged him to the ground as the two of them collided. They wrestled for dominance, locked together in a tangle of soaked fur, claws, and teeth. Each time Onestar felt he had his son pinned down, he felt a sudden jolt as if he were weightless, as Darktail flipped him over. Dimly he became aware that they were rolling down the shore toward the water.

I should be panicking, Onestar thought, seeing the glimmer of water mere tail-lengths away. But he was not. The closer his last death came, the lighter his heart felt.

Still locked together, father and son rolled into the waves that lapped the pebbles, turning over and over, deeper and deeper into the water, until Onestar felt the lake bottom fall away from under him, leaving him and Darktail floundering out of their depth. For a while they floated, still lashing out at each other, until Onestar hooked all four of his paws into Darktail's flanks and heaved, dragging them both deep into the lake. Water swirled around his whole body, and he had to fight the urge to open his jaws and take a breath.

From the shore he heard the muffled sound of a single warrior's voice. "Onestar! Onestar!" He thought that it was Heathertail, but he couldn't be sure. He felt a brief regret that he couldn't respond, couldn't go back to her, but he knew his time with his family was over.

Now I have to save my Clan.

As the fighting toms sank lower and lower, Darktail kicked and writhed, desperately trying to break free. For a moment he almost managed to slip from Onestar's grip, powering toward the air. Onestar's instincts told him to let him go, to swim upward beside him so that he could breathe. He kicked out once, his gaze fixed on the wavering light above his head.

But before he could reach the surface, the impulse passed. His life was not important now, except that he could give it to save the Clans. He wrapped his forelegs around Darktail's tail and hind legs so that they began sinking again, and he clung to the evil rogue with all the strength of his last life. He could not let Darktail escape his clutches. He could not let Darktail get back to the surface.

Gazing into his son's eyes, Onestar saw a different emotion there. The frenzied madness had been replaced with a frenzied fear. He felt a jolt of triumph, spreading through his whole body, at seeing the Clans' latest enemy truly defeated, once and for all. He was glad that Darktail knew now he was no match for the Clans. He hoped that the rogue regretted that he'd ever come to the lake.

But in his last moments, Onestar's triumph and his gladness faded. He could not deny that his own heart clenched with grief and sadness that it had to come to this. That Darktail had set his paws on the path that led to his inevitable fate; that there was no helping Onestar's errant, wayward son . . .

I'm sorry, Smoke, he thought as he began to lose consciousness. A series of memories seemed to float past him. His kithood in the nursery with Wrenflight; his time with Smoke; the Great Journey and Tallstar's incredible decision; his visit to StarClan to receive his nine lives; his time with Whitetail and Heathertail . . . He had lived a full life, he reflected, even if he was paying now for his mistakes. Gratitude filled him for all that he had experienced.

And then his memories were replaced by images of the days still to come. The days after his time. He saw Harestar leading a thriving WindClan to a Gathering of all the Clans—so many cats, more than he could count. He saw Whitetail helping Heathertail with her new litter of kits, while Breezepelt and Crowfeather hunted side by side. He saw Kestrelflight at the Moonpool meeting surrounded by the starry spirits of their warrior ancestors.

The Clans were going to survive, and thrive. And Onestar had made it happen. It hadn't been too late for him after all. . . . He would not die a bad cat.

I have saved all the Clans.

Epilogue

Onestar had waited a long time in the hollow on the moor. The gentle breeze had gradually turned colder and colder, in a way that seemed ominous.

At last a cat appeared at the top of the hollow, outlined against the sky. Onestar immediately recognized Tallstar, from the set of his head and his long tail pointing straight upward.

The former WindClan leader padded slowly down the slope to Onestar's side. His expression was unreadable; Onestar's belly lurched, assuming that meant bad news, that his warrior ancestors had decided that he would be sent to the Place of No Stars after all.

"Have you reflected on your life?" Tallstar asked quietly.

Onestar dipped his head in deepest respect. "I have, Tallstar," he replied. "I have reflected, and I realize that I have much to be ashamed of. But I have tried so hard to atone for my mistakes."

Tallstar did not disagree. His measuring gaze rested on Onestar, sending a chill through him from ears to tail-tip. "*That* is the true mark of an honorable cat," the starry warrior responded at last, "and those efforts are what has earned you your place in StarClan."

Onestar gazed at him, stunned, unable to believe what he had just heard. "Are you sure?" he asked hoarsely. "Do you mean it? You haven't made a mistake?"

Tallstar shook his head, a gentle amusement in his eyes. "I haven't made a mistake," he repeated. "I always knew that you would keep WindClan safe when I was gone. And you did . . . no matter what it cost you in the end."

Onestar ducked his head, his throat too choked for him to speak. Now he would be able to live in StarClan with Tallstar; he would see Firestar again, and put right their broken friendship; he would be able to watch Heathertail and her kits as they grew; he would be with Whitetail again when her paws led her on the path to StarClan. He would be able to watch the Clans recover from Darktail's cruel leadership, and see how SkyClan settled beside the lake.

Even after my death, I'll be a true Clan cat.

Tallstar stepped aside, beckoning Onestar with a wave of his tail that seemed to leave a frosty glitter in the air. "Come now," he meowed. "It's time to rest. You are going exactly where you belong."

READ ON FOR AN
EXCLUSIVE **WARRIORS** COMIC . . .

CREATED BY
ERIN HUNTER

WRITTEN BY
DAN JOLLEY

ART BY
JAMES L. BARRY

FIRESTAR'S RIGHT. I WASN'T A **TOTAL** FAILURE AS A LIVING CAT.

MAYBE AS A STARCLAN CAT I CAN KEEP MAKING UP FOR MY MISTAKES.

WALK WITH ME.

YOU **HAVE** PROVEN YOURSELF AS A LEADER. OVER AND OVER. AND SOON YOU'LL GET THE CHANCE TO PROVE YOURSELF AS A STARCLAN CAT.

AFTER ALL, HARESPRING WILL BE HERE SHORTLY.

IT'S TIME FOR HIM TO RECEIVE HIS NINE LIVES. TO BECOME HARESTAR.

LISTEN... YOU WERE A LEADER YOURSELF, SO I **KNOW** YOU KNOW HOW DIFFICULT IT CAN BE.

BUT IT'S **DOUBLY** IMPORTANT THAT HARESPRING BECOMES A GOOD LEADER...

BECAUSE THERE'S TROUBLE HEADED FOR THE CLANS.

GRAVE TROUBLE.

MAYBE THE WORST PROBLEM ANY CLAN WILL EVER FACE.

WH-WHAT? FIRESTAR, WHAT ARE YOU TALKING ABOUT?

I'VE HAD A DREAM. A **TERRIBLE** DREAM.

A VISION OF A THICK, HEAVY MIST FALLING OVER THE LAKE TERRITORIES.

DO YOU MEAN — ARE THE CLANS GOING TO HAVE TO LEAVE **THE LAKE**?

MAYBE... MAYBE IF I CONCENTRATE, I CAN SEE WHAT FIRESTAR SAW...?

NO. I TRY AS HARD AS I CAN... BUT THERE'S NOTHING.

NO... NO. I STILL FELT THE CLANS' PRESENCE, UNDERNEATH THE MIST. BUT I COULDN'T SEE **THROUGH** IT.

IT'S BEEN TROUBLING ME EVER SINCE.

SO THIS MIST — THERE'S NO LIGHT AT **ALL** BENEATH IT? IT'S JUST **DARK**?

WELL... NOT EXACTLY, NO.

I DID SEE A **FAINT LIGHT** SHINING.

AS IF TRYING TO BREAK THROUGH.

I DON'T KNOW WHAT THE VISION MEANS, ONESTAR.

BUT I DO KNOW THE CLANS ARE GOING TO HAVE TO BE AT THEIR STRONGEST. THEIR **MOST UNITED**.

WHICH IS WHY YOUR SUCCESSOR MUST BE A STRONG, CONFIDENT LEADER.

AND HE'LL NEED YOU FOR THAT.

THERE HE IS —

HARESPRING!

ALONG WITH THE WINDCLAN CATS WHO'VE COME BEFORE...

HERE TO GIVE HIM THEIR GIFTS.

SO MANY BRAVE, HONORABLE WARRIORS...

AND TALLSTAR AMONG THEM! HE LOOKS SO STRONG!

I RECOGNIZE **WINDSTAR**, TOO...

...AND GORSESTAR...

...AND MOTH FLIGHT...

WHO AM I, COMPARED WITH THESE CATS?

I HEARD WHAT FIRESTAR SAID. I **DID**. AND YET...

DO I **REALLY** DESERVE TO BE HERE? WHAT CAN I POSSIBLY GIVE HARESPRING?

UNLESS...

FIRESTAR SAID MY **BIGGEST** FLAW WAS COVERING UP MISTAKES WITH LIES. THAT IT ALWAYS SEEMED TO CREATE EVEN **BIGGER** PROBLEMS.

ALL RIGHT. YES.

I KNOW **EXACTLY** WHAT GIFT I SHOULD GIVE HARESPRING.

ONE OF THE **MOST IMPORTANT** QUALITIES A LEADER CAN HAVE.